SPITE

or Wounds That Wouldn't Heal

SPITE

or Wounds That Wouldn't Heal

ALEXANDER THEROUX

REDFIEND PUBLISHING
Royal Palm Beach, Florida

First Paperback Edition
ISBN   978-1-963761-14-6

Library of Congress Control Number: 2025948242

REDFIEND PUBLISHING
Royal Palm Beach, Florida
www.redfiendpub.com

To Sarah, Shenandoah, and Shiloh,
and to the memory of many battles fought in the silence
of the night before ever I knew you.

Contents

"Let them not say: we did not see it.
We saw.
Let them not say: we did not hear it.
We heard.
Let them not say: they did not taste it.
We ate, we trembled."

Jane Hirschfield

"I need retribution, otherwise I will destroy myself. And retribution, not somewhere and sometime in infinity, but here and now, on earth."

Ivan Karamazov

Take Me Out to the Ball Game

Search for the wall? Seek the decree? But it wasn't necessary. I had it all by heart, for I have a stark and pressing memory, an aspect of an inner drive in me to try to locate myself —for identity—among the loud echoes, mostly sad impressions, especially early ones, that I have had to face, one of them, a major one—the major one—being the subject at hand. I grew up in a large family, where playing outside with goofy friends involved inventing new games and showing off. We had no television. We read comic books. We had crayons, loved drawing, and enjoyed scribbling on the flat surfaces of a cement wall that was the back of an old empty garage that faced Newport Ave. It stood behind to the right of our brown house, located catty-corner to it.

Drawing what? Silly semi-obscene cartoons. A fat man throwing up, balloon head, black hat, arms behind him. Pigtailed girls. A stick-figure nutcase running in front of a trail of sequenced drops of poo comically falling out of his bum.

Many of the things that I drew were disclosures that by acknowledgement became like diaries, subtexts, if you will, of what I felt, what upset or angered me, less spoofs or send-ups than impressions of my hurt.

I was good at composition. Delineation. Much of my life, in fractured designs and diagrams, could be found on that wall. Traced portrayals, sketches. Our scrawls—writing was hardly the word for it—were foolish squibs, basically hen tracks, cacography, always vulgar, semi-literate, scratches constituting confessions.

Let me state here, up front, that what you are reading is in fact a confession, nothing less—a disclosure, actually, something I have felt compelled to write for sanity's sake. Call it the unbosoming of an ongoing deeply remembered insult that has, had, burnt a hole in my sleep for decades, still does in an angry way, one that has set the tone for, if it doesn't directly explain, my life of collapse and defeat, of foolery and endless frustration. If you find in these disclosures of insisted-upon assertion, please understand I don't claim I am a well-balanced individual. Whether you accept it or not, in any case, I don't care.

The justification of my report here is supported by what has sustained me to state. It also explains, more or less, how I resolved the problem, whether to your satisfaction or not, I will let you be the judge. It is about revenge.

Spite.

In the fourth grade, I was a brave, confident little fellow, walking about wearing thick corduroy pants and goofing around at recess with imitations of radio dialects I'd heard and making other kids laugh with jokes I'd found in cheap little books like *Brand New Cartoons* by Jimmy Hatlo, a paperback that fell into my hands somehow. I used to climb to the top of a small tree in my neighborhood and tell stories to my playmates down through the leaves. I did comedy routines and put on hand-puppet shows in our basement. I took trumpet lessons, once built an outdoor camp site with hammer, nails, and lumber pieces, and presided over hamster funerals. I was a shepherd on stage in a Nativity scene one Christmas. I lived for April Fool's Day. I was a lad born to celebrate Hallowe'en. I loved pranks. I suspect I was needy. No, I *know* I was needy. A teacher once read something of mine in my presence, looked up at me, and—apparently on the basis of nothing more than what I had written *and the way I wrote*—declared, "You want to be loved." I am a second child, squeezed in between the older, preferred one and those needful below who tend to be cherished, if that's the right word, or at least somewhat pampered.

I was a fairly popular boy—or had been. I told various girls in class I could see and talk to deceased relatives and angels—that I had memorized every word in the spelling book by sleeping with my head on top of it rather than reading it! I was lighthearted, frisky, enjoyed "showing off," as a way to get attention, liked to "lark" and "romp," to repeat the very words teachers often used to describe me. Maybe I was too energetic. I had fun, backmasking noises. I knew stuff. "There's a mask on Mars, an enormous Sphinx-like face staring out into space from the Cydonia region of the Martian landscape," I told Marilyn Piontowski. Carol Daley said I was a genius. So did Barbara Stuffle.

We had school assemblies. There were those that involved the whole school. But we also had special occasions for our own in-class activities, certain days set aside for visiting teachers to come by for select activities, one to teach us art, another to explain the rudiments of tap-dancing, and at other times a teacher came by with a slide projector, a set-up screen, and a carousel of old slides that she fed into it, usually boring travelogues of Uruguay or Guatemala or Peru for which she provided a narration. Between discs, at a blank white screen, I would leap up to provide hand-shadow puppetry of animals—butterflies, dogs, ducks—to amuse the girls. One such group activity was a music class, with Miss Yeaow, a tall, pretty lady who, after arranging us into separate boy and girl singing clusters, always amused us by stopping to give us the right key to sing in by blowing into a Hohner pitchpipe. I loved even the round shape of that gizmo, a great invention We sang all sorts of songs, "Side by Side," "Take Me Out to the Ball Game," "Shine On, Harvest Moon."

Always before the music classes began, Miss Sharkey, the school principal, used to stop by every time to make sure the door was shut. A tall, dry, humorless, no-nonsense woman whose authority was never gainsaid or contradicted, she was a strict disciplinarian who ran the school with an iron will and carried within her a strong relish for spite. Hard bark. Unmarried. Late middle age. A tight bun of gray hair, severely secured by combs. A fierce face, dark eyes, with deep sunken patches around them that bore into you with accusation. Heavy black shoes. She also wore a long black heavy overcoat and gloves. She was the embodiment of the school's rules, which she saw were strictly met and ran the place something like the diocese or precinct of a pompous bishop. She drove a green car, which was always parked in a prime spot at the front of the large, imposing, towered brick school.

Both groups had separated. Miss Yeaow took out her circular pitchpipe, blew a note, and nodded. The girls were the best, about nine or ten of them—saddle shoes, plaid skirts, cute bows in their hair—who sang, giggling, "Baby Bumble Bee" and "She'll Be Coming 'Round the Mountain." Next, it was the boys' turn. We sang "Home on the Range" quite sedately. "Take Me Out to the Ball Game" was our second song, one that I loved and had often sung at home. More exciting, it went well. An antic side of me has always been as constant as habit. I was at an end side of our group, as we stood up front, and with each phrase made appropriate gestures by way of comic commentary. At the words "ball game," I gestured by swinging a bat, and at "Buy me some peanuts and Cracker Jack," I pantomimed eating, and as we sang "I don't care if I never get back," I impishly wagged a negative warning finger, all in good fun. Miss Yeaow stood by, fairly amused. At one point the door had opened. Miss Sharkey appeared, standing there. The girls seemed to be thrilled at my daring. Applause followed, and of course I took a bow, as I believe the other boys did by way of classic tomfoolery.

But the principal's disapproving scowl had chilled the room.

She was a fearful old stick, an imposingly tall harridan slightly bow-legged who always wore what seemed like crabbed out-of-date 19th-century dresses. She presided over fire drills, rang recess bells, and addressed students at class assemblies, speaking with precise diction with sundial-style mottoes: "Today Is Yesterday's Tomorrow," "Make Haste, But Slowly," "Spring Is Not Always in Bloom," "While We Have Time, Let Us Do Good," "One Hour Will Give What Another Has Refused," "Time Takes All But Memories," and "Time Devours Things," which often gave me to think *I wish it devoured you.*

"Young man, come here! *Yes, you,*" ordered Miss Sharkey, pointing to me, then down to her feet. "You're so talented, you like to show off, don't you, so, now, guess what, now you can sing it alone. Come over here," she repeated, with a cruel, beckoning downward turn of her finger to a spot on the floor just in front of her. I fake-gestured to myself, inquiring as to what she meant. "Over *here,*" she repeated.

The class went utterly silent. I cringed and moved defensively backward. "I want you to go and stand *exactly* where you stood before—no, up front, go back there, up front, before the whole class, and it behooves you not only to listen but obey me. Do you mark me? I can see your deportment betokens a feverish interest in performing." She dismissed the others in the group with shooing hands and directed her attention to me. "Now you, you alone, stay there and sing 'Take Me Out to the Ball Game' for all of us to enjoy." *Behooves? Betokens?* I hadn't a clue what the words meant, never heard them. They were principal's words. Princi*pal:* that word alone, severe, three barks, scared me.

She marched over to me and grabbed me by the chin, thumb and forefinger tight on my jaw, and squired me to the front of the room.

I grew hot, but I was worse than embarrassed. I had been caught as a thief and been revealed. Laid bare. On display. *Exhibited,* in fact. I experienced an immediate disorientation new to me and suddenly could only see wavy lines in front of my face, not the faces in the class. Aphantasia is the inability to visualize. But I felt that I saw, terribly, that I had been literally pushed on stage but given no words to speak

I swallowed, mortified, and pitifully sang the first two words of the song. Almost inaudibly.

"No," a nettled Miss Sharkey interrupted, wagging a finger. "Do it with gestures! Like you did before. You can do it. You're a comedian."

I began to weep, visibly shaking, then became mute. I actually lost my voice out of pure fright. I was impaled. It was an experience I'd never felt before. Although I felt unmasked and exposed, in my abject panic and alarm I felt also weirdly *concealed*, and, with a dizziness, felt almost invisible, upside-down, hot all over with terror. I was almost levitated in apprehension. I had read about a hypnotist named Hart the Laugh King who once did so. Boys began to laugh. Marilyn Piontowski turned her head away. So did Carol Daley and Barbara Stuffle.

What happened, then? Let me tell you. The answer is simple. I can't. I cannot. The waking world disappeared for me that day in as if it seemed an evil magician with consummate powers made it so. I remember walking home alone, the wrong way. But wait, there is one thing that I do remember from long, long ago, from the distant past. I thereafter cultivated small dark fantasies about retaliation and over and over in my cheerless and brooding hours learned to practice and practiced to learn just how to keep my thumb out of my clenched fist when punching Miss Sharkey so she wouldn't break it!

By the age of nineteen, being well out of high school, I had become an aimless and unfocused person with no direction. I got mediocre grades. I had played no sports, attended no rallies, joined no clubs. I tried out for nothing whatsoever. To any of the field trips our school took I gave a pass. In the class group graduation photo, look for me in vain.

I never knew what to do with myself or my life, where to go or how to act, or why. College was out, as I had no money. In my senior year, I had not gone to the prom because a girl I had a crush on ignored me, badly hurting my feelings, and I'd spent that night alone. That was the way that I had wasted all my time, lost as to endeavor and having no plans, walking around apathetic and barren. I attended a few rock concerts by myself. Radical punk groups. I lived generally unfocused and apathetic, a disorder I trace to that brutal day when I had been forced to stand up in public to sing alone. I felt never the same again, never. The effect that had on me, crucial, seemed to have determined the nature of my emptiness, leaving a black hole within me.

Adversity was the narrow portal through which I now saw the world. I was concave instead of convex, shrunken, withdrawn, suffering year in and out an approval addiction, transmogrified into a morbid, sheepish personality that was thwarted like a flung horseshoe at a missing stake.

I'd become a shy, awkward, timid, even reticent person, much less confident than ever I had been before, even my brothers said so. Whenever I was home, I kept to my room, slept, or looked at the ceiling. I took a job in a small, local stationery store for a time but then quit. That was followed by work as a hand on a lobster boat for almost a year. I was going nowhere. I hated it. It was a "Negro's holiday" for me, an old sailor's name for a Sunday at sea. Although it meant to be a day of rest, work on a boat had to be done. Negro slaves on old plantations had to work a full day on Sundays as well as weekdays.

It was terrible to face. I who was once a smart, perceptive little boy with bright eyes and lots of psycho-energetic ability had no sense of community. I dated no one, later, in high school, felt no longer confident in doing so. I wasted time, attending idiotic rock shows, often drunk, took up smoking and entertained morbid thoughts. The space which I inhabited, wherever I stood, seemed less bleak than empty. A vacuum. I had for a short time been an altar boy but quit. A priest told my mother I was "ensorcelled."

To this very day, I cannot help but estimate my personal character as having a kind of shortage. Deficiency. That scold of a principal kicked a rock that, in time, caused a landslide or avalanche, put it any way you want. I once read that the Italian painter Michelangelo supposedly said that, after completing a sculpture, the artist should then roll it down a hill, to allow whatever part or parts not necessary to break off.

Right there! That was me, exactly. One hundred percent. Something had snapped off.

For me it was a wound that all through my life never seemed to heal. I practiced with paradigm-shaking force being defensive, simply in order to recognize myself as the misfit I was to face up to what I couldn't deny and so had to handle—to survive! Any mood of self-pity was a dinner bell for me.

The tracery was straight down and abject. No lost to found, blindness to sight, wretch to born again. It was exactly the reverse. I had been stomped hollow.

With my life being purposeless, I began to stay home a lot, like a little kid, except it was so noisy there I was always driven to go out. I began to read over and over the works by Charles Baudelaire. The French poet? I loved his stuff, poems, essays, too. He spoke my language, straight from the shoulder. I began taking his books out of the library, reading up in my room alone. I believe that I read his every word.

I had failed at everything I tried, booted chances to develop. I rode buses. Sat in diners. I brooded. Was that going to be my life? I would sit out on the back steps, smoking, brooding, idly facing that gray garage wall, the one with our graffiti plastered all over it. One evening, idly and for no particular reason, the way I did everything, I decided to walk over to take a look at that neglected old wall with its stupid array of stick figures and poltroons, piddling evocations out of my past, that had compiled there. I realized that what *I* was inspecting paradoxically scrutinized *me*, monitoring my behavior as if as a field study.

I suddenly noticed on one particular segment that stood out on the far left wall, I had drawn a face, along with scribbled thoughts, such as they were, a garbled bunch of written words that I must have memorized from a cartoon book, one of many I had read, in Jimmy Hatlo books when I was in middle school. I took the time to read them closely and which, herewith, I quote in full: "A mullet-headed, mule-eared, wall-eyed, hog-nosed, 'gator-faced, shad-mouthed, screw-necked, goat-bellied, puzzle-gutted, camel-backed, butt-sprung, battled-hammered, knock-kneed, razor-legged, box-ankled, shovel-footed ass-wipe." I looked closely into the cruel, sharp-chinned, bespectacled face above it, a whole melon head, one I'd not looked upon for as long as a decade, then I remembered being its creator.

It lurked there among images of caves, funny ladders, a fire engine. Farting stick figures. I saw the word *CROATAN* written in large caps There were bulb-headed UFO creeps and creatures. But it was the face that took my attention.

I stood there engaged in an epiphanic moment.

The mind lives in faint, half-remembered experiences of uncertain valence, where self-deception, often bordering on delusion, twists memory further from truth with every passing year. But of this one event I had solid certitude.

The woman's eyes on the wall glinted, squinted. The jutting ears suggested extraterrestrial activity. That protruding chin. The grimace, the glower, the frown. It came to me suddenly that the brain with a search image is like a barracuda seeing shine.

A predatory barracuda glimpsing shine always strikes.

I looked closely.

No question.

It was the face of Gertrude Sharkey.

The Chinese can tell the time by the eyes of a cat, or so Baudelaire wrote in his essay "The Clock." In a very real sense, I gauge time by that unforgotten, unfathomable, unforgiveable event, as if it, too, were a timepiece or chronometer.

I was made the fool I was by what I made myself to be by not protecting all I could have been. We approve of what is done to us in life by permitting and so allowing the instrument of humiliation to walk away scot free. I became an old man, young. The role of lap dog is a frippery the historian who is myself cannot abide.

I confess that I abandoned mercy to its green solitude—or to the rats, if you will. I will let you decide. There's a chapter closed. A new one opens up, not unlike a declaration of independence, at least for me. Allow me the decency, if not decorum, to snatch some deliverance, if not sovereignty, from a nightmare that has plagued me from youth. It was the beginning of a not-me that changed my life. To me, nothing jars an obscure sense of justice more than those pigeon-spirited weaklings who prefer to carry in their heart emotions unexpressed, feelings unspoken, and the scars and losses craven memory would erase in the name of forgiveness or exoneration, tolerance, or pardon. I have only words to play with but am not inclined to forego this distinction for the sake of some arseless respect or heart-withering, brain-muddling comment on how good I am and so, so willing to forgive!

I could tuck my terrors away into an undisturbed corner of my mind, where they may gradually be covered by inevitable layers of dust, but when a suddenly new set of miseries and torments, directly born of them filter their way back into that corner, only to find again the "tear-filled eyes of a dog being beaten," to quote my friend Charles Baudelaire, "the dust is shaken off and the monster of memory remains." I could exhaust myself quoting, "The wolf dies without howling. But not I!"

Be appalled, should you so choose. Live with it! This is a cruel business, revenge.

I prefer the words retribution, reprisal.

Repayment.

I ended up stranded on the beach, run aground, ship-wrecked, high and dry, shanghaied, abandoned, on a cruel and distant shore.

As the poet Tennyson observes,

"I held it truth, with him who sings
To one clear harp in divers tones,
That men may rise on stepping-stones
Of their dead selves to higher things.

But who shall so forecast the years
And find in loss a gain to match?
Or reach a hand thro' time to catch
The far-off interest of tears?"

Grief is an indulgence.

I admit it, but so what?

Worse, even. I had actually fostered it, and also cultivated the insult I saw by ignoring it. If misery is heartbreak, I now say, put not bereavement into play but force your desperation, oblige it, compel it, drive it with a strong arm—frog-march the goddam thing to the cause of it, and immediately demand a rejoinder.

I got an idea. The idea I got was immediately confirmed, hardened immediately into a resolve. I would like to say that it came out of the blue, but it did not. Instantly, I knew what I was going to do the exact minute that I'd witnessed that face on the back garage wall. It was as if a dark, overarching angel had prodded me finally to reckon with everything I was not and to explain why. To say that the face brought back hateful memories is not sufficient enough. An utter void had opened up in me. An abyss of horror. A merciless sting of infinite reproach. Try as I might, I cannot explain—even to myself—quite the nature of the inner rage I felt as that image on the wall flashed before me, *at me*, its frowning mouth, scowling pout and bedraggled hair, or how at the crest of that insightful epiphanic moment, all of the loathing, the resentment, the utter detestation, the ice-cold enmity coupled with disgust—*and, crucially, much of it against myself*—crowded into my brain for the humiliation that woman had caused me at nine years old, fairly raping me of what innocence I had.

Grief, of course, is also a specific kind of pain, for something that is lost. What was explicitly lost was me in a whirlpool of anguish, a suck hole or vortex revolving twisting and spinning me in a descent I didn't deserve.

It was beyond mortification, deeper than shame. It was literally a repudiation of *what the world itself was*, because for the very first time in my life I had a glimpse of ice-cold reality for exactly what it was, suddenly losing not just my faith in mankind but any hope of decency in myself. It was worse than a loss of face. I was as a child wiped out, wholesome and modest even if silly, blameless and above suspicion.

More than anything, it was a species of theft—and still within me lingered remnants of the cold eyes of that crumbling and remorseless old maid, a prison warden, domina of a child-slave empire so many years ago. *Wretched underlings!*

I saw that if once I was intrinsically illimitable, I had now been made worse than a fool, a numbskull. I had been captured in a sense, incarcerated, jailed in a way, schooled to feel subjugated as an image, snared *in* an effigy, a boy utterly unaware—oblivious, uninformed, unsuspecting, and inattentive—rendered a simpleton by the mere whim of a cruel, supervising, hateful adult, exposed to ridicule not just on that day but fitted out with an ongoing identity as an anti-model of duncery, scant and worthless for life. But I came to feel what I saw I had to learn. What I was holding on to was precisely what I had to repudiate. Maintaining grief, clasping it and clutching it close to you, only aggravated, sharpened the loss.

Let me disclose something here I did that day that I had seen my own mother do when facing fateful decisions. I took out the family Bible, closed my eyes, and randomly pointed to a page. At my fingertips was Proverbs 30:33:

> "For as churning the milk produces butter,
>   And as twisting the nose produces blood,
>   So, stirring up anger produces strife."

It immediately confirmed in me an idea that at the same time I could blame someone for the very advice it warned me against.

Some boob once said that no one can make you feel inferior without your consent. You know what I say? I say, it's a lie. What harmless little kid with a cowlick and a snotty nose when badgered and buttonholed by some menacing adult can find even a word to resist such an attack? Has recourse to any defense? Can repulse an assault? Exactly how, may I ask? What, do what—make puny fists in his corduroy pockets?

My mother, when seeing me off to school in the early grades, used to smile at me and say that a boy doesn't need a rich boy's pair of pants—I wore old knee-pants and socks—and that a famous lady in the fashion world once said, "Elegance is refusal." She meant that it is best to skip big watches and rings in favor of simple styles made from durable fabrics that one could wear forever. What did I refuse?

I refused to succumb! I refused to yield! I refused to give in! I bloody refused to knuckle under! I consented *not* to feel inferior.

How's that?

Will that do?

Virtually ten years to the day, I went back to the Washington School, visiting the place where I had spent my first four grades. I walked up the front steps, opened the large green wooden door, passed a central stairway, and, entering the main office, smelling of old varnish, humbly inquired, on the pretense of a making a friendly visit, as to where the now long-retired former principal Miss Gertrude Sharkey now lived.

Without being questioned, I was given her home address. I knew the area well. It had been virtually decided that I was going to be a bad actor. For the visit, I chose to wear a black Insane Clown Posse long-sleeve T-shirt. The songs of that group, the titles of their creepy songs, would resonate in my mind all that day, invigorating me with an apposite madness I craved.

It all fit, as far as I felt, as if artfully fashioned. Hadn't I read somewhere about a thing called "coordinate geometry," whereby a system of two perpendicular axes (the x and y axes) could be used to plot points in a plane? To me, it provided a comfortable, apt, and enabling visual. I have always been intrigued by correlations and equivalences, the balancing need for compensation, which leads to recompense and payment. Justice!

I chose an early Sunday morning. I drove over there, turning up high the CD that I had jammed into the car's console, the satanic AC/DC song "Thunderstruck," all of this, I have no doubt, with a crazed look in my eyes—"run the easting down," an old sailor once told me about wind—and a harsh, almost bitter, inexplicably metal taste on my tongue. Frivolous and indeed irrational, you'll insist I had become. Correct. I will add that I'd brought along a gun, Smith & Wesson 44 .38 special, loaded. I don't know why. I can't fully explain. It didn't seem right. I'll admit that. But I saw no wrong in it, either, OK?

Thunder, thunder, thunder, thunder
Thunder, thunder, thunder, thunder
Thunder, thunder
I was caught
In the middle of a railroad track (thunder)
I looked 'round
And I knew there was no turning back (thunder)
My mind raced
And I thought, what could I do? (Thunder)
And I knew

I was soon knocking on a door of an unprepossessing low-slung apartment building and stood waiting for what seemed ages. It turned out that Miss Sharkey was no longer there but had moved away. Why was I not surprised, as it had been a decade since I had seen the woman in those hard black shoes, scolding heels, who had taken me by the chin with that prehensile claw of hers to squire me to the front of the class, me alone, all by myself like a limping heifer selected and about to be slaughtered. I hastily wrote down the new address that had been given to me, this time in the west part of the city, and headed that way, resolute, car windows closed, with my CD still playing at full volume.

You've been
Thunderstruck, thunderstruck
Yeah, yeah, yeah, thunderstruck
Ooh, thunderstruck, yeah
There was no help, no help from you (thunder)
Sound of the drums
Beating in my heart
The thunder of guns
Tore me apart

You've been
Thunderstruck
Rode down the highway

It wasn't long before I drove up to a tall, forbidding Greek Revival house on a lot by a train track. I knocked on the door. *Chop chop slide*, I thought. I had to knock three times. *Bang! Pow! Boom!* It crossed my mind as I stood there that the last visitor to this house was probably born in Sumeria or ancient Mesopotamia or had come from centuries long past where people wore togas and ate food lying down next to tables and traveled by horse and chariot. I knocked again, hard. An old bone-hard grizzled frownface, death thin, peered around a half-shut door, the quizzical look I recognized. I asked, "Miss Sharkey?"

To Catch a Predator.

I had expected in my recurrent dreams and premonitions not to question my determination here. Let me put it more strongly: I was foreordained to try it.

The old lady conceded this with a cold, unwelcoming nod. She had egret's eyes, that bird's scruffy head.

"What is it you want? What are you doing here?"

It was amazing. I felt myself drop into the face I needed to meet my goal, express my purpose, without a hitch or hindrance, the specific features, facets, portentously framing themselves for the demand, for my visage, my cover, was not dropping the mask of humility, abjection, I had so long lived with. but had become the bold frontispiece that was really me.

"You won't remember me. I was once a student of yours." I saw no reaction. "I mean, at the Washington School." I pieced all of it out slowly, so she could comprehend. "I was one of your pupils there." No answer—or acknowledgement. "I was nine years old when last you saw me." There was no smile, no apprehension. She looked icily past me, for how long I can't say, trying to figure out what was going on, perplexed, a bit disoriented. Questioning came slow. She cannot have had many visitors. Her probing eyes looked to be debriefed. It summoned up an old Mother Goose rhyme "Old mistress McShuttle/Lived in a coal-scuttle,/Along with her dog and cat; /What they ate I can't tell,/But 'tis known very well,/That none of the party was fat."

Yet there is a shrewdness in scrawn. Gauntness is often alert. It was a bold intrusion, a dark and unlikely happening. I shifted my feet and still prodded her. "Fourth grade? Washington School? Remember? You *should,* you were the school principal," I almost shouted. "You drove a green car. Don't you—remember?" *Do you remember anything?* I wondered.

At that point, even then, I seriously could have "thrown her out of the window like an empty bottle," following Baudelaire's ingenious suggestion in his prose-piece, "The Wild Woman and the Fashionable Coquette."

Who was it that said coincidence has a tendency to occur only to the mind that is prepared to notice it? It is a serviceable saying and one my temper corroborated, for I saw that Miss Sharkey was regarding me with the very same peevishness that she had in the old classroom, and in precisely the same hard way, drab and joyless, fist-faced and bitter.

The cadaverous principal had gray scraped hair, partly urine yellow, smelling of stale bread, and was wearing a sort of wrapper, a dull housecoat, which she pulled tightly against her veined throat. She would have been about seventy-five years old, close to eighty. "May I come in?" Clutching the door with tight fingers, she hesitated, but then allowed me that, as the door creaked wide. I entered a dark, musty room and stood there. Brownish blinds drawn, dirty. Dwarf plants in pots. An accidental stillness.

Finally, I was here beholding a large part of a bygone era who was the better for being gone. I looked back over the passing years and glimpsed the boy small, flimsy, and feckless who was me as I looked into and *through* the scrawny, chalk-skinned, white-straggle-haired crone pathetically hunched down there before me to the large, imposing, shoulder-wide harridan, decades tall, whose massive features, grim when seen in profile and from below, were incongruously bordered by a wide black-bat hat, a memory, let me say, not zealously treasured.

The characteristic deadliness of merely walking into her company taxed my brain, recalling for me lines that I had memorized from Baudelaire's "Comes the Charming Evening," part of which goes,

> "The solitary student now raises a burdened head
> And the back that bent daylong sinks into its bed.
> Meanwhile darkness dawns, filled with demon familiars."

I never sat down.

A cynical jingle played inside my head as I stepped into the close, latrine smell of that cavern of an old room, a crummy flat in an anonymous quarter of town, where a guest or visitor hadn't appeared for a decade:

> "Turning the tables, now let me do—
> as you betrayed me, I'll betray you."

What was it that they called it in old books, a mausoleum or necropolis? It resembled an unwholesome and disagreeable burial ground, anyway.

Seeing this woman suddenly, being there, I was back again in front of the class. It was a phenomenon I couldn't quite believe. I immediately recollected the gluey hothouse smell of my old closed-in classroom, its stale musty air, the swelter, the ghastly iron radiators that seemed like massive teeth, the rolled world maps teachers would un-scroll, the moldy shelf where the pencil sharpener sat by a high window, all as if in an unaltered old photograph.

Students' possessions were strewn about their desks. Anticipation ruled everywhere, punches and giggles and chatter, as I stood, a lone boy before them all, cringing inside.

On this particular day? I was never of two minds, which is to say, I had no intention whatsoever of listening to pleas of sentimentality or find myself open to anything like the cheap reliance of an appeal to my noble emotions, certainly not if it sought to overrule my crucial and far too delayed mission of redress. My mind was a bonfire, aflame with broken wood, splinters.

I proceeded to identify myself further by name, framing the occasion for her in primary terms of what once was the old *mise-en-scène*, a grammar school classroom, mentioning Miss Yeaow, the music teacher who weekly visited our small class to give us lessons in singing and chorus. I paused here to mention to the old lady some of the songs that we had sung for her. I prodded her. "I remember singing 'Take Me Out to the Ball Game,'" I said. "I can still see the classroom in my mind. Can't you? The gum under the desks? The old fabric Denoyer-Geppert pull-down scroll map in front of the classroom over the blackboard? The ink holes in the bolted-down desks? The steel ink pens?"

She blinked like an owl.

"Fourth grade," I repeated—I believe now I snarled.

I paused and waited. There was a nodding hint of recognition in her pale face, her gaffer's head inclined, a sort of lethargic inclination, the barest hint of a condescending—well, it was not a smirk but a simper, a glare, something of a hesitant sneer. I can say that I felt I was in the presence of some hot coal or burning ember straight from the furnace of hell. "Do you remember that song?" I delayed here. "Please, look at me. No, look at me! Do you remember that I sang that song, with gestures, alone?" To demonstrate, I held my own chin as I sang—loudly—the first line of the song, openly shocking her. With an antic display of simulated action, I took a wild open swing with a hypothetical bat. It came near her nose.

I shall never forget her sudden look now of utter panic.

Was my motive an instinct to emend what one might call an elementary right and wrong, or simply out-and-out revenge? My reply? Do me a big favor, any pious or self-righteous attendees who wish to weigh in here. Fish out your own damn answer, take off *your own* ugly, misshapen hat, and search the inner brim or its crinkled own border, the better to read it, OK?

I sang the first line once again, adding a moving up-and-down finger under my eye graphically simulating the tears I'd once shed singing it. As I made weeping noises, it updrew emotions, and I wanted to punch her.

She quickly perked up, I saw—actually felt it!

I can say that I positively reveled in her sudden perception. It was a lightning bolt of awareness. *She had recognized me.*

Purposely I now kept quiet, allowing the extended moment to sink in, a long pause allowing for the horrifying, terrifying intimidation of silence to reach her, an interval in which I saw that, with nervous gestures of her bony hands, as if she were soaping them, she was waiting now to ascertain the point of my visit.

I like to think that she had not only recognized me but that she had also in some kind of cosmic reduction also now recognized herself.

My mood refrigerated.

I leaned into her, crow-black and deadly serious.

"I have come here—*pay attention to me!*—I have come here to remind you that you were once a savage to me," I said to her in words as bitter and bleak as I could make them. *In Yo Face.* "You abused me as a child. Do you remember how you did it? You made me stand up in front of everybody and, against my will, sing a song all alone! You shamed me—you, you, you put me to shame! You—debased me. Do you remember? *Crushed me!*" Even as I spoke, I assure you, it was as if the very soul inside me on the cusp of re-recognition was re-living—*suffering*—the ignominy of that evil, wretched day.

I spoke slowly, clearly, so that the woman could get it. I pieced it all out as if I were giving her the kind of lesson that she gave me. A hand flew to her mouth. She'd not expected this. She had expected anything but this. People do not like to learn—to be taught—what they do not already know, a paradox of cognition. And who on earth is more hidebound than a crusty old, authoritarian grade-school principal?

I continued my narration. "And during all of it, all the while, you stood by like an evil monster, a fucking monkey"—here, she jumped back startled with the queerest imaginable look on her crumpling face—"with your arms folded and with smirking delight demeaned me! With everybody else watching, some pitying but others mocking. *Mocking!* The Washington School. You were the principal. In a fourth-grade classroom. Ten years ago." I tried in summing it up to recount for her in detail exactly how it had happened and when it happened and what had taken place all those years ago, mincing no words, to convey to her that was the principal agent, tearing it off strip by strip. I pointed directly into her face. "You molested me, is what you did. Violated me. You took advantage of a small boy."

The woman's face was positively ashen, as she sat slumping, the dusty wrinkles in that termagant's shocked face withering under my scolding reprimand. But my rebuke had only just begun. I rose like a tide to lambaste her.

I coldly and carefully followed the train of the unreasonable.

"Think back! No, stay there. I said *stay right there*! Don't get up. Do. Not. Get. Up." I insistently moved closer into her vision. "Now, go way back in your mind to consider how in a perverted sense you took pleasure in humiliating me. What is worse, I witnessed the delight you took, the arrogance, in making me cry." I took in her face, while revisiting my mind to call up the image on the garage wall and the vile things she had made me scribble there, having forced me to be complicit in her adult ugliness. "The delight," I repeated, "the relish, the rapture, the entertainment, that you felt in appropriating me!"

"Now," I said, my eyes sharpening, "it's your turn, all right? Now *you* sing, 'Take Me Out to the Ball Game'—loud."

Came a long pause.

"W-what did you say?"

She was blinking like a hamster, protective hands squeezed on her bosom.

"What d-did you say?" she repeated, her voice actually trembling.

I felt weirdly, purposefully, *justifiably*, almost giddily alive and awakened in my wrath and reminded myself with Baudelaire, "Minutes, blithesome mortal, are bits of ore that you must not release without extracting the gold! Remember, Time is a greedy player who wins without cheating, every round! It's the law. The daylight wanes; the night deepens; remember! The abyss thirsts always; the water-clock runs low."

She went to move. I quickly moved, to follow. To hedge her. She started to bolt, and I sharply stepped to intercept her, shifting, blocking any exit. She reached to grab the telephone on the stand. I angrily kicked it over in a crash, knocking the entire apparatus onto the floor at her feet and punted away the receiver. At the noise, I heard a howl like the eastern spadefoot toad, a wail like a soul on its way to perdition.

Hate Her to Death.

I shook my fist in her face and ordered, "Sing!"

"No," she said flatly. Her eyes contracted evilly.

"Sing," I bellowed.

"P-please."

"Sing the song, goddammit!"

I went to reach to grab her chin. She backed off into the tall chair, cringing, and hissed, "Something is w-wrong with you! T-terribly."

"Yes," I said.

"What?"

"You!" I declared. "*You're* what's wrong with me. *You.* You who took advantage of a child! A grown woman in authority. But now it's your turn, don't you see? I'm in authority now. It is your turn, granny lady." I moved closer to her. She twitched in fright. "Now do what I tell you to do. It betokens you not only to listen but to obey me. Now, *sing it.*"

She squinted at me hatefully,

Icily, she rose up and spat fury. "*I willll nottt.*"

It was then I took out my gun and aimed it directly at her. *Night of the .44.*

If what I did seemed a childish thing to do, I did in rueful remembrance of the fact I was a child and that was the child I was. I did so to redeem that child, to remind the child that his regrets and his dire recollections had not been lost on me. Box it about, OK? Seeking to forget creates an even greater estrangement from the self, allows a wound to fester, and only lengthens exile. The secret of redemption lies in remembrance, but only if the recollection it serves to remove is a studied recall to savor, to stop, to stifle. I had enough of letting a little boy weep against the walls of his heart, consumed by his pain.

My struggle with memory was *against* forgetting. The obscene thing is to allow regret. To relieve repentance, kill remorse.

The weapon caught her attention.

Nuttin' but a Bitch Thang.

She began to cry, blubbering, just as I had, snatching at a swatch her grey hair, seizing threads of it with a pulling fist of desperation and utter horror and alarm, as she haplessly slid down from her chair, almost ready in her trepidation to try to kneel in humble fright. I could hear hiccups as she stuttered to talk, but nothing came out.

I mocked her memory "Spring is not always in bloom," I said. "Right?" "That's what you always told us at school assemblies. "'Time conquers everything.' *Tempus vincit omnia.* See? So, now it is time for you." She was cringing.

"Now sing!"

Nothing.

"Sing!"

I was howling now.

Screeching.

It was then that I heard from her, mouse-low, the words I listened for in a meek, pathetic voice rinsed of rancor by a terror of death with each pulse barely a beat. This was no school principal now but a near cadaver, blenched.

"T-take me (sob) out to the—nmmbaaall game,
Take you m-me out to, in to—with the cruowwwd . . ."

"No," I said. "You're not doing it right."

I wagged the gun.

"With gestures."

She looked up, horror-struck, almost petrified.

"Sing it with gestures!" I ordered.

Ask, had I pang of conscience, remorse, any hint of anguish for what I was doing? Did I feel at that moment a single jot or tittle of self-rebuke or shame or compunction as this cartoon hag in a housecoat dribbled the lyrics?

None.

Or as snot dripped from her nose, even when her wrinkled old hands twitched at her dirty wrapper and the feeble gestures of a bat swing was but a flay swat?

Not a bit.

"T-take me (sob) out to the—nmmbaaall game,
Take m-me out to, in to—with the cruowwwd;
Buy (mewling) me some . . . dougnhuts"

"—peanuts," I snarled, correcting her. The gun was on her.
The Shaggy Show.

Tears were now pouring down her cheeks.

"—and Cracker Jack"

"and C-cracker (blubber) Jacks, I don't care if I n-never get back.
Let me root, root, root for the home team, If they don't win, it's a
shame"

I menacingly stood above the old crone as I sought to leave.
"As J. Wellington Wimpy would say, 'Thank you too much!' Or 'I'd
like to invite you over to my house for a duck dinner—you bring
the ducks.'"

Her head was down, lowered. Sacrificially. Mortified.

"Say it, say the damn line" I said, icily. "Repeat for me what
Wimpy said, say out loud the words that Wimpy said," and I quoted
the words to the accompaniment of my waving gun, wildly, up and
down, as if I were directing a school chorus. "Say, 'I would like to
invite you over to my house for a duck dinner—you bring the
ducks.'"

I could see that she was hyperventilating.

Down with the Clown

Bent over, Miss Sharkey in a low whine was on her knees,
crouched and wheezing, but no longer sniveling, and yet totally abject, whispered, 'I'd l-ike to invite you vover to my hicehouse for a
doduck dinner—you . . .'"

"Bring the ducks," I coldly, helpfully, added. I stepped
closer and repeated the words.

She was barely breathing.

"'Thank you too much,'" I insisted she repeat. "Say it."

She did so in a low mutterance, an undertoned mumble-mutter, scarcely to be heard, almost a susurration that could be taken for a purr.

"Louder."

Miss Sharkey gleeped, "Thinnks . . . thank hoo ou too much."

I shoved the gun into my pocket.

I took one last look at the old lady and, no longer needing to forget to do something after realizing I was past it, slammed shut the door, and walked away.

The Trials of Qwert Yui Op

"All emotion is involuntary when genuine."

Mark Twain

A very rare few people are born without emotions. Any sentiment. Passions. Feelings. Responses. Soul. Surely, it's common for all of us to express our emotions, even if for a time, in many different, and under a variety of circumstances. Is it true, as some say, that physical traits are achieved through personality? That our shapes as humans grow from attitudes? I have even read that good deeds can create beauty in a person. Natural instinctive states of mind derive from one's circumstances, mood, or relationships with others, no? When I was growing up, I knew a man whom I can openly state had no emotions.

None.

The human mind in its odd twists and turns can truly be the most horrifying and gruesome thing of all, or at least I'm sure most people would agree. Remember the crow-counting rhyme: *One for sorrow / Two for mirth / Three for a wedding / and Four for a birth / Five for silver / Six for gold / and Seven for a secret not to be told*? The person I am talking was the secret not to be told. His laundry was located in a shop on Forest Street. I once worked for him as an odd-job boy for seven weeks.

His name was Qwert Yui Op.

My name is Ralph Pencil and to say that I knew this man, as an identifying detail, is woefully insufficient. When I was fourteen, I took an afterschool job there, cleaning up, under strange circumstances that I will soon tell you about, working for him three

times a week after school, but even before that, whenever my
mother used to send me to his shop either to drop off or pick up
our dry cleaning, I would shake like a leaf doing so, simply because
of the silent, mysterious, shuffling person he was—he never said so
much as boo to me—and it was no different when I did small tasks
for him. He would remain wordless until simply reaching into his
sleeves for the $12.50 that he paid me weekly.

The location of his small business was just down from the
local high school, a drab little shop but anonymous, without a doorbell or a knocker, its sole purpose identified by a small white sign
with his name hung from a hook. Inside the stifling rooms one
could smell the odor of steam, noodles, and fresh laundry. He had
no family that anyone ever saw. At night, he slept in a cubbyhole in
a space cleared of absent emotion.

What caused in him those truant feelings, missing reactions,
and lack of sentiment—self-pity? Deep wounds? A sense of loss?
Dislocation? Past anguish? Natural gloom? Had some unspeakable
thing happened to him?

Was he devoid of any natural gift for caring?

I have no theory.

But there was a livid wound in him that never healed.

Morning and afternoon, students—kids—in their way to
school would pass his shop, often stopping to peer into his front
window as they walked by, older, tougher high school boys often
with their fingers raised cruelly, making a pinched insult of Asian
eyes. as they ridiculed him. Some mockingly called out "Ching
Chong Chink," others "Rice Burner," "Slope," "Slant Eyes," "Banana," "Buddha-head." It was an appalling assault, and I felt so
even as a kid. They called him a "dink" and a "gook" and "Charlie"
and a "Jap" and "kimchi." There was "Nip" and "Wonton." I also
heard older people often snicker and refer to him as "The Key-
board." My own mother, who was never uncharitable, to anybody,
found it in herself to call him "Far Flung."

Qwert Yui Op had tons of folk wisdom. I had a deep splinter once. He haltingly explained—by gestures, sometimes by a quick sketch—that a simple potato can help pull one out embedded too deeply in one's skin to extricate with tweezers. He was willing to take the time with me but was always impassive. He placed a smidgen of grated potato onto a piece of gauze bandage and taped it over the splinter, until the potato had time to dry. We waited a day. As the potato dried, it drew bodily fluid to it. It worked. The moisture carried the splinter to the surface, so that it was easy to remove. I could swear, he was a magician!

He put salt pork on small cuts, butter on burns, black tea on tender, smarting eyes, used strips of a brown paper bag soaked in cider vinegar to heal reduce swelling or heal bruising, curiously suggested chewing turnip root to treat chills, and to soothe it swabbed a sore throat with a feather soaked in—yes—kerosene. Can you believe it?

He was an odd duck. I've seen him clap fistfuls of the herb borage into his mouth as an anti-depressant. Herbs figured in much of his thinking. He told me he believed parsley both repelled head lice and attracted rabbits. He shook tarragon into his shoes to give his feet strength. He took a teaspoon of mustard to relieve a cough, Witch hazel, he said, shrunk hemorrhoids. He cleaned the drains in his sinks with baking soda and white vinegar. I learned all of this by way of his fumbling gestures, a swift drawing or two, his acting out a teaching pantomime. He smeared peanut butter on his metal tools as a winter preservative. He made elderberry syrup in a saucepan once a week. He broke eggs into lightly oiled ice-cube trays, then stored the frozen cubes in containers. Thawed, they cooked and tasted like fresh eggs.

People in town claimed that he ate cats. They reported that in his freezer could also be found chicken testicles, turkey feet, pig brain and scorpions, black eggs, fried water dragonflies, and that he breakfasted on bowls of snake soup. And for dinner living newborn mice. Nothing was too outlandish to ascribe to this solitary man who met his customers without a word. I later in life heard of an Associated Press report that people in southern China's Guangdong Province (population just over 113 million) ate 10,000 cats per day. I never saw Qwert Yui Op actively eat. But I do know what he ate, simply because what he ate was exclusively always the same thing all the time– a weird-looking, oblong green fruit called a "bitter melon." Oblong, with a warty exterior, it is hollow in cross-section, with a relatively thin layer of flesh surrounding a central seed cavity filled with large, flat seeds and pith. The fruit apparently is best eaten green or when beginning to turn yellow. At the stages I saw, the fruit's flesh was crunchy and watery in texture, similar to cucumber or green bell pepper, but way more bitter. I once secretly nipped it, see? The skin was tender. Seeds and pith appear white in unripe and less intensely bitter and can be removed before cooking, which he did at times.

When he ate, he removed himself and went alone and separately down in—I was going to say, in his basement. But it wasn't a basement. It was a dark, damp cellar with a rickety wooden staircase, mis-nailed and half-broken and splintery. I could hear him slurping bitter melon in the shadows down there. I dared to descend there once. It was remote, like everything about him. Mr. Farfaraway—hey, he *was* far flung. *Isolation* was what he was all about. Cut off. Un-get-at-able. "Go back where you came from," many mean people would shout at him. "Take a hike, yellow man!" "You don't belong here."

Anyone could see his identity was stolen, because his identity was lampooned. Asian men are not immune to racism. Historically, film and television depicted such creatures as villains or sly, desexualized and effeminate secondary characters. While the more contemporary pop cultures I had both grown up with treated them as desirable leading characters, the cruel stereotype of the cunning, secretive oddball persists.

I would find myself in my adolescence often wondering about the personal nature of his mystery, of his secrecy, its distance, the width and range of his separation from people, and trying to gauge if it was weakness or strength. The whys of it nagged at me. Was he aware of the riddle he was? Did he understand himself? Do any of us comprehend ourselves in that we know what we want and so live our lives in that direction, or is what we are so infinitely deep down in us, so far from our desires, that we simple take refuge in what we are supposed to be, as he did not? He represented that odd oracle to me.

What I mean to say is that for the very first time in my life he made me come to look at myself from within, since that was the only side of *him* I never saw, and so having to recognize myself by way of that interior look—the only kind *he* seemed to deny—I came to see that I often appeared indifferent while feeling otherwise. It made think I'd thought the wrong way before learning that the other way mattered, as well.

I had the ogling occasion once to see him in an argument, a one-sided confrontation with an angry customer, a man he nearly killed, although once again I can promise you that in the encounter he spoke not a single word. It was before I worked there, when I was about eleven years old and bringing a coat to be dry-cleaned. I suspect it was part of the reason he hired me, as a weird kind of alliance to shut me up.

Being howled at the silent but hard-pressed merchant for gross ineptitude and lapsed work in having poorly cleaned an expensive suede jacket, Qwert Yui Op stood faceless, berated, as he heard *"Look at what you've done! Look at what you've done!"* The customer was banging the counter, slapping it. Impassively listening, looking past him, the small owner from nowhere brought a thin knife down with a flash—I was shocked, actually grew dizzy—to miss the man's hand by what had to be a scant inch! I could not believe my eyes. Screaming, the man ran out. Abashed, I silently swapped the coat for my laundry ticket.

I was trembling. Qwert Yui Op noticed it. That is when I was hired to work there, part-time, after school. It took almost ten or fifteen minutes for me to understand that he wanted to hire me as part-time help. Mainly with gestures and mumbles, by way of pantomime, roleplay, he picked up a broom and pointed to me. He laid out $12.50.

His face was a plate. He was short, still wore his coarse hair straight, coal black, like a rope in a queue, with narrow eyes, monolids, tapered double eyelids, with strong epicanthic folds, and sparse but high flammulated eyebrows like insect antennas, and he bobbed when he walked in a tick-tock fashion. I never learned, because I never dared bothered to inquire, whether this man was Chinese or Tibetan, Korean or Vietnamese—who knows, maybe he was from Mongolia—and although later, when I was in college, I did think about trying to find out but never bothered to do so. I saw snuff bottles on his shelves, porcelain stem bowls, an incense burner with two dragon-head handles, a painted prayer flag showing a snow lion, a white copper teapot, a conch-shell trumpet—weren't they used in prayers?—and a crystal statue which he once pointed to and mumbled, "*Shakyamuni.*" The tiny, seated figure wore a blue beanie and had pendulous ears. I peered closer and asked, "The Shaking Mummy?" It was the one time I think—*I think*—I detected a trace of a smile.

He had such high seriousness—far, far less of gravity than ferocity—as if in that weird, uncompromisingly locked, compact, rigid, and, in its intensity, terrifying and *pincering* stare of his, abstractly fixed nowhere, he was constantly concentrating on some past wound or trouble or deep, elemental disturbance.

He showed no fervor, no fire, excitement, or spirit. He was a closed book. A machine. What had he undergone? Suffered? Where and how and when? Those are questions that I dared ask myself only later in life. No one could account for his rigid lack of personality, but it became the occasion of rumor, anger, and abuse. One rumor was that, arbitrarily, out of anger or mere whim, he often threw away certain customers' clothes. He came to have to live by the spite that he felt he needed to have in order to survive, but at the same time he simultaneously had to cope with the wrath he came to find his antagonisms generated.

Who in earth could possibly explain it?

Who knows, maybe his strange, inexplicable behavior was the result of all the bitter melon he ate. The fruit's bitterness, or so I read later, unlike his missing personality, is said to decrease with age. A Chinese variety was best harvested when green, possibly with a slight yellow tinge or just before. The pith becomes sweet, intensely red, and can be eaten uncooked in that state. It is a popular ingredient in Asian salads When the fruit is fully ripe, it turns orange and soft and splits into segments that curl back to expose seeds covered in bright red pulp—red like the kind of fury I had seen that one time. It seemed to me at the time in a fury he would spin himself into the ground like Rumpelstiltskin!

In any case, I had taken another job when he didn't need me anymore. After the seven weeks I worked there, which was next door to Lepore's shoe shop, I was hired by them to do the same kind of errands and business of cleaning up because the cobblers saw I was a hard worker. There had been nothing much for me to do at the dry cleaners, and my Mom insisted that I keep a job after school—I was a high school freshman—to earn a little pin money and to keep out of trouble. I used to see Qwert Yui Op daily in summer coming and going, opening the shop by clockwork at 8 a.m., and closing it down at 6 p.m. He would fumble with his keys at the door showing no emotion—apathetic, unmoved, reserved, inscrutable, you choose the word—looking neither right nor left. Whenever he saw me, or did not see me—who could say?—I never knew, because his look was unfathomable.

Whether he looked past me or through me or beyond me became all the same in its expressionless inscrutability. That is simply the way he was. Whenever the front door of his little shop was opened or left ajar and, because of where I worked now, I could often hear next door his various transactions. Whatever, he was as perpetual foreigner.

I had seen him rub salt in fruit-stained clothes while still wet, then put them into the wash. Salt, he loved. To clean his sticky clothing iron, he would sprinkle salt on a piece of paper and run the iron over it a few times while the iron was hot. He dashed salt on carpets to dry out muddy footprints before vacuuming them. A paste of salt and water he ingeniously used to take out perspiration stains, and he also refreshed sponges by soaking them in cold salt-water for ten or fifteen minutes. He infused the laundry—just for special customers—with lavender by stuffing a muslin sachet with dried buds, pulling it tight, and tossing it into the dryer with a load of damp clothes, and let the scent sweeten the lot.

Many customers came in with stained clothes that he hated. I had seen his steam guns, because I once had to box some leather in his shop to be cleaned by them. Leather is the most expensive item to clean, around $100 for a coat, so you're paying more for that material to have it cleaned. While many dry cleaners rarely ever work on leather on their premises, preferring to send it to a third-party leather cleaner, Qwert Yui Op did all his work on premise. Also, there is no special leather dry cleaning method. Leather is simply lightly spot cleaned with a dish-soap leather formula and then hung to air dry in a moisture-free environment overnight. You're essentially just paying for the labor charge. To save money, you could lightly go over the jacket yourself with liquid soap, water, and a microfiber towel.

He also did a business in carpets and rugs, which he chem-dried and steam-cleaned. He had a truly malicious-looking steam gun. It was a hand-held, high-pressure, high-temperature textile spot apparatus that looked like a large cobra, its brush a serpent head. In a dingy back room, there with all sorts of utensils, brushes, and rows of jars filled with scouring compounds was an old broken push lawnmower filthy with rust and grime that had frozen gears. I was sweeping in that room once when he pointed to it. I looked at Qwert Yui Op and gestured to it myself with the obvious question. He did not provide a yes or a no, just pulled his index finger in a snapping motion toward himself: *bring it to me.*

I was astonished to see him immediately snatch up his steam gun—I came to see it was a special tool of his, a favorite instrument or rattling contrivance (a vengeful device in his damaged mind against mankind?)—and in an instant so perforate the iron-black gubbins of that lawnmower's cogs, blades, flying pins, and gearwheels with the loud force *sneeerwhhooooosh* of that burrowing drill that I positively gasped. I could not believe what I saw. *He positively shredded it!* I should perhaps add I also saw hate in his eyes. But there was nothing in his eyes.

A long, extended clothes steam press stood in another room, along with no end of flat hand irons, including an ancient oak textile clothing press; an antique alcohol flat steam sad iron; and a coal cloth ironing board. The place could have been a museum, for all I know, of original dry-cleaning tools and stuff. There were seventy-five or so bottles of spotting chemicals, with a great risk of fire and explosion for any dry-cleaning shop that used petroleum-based solvents in their machines, which this did. Not only bad for the environment, perchloroethylene (PERC), the most commonly used dry cleaning solvent, I have since read, is a potential human carcinogen. Symptoms associated with its exposure include depression of the central nervous system, damage to the liver and kidneys; impaired memory; confusion; dizziness; headaches; drowsiness; and eye, nose, and throat irritation.

Anyway, the little place was nothing if not quaint, weird in the peculiar way of a foreign-run business, full of unexpected turns and unanticipated events.

Qwert Yui Op was a very fussy person, fastidious in his own exacting way, and, like all mulish types, especially one from a foreign country, he was stubborn, self-willed, and pigheaded and selective about certain fabrics and materials. Down jackets, take for example, are rarely dry-cleaned but laundered, and hung out dry overnight, and then placed in a dryer for a few minutes to plump out the feathers, when they are good to go. Down coats, down items are not pressed. So, it can cost a pretty penny for customers to have such a coat cleaned, as they have to be washed by themselves, lest they spill feathers onto other items, which is why they are so expensive, to ensure profit from the isolated load. Down jackets need to be dried in a dryer with a tennis ball in order to prevent the clumping of the feathers.

Quirky, my Asian boss hated taking in wool sweaters, as dry-cleaning chemicals can often be abrasive on finer wools, when customers complained. He refused to take in items with rust stains, oil-based paint stains, or stains by permanent markers and spurned all silk shirts and cashmere sweaters. Peacoats, he disliked, but occasionally took. Peacoats are notorious for getting lint on them when they are dry-cleaned, and he often had me remove the clinging lint from them by scraping and shaving the fabric to look nicer when picked-up. Baseball and hockey jerseys cannot be dry-cleaned as it will melt the logos; they had to be laundered. He also found it irksome to accept men's button-down shirts unless they could be laundered by the bulk and then heat-pressed on their own machine in less than twenty seconds. Dry cleaners made little money of this, so it's a great value to the customer.

Never bring a good comforter to a dry cleaner unless it specifically states "dry-clean only." Couldn't customers in their dunderheaded thinking realize that? Dry cleaner owners will not dry-clean a comforter unless they have to, because it is cheaper to launder. Comforters can range from $50 or higher and you're getting less quality than you would at a laundromat. Comforters are rarely ever spotted for stains, and they're laundered in a basic commercial wash machine with a standard setting, hung to dry over night to save on drying time, then placed in the commercial dryer, and then finished. If your comforter had any bad odor before you brought it in, it probably is still going to have that odor! You're better off paying $5 at a laundromat and choosing your own cycle and spin settings.

Qwert Yui Op had seen it all: food stains—blood, gum, red wine, baby food, berry juice, chocolate—but, even far, far worse, starched-in armpit yellow, body perspiration, motor oil, grease spills, lipstick, smelly gloves and hats. Tannin-based stains from substances like wine, coffee, or tea, when fairly fresh are often manageable, but old or untreated can become deeply embedded and often harder to remove. Customers can be stupid and lazy and ignorant. Why bother going to a dry-cleaner if it is either unnecessary or hopeless. I came to see, even though I was a dogsbody for my boss, that many customers never check or understand their "care labels," and dry cleaners love that. Some formal dresses fall into "spot-clean only," which means they can't be washed in a conventional way. You bring in fancy sequins glued to a fabric? Forget it! Dry cleaning will melt and damage the dress. Dry cleaning, oil-based, will melt glue and plastic. Dry cleaners, when they can't clean it. may charge you major dollars regarding all fancy dress. They may go over the spots and individually try to treat them, or hand-wash the item by soaking it in cold water, and hang drying overnight, nothing you can't do at home. Again, with the fancy sequins, such items typically cannot be pressed.

Anyway, my second year at the job at Lepore's, I was one day pouring out some old saddle soap into the street gutter and walking back toward the front door, when a fat, rough man whom I knew parked his big black Buick directly right in front of both shops—no one *ever* did that—and walked into the dry cleaners with a long parcel box. I heard the exchange. Wait, give me a minute. Exchange, did I say?

Wrong.

The laundry man said not a thing.

"You there? C'mere! Look. See? This here's my daughter's wedding gown," barked Mr. Battaglia. As I say, I knew the guy, well, I mean I had seen that guy, a frightening sort of bully, simply because he was always seen hanging around at the Mustang Café, lounging around and talking in a loud raucous voice and grabbing kids to go buy him cigars. He was well known in the neighborhood. What to know was, he was not to be ignored, in any case, being a fat and bowlegged lout with a broken nose and punishing voice. An Irish guy, another punk who hung around the café, once called him a "goombah" or a "guido," words mocking Italians, whereupon in the flash of a response he jumped the guy and punched him out cold. It was rumored he carried a gun. I myself would believe any damned thing they said about him that was bad. "Loogadid-whydonthcha, K? It's a wedding dress from the 1960s, feel it, kind of an A-skirt type a thing, tea-length dress with lace and stuff. Vintage. You can't hep but see so, right?"

Battaglia was getting exasperated.

"I got the box here, look, ev'yting. This dress inside here, as you can see, is hung or wrapped whaddyacallit in dry cleaner's plastic sheets on it from the old days, fit and fashioned to take care, but now it's all yellow, for you can see what time done to it, OK? Tell me, you being a dry cleaner, you can do something to bring it back to white, right? I don't know what to do with the dress, and I'm fearing to try anything myself in case I ruin it, see?"

Mute, unforthcoming, Qwert Yui Op with a single raised finger pointed to a sign in the wall. There were signs, prices, paneled everywhere, a sort of facade of explanations that spoke for him, but they were also intervals of barriers that afforded him silence. There was no talk required. He needed none of it. The scrawled signs were fortifications, ramparts.

I looked scarily sideways to see the thug peer into a price chart. "What, so wedding dresses gonna cost me more, you tellin' me? A few more bucks, that it? No biggie, OK? I could give a good goddam. You do what you do. But wait a minute, it says here"—he pointed—"you don't clean wedding dresses." He did a double take "So, you sayin', what? Say it. Say sometin'. Can you talk?" He shoved forward butting his belly into the front desk and, leaning in over the counter an inch from Qwert Yui Op's face, tapped the counter with a forefinger five or six times. "Or you tellin' me instead to, what, piss off and you do nuttin', and with this dress I should take a fuckin' hike and walk?" He waited. "Is that it?" He waited. "Like this is a game of parchesi or somethin'? He burned. "Like I'm some kinda goddam *cafone*?"

A local cop, passing, noted the big automobile in front with an unfed parking meter and poked his nose through the laundry door to ask, "You—are you parking here?" Impatient, angry, Battaglia shouted back, "*Si! Parcheggio sì, quella è la mia macchina. Ma sì, tanto sto giusto due minuti! Rilassati, va bene?*"

"*Sticazzi!*" the thug barked.

He turned back to the dry cleaner.

Qwert Yui Op, unmoved, was staring at this customer with a closed face. Not a single show of human emotion. His face never changed, to cope or to cringe, He stood unemotionally in place, his hands folded deep in his sleeves, not *Four for a birth | Five for silver | Six for gold | but Seven for a secret not to be told.*

Slowly, angrily, Battaglia held up the old wedding box and in a raspy voice pieced out the cold words, "Take a look at this dress. See? This here, the one I'm holdin'? You know about yellow. Dis ting here you see is yellow, which you should know about, right, yellow on the outside, white in—like you, Banana. This here's the reason why I come here to bring it to you, Wun Dum Fuk, do get it? Catch? *Capisce?* Let me spell it for you again, one time, once, OK, Fuzznut? This here is to be my daughter's wedding dress, like I say—I couldna make it clearer—so you just standin' there and being a goddam *chiaccierone* about it don't go down right, an' I'm not gonna take a dive like a *cozzo* for you and just say fuhgeddabouudit, OK? Sorry, that ain't the way it's gonna go. Main ting, see, you gonna make this clean, you hear, Chow Mein, you china-faced bit of macaca, and f*ix it right—or else!*"

Battaglio hung fire.

Not a word was spoken.

"So, what is it you're sayin', *walio*—no dice? That it? *Schifosa! Ammazza*" He raised and bit the knuckles of his hand, a curse gesture. "*Porca miseria!*"

Knowing that Battaglia guy, I suspected trouble, and it would come later, but at that point, I tell you, from sheer fright I fled. I raced over to Lepore's, said not a word to anyone, and closed my eyes, closed my mind, closed my ears, and sat completely quiet, silent, behind a large shoe display there, looking busy, a tall merchandising rack of shoe risers, accessories, and shoe forms. My heart was beating hard. I cannot tell you just how long that I stayed right there, but I never went outside that day again. But wait. When I did leave to go home after work, that big black Buick was still parked out front, in the same spot. I even told my mother about it. It was well known in town that Carmine Battaglia was not a person to fool around with or to provoke.

He was very short-tempered. He was also "connected," as they say. As I say, he was short, fat, round, muscular, whose olive skin was more the color of mahogany. His brother Vinny was in my homeroom. I used to see him in the submarine sandwich shop after school, getting free subs because the owner was afraid of him. Me? I myself was afraid that in a fit of anger he might try to hurt Qwert Yui Op, do him some danger.

That Neapolitan slang word "*walio*"? I heard it all the time. The actual word, the one it misuses—the original word—is "*ouaglioni,* which means "guy." Are you surprised? Don't be. I grew up fascinated with words and later become a writer. I believe that I even heard that Blacks hearing it, derived the word "yo" from it.

My mother once told me that wedding dresses and that kind of exclusive finery could cost up to $200 to be dry-cleaned, and no, were not to be treated the same way as a cheap $6 pair of pants. When I went and mentioned that particular parcel to my Mom about wedding dresses, she said something about them and a preservation box, which for a thing like a wedding dress is specifically designed to safeguard the gown, look after it, protecting it from environmental factors like dust, light, moisture, and wear that can cause damage over time. "If you ever buy a wedding dress," she said, "*never* opt for the preservation box. Dresses cost more, you get the preservation box, which adds $50 or more to the cost, and dry cleaners *do not* press wedding dresses that get placed in such a box, which can have been stuck in there forever. See? I mean, by the time the customer opens it, what, three or ten years later to notice it isn't pressed, it's too late to take back to the cleaners for a redo, all right? So, you're paying more money for the dress *without* the pressing. You get more for your money if you buy the preservation box elsewhere and put it in there yourself after you get your dress cleaned and pressed."

She was absolutely correct.

I was not there that day, but Mr. Lepore told me you could hear the argument—single-sided, for Qwert Yui Op never said a word—for almost half a mile away! There was only the noise of a single outraged voice—a spate of one-sided barks and threats. Apparently, the thug had threatened him, said he was pressed for time, and that he had not made the trip down to that shop to be rebuffed. Impatient, annoyed, provoked, Battaglia badly received the news

that the old wedding dress could not be cleaned. Not at all? It was
out of the question.

A cousin of Battaglia's, Sal "Doggy" Gnazzo, I later heard,
set fire to the laundry bins out in the back alley just for fun of it,
but it was in reprisal against the foreign owner. Whenever I stopped
at the High St. café, I would often, but nervously, watch a group of
them from a corner booth, gathered to talk, always with hand gestures, Johnny "Black Rain" Malinconico, Wag "Fig Newton" Podargoni, and others in the group—a *"raga"* was how they referred
to themselves—with names like Falaguerra, Calcagno, Cicci-
obomba, and Abbatemarco. They virtually owned the biggest cubi-
cle there, where, all crowding around a table, they wolfed down big
platters of ossobuco, veal shanks sawed cross-wise—it means
"bone with a hole"—even slurping up the gravy uptilted from the
dish. Wimpy "Duck Egg" Selvitella was famous for having spent
six years in Alcatraz. I once by brought Podargoni from the counter
a dish of *struffoli*, or honey balls, that he had asked me to get for
him, an order as I interpreted it, and he slipped me a half a dollar in
thanks. You obeyed them. Trust me. Gave them space. These were
guys you didn't want to cross, or even look at.

Without a doubt.

No question.

Crossing the Craddock Bridge one night, I once witnessed
out of the corner of my eye Anthony ("Tony Skiball") Scibelli being
almost beaten to death in a tow path practically right in view of St.
Joseph's Church.

As I say, Qwert Yui Op was a difficult and exacting person,
very choosy and selective about what he would and would not take
in to clean. Half the time, customers themselves knew absolutely
zip about the whole nature of cleaning., what's to be done. Take
professional-grade pressing, for example, if your item cannot be
pressed, you are often paying more for an item you could be doing
yourself. Bottom line? To get the most for your money, if you drop

something off at the dry cleaners, make sure it can benefit from what you're paying for. All right? Regarding the impossible, however, like cleaning an old crusty yellowed wedding dress? A brittle, friable, decaying, and damaged shred of textile, soiled and begrimed, left over from nuptial years past, having been ignored in a dry dusty box in attic? Forget it.

Did I say forget it? Some don't.

Which brings me to my point.

About Mr. Battaglia, I mean.

For that was exactly where the problem began. There was a big police presence on that city block of shops for almost a week. They even came into Lepore's to question them and me about the car, the Buick, as to who owned it or might have left it there. Why was it parked there for so long, overnight, on so many nights? I had observed both Phil "Backwards Chris" Scarfo and fat Freddy "Alligator Arms" Bursacola in the vicinity the very night before—I got scared, what the Italians call *impaurito*, their word for it—but said nothing, *because you don't*, and stayed totally mum. The investigation took that amount of time to discover the murder. The corpse, if that is the right term one should use, for the body—in pieces—had been dismembered by steam gun. I spent much of the time that week watching, across the street on a stool eating ice cream, sitting at a United Farmers Dairy counter. To say I was concerned would be an understatement. The event changed me. As I've said, when you truly come to see yourself within, you can no longer appear indifferent while feeling otherwise.

"What exactly did they find down there?" my mother hesitated to ask, although she did so apprehensively, almost not wanting to hear the answer. The newspaper she'd avoided reading was full of lore and gory details, no small thing for a small town, having reported they took out bags from below the stairs.

I sat down next to her.

"From the dark basement, I mean?"

"Cellar," I corrected her.

"Cats?" she offered tentatively and waiting, pulled the top of her blue sweater protectively up to her mouth in horrified expectation. "*Dead cats?*"

I slowly shook my head.

"Bags of chicken testicles?" she asked. "Pig brains? Turkey feet? Scorpions, black eggs, fried water dragonflies? Living newborn mice?" She couldn't believe her own voice. "Not bowls of frozen snake soup, I hope, please God, tell me no!"

"No."

"Then what?"

I shrugged. "Battaglia. Carmine Battaglia."

I remember the day that Qwert Yui Op was executed. It was recorded on the front page of all the papers. My age at the time was twenty-three.

Portrait of Geraldine Oikle

> "Pity is treason."
> Maximilien Robespierre

Donn Croivak, an art teacher at Ethan Allen Academy in Vermont, lived alone with his black cat, "Rat," and a parrot on a small road, just off-campus. He was described by his colleagues, after he left the school, as a "deeply eccentric man" who "lived like an ambassador from the kingdom of ridiculous notions" and who "had an odd sense of humor but often smiled." He was a follower of phrenology and spiritualism and fad diets and didn't believe in refrigerators or ice cubes because he felt cold food was bad for the health. A fellow of impulse and passion, he lived to paint and loved to teach, as well, but deeply energized by the need to master his craft and feeling the requirements to do so, yearned to spend more time alone, as he had growing up in the nearby mountains of that beautiful state.

He was affable with his colleagues but disliked the social obligations that a faculty living community demanded of one. He was a dreamer, traveled a lot, bought reasonably priced paintings when they were both good and when he could afford them. He loved gardening and classical music, especially Mozart, and was a rabid reader of books. He drove an old Triumph TR4A and lived in a school-provided house on a hill.

He stayed predominantly by himself. He was not social. He felt all the insecurities that come with being human. He had ideals but disliked people who arbitrarily flaunted them, for to him they registered as nothing but phonies. He took the world to be absurd, which seemed to him to be a prime premise in life. He resented all forms of political gatekeeping and cancel culture. If he had an interior life, it was essentially the secret life of the mind. He tended to believe most things were a delusion, that serendipity reigned, that chance and hap prevailed, informing not only the crucial decisions one faced but also their outcomes. A simple corner that one turned, or failed to turn, could affect one's entire life, whom you met, or did not. When one comes to see that the living of life is a mystery, a dream, that it is basically an accident, or coincidence -- call it fortune, providence or happenstance -- one could still make a life for oneself, for in the final equation that in fact was the trick of the thing, opening up possibility, giving one a sense of freedom. It wasn't a deep philosophy, merely a settled and uncomplicated approach to living, a subtext that interpreted fate as the kind of funny performance he had long concluded it was. Himself, he never took too seriously. What predominated was his painting. Politically correct people drove him mad, but he was always open to hear, willing to be patient with, the outcast, the fugitive, the exile, which in many ways was the way he saw himself.

He took dinners at the school dining hall and dined out as infrequently as possible. He hated telephones, impromptu visitors, keeping office hours, being observed. What he yearned for in painting pointed his direction and became the way he lived. Years before, however, on a stay on the island of Santorini, unfortunately, he had managed by default foolishly to get an amount of white lead in his left eye, a toxic pigment of lead carbonate and sulfate, which he had ignored. He was an Aries—enthusiastic, full of pride and drive, with a touch of impetuousness.

He was also blind in one eye.

The black patch he wore gave him the look of a pirate, with somehow the romantic connotation of a dashing, dangerous buccaneer.

Being single, he was one of the few professors at the prep school who was available, and the few friends he had in the art department were always trying to fix him up with dates. His students loved him, and many of the girl students at a romantic age loved to stay after class to be close to him. With striking looks, tall, with natural charm, as well as being open and personable, nevertheless he had had few if any long-lasting affairs. He had been in love once or twice, and then he wasn't. It proved that the worst thing in his life was not the eye injury he had suffered in Greece but rather an arachnid which began to plague him for what seemed forever, a series of events that would change his entire life.

And her name was Geraldine Oikle.

She had been a student of his in two of his classes and almost from the very first day in both of them, proving herself needy, disadvantaged, even pauperized in ways at the time that he could sympathize with but could never quite fully understand—being deprived of attention was at its root—came to be dependent on him in crucial but elemental and imposing ways. In class, for example, that compulsive need in her manifested itself by asking too many questions, which forced him to have to call her aside at one point to explain it was excessive. It seemed to him at first that she needed a surrogate father, but it was soon made clear she had an adolescent crush on him. She would wait after class for special attention. He remembered having met her father and mother the day Geraldine first appeared at the Academy, 10th grade, when they called out from a car to ask directions.

An obese, slope-headed, unprepossessing, pear-shaped man whose flushed cheeks had the same blue-green threads of a Roquefort cheese, her father gave the distinct impression that day that he was unloading a troublesome girl rather than companionably or even proudly conveying a loved daughter to a new school, the concomitant unhappiness of the ungainly teenager even then singularly in evidence.

The young girl gave off something of the humid odor of a neglected hothouse rafflesia that in a peculiar way affected her teacher with a vague sense of sadness whenever she stopped by his desk, usually for no reason and always without the slightest apology or by-your-leave. He could intuit a marked futility in her. He had the gift of restraint. It was an aspect of him his students loved. Not an anarchist; he simply had a preference for liberty, which he tried to foster as an important quality in his students, for he disliked many rigid rules he found at the school when they inhibited originality, believing with Picasso that all children are born with original faculties but tend to lose their gifts.

"All children are artists, but they are educated out of it," declared the great Andalusian painter from Malaga. Picasso's openness and trust in this case, however, left Donn vulnerable to anyone who chose to exploit it.

Compassion came quite easily to Croivak. To instruct and to enlighten he found less effective in helping people than heartfelt and spontaneous kindnesses given, especially when a patient understanding was required, as so often it was in teaching. He had long held to a core belief of what is called "meliorism," an unswerving conviction that, through the small, humane, and benevolent actions and altruistic intentions of individuals, the world might gradually become a much better place. However, he soon came to see her visits to, and in fact her dependence on him, did not augur well. In what Graham Greene novel that he'd read, he wondered, was it proved that pity was a vice?

Croivak who noticed that in her strangely demanding and desperate clinging way she needed as much attention as affection, quickly recognized hers was a world in which illusion cast a long shadow, a realm in which reasoning and logical thinking were nonexistent. She was lonely, spiritless, insecure. That, coupled with several acrimonious dreams that she related, did not bode well. It became a bit disturbing, and, knowing before anything that it had to end, he sought to put an end to it.

In her inveigling way, Geraldine told Croivak, "You're a genius." There seemed to be envy in the remark, the *soupçon* of resentment that often exists in high praise, and he could sense contempt in her admiration. Albert Einstein once said an individual could choose to see life as a miracle, or decide it was the opposite. The latter was Geraldine Oikle's view, with no miracle ever tendered her. Were such blandishments born of admiration or blarney, sincere, or wheedling larks to insinuate herself into his favor?

"I am not even close, nor is my painting," her teacher raced to reply, waving away her remark. He hated flattery. "Frank Sinatra softly singing 'Once Upon a Time' or crooning his up-beat version of the song, 'All or Nothing at All' is genius. So is the poetry of Wallace Stevens. And Milton's poem "Lycidas." A perfectly roasted blackberry balsamic red wine dish of braised short ribs with parsnips. That's genius!"

Once in a classroom, he had discovered to his shock and no small embarrassment written on the blackboard—inside the drawn shape of a large valentine heart—the linked names "Donn and Geraldine." Was it in her hand? Someone else's? Whose? But did it matter? Good god, he thought, hastily erasing the whole thing. He soon learned that Geraldine and her gossiping companions, gum-chewing hoydens like Carolyn Martin, Phelony Coon, and others, who often discussed him as a subject, also began to mock him, exchanging smirking glances with each other in class and on "visits"—was it because he was unattached? half blind? too liberal? simply male?—all of them feeling, as she did, that it was their presumptive right to stop his house—as if it were their private headquarters—by twos and threes, a cadre of cohorts whose jittery company he quickly saw was shot through with all sorts of rivalry, competition, and childish dramas.

Take, for example her name. She obstinately insisted that she never be referred to as *Gerry* and that her full name was a noble one and etymologically meant "spear ruler." It was an exigency, part of her need, carrying with it, regarding her and her outlook, all the unfortunate and dramatic characteristics associated in its theatricality with all of those mythical Greek goddesses like Daphne, Calliope, and Hebe.

And he obliged her.

But it was then that Croivak remembered the Greene novel indicting pity as a vice was *The Ministry of Fear*—also *The Heart of the Matter*. Pity is cruel. It destroys. Love is never safe when pity lurks about. It is less than sympathetic sorrow, he saw. Pity made suffering contagious! Worse, even, it also bore within it implicit feelings of superiority, for pity can be—and sadly often is—an expression of monstrous pride.

At one point, Donn shared his concerns with several of his young department colleagues, one of whom told him, "Oikle? I've seen her, yes. Something of a lump, as I recall. A pouch of a face. Do you watch TV—that vapid program *Hollywood Squares*? The center square character Paul Lynde, a cynic and something of a wag, was once posed the question, 'When a man falls out of your boat and into the water, you should yell "Man overboard!" Now, what should you yell if a woman falls overboard?' Paul Lynde's response was, 'Full speed ahead?'"

"I've also met her," put in another teacher. "She has a sharp pointed nose like the poet Edith Sitwell. Overbearing and bad-tempered. I chastised her once in the dining hall for pitching butter pats up to the ceiling, she and her misfit friends. Three of my students run with her, Pennycress Jarvis, Clayton Danielle Webster, and Bourne Fulton-Bayer, a real handful, who at the age of seventeen is already taking Botox injections!"

"What about Skye Poulter, Louisa "Weesie" Van Der Kamp, Oveta Culp, and Thymine Chargoff? Hellions! A Chinese moocow named Sheila with a twisted brain like the double-helix I would expel in a yoctosecond."

"Did you happen to notice that tall elegant upper, or maybe a senior, Meroë Nizam, who played that violin solo yesterday at the school assembly -- her parents having nobly named her, no doubt, from the ancient city on the east bank of the Nile? I heard churlish Geraldine Oikle remark to a friend upon leaving, when they were all walking out, 'Let's get her!'"

"Right. I have also heard that Judith Crippen, Phelony Coon, Thisbe Geerdes, Aurora and Dawn Hollyoak, and another asinine chum of hers, Mimi something or other whose full name I didn't catch, stole an expensive camera from audio-visual and were put on report. They're a bunch of yahoos."

Said another, "If we up and killed all crazy, emotionally immature pubescent girls for their behavior, all men would be murderers."

"Who of them *is* well-adjusted?" asked someone.

"Well-adjusted?" asked Donn Croivak. "Does the word even apply? You can't be serious! If Geraldine Oikle is normal, the Statue of Liberty is my Aunt Gert!"

Geraldine eventually began to take up far, far too much of his time. He was reminded within weeks, touching on her visits, of the snide question "How much does it cost if it's free?" In his amateur way, to find an answer, he went so far as trying to diagnose her—and failed. She would weep, then sometimes laugh hysterically, moodily act hurt and go eerily quiet. Sharp chin out sometimes, unbudging, but then on a given afternoon timorous and fearful and quaking—or at least outwardly, for after not very many weeks, maybe a month, he concluded that, deep down, she was hypocritical and two-faced. It did not take long for him to conclude that her problems were much deeper and far more encompassing than an adolescent one—depression salted with rage—and that she had been seriously infantilized by her parents. Reason rarely works

with a troubled adolescent. Loud arguments soon ensued, and resentment followed. He was forced to ban her and her friends from
again visiting his house.

It was at this stage that an exasperated, even nettled, Croivak bothered to stop in at school admissions to check into her dos-
sier, detailed records on file. Anxiety spirals listed there by a recent
therapist confirmed the very same riptide of dark feelings, rage, depression, that, in her insistent and whining way, she had demonstrated to him. Mention was made that she was beset with dread
and bedeviled by rejection, that she was even obsessed with autoka-
balesis, which means jumping off a high place, building, bridge, or
mountain. She had obsessions. Or were they delusions? But she was
petulant and fatuous, her teacher was fully convinced that out of
vanity she used drama to evoke self-pity. Apparently, her parents,
although fairly young, fought a great deal and were badly at odds
with each other. He also learned that Geraldine was also undisguis-
edly jealous of a much prettier older sister, a sometime junior
model. Hydration, more exercise, mindfulness and meditation, nu-
trient-rich foods, gratitude lists, and keeping a journal to cope with
her anxiety were registered.

Croivak's simple request to her, that she no longer visit his
house, went nowhere. She proceeded to come by now more than
ever. She had listened as if she had understood, but her insistent
resolves to mend her ways, stark and bald as a timetable, were nothing but blatant lies. Her conflicting behavior was clearly hostile.
There she would be, unremitting and pushy, sitting on his stoop.
She wore white maxi-dresses. No fine manners, no communication
of worth, she was little used to fellowship or communal behavior.
She said she wanted to read his palm, but he refused. She drew up
astrological charts, not that he wanted her to do so, for she boasted
that she had a gift for reading them to determine what in his life
could be pre-determined.

He now wanted to be fully shut of this person. She was a hazard in a hundred ways. In a private school such as this, full of unseen pitfalls, with so many emotionally imaginative young people, every one of them enjoying—or suffering—a sunburst of puberty. Proximity by its very nature was a hazard and allegations of blame were rife. Croivak had quickly divined her resentment, easily read her vexation, no mystery there, and, in truth, the world offers nothing more childish than an angry and embittered—or alienated—teenage girl.

There is often found in elegant private academies, where a good many students are from wealthy, over-advantaged families, an element of permissiveness—an aspect of snobbery—an *école fainéantise*, a kind of moral laziness.

After Geraldine had graduated, she kept in touch, sporadically. Occasional letters. A note. She would telephone at different times, sometimes at night, mostly at odd hours, often from various and sundry call boxes, and always for no reason. Whereas once he acceded to this, it soon became a burden. She had met someone in college, decided to get married—a short, red-headed Jewish computer person. Donn had been invited and out of deference, and not without a feeling of solace, indeed relief, had attended the small, undistinguished, awkward, nonreligious wedding, which her parents had paid for and was held at her family's house. As he watched the pair that day, not much wed as conjoined—who of the two articled by whom?—he reflected that what is a pair is not necessarily who is a couple.

He left teaching at Ethan Allen Academy. Two years or more had gone by after that marriage when Geraldine once again, unannounced, like an evil elf or sinister drow from some sub-race of the chthonian, subterranean underdark, suddenly appeared at his new house in Hingham. It seemed to Donn, in utter disbelief and before he could that gather his senses, that his bad eyesight had misconfigured. There she stood in black slacks, arms folded, with

God-knows-what kind of expectations. She seemed shorter, wider, with outsticks of frazzled hair and long feet and incapable, inescapable hands, twisting, and a much louder voice. One little wad of hair about the color of last year's July grass, sprung away from her head in a sort of fall of scolding-locks that curled down the left side of her neck.

Older, nervously impatient, no longer a high school senior, a charmless individual with expectations thwarted who betrayed something of an edge—she was not wearing a ring—she had grown into something of a long-nosed, peevish harridan, and her head, a spherule of mad tousled hair, actually made her look even shorter, stunted, fire-hydrant small, as she stood there highly strung, working her mousy hands.

She was again visibly unhappy and, with no qualms at all to try to hide it, had the same droopy vulnerability she'd always shown. Croivak tried to be hospitable, forcing a smile, feeling his tight face stretch in protest as he did so, for she was about the last person on earth he wanted to see. Disconcerted, he moved about nervously straightening cushions to give himself employment. There is nothing so defeating to ease of manner as showing grace to someone you have foresworn and deeply in mind repudiated. Such an abrupt visit obscured a looming end. A pain in his blind eye throbbed. She stood there boldly, a cold-call visitor, unannounced, typically expecting of course to be invited to sit down, looking as if, expecting the worst, she was steeled to meet it. She was now wearing eyeglasses. She ground away in sepulchral tones about a pretty sister—she was envious—for she had three siblings. She then low-rated her husband out of the blue, declared that she hated her whole family, was being treated for cough variant asthma, hadn't found a job, and said, "Do a painting of me."

Trying to take it all in, Donn offered her a seat and poured her a drink and asked after her husband. He found it disconcerting that, as she sat far too comfortably there, she was running her fingers along the cover of one of his books, as though hoping to absorb transdermally some of his essence. To witness this kind of appropriation was unsettling. This eerie, blood-curdling aspect of adsorption as possession he felt again, a feeling in her presence he always felt. She had once stolen a pen from his school desk. Again, he asked about her husband, irked that she avoided answering the question. Geraldine replied that he was in Palo Alto, on business. What did he do for work? She said he was a systems analyst, whatever that was. The fact that she was not wearing a wedding ring spoke volumes, and he left it there.

"I cannot do a painting of you," he softly replied—she immediately jumped off the sofa and marched to the window, her back to him—"not only because as it is I am badly overworked, but more to the point, I don't want to." By now, he knew the drill quite well and all of its many ramifications. He paused. "Does your husband know you're here?"

The answer she gave was positively chilling.

"He knows about you," she said enigmatically and turned to look at him. He could only guess, what on earth was this all about?

Geraldine immediately sensed his disapproval.

A coldness hung in the air. She looked unhappy. Or whatever gradation of unhappiness translated to or was reiterated by rebuff, rejection, refusal, or, if you will, being spurned. She had turned quiet. He saw a connection had been severed. He was struck how she looked at him then, as if she had the answer to a question that he hadn't thought to ask. It was not the usual kind of immature, undisguised anger that once or twice he'd seen in her face when in a petulant moment, losing what little self-control she had, it became the color of baked brick, her forehead wrinkled into a horizontal flange. He had by now long detected a trace of shrewdness, artifice, the lineaments of a settled cunning and craftiness in evidence, as if a decision of note had been determined by a firm chin making some sort of resolution.

Instinctively, automatically, intuitively, as if without having to think, he resolved right then she would never again appear in that house. Iron-clad! It registered by way of a vow as if with a force announced by angelic messenger.

Geraldine Oikle was from first to last a demented actor, a depressive possessed by this, that, and the other thing. She had impressed her teacher as a lost soul at the beginning, but then soon a loose cannon, a self-deluded person having no unity of character, no principles, no convictions, nothing in her head that, when she laid it on a pillow, she could sensibly expect would be there in the morning. There was peril in the association. She seemed to live only in a kind of role without which she was lost. She carried a remoteness inside of her that she seemed, at the same time, willfully trying to re-shape. It was a paradox, that she was empty within but at the same time self-impelled. As she could not find the inner Geraldine, if indeed there was one, there was nothing for her, at grievous moments, to retire *into*; she was compelled to merge herself, or be merged, in an imagined and fanciful and super-imposed life. She could be anything you expected her to be or anything you didn't expect her to be, and she could maintain that role for weeks. She was an empty vessel—yet *inhabited!*

He had understood fairly early she was an emotionally unstable woman for whom reason was as abhorrent as cold water was to a cat. She had once told her mother, who in turn had told him, "We are both very much enamored of each other." (She often spoke in the self-dramatizing style found in bad and basic fiction.) Her mother was no better, a crass, unkillable force of nature who in her ice-cold manner had often reduced her daughter to states of flustered impotence. The defaults of parentage—how they loom! One Christmas. she attempted to invite herself to a dinner at his house. He had been dead asleep when he had heard calls, his name, then shouts from below his bedroom window.

She stood down below, brazen-faced, squeezing her hands, hair all toneless and wild and askew, Gorgon-like. She was toting a large bag and wearing black-framed eyeglasses and a dark, purple leather jacket. Her body had turned to limp schlag. She asked if she could spend the night.

Could he have possibly heard right?

What. The. Fuck. Are. You. Thinking?

Geraldine stood there, looking up, an intractable spirit-beast, a demon. She confidently asserted, "I thought that something like that was possible, maybe." Her teacher was colder than camphor. His doorknob grip was almost a throttle. "Everything before the apostrophe is unthinkable," replied Croivak, truly out of sorts. "Your last adverb is nonsense."

Croivak had tried repeatedly to warn her off, once racing downstairs to confront her on the front steps in the dark at past midnight. The horror of it all, the futility, beyond belief. He stared at her, in silence, for twenty seconds. He turned to the street and, before locking the door, sighed. "What a beautiful night." He walked back upstairs in the dark. It was the beginning of her stalker life. For after five minutes, she actually rang the front doorbell again. One accepts that human emotions are never neatly ordered nor always—if ever—rational or predictable or uncluttered. But this was beyond the pale.

He went to the door, opened it, and said, "I permit myself only one day in a calendar year to order an individual to stay away from me. And I'm taking it now." And he slammed the door shut, closing his tired eyes as wearily he leaned against it. Waiting for the noise of her leaving was an eternity.

Later that year, on an occasion of great grace, in the Vermont Studio Center in the town of Johnson, where he had for several consecutive seasons taught painting two weeks in summer, out of the blue and God's intervening grace Donn met the love of his life—a kind, beautiful, talented woman, and within a year got married.

In spite of its high point, that became a paradoxical situation in the puzzle of life, for of all events that was perhaps the black fact which became for Geraldine a—the—transformative moment, an irreversible game-changer, for in the following days it was an unalterable conviction of his ex-student that Donn Croivak had *jilted her.* Was it possible? And in consequence? Men were traducers, schemers, got in women's way, base betrayers, and in the end felons of the heart who deserved to be punished, or so she'd resentfully concluded, having become convinced that the human male in every way, shape, and form was (her words) "hostile to the female spirit." You just don't do that. People have to pay.

It was not long before at all hours that Geraldine Oikle now began telephoning her teacher at his house. It might best be described as an offensive, even an assault. Repeated calls, with the telephone loudly ringing, at all hours. At first, came cryptic hang-ups. Other times, he heard tapping, as of as code, or breathing. Midnight calls, some later. Occasionally, he heard breathing or giggles, implying she had girlfriends by her side. Croivak was utterly confounded, soon, in the extreme. What was this all about? Had she heard of the changes in his life? And, if so, how so? Had she been secretly somehow tracking him? Stalking him? Communicating with his friends? Vetting his mail in some weird way? Stalkers in the grip of this hectoring vice are motivated by a desire to control their victims' actions and feelings by the need to maintain any type of connection—regardless of the wishes if their prey—through manipulation and control. Was it mere infatuation?

A delusion has wings. What begins as a habit can become a preoccupation and soon a passion, then a studied compulsion, an addiction approaching mania, and—who'd deny it?—eventually transmogrify into an obsession.

The situation became serious enough for him to have to call her mother and father to ask for a meeting, hoping with a plea as much as a warning that their intrusive daughter might immediately desist. But that family had moved. He was stuck. At first, after one or two normal telephone calls, Donn had been polite to Geraldine, courteous and diplomatic, but discreet, willing to talk about her several classmates, references to school life, what reading she was doing, any new or unique interests of hers—there were none—trying in a generally lighthearted way to try to appease, so outfox, the uneasy and disturbing kind of insistence he noticed that infected every call. That was his great mistake.

The rabid telephone calls, assertion as protest, were a flurry, then a rash, finally an outbreak. It was an assault more than anything, a propulsive act of a kind of craft done with sheer cunning. Only an amateur self-regarding mind in its ignorant bloat could find such repeated lunacy at all effective. Her conversation—always all about herself—was basically the buzzle-muffle of aimless chatter, rapid talk, prattle. Basically, all talk is confession, even among the best of us, he came to realize. But all of this was a new bewildering experience with him. He could hear without any special gifts for analysis the lineaments of ill-will at every juncture. No hope of finding happiness ever centered her pathology. Her scornful laughter with the ripping sound of tearing sheets truly had something in it of the satanic, with screeches from hell that seemed to come from the base of all outrage. No two calls were the same. It was now cackling laughter, then tears of vague regret.

At other times, when picking up the phone, shocked awake, bleary-eyed—two in the morning—ominous silence held, at other instances stertorous breathing. Scandal didn't matter to her, whether or not in her misguided lust for revenge she'd been identified and dragged into the open. He would hold the receiver at arm's length. Escalating volume increased with her when she charged him with gross neglect and indifference.

What had been passingly frenetic was now fiendish, what sporadic now satanic, what was crazed, now an infernal and fully unhallowed, hellish assault.

She had positively become a viper.

The loud telephone rings would come at all hours, insanely intrusive, and, by way of repetition, he began mercilessly to come to expect them. "You went and married some rich pig, right, and only for her money?" she screamed into the receiver, "and any moronic kids you have will grow up to be fucking monkeys as blind as you are! And I say good! *Goood*! I would never want to grow up like you, a total phony, you and your crappy art! *Why don't you shoot yourself! I hated your stupid classes. Your right to not have your face punched in ends when you infringe people's rights, you pervert! Hear me?*"

The onslaught badly began to take hold of him. The nights he lay awake with the expectation or premonition of a call were not as bad as the spasmodic, disconnected dreams—nightmares—he fitfully fought on many a night. He visualized kiting falcons, boulders with holes for mouths, menacing caryatids, strangers peering from half-closed portals, sets of demonic teeth about to bite, waterfalls of fire, the Zapotec God of Death, tricephalic creatures with pointed heads and mummies, lepers and cripples, almost all of it with gray backgrounds like a saturnine lead linked with the sackcloth and ashes of penitence.

We as humans inevitably come to anticipate what we hate to hear, are able to predict by a calculation of default what soon takes on the condition of a plague. It foreshadowed despair in him in the ignominy of feeling owned, predictability itself a vice. He summoned to mind in frustration Proverbs 30:11–14:

> "There are those who curse their fathers
> and do not bless their mothers;
> those who are pure in their own eyes
> and yet are not cleansed of their filth;

those whose eyes are ever so haughty,
whose glances are so disdainful;
those whose teeth are swords
and whose jaws are set with knives
to devour the poor from the earth
and the needy from among mankind."

The Jekyll in her freely acknowledged Hyde whose venom demon-dancing in her took over like a malignancy, the spirit of that monster's excesses, savagery, and imbecility shaping her utterances with a willfulness in telephone call after telephone call that never seemed to abate. It was at times difficult to believe that it was the voice of a human. She positively screeched, sometimes banging the instrument of the phone against a table, and howling, *yowling*, baying like wild beast, barked out obscenities:

"Your piece-of-shit kids should die from measles outbreaks! I wish with all my heart you and your types will disappear from the face of the earth! Do you know what scum is? Let me tell you—you're scum! Now I know the definition of what rat shit is, because I have seen it right up close—it is you! If I was driving and you were in the road, my car would have a simultaneous brake failure and stuck throttle failure, and you would be a distant memory, how about that? We don't need more Hitlers! Do us the favor of having to put you out of your misery, and overdose on a lethal dose of lighter fluid!"

The visual of the weird coven he imagined she inhabited and no doubt led came easily enough to him in grotesque images. How easily he could picture demented Geraldine, at first, impish, mischief-making—and, with her several girlfriends almost lasciviously crowding by the telephone there in some dark house sitting by her in support, gleefully whispering into the receiver, but then later, almost satanically aggrieved in the savage fantasies she fed herself, truly belligerent, even crazed, her stretched mouth crocodile-wide, barking, literally *barking*!

He was convinced she might try to kill his cat, "Rat."

Croivak could intuit she was lewdly captured—arrested!—by the instrument she weaponized. A telephone necessarily implies the presence of another, the mad ringing in its urgent, ear-splitting shrillness executing an order that demands a response, a drilling insistence for immediate attention, targeting a caller as a fired gun. Geraldine doubtless would find and feel upon each swiveling dial a sinister anticipation of dread, which in her case also involved a smutty, crude, tasteless, salacious, even pornographic thrill, for a telephone is also an instrument of seduction, espionage, and murderous scheming.

After each telephone call is made, or, say, in its refusal to ring for those *awaiting* a cherished call, however, a silent phone can exaggerate loneliness, abandonment, especially in the instance of devastating anti-climax when a stalker in getting no response abides there after each dud, the aborted black receiver limp in her revengeful but disappointed hands. One telephone necessarily implies the absent presence of another. The hateful caller becomes aware of what she has to reckon with herself that that other—again and again—is *not there*!

How often had he anticipated—dreamt of—hard-slamming the front door in her face whenever she came by to collect her vengeance! Had he adopted her own Rumpelstiltskinian tactics? he wondered, as he wished her to disappear, He was at the end of his rope. He wished her ill will himself! He wanted to spray her like some mad hissing raccoon to punish her, wipe away her skeeving, anogenital odor. It crossed his mind at one point to invite her to dinner and administer a lethal amount of hyoscine hydrobromide into her cup of Coca-Cola and with delight watch her drop dead right in front of him!

And it got worse. She once or twice pulled her car into his driveway, unannounced, rang the bell, and if no one answered, in her anger or desperation or fury or drunkenness or feelings of revenge she would call up to the second floor where she knew the bedroom was—whether his wife was there or not mattered not a whit to her—and brayed his name. Another time, she bought a gun. Erratic wasn't the word. She was unpredictable and insistent and unsettled and unstable, a vacant stare in her eyes. He could visualize her by her voice in the bitter calls at all hours of the day and night, leaving sharp and startling messages, obscene remarks, even nasty, abrupt, and indiscriminate threats.

Several times in a vengeful duet, a girlfriend of hers—some partner in the crime—was there by her side. She would knock on the door late at night, and then would disappear. She left notes on his door. She openly accused him of leading her on, of abusing her. She left items in his doorway. One frightful night, well past the witching hour, when everybody in the world was asleep, she proceeded not only to creep like a toad onto his property, but this time went so far as to dare to open the shut back door and brazenly to enter the house and to leave a note that stated, "People who betray people should die!"

Art proves itself best when it is simply handed to us.

That's when his idea of doing a portrait of her first began. It was a project, he realized, that had long been forming in his mind. And he got right down to business. Starkness—a spartan take—was, he felt, required in the undertaking. He refused to sit facing a window while doing it, lest he be forced to look at benign nature as a positive distraction. He wanted inflexible metrics basically as his art form. It was a template he had used, robotically, once or twice before when he was driven to pain when he was upset. He believed that the cross-sticks of lines, a rude geometry, recapitulated in a stringent way the dynamic, evolutionary force that governed the essence of his subject. The painting that he undertook was to be not so much a portrait as a grid—actually, a grid of a face. It was amazing how, when he set forth and began to work the paint, shaping maneuvers, quietly like a spinning dynamo, which, silent and unnoticed, raced to supply the current that drove a powerful system of moving wheels, baleful memory fed it.

Alive with a like spite that he conjured, Croivak taking up his brush fairly flew as he worked the canvas to ransack his nightmares for themes, as input, and for use as munitions to re-state or supplement the twisted and mis-proportioned aspects of Geraldine Oikle, calling up in recollection whatever of his nemesis fit. He had begun with the head and face, painting a yellow spike in the middle of her forehead as a splice in a cosmic egg which in its brooding instability he subjectively saw as a bifurcating symbol of degeneration. The very oils he worked with held the clay of her being in their rank odor.

He pondered, was that how Piet Mondrian grew into the style of his early paintings, becoming what he was, lines delineating the rectangular forms he'd put on canvas, all relatively thin, gray, not black? He wondered, did such artists shape their mad rectangles in the patterns of jail cells? He worked doing fast takes, with lines tending to fade as they approached the edge of the painting, rather than stopping abruptly. The forms themselves, smaller and more numerous than in Mondrian's later paintings were filled with primary colors, black, or gray, and nearly all of them are colored; only a few are left white.

As he worked, during this period, he lived self-contained, secluded and pretty much out of the way all day. He ate alone. His wife, Jessica, understood. She had suffered as badly from the seemingly endless spate of nasty phone calls, and it was she whose idea it was to start to record the messages, capture all incoming calls, not even knowing the reason why, at first, but with some vague hope of protection from the sudden complicated witchiness plaguing them. Blocking all calls had proved impractical. They bought an audio recorder that came with a device integrated into the phone unit. It was Jessica who had also learned of the scandal-tinged history of their intractable intruder which recapitulated in rashness

Geraldine's fractious ravings over the telephone and her creepy messages, for she had been twice arrested for shoplifting, leaving graffiti on walls, and once burning a tennis court net.

They were forced to bring the recordings to the police, tapes which two cops took to another room for a half hour to listen to, only to come back to confirm that the messages boded trouble and probably required a restraining order or some sort of injunction. They filled out the requisite papers and took down information. In due time, her parents were tracked down and a detective, visiting her house, notified her of a restraining order, adding the singular warning that she was now under surveillance and that if she continued with her telephone calls or sending hate mail or coming into contact with her teacher or his wife or even trespassing on their property, she would be immediately arrested and jailed.

Croivak and his wife Jessica, many years after he left teaching, had already gone through a bad enough patch, when, out of the blue, he was notified by telephone from the Ethan Allen headmaster that another student, an obviously maladjusted seventeen-year-old girl with a long history of personal problems with her own sad, dysfunctional family—another example, as with Geraldine, of an ignored, socially impaired child, it so turned out, raised in a ramshackled and un-weeded way—who had hired a lawyer, a well-known local shyster who, taking the opportunity to plunder the deep pockets of the wealthy school, sued Donn Croivak for a sexual misdemeanor. What happened—the foul, dirty secret behind the false charge—was that Geraldine in an added fit of spite had contacted a former friend of hers from the Academy, one who was having financial difficulties, and encouraged *her* to file the suit, promising to coach her with all sorts of phony evidence and the promise of a big payoff if she succeeded. This girl had not been one of his students, and he had seen her but a single time in the four years he had taught there when she and several other girls had stopped by his apartment for less than five minutes to see his pet parrot, Belladonna.

The two miscreants, he also learned, had also viciously reported to the headmaster, as well as to Oikle's lawyer, of a carnal mnemonic that he had once innocently given them in class as a help to recall or remember *colors*—to assist their memory by rhyme—which went "Bad boys rape our young girls, but Violet goes willingly," charging their teacher of salaciously and purposely trying to offend young girls.

The scandal of the crimes was made public. It funneled throughout the school. It was in the newspapers. It was mentioned on the radio. It was a stain on his record. Croivak had to sit through two humiliating depositions and inquisitions and in the end was officially banned for life from ever entering the grounds of Ethan Allen Academy, under a penalty of immediate arrest. It was a wound throughout his life that never healed.

"Unwholesome" is the word one constantly hears in prep schools for unsavory behavior or poisonous relationships or such activities. Dysphemisms are avoided as being coarse and unrefined, even for criminal conduct.

Prep school can be a minefield of social complications and scandals. The charges cost Croivak as much as $50,000 to settle, legal fees included; he would have been facing a preposterous six times that, or so he was told, to fight the case in court to defend his reputation, of which nothing was more important, far more money than he had or ever hoped to have. It was that ordeal that confirmed in full for Croivak, regarding many if not all attempts at good will, never mind in teaching, could be turned to evil as opposed to good by mere whim, that any such endeavor is utterly powerless against blithe misuse.

Donn Croivak, with each brushy addition, each stroke, followed the clues that he had picked up of what he had noticed in Geraldine Oikle from the first. As was probably the case with most artists or illustrators, it was inevitably his habit, almost subconsciously, to examine, to appraise, the pictorial possibilities of whomever he met. In her case, he came to see a fretwork in character, the tracery of a grid, and by underpainting he reduced her to a kind of scaffolding, not as brainless structure, that is, but one, visage-wise, with a pattern to frame a scold, the construct of the peevish, reckless evil of demented anti-romance, with the scowl in flesh of inexact facial boundaries, an interrogating mask with an edge of red lip, its curl, like a wet question mark. It wasn't that a face didn't form or a body.

It was "reality" he wanted. To approach the spiritual in art, one must make as little use as possible of reality, because reality is opposed to the spiritual. He wanted the indecency of the actual, its *shapes*, its starkness, its sense of sin!

He had imbibed this concept of art back in Greece when in Santorini he walked the island, wandered the gray volcanic sand of its beaches and ramparts of its bright white cliffs, studying, in a casual, non-academic way, its landscape based it on the pattern of the "coastline paradox," slowly having made the counterintuitive observation in his wayward ramblings that the coastline of a landmass does not have a well-defined length or even the exactitude of a boundary, as such. It is the precise recapitulation in form of any raddled organism—whether gaunt, drawn, pinched, exhausted, worn out, embattled, or battered. It is the nature, imprecise and vague and off-target, of the fractal curve-like properties of ragged, serrated coastlines; i.e., the fact that a coastline, any coastline, typically has a fractal dimension.

Please! Was there any better definition of a depraved human personality than that? Could any more comprehensive or disproportionate state in extent or magnitude be better realized even in fantasy than this geographic description of a craggy, serrated mass? Could any personality be found more shaped to fractal non-dimension than this hectic bitch?

It was to be a full portrait, head and shoulders, on an eight-by-seven-foot canvas he had specifically chosen and mounted for the half body. He began with the face, malapert and subtly audacious, and the spread of untamed and slightly disorganized hair that crowned it in a cowling of open disapproval. Her challenging shortness he caught perfectly in the meaty neck, pivoted forward with a kind of yearning insolence and deceit, her raddled eyes smeared with glints of hesitant gray that revealed an impulse toward motion, a restlessness that seemed led by that pointed and impudent nose that conveyed fury merely by dint of its length. He batted about and revised the wet paint, prodding parts of it into shape with a correcting thumb like feeling a nap of worsted. He succeeded in capturing the complicated mood of defiance he wanted in the general physiognomy. A subtle curving polygenic line of her forehead registered in a perfectly insulting and peevish way an attitude of cynical doubtfulness and cross-hatched fury as if the viewer were literally but punitively invading her space.

At key points, in the flesh, he gave the painting a heterodox touch of the abstract, a sparse black line or band with a primary color, knowing Cézanne's elemental, game-changing translation of visual reality into equally emphasized lines and daubs had always electrified him, as it had, say, Mondrian. Perhaps this is why Mondrian characterized his style in painting as "abstract real," not the oxymoron it seems. The "look" didn't matter to him. What did signify was the self-abnegating intensity.

As Croivak worked away on this canvas, he played on his phonograph Mozart's Symphony No. 40 in G Minor, K. 550, sometimes called the Great G Minor Symphony. Composed in the summer of 1788, it was finished at about the same time as his Symphony No. 39 and Symphony No. 41, marking a period of productivity exceptional even by Mozart's standards. Hearing this inimitable music reinforced Croivak's intent and strengthened his resolve to finish this dark task. It is one of only two symphonies that Mozart wrote in minor keys and reflects his interest in the artistic movement known as *Sturm und Drang*, in which darker and stronger emotions were showcased.

The composer soon revised the piece to include clarinets and made other changes to the instrumentation, and it is this version that is often performed today—and that is considered one of the greatest of Mozart's works.

Croivak almost smiled. The painting soon loomed with confrontation and provocation and dissent. Had the subject willingly sat for him? Submitted voluntarily to whatever variations she trusted he'd do with his brush? The answer was *yes!* She had indeed sat for him, *for years*, of her own sullen volition, by her actions, with her insolence, in her freakish, intemperate phone calls. The painting he would call *Spite,* a perfect title.

As he worked his brush over that audacious image before his one good eye (which in a weird way always helped him see, as if by isogenic lines, a special kind of targeting locus), he realized—especially regarding her insane possessiveness in hoping to absorb transdermally what she could of *his* substance and spirit and, indeed lifeblood, in spite of his subtly skewed, his blinkered perceptions—that she had given him what he needed to have, handed him outright her own disabling insufficiencies as a subject, including all of its vulgar and hideous hues. With certain overriding exceptions, he kept to ochres, russets and browns. His painting was the result of a flood tide after a long ebb.

Cognition was involved. He had always painted what he also simultaneously wished to see and to discover, the very act itself in a way creating—indeed replenishing—the subject at hand on the canvas. In a real way, it might be said that it was the actual *process* of painting that taught perception rather than creator informing it, his capacity or skill or approach depending on the discovery within the act. It is *procedure* that produces, pointing the way to answer everything of the whats, hows, and whys of the craft. Art involves the revelation of uncovering, for, truly, the finding is in the seeking. Disclosure depends on the artist being ready for it, the recognition of what but awaits an informed response.

It had always been true for Croivak. Inspiration is offered to those willing to accept it and humble enough to need it, conception the need to receive, design being the breakthrough to an encounter awaiting him to be revealed. Its benison was the insight it gave the painter of discovery of the blessedly divulged. He had always understood that the case for masters like Vermeer and Rembrandt made itself, with the bold, daring, and inevitable preternatural range of their formal and iconographic leaps—forward, backward, and sideway– teaching what a painting could be made, or even dared, to do. He particularly loved Mondrian. The brief for him is harder to exempt him from cookie-cutter modernist narratives ("Next slide, please") of marching, of parading styles, from his earlier modest-looking Dutch landscapes to the riveting abstractions that he made in the decades before his death, as a wartime expatriate in New York, in 1944. But style for him, from first to last, served a quest first to seek, then manifest soul-deep spirituality as a verifiable fact of life. His aim, he said, was not to create masterpieces, though he did that, too. It was "to find things out."

A figure on Croivak's large canvas he saw had slowly emerged. All corporal integrity in the subject was fractured, as if animated by the impertinence of its facial attitude alone. In the lineaments of the rude being in the portrait, as if foreordained by some devilish fate or doom of circumstance that had mandated it, a creature had taken shape—uncivil, brassy, and contumelious—and it boomed with unstoppable malice as if it had literally come to life. Contumely had created what was contumacious. The insubordinate body was a willful landscape, the unprepossessing quality of its naturalistic flesh tones, mottled and marked with contour lines, bewildered in greenish purple swipes, revealed a being raddled with discontent, the hunch of shoulders patina'd with added brush strokes in a fraudulent yellow to show hostility. The fleshiness of the pouting but still aggressive mouth, with a sulking lower lip sagging, looked if the woman had just wiped it with the back of her hand, the chin braced to be misunderstood. The midsection of the figure, scrambled into colored marks—he used crayon and oil sticks—gave off surrealistic notes. From the upper arms the shoulders, she was all haunch, a human grenade. The figure's midsection was scrambled into colored marks—he used crayon and oil sticks—that gave off surrealistic notes. From the upper arms the shoulders, she was all haunch, a human grenade.

In this undertaking, Croivak had wanted to come as closely as possible to the truth in aiming toward naturalism, in spite of abstract details—for no one in all truth can deny that much of portraiture is retaliation in the same way response is reaction, reply to redress—and extract, abstract everything from that, until he reached the foundation of his subject's substance, the pith of her unprincipled pettiness, and in places, for he believed it possible, through horizontal and vertical lines constructed with awareness, and with calculation, led by high intuition and the misery well remembered by his infuriated hands.

He felt contrite, almost apologetic just prior to showing the ruthless portrayal to his wife, that instead of the devilish rendering he had painted, he had not had the chance to take for a subject a beautiful woman with the curve of gold wings behind her shoulders like a Fra Angelico angel or a goddess with a lavish blue veil as worn by a chaste *cinquecento* Madonna.

It was less a painting than an encounter. Retaliation—justice—never drew its own portrait with a straighter stroke. Upon seeing it, his wife Jessica said, "I am astounded by the facial immorality. There is also a leakiness in that guiltily dropping left hand alone. Beauty—is it not?—is usually the male image of the female body, as they say, but in the disconcerting ugliness rendered there— I have had the bad luck to have seen this person only once, a fleeting glimpse from a window—you have nailed her contempt in a single unforgettable image."

The painting was almost finished. Croivak sat entirely alone one full day studying what he had done. Its origins he deliberated with mixed emotions, as he listened to the Mozart masterpiece Symphony No. 40. The composition year 1788, he knew, was a dark one for the thirty-two-year-old composer. Viennese audiences had proven less eager to hear his concerts, recitals. Large bills were piling up. His infant daughter, Theresia, had just died. Letters to friends reveal that he was finding it difficult to look beyond the threatening shadows, and some have suggested that this fact influenced this unusually anxious symphony.

The painter knew in his heart Wolfgang Mozart had loaded his somber feelings into this one work, though even here, all is not sorrow. At no point in his career would this composer allow music to stay long in sober moods.

Croivak's final surveying look of course was done with one eye. It had robbed him of depth-perception. People were constantly asking about the black patch he wore. He had long felt that one eye was sufficient in its glance to approve what he felt two eyes might have altered. With one eye, the brain only processes input from a single visual source, which can simplify visual perception and reduce sensory overload. As to adaptation, many individuals with one eye learn to adapt their other senses, such as hearing and touch, to compensate for the loss of depth perception, often enhancing their awareness of their surroundings. As to having one eye, there was also a reduced risk of eye conditions that can affect both eyes, such as certain types of glaucoma, or cataracts.

He knew very well that people with his condition sometimes managed develop a heightened ability to focus on small details as they learn to rely on their remaining eye to gather information. Having two eyes instead of one is advantageous in at least six respects: the danger of blindness is decreased, the visual field is enlarged, stereoscopic depth perception is possible on the basis of binocular disparities, the position of the eyes relative to the head can be computed from the images of both eyes, visual obstacles in front of the horopter perceptually shrink, and the signal-to-noise ratio is increased.

Croivak realized with justification, as he looked at the sulking, scowling mouth, the source so often of his baneful oppressor's insistent and maniacal abuse, that he had managed to produce a cooperating, countervailing balance to that subject's maliciousness and spite. In a moderate way, he felt explained, if not defended. He sensed deep in his heart he *needed* to have such a painting done. As Virginia Woolf once declared, "Nothing has happened until it has been described."

There were a few last adjustments to be made in the subject's cruel mouth and one of the grasping hands, which Croivak fixed with several passes, done as if by scheme in an air of musical tension he had been listening to in one of the dark passages of the symphony, never of the sweeter light ones, rather a soaring movement shot through with urgent and fretful turns. In the middle of that movement, a section where the orchestra concerned itself with bleak ideas, never quite fury, but blended into an intricate mix, the painter put aside his brush.

Standing back to take a final survey of the work, Donn Croivak couldn't help but recall the words Representative Preston S. Brooks of South Carolina who unapologetically declared after having physically beaten Senator Charles Sumner of Massachusetts with his gold-headed cane in May 1856, virtually killing him: "Every lick went where I intended." Her teacher had become the re-incarnation of rancor and antagonism, of which Geraldine Oikle was the model, the very paragon and manifestation of spite.

And it was on that note that Donn Croivak finished the painting. So demanding had been the emotions of that work drawing on him that he then immediately set it aside. He and Jessica traveled to Estonia for a year, for his wife had earned a Fulbright grant in literature, giving them a deserved respite. To his surprise, after the painting had been taken by a New York gallery, it was purchased within two years of its completion by the Museum of Fine Arts in Boston. The financial outlay let Croivak and his wife move out of the state and away from the school, not without great relief. The portrait can be seen today at the Museum of Fine Arts, room 447. It was, paradoxically, a positive effect in spite of—and because if—its negative cause.

It was in ways the kind of mixed blessing in life that came at one, confirming (as well as denying) the nature of his earlier reflection that attempts at good will, like art, go out helpless into the world to be turned at whim to good as well as evil, but, still, that every such endeavor is powerless against misuse. There were all sorts of rumors about his tormentor, that she had married again, that she had flunked out of college, that she earned her living by privately giving astrological readings. He was even told by someone that she committed suicide. It was all hearsay and gossip, and he didn't care one way or another. There was nothing he chose to hear of her or her life that mattered.

The concavity of her vulgar raids on his life remained a continuing hollow, a deep dent that only returned to anything like convex when he and his wife, Jessica, had moved away and three years later when he heard that she had moved to British Columbia or Alaska or somewhere, probably with a second—or third—husband. Who knew?

To haunt Canada, screeching and spooking its purlieus.

Who could say?

But, far more significantly, who cared?

Coca-Cola Kids

"Wouldst thou read riddles, and their explanation?
Or else drowned in thy contemplation?"

John Bunyan, *The Pilgrim's Progress*

The young chemists were unique—close friends, all bright, energetic, and inventive. Poke, Spike, and Grommet, fraternity members of Beta Omicron Pi, each of them a chemistry major and now full-time graduate students, had bonded and been close from the first day they met at freshman orientation at the Atlanta Institute of Sciences, bosom friends, seen together constantly, and inseparable to a degree that most everyone, groups who both knew them and did not, when they did not assume they were literally brothers, bruited it about that the three of them were ambisextrous—each queer as a blue gnu.

Spike always chewed his necktie, had inflamed eyes, and boastfully claimed he could prove an electrochemical cell could reliably perform organic redox reactions. He was brilliant, something of a math weirdo, played the clarinet, and as also an expert on glues. He had hard hands, smoked small cigars, and liked to sing. Among other gifts of his were he loved to juggle and could reproduce—with an amazing exactness—John Hancock's paraphed original signature. Poke, a redhead with a dimpled chin, was a self-amused bumbler who radiated a kind of innocence and always wore a bowtie. Known for having a somewhat conservative bent in politics and given to a febrile effort defending it, he was an exuberant cascade of opinions. He also held a part-time position at the Fleischer

Biomedical Spectroscopy and Imaging Lab (BSIL) at the Emory University School of Medicine.

Grommet, a Catholic who directed a church choir and was a licensed pyrotechnician who annually organized July 4 festivities, was skilled in pharmacy, as well, and as a side-hobby researched the geometry of the fourth dimension. He had been on the ground floor, scientifically, even as an undergraduate, by way of his father's connections as a doctor, in the importance of determining different color and shapes in pill medicines. He could be bossy but was always gentle. He liked to drink. In conversation, he was direct, intense, and candid, but was often in a way too methodical to make small talk. With a penchant for them, he was in the habit of uttering cryptic Zen-like pronouncements, such as "A wet face cannot get wetter," "Geometry is the science of cutting pies," Do not beat the drum with an axe," etc.

Each of them, a bonding factor, possessed the ability to hyperfocus, and in that regard, saw themselves as geniuses, or at least so claimed to be.

Closeness alone didn't do justice to the trio. Spike had dated Grommet's cousin, Tabitha; Poke who lived over in Johns Creek and had grown up in a big family became friends with Jackie, Spike's younger brother—they lived nearby and drove him to downtown Atlanta every Sunday to Grommet's church to sing; and it was through Grommet's singular efforts that both Poke and Spike became frat members. Their affection was unbounded. They socialized together freely. They shared with each other all their chemistry theories, benevolently shaped experiments, had published three papers—jointly written—in the *Journal of the American Chemical Society* and *Modern Drug Discovery*, once all traveled together by car one summer to the Black Hills of South Dakota, and virtually fought to pick up checks in restaurants.

They were each of them in their easy alliance, and by a nat-ural affinity, guileless, simple, and straightforward, as open as the sunrise.

One night, Grommet, wearing a closet smile, said, "Pay at-tention. I know how we can become famous, maybe even rich, and crash the world headlines."

"How?" Poke and Spike chimed in.

"First off, we all know Coca-Cola syrup is distributed to in-ternational bottlers who combine it with carbonated water to create the company's flagship soft drink, which is a closely guard-ed riddle right?" He opened the palms of both hands. "But what about the secret to that formula?"

"A history of mystery," said Spike.

"This is news?" asked Spike.

"Hardly," piped in Poke, huffing. "But before you go any further, save your breath, OK? I have traveled down this well-trav-eled road before. My brother, a lawyer in Washington D.C., did legal work in China all through the 1980s for Pepsi-Cola and in the course of his stay there happened to get connected with higher-ups in management and learned the secret to Pepsi, or as close to the secret ingredient of Coca-Cola as the two of you sitting there with your thumbs in your bums can get—sweet bay, Grecian laurel, *or-ganic Indian bay leaves!*"

Grommet laughed out loud. "So goes the rumor."

Then he grew serious.

He had a haughty face but cared for his pals.

"I have bigger fish to fry. What I am suggesting is that we get together, no bullshit, use our chemical know-how — 'Skill is expertise, aptitude is required; what morons fail to now is, chemists don't get tired.'" They all guffawed. The boys, owlish, superior, didn't merely assume they were the embodiment of cleverness, they knew it. Indeed, they were nerds.

"Coca-Cola is like the U.S. Constitution—we'd be de-constructing it!" squealed Poke who, reedy, weedy, and thin with an elongated pipelike neck that called comic attention to an extra-large Adam's apple, seemed perpetually astonished, with the stunned look of some kind of pop-eyed avian creature who had just swallowed a cricket! "I see the task at hand as patriotic! A fat, idle government big enough to serve you is big enough to take it away, right? We would be simultaneously subverting every weak Liberal who claims government doesn't go far enough, constantly demanding it be expanded!"

Grommet asked, almost rhetorically, "In this hunt of ours, should I be telling you, don't make much of what's not made much of? No, *quite the opposite!* I tell my Sunday School kids, 'Read the Bible not devotionally, but *devotedly!*' Get the difference? Assert by what's guided by probability, not merely allege with certainty, a notion that comes in handy, because that way it allows one to contradict oneself—being self-critical, see? That can be a virtue, healthy mistrust, not hewing stubbornly to one voiced opinion that may prove bogus."

His colleagues all agreeably nodded.

"We're looking for the black swan, OK?"

Spike offered, "Atlanta here is obviously ground zero for Coke, and so we happen to be located at the Los Alamos Proving Grounds. There's that. Let's not waste time, it is a given in Coca-Cola circles that the key ingredients that go into Coke syrup are well-known, arcanely, as 'merchandises,' and this I happen to know from my fat cousin Shirley, who had two or three aunts who for ages worked over at 1 Coca-Cola Plaza NW." He was excited. "I often do science over at the sub-lab of NASA right near there on the subject of rotations in space."

A specialty of Spike's, with a side-interest in geology, were details on the mineralogy of the rocks on Mars where he was also investigating the dark specks a few-thousandths-of-an-inch- wide within the mudstone, specks containing, to his surprise vivianite, an iron phosphate mineral surrounding off-white centers that included greigite, an iron sulfide mineral— an astounding biosignature discovered by a Mars Rover!

"The Dixie Coca-Cola Bottling Company plant is still located right over there on the southeast corner of Edgewood Avenue and Courtland Street, hard to believe," said Grommet, nodding his head. "The small, two-story Victorian commercial building was the site of the first Coca-Cola bottling plant in Georgia. We have passed it a thousand times."

"Right. And the first glass of Coca-Cola," observed redheaded Poke in a singsong manner that mocked the speech of rote, "was sold for a nickel on exactly May 8, 1886, at Jacobs Pharmacy, a popular Atlanta soda fountain, where it was sampled, pronounced 'excellent,' and placed on sale for five cents a glass as a soda fountain drink. Coca-Cola was created by Atlanta pharmacist John Pemberton in his laboratory just a short walk from this location at Marietta St NW and Peachtree Street."

"You got the dope down!"

"The company went public in 1919 at $40 a share. A single share bought then would have multiplied to a staggering 9,216 shares today and would be worth about, what, $635,904, at least. Not only that, but you'd be bringing in almost $17,900 in dividend income *every year.*"

"There's a location marker there on Edgewood Ave., Dumb-bell," noted Spike, wagging a satirical in front of his nose, one of his quirky habits.

"Do you want to spend the weekend at the testing room labs with me?" asked Grommet of his fraternity brothers, holding up a three-ring binder. "I'm keen to share here the results that I've begun assembling." The boys had nowhere else to go. They didn't bother to date, they spent almost all their time at the science and research lab testing rooms. "We breakdown the drink for all its elements and broadcast the results on nationwide television, CBS, NBC, and ABC, and in the process make history as explorers!"

They all laughed.

Grommet was in full fettle. "Coca-Cola as a drink is a *personality*," he said. "It has manifold aspects, like human beings, who are numerous in terms of identity, and who would—I mean, who could—deny it? Every human being is a collaboration of personalities. Each one of us has several selves, which we labor a lifetime to configure, even if not wanting particularly to examine them all. We're multiple. In being true or, say, attentive to only a single image inevitably means being false to several others." He added, "I've already done major work on this."

"Include me in," said Poke Chambers.

"Me, too," hooted Spike Aguilar, clear-eyed, handsome, and aggressive, making a victory fist.

He heartily grabbed Poke's hand, whose handclasp had no vitality. There seemed to be no bones in it—it was soft as duffel! Warm and moist. He jumped back. It was like shaking hands with a buttermilk biscuit.

"Done," pronounced Grommet Bateson.

It was mid-September. To get started, they met in the college science lab on Friday night. Assignments were meted out, agreeably. "Here, this is for you," said to Poke to Spike, arriving a bit late and handing his friend a beautifully wrapped gift. Unwrapping the ribbons and paper, Spike was staring at a brand-new Omega watch. "Oh my God,' said Spike, overwhelmed, "you are one loving guy. I *mean* it." He held it up and waved it proudly. "They should call the two of you, a conjoined being dubbed '*Spoke*' by name," said Grommet, smiling.

"But I've not forgotten you, dear man," declared Poke to Grommet. "I recall a few days ago you expressed a wicked craving for a pair of surgical magnifying loupes with 3 X magnification portion to significantly amplify by microscope all tiny objects up to 20

times that—here, this is yours—plus a pair of battery-powered head
lights, built in." "I don't believe it," said Grommet, almost blushing
with delight. He grabbed Poke's hand, squeezing it.

Spike joined in, to make a trilateral hug. Bonhomie reigned.
They were instantly excited and charitably disposed to group par-
ticipation. "What a privilege it was to zero in on this troubling
brainteaser at last!" he said, lighting up a celebratory cigar. "Back in
the old pioneering days—have you heard this story—Plains Indians
always used to mutter, *'Follow cigar smoke, fat man there.'* They all
laughed.

Grommet grew serious, "We have to hit on all twelve cylin-
ders. An itinerary of discipline, facts, neither whim nor interpreta-
tion! What doesn't fit, throw out, just what St. Paul did during a
terrible storm at sea to lighten the ship, pitching even *wheat* into the
sea, which reflected their serious desperation, the last essential
cargo of the ship after they had already lightened the vessel previously. Check it out—Acts 27:18!"

Within minutes, the guys were already taking notes.

"The beau ideal here is that we happen to be friends, a sym-
metrical, top-down force field, not a lame, robotic ensemble hopelessly tied to rigidly mandated workplace 'efficiency.' Such a climate
works! Understood and acceptable?"

They were all smiling.

"Now, let's synchronize ourselves and not waste time, OK?
Route step. Steady pace. Rifles shouldered. Nobody rides," declared
Grommet. "Above all, let's be open for anomalies. Smooth seas do
not make skillful sailors."

He excitedly clapped his hands.

"Remember, luck is a residue of design!"

Weeks went by. Graduate courses were demanding. But the
special project that they agreed to collaborate on was in full swing.
To get off on the right foot, Grommet had generously ordered and
paid for three full cases of Coca-Cola for each of them—to drink,

to taste, to savor, to test, to think about. That very first night, characteristically getting right down to business, Grommet confidently stated, "'Merchandise 7X'— let's get this right out of the way, as we set out to try to examine, scrutinize, probe, and reconstruct, then of course test, and appraise, judiciously weighing every detail—is recognized as this famous soft drink's exact formula. No. 1 in 'Merchandises' is sugar—"

"But look, we all know—"

"No, no, let me finish, No. 1 is sugar in the form of, well, some say cane, but generally high-fructose corn syrup, No. 2 caramel coloring, No. 3 is caffeine, and No. 4 is phosphoric acid. The identities of numbers 5 through 7 or 9 or whatever are a matter of debate—particularly the last bungle of 'merchandise 7X' (the X has never been explained), which is thought to contain a mixture of essential oils such as orange, lime, lemon, and lavender. It is well known that originally this elusive No. 5 was a mysterious blend of three parts coca and one part cola. Beyond that, however, from where we now stand, all is hazy except—"

"See," noted Poke, "right there -- there is the sticking point, No. 5+ is an unexplained mingle of components. An amalgamate. Mysterious ingredients."

"Actually, it's a coalescence," posited Spike. "Technically, amalgamate refers to the alloying of mercury with another metal."

Poke shrugged. The two cordially swapped smirks.

Grommet began, saying, "Ol' 'Doc' Pemberton—John Stith Pemberton, that is, the American pharmacist and Confederate States Army veteran who, as we all know, is best known as the inventor of Coca-Cola—"

Poke interrupted, to add, "He suffered from a bad saber wound that he sustained in April 1865, during the Battle of Columbus, and, curiously, his efforts to control his chronic pain led to a very bad case of morphine addiction. In an attempt to curb that agony and to meet that terrible need, he began to experiment with various painkillers and odd toxins. His development of an earlier beverage—his first recipe was called 'Dr. Tuggle's Compound Syrup of Globe Flower,' yes, in which the active ingredient was derived from, yes, the buttonbush, and—"

"Right, well, what I was attempting to clarify, Poke, before you butted in, and, for your information, I knew about his Civil War wound, and it was, I believe, specifically to the chest, incidentally, which you didn't mention—"

"It was wound to the stomach, at least the way I heard it," interjected Poke, "and he soon became addicted to the morphine used to ease his pain."

"—anyway, it was on May 8, 1886 specifically—we happen to know the exact date of the famous experiment—that he used a wooden oar in a big brass kettle to stir up a strange new concoction of caramel, coca leaf, vanilla, lime juice, and, in an attempt to reproduce a perfect brew, began to experiment with coca and cocas wines, eventually to create a recipe containing extracts of kola nut and a wild Mexican shrub known as '*damiana*,' which he then humbly christened 'Pemberton's French Wine Coca!'"

The guys were all Georgians, the three of them, specifically, pointedly, from Atlanta. They knew the lore, they knew the learning, they knew the legend. What they all shared, beyond that, like all perspicacious boffins, was not only the secret delight in finding accepted wisdom proved wrong but also, concomitantly, the ongoing, compulsive, and irrepressible conviction that it was their lot—their just due—to right it.

"Coca-Cola is designed, take note, to produce drinkers capable of examining it—a remark which is not the tautology it seems," said Grommet, "for it offers a taste virtually asking how to be decoded. Ours will be a provoking task."

"And a big one," said Poke, laughing.

Spike quickly demurred. "You call this big?" he asked, "a considerable labor? King Mohamed Al-Faisal planned to have a 100 million-ton Antarctic frozen iceberg moored off the coast of Saudi Arabia to produce water for that arid land to arrange for more water than the Nile could ever provide. Now *that*'s big! You want big? Australia engineers plan to build a mountain, 3000 foot-high, out of Teflon several thousand miles long, running north-south across Australia with the solid reasoning that clouds would form by air being forced to climb over this artificial mountain, causing turbulent weather thereby created to give rain, which would then make the deserts bloom to yield up fertile land that would lead to a vastly-increased population, which would soon make Australia fabulously wealthy!"

"Of equal precedent?" asked Grommet. "How about Jesus, living in the far remote, isolated, and improbable little country of Palestine two thousand years ago, selecting a few completely uneducated and illiterate Galilean fishermen who went on by a miracle to change *the whole world*?"

"It can and must not be forgotten, and especially not by us in this undertaking, that Ol' Pemby flavored it with a mix of exotic oils that he later dubbed 'Merchandise 7X,' then sent the syrup to Jacobs Pharmacy, where a colleague added water and carbonation to create the first taste test. An entrepreneur named Frank M. Robinson, who was Pemberton's partner and bookkeeper, people forget, invested with him— it was this same Robinson, to whom major credit should be given but rarely is, the guy who actually named the now famous beverage, even designed the distinctive Coca-Cola script and logo — and traveled around the Atlanta area, peddling the syrup as a new fountain drink for drugstores."

"I actually heard from a chemist friend a month or so ago that a recent study identified and measured as many as fifty-eight aroma compounds—*fifty-eight*, mind you!—in the top four or five U.S. brands of cola," said Spike, "so just fathom the amounts of essential oils in Coke of cinnamon, nutmeg, orange, and vanilla."

"I've heard that coriander is added, as well," said Poke. "Mass spectroscopy should give us the No. 5 blend."

"Spectro is often paired with chromatography techniques, as you all know, in order to separate them. Exactly," declared Spike.

Poke offered, "NMR—nuclear magnetic resonance—is matchless for good information—rich, non-destructive analytical technique. That would be the way to go."

Grommet wagged an admonitory finger. "Not necessarily, my friend. MRI for chemicals may prove to be best. It handily re-capitulates the electronic environment surrounding each atom, which can be used to determine structure."

"No, but wait, listen," quickly pleaded Poke, "NMR pro-vides detailed information about molecular structure, dynamic pro-cesses and allows the direct observation of chemical reactions. Think about it."

"What about optical rotation?" suggested Spike. "Go that way? Beam polarized light through a sample syrup, figure out its chirality. Check its types. Chiral axis, chiral plane, a helix, whatever. Sift by rotations, translations alone. A right shoe is different from a left shoe, and clockwise is different from anticlockwise."

"Or X-ray crystallography as an alternate," submitted Poke, getting into the swing of things. "I could personally handle that, all right? Shining X-rays through a crystal and figuring out the struc-ture based on scattering."

"But remember," advised Grommet, "we must all avoid wasting crucial time on any of our tests, experiments, or probes, pursuing what is *not* in the formula, but rather what is. The sad log-ical end to defensive warfare is surrender, right? Defeat!" He waited. No one spoke. "I remain convinced that the likeliest explanation is the correct one. 'Occam's Razor,' no?—the idea that the fewest as-sumptions are always the best, which is to say that in explaining anything, in coming up with a solid solution, no more assumptions `should be made than are necessary. Let me remind you, gentlemen, that is precisely how the Danish theoretical physicist Neils Bohr postulated that electrons circle the nucleus in fixed quantum orbits for which he won the Nobel Prize, and how Sir Lawrence and his father, Sir William Bragg saw how crystals diffract X-rays, and how Melvin Calvin unraveled the key steps in the assimilation of carbon dioxide during photosynthesis, and how Renato Dulbecco extended phage methodologies to animal viruses, and that gave Linus Pauling's brilliantly insightful proposal of the α-helix as the basic fold for the polypeptide chain his greatest impact on biology. Or is that wrong reasoning? I mean, on the other hand, in our case, animated, dynamic, and competing explanations for a phenomenon may prove the better breakthrough!"

He paused to add, "Why don't each of us, separately, follow the bliss we choose—independently, privately, seek that one elusive missing ingredient?" His fellow chemists hastily agreed. "Look closely at the underside of an oak leaf—notice, above all, the intricacies of the geometry of its delicate veins. No invention devised is more beautiful, more simple, more direct, because nothing is lacking, nothing superfluous. Let us use that as the template of the missing X. Aspire to that simplicity in your search."

He then opened up his three-ring binder.

"I've done a lot of research already," said Grommet. "The secret formula for Coca Cola, Merchandise 7X, as you probably all know, was held in the main vault of Trust Financial in Atlanta for eighty-six years, now Sun Trust Banks. In 1892, Asa Griggs Candler bought the rights to the Coca-Cola business and the secret formula. In 1919, Ernest Woodruff and a group of investors bought the company, using the secret formula as collateral for a loan, and he asked Candler's son, 'Buddie'—he was an animal collector, a menagerie that included a Bengal tiger, four lions, a black leopard, a gorilla, baboons, and six elephants, by name, Coca, Cola, Pause, Refreshes, Refreshing, and Delicious!—to write down on paper the now precious secret formula, which he placed in a vault in the

Guaranty Bank in New York. But what happened was, when Woodruff eventually repaid his loan, therefore redeeming the secret formula, he brought it back to Atlanta to place it in the Trust Company Bank.

"In 2011, after 135 years of heritage and intrigue, the secret formula was moved to the World of Coca-Cola Museum downtown here, where thousands of people visit the 'Vault of the Secret Formula' every year. It is never touched. Instead, the formula is passed on by word of mouth, almost as if it were the secret cant of a special fraternal order."

"Like us," said Spike, hugging Poke.

"It is only one of the—maybe *the*—most closely guarded secrets in history."

"Them's the facts, brethren. The Coca-Cola Company's by-laws specifically dictate that *only two* Coke executives—designated keepers of it—are officially allowed, *sanctioned*, to know the actual formula at any given time, by tradition, by rule, by principle, two alone. Passing on the recipe is a verbal rite."

But Grommet scotched any undue reverence.

"Let's face it, gentlemen. The so-called hallowed recipe is little more than just another chemical formula. We are not trying to decipher Mesoamerican glyphic scripts or Linear A or the weird inscriptions of Easter Island rongorongo, OK?"

"We can nail this bitch!" said Spike, excitedly.

He slapped Grommet's palm.

"You've picked the right man in me—and why? I have done something like this before, in a sophomore chem course, breaking down an old, corked bottle of Mother Seigel's Curative Syrup, I'm not joking, an ingenious country extract of roots, barks, and herbs concocted by the Shakers back in, I don't know, 1885 or so. A 'blood purifier.' Sold for dyspepsia, for people out of sorts. A digestive. I've actually seen a bottle on display at the Smithsonian, it was that famous. They were all laxative and cathartics back then."

The group began to meet, as planned, every other night. They worked separately on various phases and from varied suppositions. Poke and Grommet sometimes worked together, as did Grommet and Spike. They were fastidious, detail-oriented, selective, precise, and, as working chemists, conscientious, exacting, and thorough. Their tempers were tested. "It is not a simple right-to-left boustrophedon here. I have read that Goizueta—*Mr.* Robert Goizueta, the legendary innovative Coke president?—was officially taught how to mix the secret formula at Coca-Cola's Atlanta Technical Laboratory, almost as if it were a formal *rite de passage*. He claimed it was little more than a solid chemical equation. Still, it remains a mystery why lovers of this magical elixir so lust after it, *one billion addicts* in the world who drink it every day, not satisfied until they get their daily eight-ounce fix!"

"It is sold everywhere on the planet."

"Except," put in plucky Poke, "in North Korea and Castro's Cuba, when Coca-Cola was prohibited being sold in 1960. Rum and Coke there is now called a 'Cuba libre'—literally, 'Free Cuba'—a highball cocktail consisting of rum and I think a brand called TropiCola or something and in many recipes lime juice on ice. '*Kekoukele*' is the Chinese translation of Coca-Cola, where it has been sold as a popular brand since 1920."

Spike said, "Aristotle Onassis's daughter, Christina was obsessed with Coca-Cola—positively craved it. In fact, she loved the taste of it so much that she ordered a Coke machine installed in her Swiss high school."

"President Donald Trump, like two other billionaires, Elon Musk and Warren Buffett, are fanatical Coca-Cola drinkers. Notoriously zealous? A person named Robert Pedreira from Bahia, Brazil claims that he has been alive for the last fifty years solely by drinking Coca-Cola. A grandfather, he swallows his meds with Coke. Hasn't drunk a drop of water in half a century. As per a report from *Oddity Central News*—yeah, I read it—the seventy-year-old retiree, undoubtedly the entire world's biggest fan of Coke, is suffering from both diabetes and heart disease. I have seen his photograph. His color is flashing bright pink."

"Coca-Cola, by way of its consistent global presence, advertising reach, and cultural impact, is said to be the second most understood word in the world," said Grommet.

"What is the most understood word?"

Grommet said, "I thought you'd never ask. The second most understood word, globally is 'OK.'" He laughed. "So, do you guys want the fame of a major discovery?"

"OK!" joining in, they all shouted. "OK!"

They were now into the month of October. The requirements and demands of their official classes doubled work for them, but all three were now dogged in their separate pursuits of the secrets of the Coca-Cola formula. The guys worked mostly early in the morning, although less so during the day, getting back to the lab late into the night to work, snapping up protein bars for one-handed snacks and tasting, testing, re-tasting over and over sips of the drink, all the while taking close notes, as studiously they went biohacking the liquid for clues.

It was a world of autoclaves, centrifuges, thermometers, crucibles, tongs, fume hoods, scales and spatulas, incubators, wash bottles, beakers, funnels, test tubes, flasks, Bunsen burners. Working together began to create some tension, however. Although he was often in the lab, Poke was privately hoping to nab a room, alone, adjacent to the medical area, which had access to an NMR spectrometer, an indispensable tool, he felt, for the structural determination of molecules, molecular notions, and interactions.

Color signified in Coca-Cola, flavor made demands, there was texture, of course, balance, composition—"finish"—but tasting was the clue for profile. Even mouthfeel. Glass bottles were fine, but, together, they first concentrated on the can. Did that seem odd? Poke said, "Maybe a tin can imparts a taste to Coca-Cola, as well. Ever think of that?"

"Possible," said Spike. "Not at all plausible.

Grommet thought to jump in here.

"Let me add, please, by way of caveat," he said, "that the arrogance of any of us by insisting that any key to the Coca-Cola formula, to the exclusion of all others, means exclusively that no others are open to consideration is a mistake that closes off curiosity, perception, the adventure of discovery, and so both queers and ruins our search. Regarding the concept of curved Einsteinian space, we are at all times looking at the back of our own heads, OK? Accepted. Let's just not let that notion apply here."

"Modern cans are made from steel, lined with a transparent film made from assorted plastics, instead of tin. If one uses metal containers or lids that are reactive with acidic foods, this can cause a metallic taste. Why not?"

"All aluminum cans have a plastic liner," said Grommet.

"Actually," said Spike, correcting him, "it is an epoxy resin, a type of plastic coating that adheres tightly to the metal. It protects taste, prevents leaks, and extends shelf life. But with that protection comes tradeoffs."

"Right." observed a worried Poke. "Alarmists insist that cans of Coca-Cola along with other canned soft drinks—aluminum cans, including energy drinks and canned waters—being lined with BPA, that is, bisphenol A, a chemical linked to hormone disruption, reproductive issues, and even certain cancers, are dangerous."

"It has all been looked into, needless to say," said Poke, "but, although no one likely seems aware of it, such cans might very well be leaching hundreds of thousands of microplastics and other hormone-destroying compounds into our bodies. In the long run, who can predict the results?"

One bone of contention was their varied view of Harvey Washington Wiley (October 18, 1844–June 30, 1930), the American physician, chemist, and the first commissioner of the United States Food and Drug Administration, who had worked at the Good Housekeeping Institute laboratories and advocated successfully for the passage of the landmark Pure Food and Drug Act of 1906. It was this Wiley's advocacy for stricter food and drug regulations that indirectly contributed to Coca-Cola's decision to remove cocaine from its formula in the early 20th century. This move addressed public health concerns but has drawn modern criticism for its impact on drug policy perceptions.

Whereas once the discussion of such a subject would have been an amusing, indeed, an intriguing option to kick that can around, Poke Chambers, taking an odd conservative position, sought to school his two colleagues on the horror of such a drug being even associated with Coca-Cola, and it went down poorly. It seemed right-wing, reactionary.

"Are you a fascist?" lordly inquired Spike Aguilar, taking off his glasses and pushing two wash bottles into a nearby barrel for added comment.

Grommet Bateson uncharitably, uncharacteristically—but he had been drinking heavily lately—also put the boot in, adding, "Oh no, are you becoming one of those snowflakes and milksops who loves shag carpeting, manscapes your pubes, and, when his pet dog dies, then tearfully, wussishly exclaims to everybody, 'He went over the Rainbow Bridge'?"

"Right, and next thing we know, you'll be collecting stuffies and plush toys, wearing an ankle bracelet, and singing out like Judy Garland about Madame Crematon, the 'inventor of the safety pin,' the faggot's national anthem!"

"Exactly, along with a precious wall display of Clarice Cliff pottery."

"Me? Never heard of it," sniped Poke. "But look who *does* know about it!"

Spike inquired, "Do you also go big for 'Cancel Culture'"?

"What a peawit!" said Grommet.

Poke exasperatedly threw a towel across the room and sniped, "You guys have turned into real weasels."

"Examine what is said, not who is speaking," said Grommet, sententiously.

He then pulled out a small chart.

"And anyway, Poke, coca in this context isn't just a sportive allusion, OK? Everyone knows that cocaine was part of the original Coke recipe. It is now a Schedule II narcotic, and it's illegal to bring coca leaves into the United States, for any purpose, including the harmless use for brewing tea or for chewing it. The drink today features 'FE Coca,' which is to say, *fluid extract of coca*. After the year 1903, all cocaine was removed from Coca-Cola, making the extract just another favor component—crude cocaine left over is used by select pharmaceutical companies for medicines. Leaves used to make the extract are called 'spent' and are as safe as a leaf of iceberg lettuce at the A&P, clean, laundered, rinsed—wiped, if you will—by the billion-dollar Stepan Chemical Company in Maywood, New Jersey, I checked, the only company in the U.S. that is licensed by the DEA to import legally Peruvian coca leaves. Cocaine-free coca leaves are perfectly legal and available as an herbal tea."

Such behavior was not and never normal for them. Competition had reared its ugly head—with hurtful recriminations. "As I was trying to tell you two weeks ago, although as usual you weren't listening, that a specifically Chinese cinnamon oil, cassia by name, plays a large, if not the largest, most significant role in the Coke formula, the principle, ingredient-wise, like, try, a 1/10th drachm—0.18 g—and if you—"

"Right," retaliated Poke, "while you were interrupting me, Grommet, at the very moment I was wearing a protective chemistry fume hood at the lab table handling various benzoic, oxide, and boric acid powders. trying to negotiate the supportive value of India bay leaves in Coca-Cola. Thanks a heap!"

"To explain just what exactly?"

"Taste, flavor, the drink as a soothing digestive comfort."

"Bay leaf powders aren't worth rat-shit, for our purposes," said Grommet.

"What?"

Startled, Poke was given a turn.

"You're joking?"

"A hidden secret in the formula is *cassia leaves*!"

"So, what are you telling me now?"

"You're always so damned certain, Grommet," argued Spike. "I'm beginning to think—considering the cravings, emotional triggers, and blood sugar fluctuations of its serious addicts—that *cane sugar* hugely signifies in the formula! Think about it—it's right there in front of you, a major component but a subtle enticement in the way, say, that, according to rumor, Coca-Cola it is supposedly a hidden logo on the Danish flag."

"Oh, bullshit."

"No, listen, *wait*. I've spent entire weeks monitoring the habits, overall diet quality, hydration, and stress levels of some of Coke's, well, *users*, freaks, of you want, and almost all of them show a pronounced lack of calcium and magnesium. I don't have to tell you that back there in the 1980s, most Coca-Cola bottlers on the United States switched the sweetening ingredient in the drink from cane sugar—*sucrose*—to the cheaper high-fructose corn syrup, but you don't seem to acknowledge it, do you?

"But what in the name of Sam Hill—"

"Just a minute! Wait, will you? As of 2009, the only U.S. bottler still using sucrose the full year-round was the Coca-Cola Bottling Company of Cleveland, which serves northern Ohio and a portion of Pennsylvania, all right? Mexican Coke still uses cane-sugar-sweetened Coca-Cola."

Grommet brushed this off. "That's old hat, and we've dealt with it."

Spike voiced a reservation. "Cassia leaves? I've got cinnamaldehyde in my ingredients blueprint, had it from the jump. What's the big news?"

His adversary waved a deprecating hand.

"Cassia leaves are similar in appearance to bay leaves, Poke, get it?"—he pointed—"but they are usually much bigger and have three veins running the length of the leaf, rather than the single one found on bay leaves. See? Take a gander. They also taste radically different than bay leaves with a clove and cinnamon flavor."

"A farcical distinction, if ever I heard one," said a piqued Poke, offended, who with a fund of insecurities that spawned an abrasive energy hated to lose in the fight of a running war but yearned for the credibility of his peers.

"Wrong!"

Spike interjected, "I've read that cassia is not unlike passionflower, which is a calming herb that can reduce anxiety and improve mood, slowing down your brain by blocking specific signals in your central nervous system. But it may increase GABA, no? Research suggests that passionflower may increase GABA."

It interested Spike.

"And are you talking about cassia bark -- or cassia root, as well? I have heard that cassia oil has shown promising results with sufferers of type 2 diabetes. You can substitute actual cinnamon—Ceylon cinnamon, the real thing—for cassia in food recipes, but I believe that it should be used more sparingly, as it has a stronger, sweeter flavor."

"Any iteration. But I mean the leaves. The dried bark of an evergreen tree, native to Burma, cassia is aromatic and, yes, figures in Asian cuisine. It is also used in powder form. Cassia leaves have a ton of utility," said Grommet. "Utility is a value of mine. I don't care in what shape or form. And what, tell me, that plays into our search should we dismiss? Nothing"

"But bay leaves—?" insisted Poke.

"Come on now, gentlemen, enough of quibbling and cavilling. let's make like a proton and stay positive!" said Spike, idly juggling a handful of burette clips.

"It is *not* at all a farcical distinction," said Grommet, a bit irked, looking up from his microscope, "because bay leaves contain eucalyptol, terpenes, and methyl eugenol—essential oils—which contribute to their taste and aroma."

"They are also infamously bland." Spike had been listening. But no one said anything, not a word. "Flat as a geezer's slippers. Insipid. Vapid. Flavorless. *Savor*less."

It wasn't the first time the stress of their meetings had begun to add something of contention. As a group, they had a nagging sense, not of failure, but of success being too long postponed. "I don't see why we haven't capped this damned oil well already," said Grommet, somewhat impatiently. "Any problem can be solved using the materials in a room,' according to Edwin H. Land, the Polaroid man who not only invented filters for polarizing light but the retinex theory of color vision. And here we have the materials, and we're in a room. Right?"

"What he meant, I believe, was the character and constitution of the *minds* in a room."

"Or rather how much room was in their minds is probably more like it, you know?"

"You sound absurd," grizzled Poke to Grommet.

Spike growled at Poke, "And you, I swear to God, work like a man accustomed to leaving things behind. Cocaine in Coca-Cola you're telling us was a Soviet ploy?"

"Right-wing," added Grommet.

"Old fogyish, ossified, anti-modern."

Poke indignantly stamped his foot, "Your heads are shaped like Klein bottles—queer 3-D shapes with neither an inside nor an outside!"

"And yours like a Mobius strip," grumbled Spike, turning to Grommet, "with only one side and one boundary!"

Reciprocating, Grommet quickly countered to Spike, "At least it's better than yours, which resembles either an inexplicable Triquetra or impossible Reuleaux triangle, a crazy medley of intersecting arcs and discs no one can figure out"

"I have been using—" interjected Pike in retaliation, coughing, sputtering angrily at the unfair prodding and the provocation "—using an integrative research approach that combines chemical-analysis, LC-MS, HR-LC-MS, of small plant molecules. phytohormones, plant specialized compounds, and volatile organic compounds, GC-MS, and the impact on multi-trophic ecological networks in crop production to identify key phytochemical drivers steering ecosystem services strictly for use in carbonated drinks. *That is insufficient?*"

He waited.

"Am I talking to myself here?"

His colleagues had heard it all but ignored him.

Blithely continued Grommet, "The United States now allows manufacturers to label cassia as cinnamon, I have checked this out, without disclosing on packaging that it's cassia. Are you with me? McCormick—the spice brand people?—have taken full advantage of this fact. It is sold cheaper on the market. Coke has a distinct cinnamon flavor. Why start at zero? The primary taste of Coca-Cola, at bottom, is thought to come from both cinnamon and vanilla—you can also throw in caffeine—with trace amounts of essential oils, and spices."

"Such as lemon. *And* lavender!" said Poke. "And what about citric acid or lime juice. I have spent at least a solid week with my nose deep in NMR chemical shifts compiling for special organic compounds. A subtle acidity is a secret in Coca-Cola. What is its acidity? I have tested it, and its pH checks out to be 2.6 to 2.7, mainly due to H_3PO_4, phosphoric acid. As a fizzy drink, it contains plenty of dissolved carbon dioxide, although this makes very little contribution to its acidity. And you people don't think lime juice is involved? Impurities. Reagents! I've checked! Run tests! Give me some credit."

"What have *I* been doing, *sleeping*?" queried an irate Spike. "Same with me. All right? I have blown through the ranks of these things like a wind in wheat."

Poke could not suppress a yawn, smothering it politely with a happily fluttering hand.

"Look, I have problems with mere statistics," said Grommet. "Can you comprehend that? Data shopping. Let us please not accept blindly the notion that knowledge necessarily increases with incremental information—which is the foundation of statistical inference and may in some instances, but we don't know which ones. I'm inveighing against facile certainty, that's all. My point? Don't get married to positions to the extent that in our pursuits we push randomness under the rug. The mother of all deceptions is false certainty. Theory cannot be verified. You know who can always find a reason to fit a past event? Astrologists! There are things to gain from *disorder*. Einstein said, 'If we knew what we were doing, we wouldn't call it research.'"

"No one even mentions orange rind."

"I have looked into every damn thing, St. John's wort—they call it 'goat weed'—wild yam, ashwagandha, even licorice root." Spike folded his arms, triumphantly. "Including orange rind, both the zest *and* the pith, my friend."

"What about echinacea?"

"That, too—a flower native to North America that has been promoted as a dietary supplement. I happen to know from flowers, dear man, ignorant though you think I may be. The interplanetary ones, included. Smaller than a penny, a flower-like rock artifact was actually imaged by NASA's 'Curiosity 'Mars Rover employing its Mars Hand Lens Imager—MAHLI—the camera on the end of its robotic arm. That dramatic image was taken on the 3,396th Martian day, or Sol, of that dramatic mission."

Poke nerdishly squint-gawked, his mouth stretched into what looked like ghastly and disapproving skepticism, "*What is a 'sol'?*"

"A Martian day—or Sol—is 24 hours and 37 minutes long, Poke, your frown noted, while every Sol is different, each one is packed full of exciting science activities, observations, and discoveries, OK? Get an education."

In the lab, Spike who had felt left out, said, "I have posited the unimpressive use in Coke of exactly 1.5 ounces of caramel for color. Negligible. Ineligible. Discreditable."

"Means nothing," said Grommet.

Poke did not agree. "Coca-Cola's color is a rich dark green-brown due of course to that specific 'colorant.' Comforting, I suppose, but peculiar in a way, because, broadly-speaking, different studies reveal a general tendency for people to associate sweetness with red and pink, sour with green-yellow, salt with blue and white. Such are the quirks of humans."

"Coca-Cola, the drink, was originally green. This we know is a fact," said Spike, irking Poke.

"Coke can have a red tinge, as well, depending on the light you're in. These are 'emotional anchors,' mind you. I've actually seen *blue* in it!"

But this had been a digression. Squabbles were the last thing that this group needed. Disposition, outlook, and perspective were now going sideways. Where had the mindsets altered? "The difference between an ordeal and experience is your attitude," stated a didactic Grommet.

Yet who was listening? "You also left out neroli—"

Again, it was Spike, of whom no one was taking notice, coming back to quibble with Poke regarding his NMR chemical shifts.

"And I must say I find overrated the whole concept of cinnamon as a taste and flavor in Coca-Cola and, if you really want to push it, totally bogus." It was Spike, raising his hand with a little wave from across the room.

Grommet looked at Spike. "Wrong. Dead wrong." He turned to Poke. "And you, you haven't even so much as mentioned glycerin."

"For godsakes, give me a chance to finish," shouted Poke.

Ignoring him, Spike chimed in, "Neroli is important! And what I've been trying to point out, if you can set down that goddam beaker for a minute, Poke, is that it is not at all unlike bergamot. The 'Prince of Citrus'! It is an essential oil produced from the blossom of the bitter orange tree. Its scent is sweet, honeyed and somewhat metallic with green and spicy."

Poke raised a finger, his *digitus medius*.

"We must consider it a lead ingredient in Coca-Cola."

"How can you say that?"

"A hunch," smugly answered Spike. "Nothing more." He knuckled the table. "Instinctive thinking." He did so again. "Inborn intelligence, OK? It is never wise to disregard the sagacity if those who do not learn their lore from books."

Grommet helpfully added, "Bergamot is made using the rind of the orange fruit, rather than the flower petals."

"Did I say it wasn't?" asked Spike.

Poke said, "You didn't say it was."

"A lot of glycerin is made from animal fat," said Grommet, "processed on the very same equipment as animal glycerin or made from used oil from non-kosher establishments, rendering the glycerin non-kosher. Glycerin, you understand, would be offensive and indeed blasphemous to any and all Coca-Cola producers, because its inclusion in the drink would antagonize such otherwise irreconcilable groups such as orthodox Jews and orthodox Moslems." He laughed. "Trust me, I know everything about it. I have worked with glycerin much of my life. I alchemized in my cellar. At the young age of fourteen, I managed to concoct a powerful liquid with it that exploded on touch! My Mom went shithouse. We spread it on door-knobs, bannisters, even toilet seats!"

Grommet was ahead of them on the project and had been working for months.

"I've got it down right here in my three-ring binder, rec-orded," he said, tapping it. "Coca-Cola was certified kosher in 1935 by Rabbi Tobias Geffen, after beef-tallow derived glycerin was re-placed with vegetable glycerin. But high-fructose corn syrup used by most U.S. bottlers since the 1980s is considered *kitniyot,* which is to say, derived from grains, seeds, and legumes by the strict defi-nitions of kosher law, and therefore forbidden to Ashkenazi Jews during Passover, according to their traditions. Each year, in the weeks leading up to Passover, bottlers in markets with substantial Jewish populations switch to sucrose sweetener in order to obtain their goofy Kosher for Passover certification."

Spike knew the products. "I've worked with it before, it's used all the time in the biodiesel industries, a by-product of soaps and candles. Vegetable glycerin is a clear, fatty liquid typically sourced from coconut, soy, or palm oil. You find it in humans, an-imals, and plant matter. It treats constipation, OK? No biggie. It does not easily oxidize. A common substitute is corn syrup." He shrugged. "What's the mystery?

Removing his glasses, he added, "Glycerin is kosher—my Chem 101 professor was a Jew and a fanatic about food—that is, of course, if it is made from kosher vegetable oil or petroleum and processed on kosher equipment."

"Which it rarely if ever is," said Poke, smugly. "Did you hear me? Are you listening? And Glucksman, your professor? I studied under the very same moon-bat for a course, as well. We all suspected he was off his dot. He also believed not only that the moon was hollow and that a separate flowing aquifer exists under the Atlantic Ocean *but also hidden worlds*! Anyway, regarding our investigative work on the Ur-formula, which feeds into the new, who the hell gave a good goddam about Jewish or Moslem sensibilities back in 1886 America?"

Spike glowered at Poke.

"Why are redheads always so touchy? Is it in your genes, man?"

"And so adolescent."

"That's my natural color, OK?" acknowledged Poke, angrily. "Like General Robert E. Lee, who is frankly one of my heroes. Not a Yankee, like you, Grommet. Red-faced like all the well-born Lees of Virginia, with pale skin."

"I was born in Baltimore, Maryland, Poke," Grommet reminded him, "which during the Civil war was entirely sympathetic to the Confederacy."

"You're an only child, right?" said a challenging Poke. "Difficult. Small gifts for debate, parleying, and negotiation. Ill-tempered under pressure. I myself am a kid from a big family. We grew up learning to maneuver as a way of not being hated by our siblings. Simple as that. No, it was not good manners, it was a strategy, a plan of action, you could even call it a ploy. We would never take the last cookie on a plate."

Grommet snorted, "Oh, don't be so goddamned sensitive."

"That's your problem, too," muttered Spike, belatedly adding, "And while we are at it, I also cannot for the life of me see how caffeine possibly slots into the existing scaffolding of the Coca-Cola formula in the first place." Nobody said anything. He grumpily folded his arms, kicked the back of his stool, and asked, "What, am I alone in this room?"

He looked querulously at Poke. "No comment? I swear, I would rather have been equipped with a knowledge of people than a microscope."

Poke sourly retorted, "Oh, dry up, you nitwit!"

"I suppose that it leads to the question that we all have to consider scientifically, do people who drink Coke smoke cigarettes to combat the high? Or do they aid and abet it as an ancillary drug, its druggy near-cousin?"

"Do I have to tell you at this stage that the word *cola* is a direct reference to the kola nut—that's k-o-l-a—which is the natural source of caffeine. As far as Coca-Cola goes, caffeine citrate took its place, making the nut unnecessary."

Poke groaned.

"Oh my god, are we starting from zero here?"

Spike pointed to Poke, "As to unnecessary nuts—"

"Bite me!" snapped Poke.

"Attention, folks," Grommet suddenly exclaimed, loudly knocking on the table in the hope of stemming some of the inexplicable and highly unsettling discord, while also feeling proud to have a grand announcement to make. "Let me give you the dope on cassia leaves, dopes!" He walked over, dramatically, to close an outer door as if to protect the major secret he was about to divulge. "*Cassia auriculata* is an evergreen shrub that grows in many parts of India and in other parts of Asia. The flower, buds, leaves, stem, root, and unripe fruit are used for treatment, especially in Ayurvedic medicine. Cassia which is an ayurvedic herb isa more popularly known as *senna*. It is mainly used as a blood purifier, a laxative for relieving constipation, used to treat skin diseases. It is also known as *swarnapatri* in Sanskrit."

"And?"

"Mere foliage, right?" asked Grommet. "Sheer vegetation, moronic leafage, and brainless as a plant? Fine, except, drum roll, boys, it is definitively a part of Coca-Cola's secret formula. A major part. Maybe the major part, OK?"

"Flora? Verdure? Vegetation?"

"Right-o. Look, I myself checked this out long months ago. In India, cassia is used for everything from diabetes to pink eye,

constipation to rheumatism to muscle pain, and for other implausi-
ble conditions, but there is good scientific evidence to support its
wide use elsewhere. And I am here to say—to announce—that despite Poke's remarkable busy brother, 'a lawyer in Washington
D.C.,'" he mocked, "'who did work in China with bay leaves
through the 1980s for Pepsi-Cola,' in knowing this about cassia
leaves, we have come along way on solving part of our sacred mission. We are closing in on the formula!"

"Really, do you have to be so rude?" asked Poke.

Spike jumped in, "And aren't you yourself in your declara-
tive cassia leaves assertions showing the very 'facile certainty' you've
previously condemned?"

Ignoring him, Grommet, opening a bottle of liquor he
pulled from his briefcase, explained, "Under orders from Coca-
Cola kingpin Roberto Goizueta, to have retrieved this valuable key
ingredient of fresh, green, just-picked cassia leaves and bring them
back to Atlanta, at any cost, various Coke middlemen and emissar-
ies were ordered to travel to far off India and mainland China for
samples, often having to smuggle them folded into a fur hat or un-
derwear or wrapped inside a collection of neckties!"

"By the way," said Grommet, taking a hefty slug of liquor,
frowned and shook his head, "one of us left the chem lab a mess
last night. Retorts left off the retort stands and some still full, and a
dry distillation one. A window was left open." He looked at Spike.
"And mornings, the smell of tobacco is overpowering."

Shrugging, Spike snapped, "I use cigars. Smoke comes out.
Live with it, Grommet."

"And why this sudden and unbecoming unpleasantness?"
carped Poke

"I correct you, and, what, your neck prickles like a Bull Ter-
rier? We all have to follow rules, don't we? Spike's brother Jackie
told me you used to run red lights. In any event, that was how the

novelist Margaret Mitchell was killed in 1949, struck down by a speeding driver at the crossing Peachtree at Thirteenth Street."

Poke puffed up like a partridge.

"That's a nerd stat," he snapped.

"You're as uptight as those idiotic bowties you wear," said Grommet. "Isn't it a common fashion accessory from the nineteenth century?"

"Time was, when you used to compliment me on them, *friend*," said Poke, throwing aside a pipette in disgust and walking out of the room.

Defending the belittled Poke, Spike said, "Sir Winston Churchill wore bowties. As did President Franklin Roosevelt, Le Corbusier, dancer Fred Astaire, Stan Laurel, Vladimir Horowitz, Groucho Marx, and Alexander Fleming, the Scottish pharmacologist who was a Nobel Prize laureate."

"So did Pee Wee Herman, along with that total arseless idiot comedian Jerry Lewis, and the Penguin in *Batman*," scoffed Grommet impatiently.

"And Donald Duck," hawed Spike, jeering.

Poke, fighting rage, turned to Spike with the same sort of muffled animus, "My cousin, Tabitha, incidentally, once let it slip that you took her to a band concert outdoors at Piedmont Park one time and smoked weed all night."

"'Clowns to the left of me, jokers to the right,'" responded Spike, sitting there sullenly. "'Stuck in the middle with you.'"

"You disappoint me," said Grommet. "So does Poke."

Spike shouted, "No, the truth is, you frustrate and discourage and fail us."

"Poke said the very same thing about you!"

Nerves were now badly frayed between them, petty attention given over to problems they once sloughed off. They were now repeatedly getting into unpleasant and even offensive debates, at first mild, that became pointless and unproductive bickering, burning disagreements that they stubbornly maintained, creating bitter and insurmountable discord.

Each man arrogantly came to feel he and his singular discovery was the flywheel of the breakthrough. Over the months were the findings disseminated? Never, not once. What were left were fragments without context, seemingly private jokes, missives designed not to persuade or even to be broadly intelligible but simply to circulate. In insular internet worlds, this style of communication *is* the point. And it produces an epistemic fog that can obscure the meaning of even the most intentional of gestures.

It was very late, almost midnight. Leaping up on top of the lab table, a proud and slightly tipsy Grommet—he had opened a bottle of Wild Turkey and had guzzled a good half of it—loudly pronounced, "Ladies and Gentlemen, I repeat, I am here to announce that the elusive and mysterious element comprising No. 6, maybe 7, of the secret 'Merchandise 7X' that goes into the making of Coca-Cola syrup is—cassia leaves!"

He hiccupped.

"Other theories of yours?" He belched. "So wrong for so long!" He burped. "All ping but no pong!"

That Grommet had not bothered to share the bottle in a friendly way with either Poke or Spike went not unnoticed, as had very little in the intervening months in the matter of comradeship, team loyalty, or solidarity in what initially had been a team pursuit. And when it came to singling out and seeking the elusive No. 7 of Merchandise 7X, the young chemists who'd been faced with an enigma that each struggled to penetrate—for long months now—had an equal but more perverse problem by way of withholding information from each other.

Was it the result of flat refusal? Coyness? Selfishness? Diffidence? Willfulness? A fear of repudiation? Or just plain spite?

Grommet, still standing on top of the table, read the room and, insulted at seeing nothing but the backs of his fellow chemists, expressive of sulks and sourness, he punted into mid-air a glass beaker that split open and shattered. Did he think he was on stage? If not, why did he throw open his arms like a Shakespearean tragedian—ridiculous—and bellow, "'I'll find the secret, if it not be now, yet it will come. *Ripeness is all!*'"

Now he was half-bombed. "M-may I mention here, awkward"—he loudly burped—"*up, wkwardoc*, I mean aw-kkward as it may be for the th-three of us, but s-since we are now being frank with each other, what about those floor-fo-our or f-five full cases of Coca-Cola I bought you a couple of months ago?"

"There were *three* cases," cracked Poke, coldly correcting him, not even deigning to turn around to say so. "And mine was missing four bottles."

Cheeseparing.

"I don't care if there were *fufty-fify fitty or fifty*— or eleven," Grommet managed to get out, wobbling on the table with unsturdy legs. "Not one of you took time to acknowledge the gift or even b-bothered to thank me."

Perverse, inappropriate, and embarrassing, it was a sad scene, but typical, as a final salvo to this wayward, misbegotten enterprise. The lab doors were then slammed shut in a final ignominy, and all participants went home.

As the trio of chemists had come to see, the mystery in and of this universally touted soft drink lay precisely in the intricacy of swirling and unidentifiable oils, hidden deep in the fizzing deep, dark, depths of pure carbonated cola.

For that was the rub. The man to whom guardianship of the secret formula had been chiefly entrusted, Dr. Orville E. May, one of the most notable figures in the distinguished firm, as well as the 1948 recipient of the highly prized American Institute of Chemists Gold Medal, had disclosed many years ago—at a private Coca-

Cola Partner site, composed of a select in-group of twenty-five men—why it was that the drink has managed for so long to defy with such frustration determined assaults upon it by analysists in trying to penetrate its secret.

"You cannot take a mixture of citrus oils and tell which ones are present, or in what proportion," the authoritative May had boldly proclaimed. "Neither chromatography nor infrared spectrum analysis can give you the answer. And when you realize that lemon oil alone has as many as twenty-six constituents, and that other citrus oils are equally complicated, you can see where outside chemists run into trouble." It was a humiliating and discouraging anti-intellectual pronouncement.

Running into trouble was what such a quest was all about. It was only a few years back that the Faculty of Pharmacy at the prestigious Université Paris-Saclay in Orsay, which had been asked by its national government to investigate the enigma of Coca-Cola and the notorious mystery of its ingredients, in the end concluded, lamely, that the drink was nothing more or less than "ordinary lemonade."

They were greatly mistaken, of course.

Had that French group been as tenacious as the three dug-in chemists from the Atlanta Institute of Sciences, they might have succeeded. Grommet, after private experiments—he saw that with his solitary work in the lab as he experimented on his cassia leaves—had become convinced that he had the final solution in his endless observations of various mixtures, blends, emulsions, suspensions, and colloids he had tried out.

What is curious, so did Poke, who felt the same, working in the wee of the mornings when not a soul was about, the sole condition now with which he went to work. But had their scope on reality suffered as well, their range, orbit, and sweep so narrowed that lunacy prevailed? At one point in mid-November, Poke discussed breaking into the vault on the grounds of the World of Coca-

Cola in Atlanta to find out the secret ingredient, representing 135 years of heritage and intrigue.

And yet even more astonishing was the lordly conviction held by Spike that he had personally determined what that last missing element was. He confided to no one that, after months of study and scrutiny, trials and tests, evaluations and examinations, it had crossed his mind one night that, masked, anonymous, he thought of actually kidnapping a member of the board of Coca-Cola and at gunpoint extracting the secret. It would be easy. One night. No dire threats. Simple. Take him for a long ride. It was only a last-minute recollection of the depressing reflections of Orville E. May about the confusing mixture of oils recently explained that saved Spike from engaging in that rash act.

"The last thing we need is being criminally prosecuted!" cried Grommet.

By then, at any rate, fractures to their friendship had become far too deep to mend, testy mood changes breaking all pacts. Over three months, intense rivalries had subtly crept in like fog, the inevitable nature of each working independently. Weeks before, Poke picked up all his gear and Coke cases and removed to his room near the medical area. Opting for another method, Spike in a separate building managed to access a polarimeter to test his fluids, even other soft drinks to compare under what is called circular birefringence. Grommet alone stayed in the main lab. He hesitated to stop in to see his colleagues.

They each had a passkey to the lab. Only Grommet used it, no one else. Thanksgiving came and went, with no intervening communication between them. No messages, no dispatch, no reports, no bulletins, no memos, no news.

No turkey or stuffing—no sharing of food. No congenial table around which friends warmly sat.

It was now mid-December and growing cold outside. Poke and Spike never came back to meet in the science lab, as inevitably they had no reason to so, or at least they so felt, which seemed odd in not wanting to share with each other—or even inquire—what each believed was the missing portion. It was the strangest thing, as if climbing a high mountain together they were now each descending on three sides.

Three separate sides.

Anonymously.

What precipitates rivalry? Relations.

Who was it said that one friend in a lifetime is much; two are many; three are hardly possible? Maybe it was true. Dislike is at the heart of it. Rivalry, which is the competition for superiority, involves the motive to compete based on contention, the inflated pretension to be above what in fact is an emotion or mood riddled with pusillanimity, the need for having the whip hand traces an ache for control. Why is this a mystery?

Was it not the heavenly angels who became demons?

The compulsion to drive the other fellow out, the obsession for control? It is as deeply corrupt as the fool coign of vantage. Mastery is the one direct path to ascendancy, command, supremacy, superiority, and inevitably domination.

Overreaching?

Regarding Coca-Cola?

In a historic scandal, a certain Joya Williams, forty-two, a secretary to the global brand director at Coca-Cola's headquarters in Atlanta, tried to steal the formula and faced up to ten years in prison on the conspiracy charges of her failed scheme—along with two of her accomplices, Ibrahim Dimson and Edmund Duhaney—of conspiring to sell the confidential trade secrets, yes, you got it right, to the rival Pepsi Cola Company for $1.5 million. Talk about the steadfastness of tomfoolery! The reason that the criminal ruse failed was that Pepsi refused to capitalize on the opportunity but instead went ahead and reported the illegal offer to both Coca-Cola and the FBI. The FBI set up a sting operation, posing as Pepsi

executives, leading to the arrest of Williams and her two confeder-
ates. Public prosecutor David Nahmias praised Pepsi for doing the
right thing, stating, "They did so because trade secrets are important
to everybody in the business community. They realized that if their
trade secrets are violated, they all suffer, the market suffers, and the
community suffers."

The chemists had now each of them become more mono-
syllabic than fluent or articulate, wherein every exchange—there
were no more conversations—was generally met with a quick snap
or an abrupt dismissal, and, whereas in their earlier communications, each insight, even an extravagant error, became a vital portal
for a new discovery, any aid to a deeper understanding of a subject
at hand by now had long dissolved.

By late December, the chemists, who were no longer stuck,
were yet disagreeably at odds. After three months of work, each
remained hidebound touching on the discovery of the secret ingredients none of them would concede to throw out, yet the facts of
which none of them would share. They had become short-tempered, unbudging, indeed spiteful, and, along with their heavy
school workload, the trouble they had faced—the lab work involved, the disputes, the disagreements, the altercations, even bickering, frequently over nothing—had taken a final toll on all of them.
Being at variance with each other, which had often led to a war of
words, had long become a glacial and exclusive silence, a raised bar-
ricade, a disharmony in a once cordial relationship they had never
known before.

On a bulletin board, one of them had posted on a card, "I
have worked out the solution to No. 7 of Merchandise 7X." No
name—anonymous.

Below it, another card: "So have I unriddled ingredient #7."
It was signed with a dramatic replica of John Hancock's signature,
with full flourish.

Then yet a third, incognito. "As have I."

When Christmas Eve arrived, as a gentle sifting snow fell, in a low wind, the laboratory at that late hour sat in the looming, unoccupied shadows locked tightly shut and unlighted in the soft blowing dark, the breach among the three chemists being complete, with their work wrapped up but without a remnant of any bond or friendship left among them. That entire month the sky was lurid with sleet and thundersnow.

There was sadly not Christmas enough to save the day, not enough Christian kindness sufficient even to make it bearable. Squirrels chasing each other up and down the tall elms on that lonely night was the only life in evidence. No one was on sight, not a soul abroad. The tall windows of the untenanted laboratories that once burned hot like fire when the sun shone brightly through them, peering into research and creativity, were now vacant and silent dark spaces as hollow and as empty as false promises, bare, and desolate, except for the bickering and rivalrous sheeted ghosts up from the cellars inhabiting the purlieus of the vaulted darkness there but mercifully unhelpful to each other with eerie whispers as fruitless and void as the wet waves of white wind through which they passed unseen.

In the end, the anomaly was that all three chemists each fully believed that he alone had discovered that one, final, undisclosed secret 7th of the Coca-Cola formula and had done so by sheer stealth, that last rare, venerated but maddeningly elusive ingredient of which at that point only the company's two executives, top technical officials, were the designated keepers. As to the sacred matter of passing on the verbal rite?

It never happened.

Ironically, they had all accomplished the hard work by three different methods and as many different approaches, private, well-concealed schemes and strategies with none known to the other, never mind to what degree or development, with each now in possession of the full and complete formula. The tragedy?

They all flatly refused to share their secret with each other. The relationship between the men had become so toxic, so venomous, that none of them would share, split, divide, or divulge the solution, which remained unsolved.

Such was the craft of their sullen art, they would apportion nothing to each other, even a nod or a hello or a passing look. They took care to see to it that they each used different, separate entrances and exits to the lab building.

Out of sheer spite, the three chemists preferred walls to bridges. Ironically, the secret formula, known only to a few, was closeted as if locked, and never divulged.

They found not fame, but infame.

It was unavoidable, perhaps inevitable.

The three of them never spoke to each other again.

Duet in A Minor

Day by day, year by year, one's story unfolds, your life story. Things happen. People come and go. Scenes shift. Dramas take place. Time runs by, runs out. By any true definition, the unexpected is its singular, primary feature. A good dream. The odd coincidence. Perhaps even the smallest events hold the greatest clues. The unforeseen. An unanticipated visit by an outsider. A chance encounter out of the blue. The abrupt. The abnormal. The sudden. The unplanned. The unexpected sound of your name on somebody's lips, a stranger's, say.

Does that come across to you as peculiar or unusual, atypical or unfamiliar? I had that strange, unexpected experience, this last one, just recently.

It was a sexy voice on the phone, captivating even. Luscious might be too strong an adjective, not to say embarrassing, but it was warm. I detected a kind of dialect, or was it a lisp? Was I being rash or impulsive, jumping to conclusions? Yes, of course. A fat person can have a nice full voice, I knew, and possibly that applied here, I thought, although it is probably the last thing one would use to describe a person in endorsement of them. It was hardly original of me to observe that a low, smoky, sultry voice is most often associated with femme fatales, bombshells, and others who sound deliberately sensually, inviting.

But I have to admit that's what I had expected. Few intelligent men can resist a desire which has nothing to do with his

intellect, but which in a deep, subconscious way is—pulls—
stronger than his mind. It was also the month of May, which, along
with the bright spring air, can often play ducks and drakes with the
chastest, most modest of men.

She led the conversation. It was her call.

"I heard you play two weeks ago in a marvelous concert at
the Strand Ballroom and Theater Center in Providence, Rhode Island. It was too glorious simply to forget." She explained she was
calling from Washington, D.C., and then paused. "It was just a
whim. I bothered to look you up online. Do you mind?"

She identified herself with a self-deprecating laugh. Her
name—and she spelled it out for me—was Rebecca Ann Horrix.

That any individual would take the time not only to attend
a concert of mine in a different state than hers but then go to the
trouble of making an effort to telephone a not particularly distinguished anybody of a cellist, namely John Reynolds, thirty-two years
old, unmarried, who lived all the way up in New Shoreham on
Block Island, nine miles south of the mainland, was surely impressive enough to investigate. So, in the light of that—since her zeal
outran my apprehension —I proceeded to invite her to come to
stay for a few days.

I drove down to meet her at the ferry, late. I was utterly
unprepared for what the dusk revealed. At first, due partly to the
rising fog, the muffler she wore hid her lower face. I couldn't see
the strong chin later so strongly revealed. She had a touch of sleep
in her profile. She was tall, high-breasted, wore strong black shoes,
which matched a sort of risqué priestess blouse, black, which
looked to me like a dirndl, and carried a buffalo plaid carry-all bag.
Only her head of thick rich auburn hair, rolled back into a severe
bun, gave her a no-nonsense look.

I smiled and stepped forward to shake hands, but she
crowded onto me with the arch and burst technique of a butterfly-
style swimmer, an impressive hug.

Mine was a modest house on a back hill, with a limited sea view from the front porch. Fronted by a rude stone wall and battered by sea breezes and salt air, the weather-beaten cedar shingles had turned from a bright gold to a pale blue gray the way that locks of hair slowly turn color with time.

The rooms were old wood-paneled, a bit of a male thing, I suppose, or at least people had said so, and I had rubbed linseed oil into the woodwork, which gave a manly scent. A Blue Willow China oval soap dish. Oven mitts, cedar shoe trees, in a corner an old Philco cathedral radio. I had a photograph on the wall of Laetitia Casta, the beautiful French model. "This looks like a fern hall," she said upon entering. "I expect to see ferns." She was frank. I sensed she had a bit of temperament. I set down her large bag as she peered out the window just before dusk. "That's a buttonwood tree," she said, nodding out to the front lawn.

"We call them sycamores up here," I said.

Rebecca appeared comfortably matter of fact. There was an intense prettiness to her honed eyes. Her sharp nose was pointed with deep calipers that measured a wide mouth with a strong philtrum above tightly fastened lips. Resilient, if sprung-wound, she was given to purposeful silences hid behind orange clouds of smoke from her cigarettes. I was rash soon enough to posit what I thought the future as she imagined it, a dubious adventure open to hap and circumstance, a heightened yet doomed circuit of quickly turned corners to avoid routines.

I brewed a pot of pine needle tea, rich in vitamin C, five times what is found in lemons. I brought it to her, sat back, and lifted up my cup to her. "Toasting with water is akin to wishing bad luck or even death to a person," she remarked. One needs to know one's audience. I looked to see if she were smiling. She was not. Oh, well. I got up to offer her a glass of beer.

I had once read of advice given to a movie star playing a romantic lead for the first time. You stand still, he was told, and make the woman come to you. You've got something she wants, it's understood, see, so she has to come to you. Always. Whatever the occasion or circumstance.

My thought? Farcical chauvinism. The opposite of charm, to say nothing of grace. I wanted to please her.

I showed her to her room. "The wallpaper you put up there? Tragic." She poked her head into a side room, "Is this where you practice?"

She was frank, unhesitating, and got right down to the nuts and bolts. "Why do you have a winter coat there? Are you growing a ponytail? How do you heat this place?" I noticed that as she spoke, rapidly, she had the yellow-brown eyes of a silver fox. "What is that figure supposed to mean?" She was pointing with something of a grimace to a bust of composer Zoltán Kodály, whose *Romance Lyrique* was the very piece that I had played on the night of her attendance at the Strand Ballroom.

Ironically, the composition was not unlike her visit, I came to see. It begins quite optimistically, simply, in a major key and the rich middle range of the cello. But the melody intensifies, and major dramatic pauses add intensity. After a surprise solo cadenza, the original genial melody commodiously returns, lulling us back to serenity. The way life should be. Unfortunately, the way life too often quite decidedly is not.

The handsome Hungarian had long been one of my heroes. His first wife, Emma Gruber, died in November 1958, after forty-eight years of marriage. Thirteen months later, in December 1959, he married young, pretty Sarolta Péczely, his nineteen-year-old student at Franz Liszt Academy of Music, with whom he lived happily until his death at age eighty-four. I always tapped the head of the bust of that dear, cross-eyed composer—pedagogue, linguist, and philosopher—every night before I went to bed.

A blessed man. I should have such luck.

It was very warm weather for May. Later, that first evening we took a quick narrated taxi tour of the ten or so square miles of the island—in the cab, she put her hand on my arm—and, very tired, she went early to bed. The next morning, we went for a walk, talked, visited a white-ribbon beach, and at one point down by Corn Neck Road at an ice-cream stand I bought her a cone, introducing her to what has since become something not only of a local but somewhat of an old-fashioned taste, "Frozen Pudding," a flavor of rum with raisins and cherries.

I must admit I was taken back a bit when she earnestly began to quiz the vendor about it, who when he told her that it contained 15 percent butterfat, she summarily dropped it, plunk, into an outdoor trash can.

Looking widely around her, Rebecca Ann pronounced, "She is a lovely and alluring island. About how many, um, acres are here would you say?"

"Since an acre is a measure of area and a mile a measure of length, you probably mean a square mile, which would then become a measure of area." Was that really my own voice that sounded so pedantic? And if so, why so? We of course managed to get into such verbal tangles, the kind strangers new to each other constantly face. "Block Island, which is seven miles long and three miles wide—and so, probably covering roughly about 7000 acres—is about ten square miles. It is shaped like a pork chop." It was a beautiful day. I began whistling. She turned to me. "You whistle?"

There was a note to disapproval

"Are you shocked?" I laughed. "There is actually a "Train Whistle" etude for the cello, for kids. I used to teach it to a young debut strings group over at the Cape Cod Symphony." For fun, I whistled a sample tune from it. "Are you aware that the practice of whistling shows up in the Bible? That's a fact. God is described as a shepherd whistling for his sheep, which is possibly what the Hebrew prophet had in mind—Zechariah 10:8—to describe how God will one day whistle to bring that wandering and scattered people back to himself."

"I don't read the Bible."

I went on to add cheerfully, "You referred to the island with the third person pronoun 'she.' I had never heard that perplexing reversal before, except once. It is a curious coincidence, at least for me, that in church the previous Sunday, I heard the Holy Ghost referred to that way. It must be one of the new trends, which become more unfathomable with every passing year." I smiled. "I must be getting along in years."

"I don't attend church," she stated.

I managed a neutral, "The more modernity, the less religion."

A wintry smile followed. "As to politics," she added, "same thing. I stand outside the ivory tower of learning."

My conjecture was that she made these remarks less to provoke me than to amuse herself, dangling whatever responses she might evoke like a mobile over a crib.

Rebecca had a cold smile—what one might call a "smize," which is to say, a smile with the eyes but not the mouth, for her mouth was more often than not a stern, over-deliberating rictus. It was part stare, part simper. As I saw it, she seemed to be unobtrusively unaware of her triggers, as if remaining abstractly, inconspicuously off-stage on the one hand, with an indifferent but unsettling detachment, kind of standing beside or above herself, immune to the off-putting effects of her withdrawals, the remoteness of disapproval, but on the other hand suddenly cropping up with a kind of bold candor that approached audacity, a tough mettle, cheek, gall, even impudence—whatever.

Later, I treated a restless Rebecca—she demanded I not call her "Becky"—to martinis at a local tavern, and when we returned to my house, we sat outside on beach chairs on the small back lawn, terraced down to the shore and the ocean and saltwater that with something of a face, while pulling a protective sweater to her, she described as mignonette green. Drab!

"And I also happen know that my surname is unappealingly frightening, so you needn't worry about it."

I hadn't said a word.

She smoked a lot. I had to keep getting up to empty her ashtrays and bring back clean ones. Prior to her visit, I had gone ahead and made some cherry turnovers. "No sweets, she said. I suggested some *hors d'oeuvres*.

"No, I not for me. Fanks."

Have I mentioned this?

She had a theta-tismal speech impediment, or defect with *f*: "firty-one," "firty-two." It was in fact a lisp, of sorts. Children have it. Strangely enough, she also suffered a bit—or maybe I should say that I suffered hearing it—of dysprosody, also known as pseudo-foreign dialect, one of the rarest neurological speech disorders. I made it a point to check on this after she had left. It is characterized by alterations in intensity, in the timing of utterance segments, and in rhythm, cadence, and intonation of words.

Pacing.

As I say, I am a cellist.

She didn't bristle. She was matter of fact. But she was frankly tenacious and defended this, insisting, "People who pro-nounce '*th*' as '*f*' do not have a speech impediment. It is a matter of accent and dialect, and for the same reason, it is not 'wrong' or the result of poor education or laziness or anything like that, OK?"

It didn't offend me, not even close, or put me off in the slightest bit. Why would such a thing bother anybody, and why, why, why was she so defensive on the subject? Was I an ogre? But I have to say, since it came up several times, that to give it any at-tention—she was self-conscious and under strain became louder and *more extroverted*—I found the tension a pain and resented all that empty difficulty. Discontent is critical. An instant dislike of her at that moment, in the way that the negative emotion of resentment as a displacement activity seeks to blame, translated into a sudden but inexplicable disapproval on my part of her lanky hands, sharp nose, and forked eyes, uncharitably calling up for me the nasty crack, "Throw a hat at her and it'll hang wherever it hits."

What was unsettling to me was that my dim experience with her thus far—I prayed it wasn't my cynicism—involved confirmations rather than discoveries.

Needless to say, the salient feature of Block Island is the ocean. Next day, she woke early. I made a large breakfast of bacon and eggs. We then took in the bright salty gusts of sea wind blowing off the high, dramatic bluffs, buoyant and refreshing. We headed down a cliff and took a long walk along the beach—predictable, huh, the very first preference lovers list in the romantic singles ads of newspaper and magazine "Personals," no?—and, when she stooped to pick up a shell, assuming—presuming—she was interested, I went on to explain that, to determine the age of a clam shell's annual growth, layers are discernible in the chondrophore, the tooth that holds the two halves of the shell together, which is to say, the cavity that supports the internal hinge cartilage of the shell of any such bivalve mollusk.

I might as well have been talking through my hat, as with a brooding, faraway look, she stood staring past me, with her arms censoriously folded, while I yammered on pointlessly. What on earth do such tedious, mind-numbing, eye-wateringly dull, and totally irrelevant facts do, in your opinion, to make you think they are worth a stranger having to hear them, I thought I heard her thinking whenever I held forth.

"You have a musician's long fingers."

"A cellist's left fingers, which often hurt, need always to be strengthened," I explained. "These digits are bone hard." She softly felt them, seemed to hesitate to let them go. What is the female equivalent of must? I swear I sniffed or inhaled it. "There are no frets, you see, on a cello," I continued. "It is basically all about ears, listening closely, the auditory—you know, muscle memory. Intonation. Bowing. Articulation."

She said nothing.

I was trying. "Any mistake—I should say, every mistake—when you're playing is obvious. One must never shift the instrument when performing."

Clouds of gulls and terns swept the sky. There were boats along the shore, some mouth-down. Wooden Rhodes. Beetlecats. A couple of Boston whalers. An unhappy yawl probably from Marblehead or Gloucester or Hyannis with a six-foot keel lay on her side, waiting for the tide to pull her out. It should never have come to Block Island, never with a keel like that. And yet how that same problem fit my seemingly bored and listless companion, her back to the sea, who seemed subtly impatient and only to be biding her time.

There was a glorious high tide. I was watching the always enchanting sight of the waves dancing in the ravenously bright-forming pale green hollows, as the air rang with the shrill voices of the wind, which then with a brave, hopeful rise breaking with lovely, blue-green, terrifying crashes, falling with a shattering violence in broken rainbows upon the beach, the dramatic uplifting and spilling swells never all of one color but with rich stripes of jade green and gentian blue, often flavescent, swelling at times in the hot sun with the mild azure of a child's eyes.

Was it heedlessness or impercipience on her part that she described this same alluring ocean, sourly, as being "mignonette green," subfusc and murky and drab?

Horrix had dated sporadically, or so she hinted at. She explained that on the night that she heard me play, she happened to be visiting New England when applying for an airlines job and that her interviewer had invited her to the concert.

"Do you like living in Washington, D.C.," I asked, "what Henry James called the "city of conversation?""

She waved at the air, noncommittally.

I could more or less intuit that by then I had disappointed her, had cast down or aside any hopeful aspirations she might have had in my direction in the way of a closer bond—or even more than that. She lagged a bit, began to keep a small and I felt disapproving distance from me, squinting at schools of forage fish.

I remarked, "Did you know that if a smelt is dried and stuffed with a wick, it will burn like a candle?"

"What's a smelt?"

"Small shiny fish. A sign of spring. Very nutritious, packed with omega 3, vitamins B. and good protein. Low fat, low calorie. The fish taken out of cold saltwater are preferred to those taken in warm water. Those that come canned in oil are delicious. Although they don't command a high price on the market, they provide a source of supplemental income due to their abundance. The smelts taken here are 'flash frozen' simply by being left on ice and then sold to fish buyers who came down the docks."

"I hate the sea," she remarked.

I had considered taking up her to have a look at the Southeast Lighthouse. It crossed my mind to show her prehistoric horseshoe crabs, their blood an eerie blue, due to the copper-based respiratory pigment called hemocyanin it contained. I'd even wanted to show her how to paddle a canoe without ever switching sides. But in the light of her remark, all went by the board.

Would she have wanted to go over to see Black Rock and the nudist beach? Probably. But at that particular point in her stay, it was all out. Who cared?

The following morning, I made breakfast, hoping she'd slept well in her room waiting for her sleepy arrival. She appeared, yawning. "An aluminum teapot. A nut grinder there, is that right?" She was surveying the kitchen. "A strange, what, 1950's metal grapefruit juicer or something?!" I tapped it and flipped the handle. "W.P.A. period. Right-O!"

"And those?"

"A couple of Foley forks, perfect for mashed potatoes," I explained.

"Oh, an old vintage cake-holder! And that, um, glass goose-bill thingie on the wall, with a spout?" "It's a barometer," I said. She pointed. "Molasses?"

"Later. For Indian pudding."

"That rasher pan—"

"You mean this one for bacon?"

"The thing's at a ghostly, ghastly 33-degree angle! *Warped!* You're a funny duck!"

"I'm a Yankee, you must remember," I told her. "Thrift is as natural to us as twirling whirligigs are to children. A golden rule up in these parts goes, 'Use it up, wear it out, make it do, or do without.'" We sat and ate quietly.

Fussification!

My running thoughts? Sorry, not for me expensive pots, rare wines, exotic flower displays, the choicest viands, the whitest sheets, or the most valuable porcelain chinaware. Ceiling fans? A hot tub? A big chill, autograph edition refrigerator with thermidors and heavy-duty shelving? A digital shower with hidden pipework to limit the need for cleaning chrome? Uh-uh. We are not rich by what we possess but by what we can do without. That cutlery sitting on the table? It is iron, not silver.

I showed her my library. Being fond of books, I found reading as significantly a joy and as strong a passion with me as playing my instrument. "Is this where you spend much of your day," she asked, archly, "um, studying the structural deficiencies of *Beowulf?* Reading biographies of composers? Worrying yourself into a grouch?" I was by now somewhat familiar with her taunting tone. Much of it was an attempt at humor, not the greatest gift of hers.

What did rather surprise me, however, was the literary allusion a snobbish and superior me hadn't expected of her. She also asked to see my record collection. She sat down and humored me as I played her various records on my phonograph, some of my favorite classical cello pieces, when she seemed interested enough. But before that, as we entered the room, she sat down, then quicky stood up, petulantly.

"Anything new with the issue I'm about to make?" Rebecca Ann Horrix abruptly asked. She pointed. "We need to correct the right-to-left layout of those three windows. There is an alignment problem." Had she actually said *we?* Had I heard that correctly? I had long steered clear—never brought up—any romantic notions.

Wisely, I thought.

Keep it unsentimental.

I knew by now her visit would be brief. Her thoughts? As with Maurice Ravel's *Boléro* she never developed them but just got—*grew*—louder and louder. Several times during her brief stay, I developed throbbing headaches, a vertigo of sorts, and to stem them opened a bottle of Meclizine tablets, which I had now begin to take every morning and night My mind seemed to clear like washed glass on one topic, however. She'd soon have to leave. Cool and crystal clear. I glanced at my watch, it was getting on toward noon, and I was hoping for time to practice my cello, as usual. I took down three or four albums.

On the phonograph, I slotted the Shostakovich Cello Concerto No. 1 and told Rebecca, "When talking about any cello repertoire," I explained, "one must not forego one of the greatest concerti written for that instrument—the Shostakovich—which premiered on October 4, 1959. You might be interested in knowing that he wrote the work for his composer friend, Mstislav Rostropovich, who committed it to memory in four days."

She seemed keen as she sat there.

"It is one of the most difficult concert works for cello, this, along with the *Sinfonia Concertante* of Sergei Prokofiev. The end of this particular Shostakovich requires the cellist to play off the fingerboard"—to get across the point, I walked over to demonstrate on my cello, pausing as I always do to tap the scroll affectionately—"reaching as high as an E7, the extreme upper limit of the range of the instrument. It is a composition filled with alien and unexpected but meaningful musical, well, distortions and, at least to me, develops a theme of Obligation and Desire, like Wagner's *Tristan*."

"Desire, as in sexual?"

I chose to let that one hang, not tamper with. I saw that a direct answer, on any level, could lead to entanglements, which I aimed to do without.

It was a long, extended composition. I might have selected too formidable a piece for her. I played the record, to a strange silence. I placed next on the turntable Vivaldi's Double Concerto for Two Cellos in G Minor. "Listen to this," I said, "a quite lively Baroque piece full of energetic interplay between two cellists. You might be interested to know I once played it with young Yo-Yo Ma up at Harvard University, when he was a student at Adams House. Although not part of a larger collection, like *The Four Seasons*, it shares the same spirited and punchy rhythms and clear, memorable melodies. Today, it remains a firm favorite among cellists and is a regular feature in concert programs."

"Is that your own recording?" asked Rebecca, after it had ended. That was her sole response. "No, it is not," I replied, curtly, I'm afraid. Did it matter—at all? "Why not" she asked, a bit irritated. I deigned not to answer.

The afternoon was passing slowly. I played another cello classic, part of the Italian composer and organist Girolamo Frescobaldi's *Toccata*, a recording which the great Spanish cellist Gaspar Cassadó had musically arranged for cello and piano, a particularly brilliant score, one I loved. I presumed that Rebecca should know something about the piece, and so went on to explain, although frankly I suspected she couldn't have cared less. "Among purists, some doubt has been cast on originality of this work—the old manuscript of which, by the way, has never been found—but, assuming that Cassadó did compose the piece in 'Frescobaldi-style'—mainly innovations in the matter of tempo—it opens, nonetheless, with a plaintive 'Adagio,' listen closely, and then morphs into a spirited and proud section full of resounding chords." I closed my eyes and listened closely to it.

She was sitting abstractly, knees up, her head turned in profile, attempting to extract scruff from her long fingernails with the corner of a paper envelope.

As my guest was close to being half asleep—overkill is my vice in having guests listen to music—I shut off the machine and put all the record albums away, satisfied that my guest had had more than her fill. Had the day generated a greater response from her, I might have played several more well-known pieces for the cello, such as Saint-Saëns' *The Swan* or Franz Joseph Haydn's Divertimento in D, a lovely work in three short movements, the opening movement, especially, a melodious Adagio, which is followed by the enchanting Minuet and Trio, and a flashy Allegro last movement, but abstained—

—for which I'm sure Rebecca Ann Horrix was grateful.

I suppose I was justifying my life when, upon reminiscing, I said to my visitor, "The first cello piece I ever heard was at a concert taken to me by my parents when I was eight years old, Johan Sebastian Bach's fundamental *Six Suites,* which paved the way for such beautiful works as Dvorak's Cello Concerto in B minor and Sir Edward Elgar's Concert in E minor, which you may or may not recall was my second offering back in Providence that same night that you attended."

I paused. "Remember?"

I walked across the room—my cello stood on a triangular stand in a far corner—and pulling up a chair set the instrument before me. "It is a hearty fellow. Beefy," I said. "The first cello did not appear until the early 1500s, with its seductive, rich, deeply layered, dark sound, built in northern Italy, evolving from a group of stringed adjuncts called *violas da braccio*, or 'violas for the arm.' Cello strings, originally made with sheep or goat gut, are fashioned today of aluminum, titanium, and chromium. Notice, the cello's neck slants backwards, not for comfort, but simply so that players can produce a louder sound by applying greater pressure to the bridge. The majority of cellos have 'purfling,' an attractive inlay around their edge. While you might think that this is mere window dressing, it actually has a practical purpose, helping to prevent the wood from cracking under stress."

She yawned, lit up a cigarette, blew out smoke, and said, "The vibrations, the pitch, volume, and timbre seem almost human in sound."

"And emotional qualities like tone and inflection, yes," I said, "The human voice is the most beautiful instrument of all, but it is the most difficult to play."

"That is quite insightful."

"Credit Richard Strauss, who said it, I'm afraid, not me."

I removed the cello, set it aside, and went to a side-bar to pour two glasses of red wine for us.

I was never a host who ever wanted to be the chief source of entertainment. But music, after all, was what brought me to her attention—or was it the reverse?—and she had seemed keen to want to hear something. There was no affiliation between us. No sense of alliance or tie, not even close. But then of course why would there be? Such things are rare. We were both more than anything like chalk and cheese. Different as white knight to black bishop. I have always conceived that an instant and true love connection—and I can't deny that when I received that first phone call it crossed my mind as a possibility—to be easy, lightning-sudden, and as smooth as the 3-6-3 double play in baseball, first to second to first. The transformation, not optional but mandatory, is clearly nothing short of an outright miracle.

"But surely you yourself are going to play for me?"

She had a way in her glee, well, not glee, but mirth, I guess, of shaking on each side of her head matched earrings that looked like a pair of metal tea-immersion balls. In any case, on that day to please her, I sat down to play the expressive and romantic part of Bach's Adagio from the Toccata in C, explicitly a passage from the popular satanic ritual scene filmed in the 1934 Karloff/Lugosi film *The Black Cat*:

My guest seemed to enjoy it.

It was encouraging—and a welcome change. She asked for another piece. I wanted to please her. So I proceeded to play for her the "Allegretto quasi Menuetto" from Brahms' Cello Sonata No. 1 and, hoping she would not be bored, followed that with Rachmaninoff's Vocalise for Cello and Piano, Op. 34. She found the latter a delight, softly applauding. "It's a simple piece, that," I said, "particularly by way of contrast to the more complicated Piano Concerto No. 3 in D minor, Op. 30 of his or, say, his elaborate "Rhapsody on a Theme of Paganini," which has something of a dazzling bravura about it, alive like wild and bounding caprine, with no end of piano variations."

I sat back. "The Russian composer was a virtuoso pianist, his technical perfection legendary even in his day. His hands were reported to be so huge as to be able to span a twelfth -- an octave-

and-a-half and could make a stretch from middle C to high G. The size of his hands, so they say, may have been a manifestation of Marfan's syndrome, their size and curious slenderness typical of arachnodactyly."

"Caprine?"

"Goats," I clarified.

I had been trying to be poetic.

But that gloomed me a bit, I must say. It was irritating. After hours of symphonic outlay for her, she could surface with just that one observation?

"Do you write music, as well?" she asked. "A certain amount, small enough to keep me humble," I replied, adding I liked the form of the *chaconne*, which allowed for melodies to be repeated with several variations, excursions through several keys and brilliant reiterations, and that I had also composed and performed an original piece called "*Ein Buschenlied aus Heidelberg*," a fraternity song in memory of that venerable old city in Germany where I had once studied for two years.

She had grown quiet.

I felt uneasy and looked for something to say.

"There have been many notable cellists, other the Pablo Casals and Jacqueline du Pré. How about President Thomas Jefferson? He used to play duets in the cello and violin with his wife Martha, who played the piano. Charlie Chaplin taught himself to play the piano, violin, and cello. Novelist Katherine Mansfield was another one who took it up, an occupation that she believed she would take up professionally, that is, until she dropped it for writing. Prince Charles, the Prince of Wales, often played the cello while he was studying at Cambridge. I myself have always admired the celebrated cellist Emanuel Feuermann, who was born in Galicia in 1902. Something of a prodigy, he toured this county in the 1930s. He owned an instrument made by Venetian master luthier Domenico

Montagnana in 1735, an instrument known as the 'Feuermann cello,' which I believe is still being used somewhere."

I plucked the A, D, G, and C strings.

"A sense of touch is important, needless to say. You might be interested to know, as few do, that Louis Braille, the French educator and the inventor of the reading and writing system named after him, was himself an accomplished cellist. Blind in both eyes at the age of five as a result of an accident trying to make holes in a piece of leather with a stitching awl in his father's harness shop, he developed his senses to a great degree, with delicate fingers. A keen ear for music allowed him to become an accomplished cellist and organist. Later in life, his musical talents led him to play the organ for churches all over France. A devout Catholic who died at age forty-three, Braille held the position of organist in Paris at the Church of Saint-Nicolas-des-Champs, and later at the Church of Saint Vincent-de-Paul, where I once had the privilege to play myself, for a wedding, under the Saint Elizabeth Window, a very moving event for me."

I duly noted, "The emperor Napoleon Bonaparte once declared, 'Music is the voice that tells us that the human race is greater than it knows.'"

"It has always struck me, regarding strings, that cellists bow to keep music aloft," I continued. Think of this way—the act is uplift, basically. The way music soars. It is about rising, ascension, climbing." I couldn't help remembering some remarks that my guest had earlier made, mainly by way of insinuation, about rejection in love. "Falling needs no explanation, in Einstein's theory, because cosmically speaking, it is the most natural thing that can happen to anyone." We both knew we were talking about romance, failure, heartache—life. "Only in avoiding falling does any force come into play. The weight one feels on the soles of one's feet is pushing upwards, not downwards."

She inquired about fame. "I am far from famous, I said. "Not even close, I'm afraid."

"Wrong. You're admired. Probably adored. I noticed it back there at the concert." She stubbed out the butt, to my surprise, in the base of a lamp. "Two standing ovations, right?" I replied, "Fame and love are at loggerheads. Desire for fame is a will to conquer. Desire for love is a wish to capitulate."

"You cavil, seem to me pessimistic." She lit another cigarette and sharply pointed. "What about Miss Model Pants over there—Lucia?"

"Laetitia Casta. It's a photograph. Diminished reality." I took a sip of my wine. "I am not relationship suitable."

"That phrase, how the words go together."

"Like mosquitos and nets?"

"Or love and hate."

"Odd, how pairs are often opposites."

There came a long, studied pause.

If the sun had not set, it had long since vanished behind cold, dense clouds, and the room we inhabited was dark, somber, except for a single lamp on the table between us, offering little of clarity regarding the conversation.

"Why haven't you given it a chance?'

We both knew very well, each of us, by way of an extended glance, almost a scrutiny, exactly and rather uneasily what subject was being referred to.

"I have done so."

She stared at me moodily, unflappable.

"Several times," I added.

An eyebrow arched, as she sipped her wine, and she looked somewhat vexed. I offered a comment or two about the unique quality—and value of—solitude, casual remarks to which she became remarkably unreceptive. Allow me to amend that. Frigidly disapproving. Aggressive air quotes here.

"You are a skeptic. Cynical."

"But not mistrustful."

"Apprehensive maybe."

"The primary obligation of intellect is to distrust itself."

"I myself once thought the same thing," she asserted. "I once married a man who treated me like he bought me by the pound. I feared I'd never be free of him. It was a hateful cataclysm I choose to forget. I was nineteen, mistake-prone, an unfortunate age—no soft wadding between oneself and the universe. I was not the best judge of my own interests."

"There is nothing final about a mistake," I offered, "except it's being taken as final."

"Being lost like that, foundering, I made a vow I would never be displaced like that again. It was like I—like I lost the keys to my car. But even worse, lost freedom."

"It confirms a truth that I have long held. Every fear is a fear of loss."

Rebecca temporized momentarily, thinking, as if on the cusp of a sudden harsh reflection. She then turned to me to ask, coldly, almost judgmentally, as if her own fears now applied to me, "But how can one lose what, what—"—she was looking for the right word and she was looking at me, "—what one has never tried, what one has simply thrown over?"

Hearing an accusation in the palimpsest, I began to comprehend with a new conviction and, I must say, not inconsequential intensity, that information is property.

The way I got it, at least from earlier dropped hints by her of teen-age belligerence, an early interest in sexual adventure may have been a refusal on her part of the established feminine role required by a family and the implicit demands of a society with its staid and fixed rules, a bold, defiant disapproval in her intractable mind of their wishes and decrees. To be willful, to be assertive, to be overtly interested in sex, was the prerogative of young men; but why should that have limited her?

Had I to choose a dog for her, it would have been a German Spitz Mittel, an aggressive breed.

She always seemed to be leaning forward, following her long strong jaw, as if resisting a high wind, her body its breathing. While it showed intensity, eagerness, even an animation of sorts, I have to add that more than anything it basically conveyed a wistfulness that I honestly still find hard to describe. She was lonely, something of an isolato, and by way of her visit seemed interested in me less as a person than as a possibility. She told me briefly that for her divorce she had stayed all by herself six weeks in Reno, at a ranch that catered to the trade which was often referred to as "Renovations." Hers was a weariness, and I could detect a desperation, revealing that she had been alone too long.

Progress requires change, however, and change creates difficulties, open to chance and hap, risk and hazards, forcing on us demands that can be confusing and, in the formidable need to adapt, poisonous options and alternatives. I didn't want to bore her with what is called toxic positivity, the idea one must always stay goofily positive as a way of rejecting negative emotions, no matter what may have happened to a person in whatever context. Shaming her for feeling blue was the last thing on my mind, a mind with too many other concerns.

It is clearly pride that makes friendship so difficult. To submit, to bow down to the other, is never easy, but it must be done for mutual understanding. No news there, surely. I spent silent hours trying to figure her out. As I saw it, hers were not tidal mood changes, as such, but what seemed to me rather a steady discomposing formality and coldness, born of what appeared as an abrupt but ongoing need to make slighting remarks, out of an inner urge to prevent anyone—me, for example—from having a mandarin position, which added up to threat.

In my opinion, the very act of *attempting* plagued her. Reach! She was forever pursued by *trying*.

We had finished the wine. I asked her if she might like a cocktail. "How about a glass of tequila? *Blanco,* bright and grassy? *Reposado,* mellow, hints of caramel? *Añejo,* rich and complex? I can give you a tumbler to sip."

She said, "I would like a charred pineapple margarita."

"I don't have the pineapple. I believe it also calls for green Chile liqueur or something like that—right?—and, as I recall, burnt sugar syrup. Sorry."

She waved it all away.

The afternoon was waning, with a slight chill in the air. I went to close the windows.

"A mist is closing in," she observed.

"'White and feathery it comes from the deep to its brothers the clouds, full of dreams of dank pastures and caves of leviathan,' I quoted, "'And later, in still summer rains on the steep roofs of poets, the clouds scatter bits of those dreams, that men shall not live without rumor of old strange secrets and wonders that planets tell planets alone in the night'—from an old H.P. Lovecraft *The Strange High House in the Mist.*"

I drew the curtains.

"He also hated the sea," I said, "and anything to do with it."

A studied pause held.

"Do you hold grudges?" inquired Horrix.

I suppose I deserved that.

But woman was not happy with herself. Her brass was a shield, but her bad behavior was like her questions, bleak. It was like an *en echelon* attack. I constantly detected latticed shadows falling harshly across her head.

As far as helping clear the table or stacking any dishes? Useless as a chocolate teapot. I really didn't mind at all that much actually, as it serendipitously confirmed in an obvious way my interest in her leaving. She dropped used wet bath towels on the floor. She made three long-distance telephone calls without asking permission. She left dishes in the sink, smudges of toothpaste on the bath towels, discarded all shed clothes on the floor. She sat smoking while I cooked. Dropped books open face down. Left lights still burning in rooms that she no longer occupied—one of my pet peeves—and her drinking glasses left several white rings on a walnut table. She left her bed unmade.

She had what is called a "wanter's" capacity—to be served, the expectation to be waited on, attended to, assisted. There is an indifference to it which is worse than apathy—icy disregard. A hot shower that she left on for almost an hour destroyed a valuable print in the *en-suite* bedroom she slept in. Being married to her? Daily I would have fought the temptation to pound her skull into aquarium gravel.

I heard with a sudden sense of remorse the cruelty repeated in my thoughts of what she'd inadvertently reminded me I had marshaled in my discouragement.

Motherhood she said she would totally abhor. I must admit that as I listened to her on that subject, praying it would soon end, I had to force myself to wrangle long and bitterly with my uncooperative and largely inactive disposition telling me not to be kind to her when she described children as "stupid as geese." But, again, what she was saying effectively made me feel rotten myself as I reflected on my lack of mercy for her.

I have a theory, which is about reversals—the way that life *can happen backwards* by rash and reckless behavior, the kind that led me out of vanity, self-approbation, and conceit to ask Rebecca to come to spend days with me on the island and that fed into nothing but foolhardy exploits that invite weird countermanding or revocable actions by madcap maneuvers.

Hers, yes.

But mine, as well!

Ours was a vainglorious duet.

Who can predict the whys of ways?

It was only a few miles outside the city of Damascus that a penalizing and angry Paul was on his way—people forget, if they ever knew in the first place—specifically to bring back to Jerusalem for severe punishment any and all members of the subversive heretical sect who called themselves Christians. A maniacal bigot and mad zealot, he presided over the stoning of the holy martyr St. Stephen and was a severe authoritarian, a pedant of the law when Christ himself appeared to him and called him by name and gave him a new faith to live for and to die for, a faith that led him to write years later, "I am convinced that neither death, nor life . . . nor things present, nor things to come . . . nor anything else in all creation, will be able to separate us from the life of God in Christ Jesus Our Lord" (Romans 8:38–39).

One fails to reckon that Paul's had initially been an errand of *vengeance*, when in an almost incredibly unforeseen turn of events he had to turn to face, embrace, a complete reversal. It is the damndest thing, Confederate General A. P. Hill always wore— *sported!*—a red shirt when going into battle, a brave announcement, yet an item drawing maximum attention. He had often said he had no desire to live to see the collapse of the Confederacy. In his case, as if to provoke the reversal, that wish came true, for Fate in turn obliged him, for on April 2, 1865, during the U.S. breakthrough in the Third Battle of Petersburg, just seven short days before General Robert E. Lee's surrender at Appomattox Court House, Hill was shot dead by a Union soldier.

These were my thoughts and my reflections. But I was going on in an attempt, almost as an anodyne, to explain my own behavior to my dubious self.

Three days after her arrival, my guest Rebecca Ann Horrix had departed.

Vanished like a ghost at cockcrow.

I had gathered her goods, we bundled in, and I drove her down to the ferry in an uneasy silence, for which I found no words to break the tension. We must have waited more than an hour. A thin warm drizzling rain down by the boat docks kept all passengers inside the waiting rooms. She smoked cigarettes, I sat nearby, needing a reprieve. She said not a word, wagged a foot up and down. You can't beat fun for having a good time. Who was it said, "One minute of waiting is a century to the hopeful." Could it have been Isaiah? Was it a Chinese proverb? No, I think it was actually Shirley Temple in one of her movies.

I went to shake Rebecca's hand, but she would have none of it. Everything had fallen apart. She was grave, aloof, her mouth set in an inflexible rictus, her eyes lethargic but then watchful.

"Oh, there's the boat!"—and she was gone.

I couldn't help but reflect on the earlier exchange we'd had in my living-room—or was it solely my monologue? Falling is the most natural way for objects to behave—and our main mode of travel through the universe and in this valley of tears. It seemed to sum her up. Desperate, most of us spend most of our time *not* falling. 'Not-falling' appears in Einstein's theory of gravity as an acceleration—a continuing gathering of speed—even when you are standing or staying in one place.

Was her trouble staying on one place, I asked myself, or its exact opposite, constant acceleration?

Had hers been a generic visit? Could it have been merely the pursuit of contact? To realize a contiguity? To find comfort in connection or communication? Merely to meet someone new for a change? A random approach? Or was it flight? What on earth was she seeking? A friend, a lover, a husband? Then again, was it to learn—or unlearn, and if so, what? Why?

Who could possibly know? Who could possibly say?

May I add something just as crucial, as striking? What had *I myself* been seeking that was so much more cogent, so superior, in having invited her? I was as puzzling, I was *almost* as puzzling, *I was surely almost as puzzling, if not more so!*

What about things given us to perceive? Didn't Kant tell us our own minds help us create the reality we experience? Argue that time and space and causality are best understood as forms imposed on the world by our own minds? Insist that the waking world we know is forged by what we encounter?

No, what I confronted, I created. That which I met, I made. Blame me for the whole enterprise.

I was more culpable than she. To shift the blame for the misbegotten week was callow and unreasonable. When novelist Henry James was once saying goodbye to his young nephew Billy, his brother William's son, he told him something the boy never forgot. Of all the complicated and impenetrably recondite things that this abstruse, most complicated and often obscure writer could have said, what he managed to say was this: "There are three things that are important in human life. The first is to be kind. The second is to be kind. The third is to be kind." I tried to follow that good advice, hard as it was to do so.

After my guest left the island on the night ferry, I drove home, rolling down the window for fresh air, and I was whistling. With a renewed spring in my step, I made for myself the Indian pudding I had intended to make for her, and then sat down in a mood of gratitude, along with sheer relief—my large intervallic leaps in highly flared bowing a sign of joy—and played Sergei Prokofiev's Cello Sonata, Opus 119. Later, it crossed my mind in the library to pull down my volume of Robert Frost's poems to read a verse from 1942 that I had been thinking of during the whole week of my guest's impromptu visit. The poem is called "Never Again Would Birds' Song Be the Same."

Curiously, for maximum self-schooling effect—*lessoning myself*—I read it aloud:

He would declare and could himself believe
That the birds there in all the garden round
From having heard the daylong voice of Eve
Had added to their own an over-sound,
Her tone of meaning but without the words.
Admittedly an eloquence so soft
Could only have had an influence on birds
When call or laughter carried it aloft.
Be that as may be, she was in their song.
Moreover her voice upon their voices crossed
Had now persisted in the woods so long
That probably it never would be lost.
Never again would birds' song be the same.
And to do that to birds was why she came.

It literally non-representationalized my visitor, almost by confoundingly direct poetic intent. How Art always triumphs over Reality!

Curiously—is God a novelist?—I received a letter from this same Rebecca the following week, post-marked from Barbados. It was filled with notable ingratitude and a rancorous spite that she had doubtless been stifling during her entire visit.

"*You will no doubt be surprised to hear from me after my disastrous week visit with you. My advice is that you get a clue and change. You hold onto ideas you long ago should have shelved, like that Laetita Castellucci thing on your dumb wall or whoever she is. That bedroom that I slept in which is the color of broccoli or kale is not the 'delightful French room' you think it is. You are far too vain about your music. Those scraped passages that you rendered playing Gabriel Fauré's 'Elegy Op. 24' were weak. I could say the same about Schubert's 'Arpeggione Sonata,' the one you played outside for me, which was really not for me, for I could clearly see so in your distant eyes. You think you're an activist for saving the planet or something like that. You think more of your shoetrees and oven mitts and precious cello more than people, citizens of the real world. You should go hug a Foley fork—or Freaky fork, or whatever the hell it is—and your grapefruit squeezer!. You tap the scroll of your cello with a love you give to nothing else. I offered you myself, but you are afraid of love and in a cowardly way sought to interpose all sorts of dopey activities between us, placing hobbles in the way to block it. That is why you live on Block Island, where you're right at home. Don't you see? You are attached to smelts. Yes, you can play music, but you are small, tiny, and alone.*

"You are a smelt yourself."

At least in the end I had been identified. During the course of the entire visit, the woman never once—not a single time—ever used my name.

Spoke it, not once.

Dogleg to the Left

"Now she's eyeless.
The snakes she held once
Eat up her hands."
George Seferis

"To do less than the ultimate is to do nothing."
William Zeckendorf

Sheriff Mordaunt Hill's wife was a shrew, and he would have gone to the end of the Earth to get rid of her. People in the small town of Edge, who knew her well, witnessed the folly and cruelty of her behavior, often repeated there was no worse a termagant or scold in the entire state of Maine, so she was scrupulously avoided. Thain, who had grown up poor earlier in life had ambitions but the life she had thought she'd find in marriage, came whistling down a stick over the years in repeated disappointment. The two had been married for fifteen years. He had in his wishes wanted to study at the university but couldn't meet the standards, and he had become resigned to the loss.

A pipe dream of his had long been to live on a tropical island or atoll by himself, the likelihood of which, he knew, was on a par of his being happy in life with a miserable wife. She had demanded he take the job at the jail—one he had not wanted—for the guaranteed state pay. Having taken the job, one retaliation of his was to stay there and rarely go home.

Her many reprisals ensued.

But Thain's many offenses, which seemed never-ending, he had long compiled. She was a sloven, fully indifferent to leaving the house unkempt. Her habits were vile. She left piles of dishes in the ink, including soiled cups with tea bags and squeezed-out lemons. That it badly bothered her husband was of course intentional. She refused to wash dishes. She interrupted him at every turn. She noisily. sucked beer from cans. She wore hair-papers, even at noon, and could be found scuffing around in housecoats. She smoked cigarettes, turning the curtains yellow, and left butts in ashtrays. She kept a pet parrot in the kitchen that she fed dead yellow jackets. Worst of all, she was argumentative and would interrupt him at every turn, frequently barging into his shed, where he'd be fixing a tool or sharpening an axe, just to point out—indicating, say, a tiny egg stain on a dish—to show how stupid and incompetent he was. She brayed when she spoke, her voice was loud, an ear-piercing shrillness worsened with a speech defect, a slushing sound with every *S* that she mispronounced.

She was an absolute, hidebound, and irremediable confrontation freak who never, ever retreated, retired, or withdrew in an argument. Acrimony, envenoming her, actually gave her life. She positively craved dispute, relished discord, and Mordaunt, an expert on her lust for conflict, knew creatures with such rage are often killed. Such aggression is inborn, in the same way circumstances alter faces.

Any individual who had truck with such dented souls can recognize almost immediately, by deduction, that they had been hated by their mothers.

And, of course, an added truth was that they hated their mothers, as well—vehemently.

The taint is hereditary, inbred, congenital.

Mordaunt had grown up in the isolated New England woods, the iron dark, grown in contained silence like one of the lonely spruces, solitary firs, isolated junipers, or forlorn oaks in that remote state. He had originally built himself a house on Monhegan, an island off the coast of Maine. A peculiar tradition, still in play, is the decree, after a bachelor has built a house, that he bring home a bride. He met Thain, who was a waitress, and without much thought married her, partly to meet the island requirement. Within a year, the house had burned down from an oil lamp spill, and they went ahead and moved to Edge.

He soon saw with a great deal of self-pity that he had lost custody of himself and now often removed himself to an outside stoop where he ruminated and stared at the elephant-ear arums the size of kitchen tables that sprang from the soil along the front of the porch and the second growth turkey oaks that formed a miniature forest across the way.

She would fret out all her ill-humors and talk aloud to the worm-eaten shelves on an angry search for a soup-cans for something to eat, one arm leaning against a sloping wall as she kicked away the cat on the uneven floor covered by an old, frayed rug the color and consistency of porridge. She loved mutton, but to her husband, it was rank and like licking a barn door. The one meal she most often made, Satan's Recipe for Burnt Potatoes, knobby russets cooked on a warped sheet pan set under the highest high oven heat with a long cooking time to evaporate the liquid—the sugars from added lemon juice having scorched and burnt them—she'd serially nibble all day, sitting sideways and barefoot on a sagging hammock in the front yard, loudly chewing and flipping through magazines.

In a tough, rustic state, the remote town of Edge was predominantly known for its hardened men and disappointed women, where independent and unconventional and relentlessly original individuals, God-fearing non-conformists for the most part, for whom the past was something to forget and the mysterious future a kaleidoscope of half-formed dreams, struggled for a better life without ever expecting to find one and where there was punishing labor or no work at all.

The folks there were tut-mouthed, rarely spoke, and when they did it was but a word or two, an exchange basically *a-yuh* and *nope*, with little inhale of agreement on one hand or a negative pip of the lips on the other. It was a hardscrabble world up there, with little to soften the days. Maine in winter can be bleak, silent, and cold. Much of it seemed buried in forest woodlands and brakes of a tenebrosity so thick and heavily, scarily concentrated, that, in a misbegotten turn, one could become dangerously lost. Air is darker up there, the sky a deeper dark, with a shadowy gloom that can tint the thick woods pitch black.

Mordaunt was not very bright. But he was tenacious. It was no secret in the small town of Edge, where gossip ruled, that he had spent some time at the Augusta Mental Health Institute when he was in his twenties. But he was reminded of it. His wife who was the occasion of such sallies never stopped talking. It is said that the average person speaks about 31,500 words a day. Thain spoke thrice that, easily -- maybe more.

But the neighbors, the uncommunicating townies, called him "The Man with Icy Eyes" and "Sheriff Morbid" and "Husband of Hellfire." Thain herself often angrily threatened to have him involuntarily re-committed. He had quirks. He always paced while thinking. He cooked squirrel. His sole reading was confined to the Bible, which his wife surmised was daft and for which she constantly derided him—to her it constituted less a monomania than living proof of his being half-demented. Hunched into some secluded hole of space, flipping through page upon page of Scripture—for what, she wondered?

It was she who demanded that he take the job as sheriff when it was offered to him, to give her "profile." For she was vain, a common vice of the facially unfavored. She had the red eyes of a gannet, something of the trace of a mustache, and a bulging belly, for she lived solely on beer and pastries, jelly donuts and pies, and nibbling her knobby russets.

Her sallow attenuated, almost impaired jaundiced color was corrugated by chronic rage and in a pinched, washed-out way matched her skin, slack and mottled, which was always revealed in traipsing half-open housecoat. She used the wrong lid color to match her eyes. Her claws were raw, unrefined. A woman's hands can betray her age more than any other feature. Mordaunt fled her company whenever possible.

Reality was a state of things she could never face.

Women love the lie that saves their pride, but never the unflattering truth. Headstrong Thain rarely bathed. She was a hopeless glutton. Her fist could reach into the tiniest of bags for nuts, raisins, seeds. She held the opinion that she could sing, a chirping, ear-piercing strung-out stridency which literally sounded like grasshoppers at night, shrill, high-pitched, and eerie—she could put only air through her vocal cords. When she drank, she followed the vulgar habit of reaching into a goblet with her long tongue and lapping at the inner 'legs'—the bands of wine running down a glass after swirling the liquid around—from the bottles of cheap tokay she hid in various places about the house.

Whenever she made desserts, which rarely she did, it was either hideous gelatin-fruit rings or half-peeled apricots sitting in a dish of sugar or a pyramid of conical cakes fashioned with potato flour, which were dryer than sand. It never occurred to her consider pureeing frozen vegetables to disguise their icy origins. No, it was slapdash everywhichway forward. Every meal with her was truly a barmecidal feast.

This very evening, Mordaunt sat, eyes closed, before a day-old battered casserole he couldn't bear to look at or smell, never mind taste.

"*Cooking?*" exclaimed Thain, outraged, bouncing a tin ladle onto the table to begin another near-fatal argument. "You wouldn't know a fegato from a plum fucking Danish, you, a Tibetan dirt salad from a Bolivian guinea pig terrine! That breaded shrimp concoction you made last Friday looked like worm fingers!"

He had unthinkingly set aside an ugly chunk of gristle—and mouthed the word *fat*.

It had offended her.

Thain used to be overweight. fat.

"Fat?" How venomously she loathed the word.

He turned his back to her. "I once saw you suck up a whole flan, pig-wise."

"You're barking up the wrong eucalyptus, Wood Panel Brain!" declared Thain, punting a frayed slipper into the air, catching it on a snatch, and then angrily hurling it directly at her husband's head. "I was—*copious*."

She rapped a hard tattoo the table.

"When I was copious, even then I didn't feel that I was accepted socially, which made *you* defensive!—try that on for size, Pee Wee. I myself could have cared less. You didn't, don't, never did accept me, so I don't accept you."

Silence—it had once been *silience*, in their early years—was almost always his repartee, the absence of *any* ambient audible sounds. But those were days in a distant past, as previous as any warmth between them

"Crone," he whispered.

Thain shrieked to hear it.

"Read it and weep, Fart Boy!"

There is nothing like living together side by side for blinding people to each other's faults, on any level. Thain, ptyalizing white spit, roared out if her chair in full fury and barged into his chair, kicking with both feet. "You got spaghetti for legs! You are a *down pillow* of a sheriff! The most excitement I've ever seen round here, you ineffectual feeb, is you on your back with your legs up playing acroyoga with the stupid cat, a game that normal people play with their small children! Your nails are bitten to the quick—to the cuticles! You are never in the swim and are a slave to khaki and a kind of barking limp blue and over-the-calf length socks and pants and trousers with broken belt-loops."

She was almost on top of him now, whacking at his shoulders and swatting at his head. "You want an honesty binge? Let's get a touchy subject out of the way. You'd never be a gentleman with an attaché case or a briefcase! You're a flop, a nobody, a dud! You're what they call a 'weeper'—a bottle with a leaky cork!" Thain strode to the sink, her back to him. "You're always in a damn hurry to get nowhere. Claimin' you need a vacation, as if I myself don't and didn't deserve it– well go ahead and take one, see if I care! Why not go down to Cape Cod, where that ol' nutty granny of yours was from, whom you're always boasting about, Foulmouth, High-anus, Wallfeet, Tororo, them places?"

Mordaunt could barely stand the onslaught of the merciless black rain. The incredible variety of her screams, often roars, the frightful deluge of a great orchestra of outbursts and keening hate, flat splats in the air like cannon firing.

Marriage. It was not to be denied that there is something awful in the nearness it brings, in the nexus it bears, in the occasions it offers. Proximity has as much a geometry to it as a rhomboid or a rectangle, an obtuse or a reflex angle. There is a configuration to it, a grid of elemental contours that can breed hatefulness. It can generate and engender evil. Thain bulked at Mordaunt in impossible ways, in spite of the fact that a childless couple, with no dependents, should have been able to get along, even if by cagey ploys of avoidance by avoiding each other. A consolation for him, he read— and knew—his Bible. In an early grade, one of his concerned teachers had once written to his parents with the, she thought, helpful suggestion, that he was abnormal and needed remedial help based on that singular fact alone, that his reading the Bible—even carrying one around with him—was excessive.

Mordaunt was in fact not really normal, not at least in ways that most people were. He had often begged her for a divorce, which repeatedly she flatly refused to grant. He read her Proverbs 5:3–4, "For the lips of an immoral woman are as sweet as honey, and her mouth is smoother than oil. But in the end, she is as bitter as poison, as dangerous as a double-edged sword." She ridiculed and mocked him. He was shorter than she was, even mousy. He told her once, *"Freedom is an obligation."*

He sought diversions. He cut wood. He spent time ice-fishing and trawled a favorite salmon run. Salmon! How he admired and deeply came to envy the resilience of that fish, its steady, tenacious capacity to survive the worst travails and strain, to live in saltwater and fresh, jump twelve-foot dams, travel thousands of miles across vast oceans to locate its ancestral rivers and spawn within feet of where it hatches. He would sit and stare respectfully at a hornbeam tree, a native Maine species, its muscular-looking trunk, its brawn, admiring how it flourished in rich, wet soil, although it never grew very large.

How and why had he not such gifts, and why so passed by? Life was a jack incident to him, unruly in cause, erratic in effect.

At times, after angrily slamming the door on his wife, rueful Mordaunt had momentary regrets, but was he not forgiven? Hadn't St. Paul himself said in 1 Timothy 1:13, "But I received mercy because I had acted ignorantly in unbelief"—*because*, Mordaunt noted—"and the grace of our Lord overflowed for me"?

He was a temperate man, never wasted money, and was in many ways old-fashioned. He carried an old deerskin purse and had one of those wonderful old knives that could crack walnuts and torque open pumpkins without risk of blade nicks. The attention that he gave his own male-oriented, personal, private pursuits, which consisted basically of fleeing her when he could not avoid her company outright, was in direct proportion to ignoring her. It was as if each morning he had to plan that day's abandonment which he needed to be sane. He would then get angry as a way of justifying the guilt he felt for lying to her about his lax, soon neglectful, then diminishing, and ultimately failed affection.

Occasionally he went out to hunt. It was as much a way of getting out of the house and away from the perpetual nag that nag that he lived with and served as a sport. He relished squirrel meat, one of the many, multiple things he never shared with that woman. Several times in the wild thickets over by Millinocket he had shot black bears—a dry sow, never having had babies, is well-known among hunters for having the tastiest flesh—bringing one down with a single blast to the heart with his Mauser, a Hornady 73-grain bullet, and another with his 375 Winchester, a 200-grain bullet, dropping each like a bag of salt. At the instant of each kill, he had angrily barked, "*Thain!*" Just to sit quietly in the forest in his small tent amid the green rushes and bushes was a soothing balm, the soft breezes, a light blue air, blowing through stands of hemlocks and pines nothing less in its embrocation than thick verdure where he sat ensconced, packed in—the perfect place for a ruminating depressive, chewing out his insides—in a natural breastworks and gabions against this hated wife.

He took refuge in truisms, excusive reflections filling his head against his troubles, such as "If your neighbor's beard us on fire, make certain yours is soaking wet" or "It is better to be the head of a mouse than the tail of a lion" or "Continue to carry bricks from your past, and you end up building the same house."

Mordaunt worked alone. He poked around in his garden, alone. He always sought to eat by himself when he could, otherwise his food stuck in his craw. How painful it was to hear Thain singing inside—*cawing*—through a window, not a fluty bravado, or even whistles or trills, but grasshopper sounds, like two pieces of sandpaper scratching together. Wheeks. Squeaks. Screeches. It was truly unbearable. He would get up at night to make an earthquake cake, which he'd then bring to his outside shed to eat with a fork in peace or over to the jail where he would sleep at his desk, slumped like a furled umbrella, snoring and glad to be away from his wife's eyes that were as cold as holes cut in an ice lake for fishing and just as dark. At times, he talked to the prisoners in his jail for relief.

But as time passed, Thain's slovenly attitude never abridged, her cruelty never abated. Unkempt, slatternly, and disheveled, she barged through rooms, kicking aside whatever lay on the floor. When she bellowed, she thundered and hit the back of the houses. She swung often and wild and filled with wreck the abysses of her husband's nether world. To live with someone like this who would not be blamed for anything? Who absolved herself from any charge whatever and remained acquitted in argument and attitude?

What dastardly things she not do? A baby daughter born in their first year of marriage died at birth. On the small gravestone, a grieving Mordaunt, passionately seeking to honor her by way of Scripture, had pleaded to have her identified by the name or Mahlah, Hoglah, Milcah, or Tirzah. Nothing obtained that way, as typically nothing ever did. Bitter Thain willfully went and had the stone engraved simply: "*Lost!*" In an inconsiderate act one day, she in a cruel and heedless way deliberately ripped out the stiff title-page frontispiece-sheet out of his Bible to serve as a floor for her parrot cage. She was negligent everywhere, left water running in the sink, broke lightbulbs she left rent in their sockets. She refused to darn his socks or wash his clothes. He had a favorite antique model 89 Remington double barrel shotgun, which she purposely left out in the pouring rain for a weekend to rust.

Amicability was impossible with her, free or open speech unthinkable. How she had fleeced him out of any comfortable features of living! And the meek docility that she demanded of him, the deliberate underdevelopment of his personality she required, the almost primordial abasement she expected.

Compliance—being submissive—was the condition re-quired, *demanded*, if he was to have even a smidgen of a chance at happiness.

Could he not be accepted, he wistfully wished, in light of his wife's hardness and deceit to be valued for at least one passing day, as a husband who needed above all other allegiances a smidgen of loyalty, decency, and truth? Was he not a man, a human being? He felt himself a worm, insignificant, a thing to be trod on. Didn't an old radical adage state that the will to command is not as cor-rupting as the will to obey?

He would stare out at Thain, snoring on the porch. She was as bad or even worse than any of the bad wives in Scripture: Delilah; Tamar; Athaliah, the Baal worshiper; deceitful and money-grubbing Sapphira; Potiphar's lewd and lying wife; and Jezebel, whom the wild dogs devoured and who was too poisonous to be buried in the ground. The wife of Job! *And how about Eve herself?* "It is better to live in a corner of the housetop than in a house shared with a quar-relsome wife" stated Proverbs 21:19, and Proverbs 27:15 "A con-tinual dripping on a rainy day and a quarrelsome wife are alike."

Not for him any cigar clubs or supper rooms or dance em-poriums or smoking lounges in which to find a mandatory refuge. There was either the jail or the back porch for him to seek sanctuary or asylum, when not a mad onrush into the deep forest, where he would block his ears with custom-made stoppers on a last-ditch frenzy to get out of the tornadoes of the rants and snarky, scathing criticisms of his crotchety spouse.

Vows desolate and forlorn Mordaunt repeatedly muttered that had her head had been a basil plant, he would have taken to it with flashing shears and trimmed it bald or even gone so far as to lop off—*utterly abscise*—the entire wrangling, quarrelsome, cantan-kerous, wrangling thinkball, *trimming to the neck*!

How desperately he yearned over and over to abide in a special place, unaccompanied, solitary, single, separated even if forsaken. Yearning was too mild a word for it, as was pining. He hungered for it, more than desired, *craved it*, felt he could kill for it. It got so bad at one point that, suffering abdominal pain and learning one day that he was the victim of a blocked colon, with a medical prognosis from the doctor that he might die, things had become so hellish on the domestic front that he actually did not care, not a whit, and he literally *looked forward* to death. which he seriously felt was far better than the life he lived, He was even grateful that a thing as real and mild as death could give one release.

A miserable person, Thain in the way she lived and walked and waddled was truly the essence of rancor, spite defined. She could never disagree without being disagreeable. Vehement and repugnant replies alone served her. The only sports she delighted in was running down others and jumping to conclusions, actions by which repeatedly she regarded herself grandly as the leaven and him a lump of dough. This he tried to correct.

For Hill was an inveterate—deep-seated—Bible reader.

Y*east* in Scripture is considered sin, he told her, repeatedly, but she'd turn her back on him. Leaven or yeast, he tried to explain, symbolized what was and is *negative*. Did not Jesus himself warn his very own disciples, as Mordaunt quoted, to "be on your guard against the yeast of the Pharisees and Sadducees," by which he meant the glib shallowness of their teaching that resulted in hypocritical and faith-denying lives (Matthew 16:6)? He told her unleavened bread symbolized and called to mind the notion of leaving old sin behind. The yeast of the Pharisees should be understood as self-righteousness, he spelled out. They held their strict adherence to the Law as proof of their own goodness. The yeast of Herod, which he lorded his position over the Jewish people, is the yeast of power. Corrupt!

Any words this way she only met with scorn. Scorn was the world she inhabited, morning 'til night. That he was slow-witted and not very intelligent and gullible and slow on the uptake and merely just a sheriff with a dumb badge, clipped on a rumpled shirt just below a plate-like face, invited only contempt.

Her husband repeated his claim. "Jesus said 'beware of the yeast, it rots and corrupts,' not just physically but morally, as well," explaining unleavened bread, then, became a cultural reminder for the Passover and when God delivered the Israelites out of Egypt, that God was their deliverer. Therefore, every time *unleavened* bread was eaten, God's deliverance from death and slavery would come to mind.

"But if you have no faith, what more should I say?" asked Mordaunt, seeking to face her down. "'For time would fail me to tell of Gideon, Barak, Samson, Jephthah, of David and Samuel and the prophets"—he was quoting St. Paul's Epistle to the Hebrews11: 32-38—"who through faith conquered kingdoms, administered justice, obtained promises, shut the mouths of lions, quenched raging fire, escaped the edge of the sword, won strength out of weakness, became mighty in war, put foreign armies to flight—"

A rant she had so often heard, she could bear it no more.

She abruptly cut him off.

Thain hurled a half-empty beer can at him and screeched, "Mental cases like you believe in any goddam fool thing they hear!" She would turn upon him on a dime. "Where is the kitchen colander? Hear? Wake the fuck up, Dearie, or am I speaking to you through my shoes?" "Look alive, explore your brain, Bugwog!" "Must you insist on dropping crumbs on the floor, Mud Puddle?" "You've got a rodeo brain!" "That's right, throw everything around. I haven't got enough to do without picking up after you!" "Now where the hell is my reticule, Yo-Yo? And that soft-grip potato peeler you every goddam day choose to hide? And my purple slipper socks? Have you gone and lost them again?" "Can't you remember to open the bulkhead when it stops raining, or are you a cripple?" "Your spouse is the goddam Bible!"

As to religion? His wife believed in precisely and exactly nothing. She had no use for the church or any of its mandates and dark admonishments, its bitter rebukes leveled at so-called sinners or the manifest greed so characteristic of them that hoovered up coppers and coins every single Sunday. It was, all of it, a bunch of goddam witchcraft! It wasn't that the endless mass of plug-ugly and petty profusion of Bible thumpers and screamy gooses and ganders of the church who put darkness forward and insist that it is light deliberately told untruths, it was that they didn't give a good goddam about truth at all; weren't interested in truth; didn't know jack about what truth even meant; demoted truth to negligible status compared with other, worthier considerations. No, on that subject, more than any others, she had planted her flag. Whenever Mordaunt pontificated or shoveled out what she described as his pious bullshit, he received her notorious, piercing "blue glare" treatment.

Her face, a patchy white, bore the veins and streaks and seams of stratification, which had the purple curd of cauliflower, and in this matter of a dead god and his taints with which had scant patience, they inflated, empurpled. She would slam the door and hasten to her hammock to wreak havoc on a pigeon pie.

Mordaunt to her was little but a grunt, having nothing at all to match the charming pictures and photos of the pillow-lipped movie heroes and sensualists with long eyelashes and bulging codpieces in the magazines that she stole from the town library, which she cut out to ogle. Her husband walked with the peculiarly rolling gait of the chronically flat-footed. He was also a stutterer and suffered from a low-grade bipolar disorder called cyclothymia. One nervous breakdown had already slowed his progress in life. That, together with his dicey, badly etiolated physical condition, had nothing but a bad effect.

Nevertheless, Thain was incandescent in her persistent and unfaltering intensity that he learn to meet her needs and obey her, or else be treated like the lackey he was. With a limitless appetite for bullying authority, she wore the pants in the family and rode herd everywhere, her ambition by way of a tyrannical bossiness—a magisterial position she automatically assumed—being strictly to assume and exert power to tell anyone she met, by shouted order, what it was they wanted, whether they knew it or not.

Still, she lived centered in a fray of innuendo—neighbors gossiped—which she refused to ignore but met head on, when and however, for rancor was her middle name and once in a market brazenly hit an old lady with an umbrella who, when she cut in front of her in a checkout line, muttered "You are a soapy vixen!" The French-Canadian contingent in town referred to her as "*Rognons*"—kidneys—and "The Moray" and "*Ecrevisse*." Townies dodged into doorways or cross streets to avoid her, on whatever pretext necessary. They referred to their house on Bone Lane, a bleak, unprepossessing dwelling with twin witch-hat spires and black gables, as "The House of the Day After Yesterday Went Away."

She also had two nagging half-sisters, Lizzie and Meegan, gnarled and dysfunctional personalities who were exactly like her and just as hideous-looking and horrible as was the hated Thain—petty, nosy, barbaric, uneducated, maladjusted, jealous, and mean-spirited—all equally nasty people from the family of Throops, who lived several counties away up in the Northland where they had been brought up in the sticks like wolverines.

It was rumored that Thain had been adopted (sources differ) from a pregnant teenage girl named Wemet, when she was six weeks old. But then did it matter? Who cared. Thain, pain, insane. There is small choice in rotten apples.

How often Mordaunt dreamt about living on an island. Alone. Faraway. In the Pacific Ocean, but anywhere where he would not be bothered, where he could be free and never again bothered by such a harridan as—he could not even mention her name, she was so damned awful. He often developed serious severe migraine headaches from his pondering reflections night after night at the jail, when the act of going home seemed pure misery. She had an idiotic cackle. But it was her wrath that had become impossible to take.

It was unfortunate for her that she married a brooder. Dark sides are important, he told himself, and should be nurtured like nasty black orchids. The ill-intentioned, like her pets, the yellow jackets, lurked like shadows in their swarming hatred. The shadow of evil in the way of its contrivances has no real substance of its own. You cannot cause a shadow to disappear by simply trying to fight it, by stamping on it, by railing against it, or any other form of emotional or physical resistance. She once called the police, enjoying the alarm when, one Sunday, he would not come out of his room, or even respond, and when they arrived, as she recounted for them some tissue if lies, they proceeded to kick down the door. He would never forget, she stood by with her bulky arms folded, smirking.

"You're a worm," she charged him. "Know what im*po*tence is? Look in the mirror. That'll tell you. See, there, look—a lump of dough."

He walked in dots and dashes like a Morse code out of the room, half weeping, having swallowed the deepest insult that could be aimed at a man. How erroneously, how falsely, how gullibly under a misconception had he for so long mistakenly enjoyed, and with what delusion, the spurious splendors of thinking himself a man of blood and valor, when all the time his wife had judged him empty as a windsock!

She had rented space in his head. He thought *one must not feel guilty about removing toxic people from your life.* He knew he was not stupid or illiterate, although he understood he was a failure and doomed to live cheek-to-jowl with a hateful wife. Most of the people in Edge, Maine, were not normal. The mood, the feel of the village, the atmosphere of its character, was ingrown, unhealthy, entrenched disputatious, daunting to outsiders, and unable to agree on questions of who, where, what or when.

Maine is a state, in fact, where the customary and the conventional, the ordinary and the usual are rarely often found. When not at work at the jail, where he often slept nights, even for full weekends, sometimes weeks, he spent time at the small-town library, late, after work, so he would not have to go home, where he would sit in a side room, alone. He once read that female sabotage is an evolutionary theory regarding the propensity of certain females to select *burdened* males of their species for mating. It was nothing but a revenge, apparently, for their own inadequacy, so they could shift the blame away from themselves for incompetence and clumsy incapacity and plain meanness. At least that's what he concluded. How was it possible to make a toxic person regret hurting you?

What were "gender norms," he wondered, as he turned page after pages of magazines there in the library's periodical room? How understand the nature of autonomy? Who was to blame, as was asserted in one dumb article that male-centered perspectives were internalized? Why was it, as he had read elsewhere, that lower rates of crime and delinquency among females reflected men's deference and protective attitude toward women, whereby female offenses were generally overlooked or excused by males? When was it ever normal for a woman to look into a fire and smile? Where was justice? What did it mean that protest was muffled by inadequacy? Why was it that the first reaction to truth is hatred? Who said? He didn't know and could not say. He knew only his spousal pain that never ended.

It was a curse. To have gone and married someone almost as wicked as the evil Nephilim, creatures who were the product of copulation between divine beings, literally, the sons of god and human women—the daughters of Adam—a mysterious race of supernatural beings briefly mentioned in the Old Testament? It was a fatal, unrectifiable mistake, his heavy cross.

Why were couples so miserably mismatched? Incompatibility in and of itself, ever bedeviling Mordaunt, became as much the source of endless thought as it was of interminable frustration. "What has straw in common with wheat?" as he recalled the Lord's question in Jeremiah 23:28. Cabbage is reprehensible with roast beef but laudable with bacon, salt fish abhors mustard but is delicious served with parsnips, and lamb, delectable with mint jelly, pairs never with ketchup. Sour citrus fruits or acidic berries taken with milk curdle that liquid and can lead to digestive discomfort. Such odd, anachronistic linkages! Beans and cheese! Radishes and raisins! Venison alone, he knew from personal experiment was one meat that accommodated anything. That was *him*, he realized, unlike other men. *Deer flesh.*

Odd. Mismatched. *Not* matched. A bookend uncoupled.

A solitary single exception!

Relationships require a lot of forgiveness, he thought, *but sadly I am not Jesus.* I am only a mentally ill sheriff of a godforsaken town in a remote village, left to serve out my days there, and not, never, on a beautiful island, alone.

A stroke of good luck, however, by a strange fluke, a coincidence finally, came his way, or at least he so interpreted the opportunity, although it took a period of time before he would realize just how. It had so fallen out the previous Fall when one night he had been called into a grim situation that had occurred in a fatal fight over lobster traps with two aggressive men, when the perpetrator, a thug down from Bangor, had severely punched another man who had fallen back and knocked his head on an iron oarlock and was killed. A trial was summarily held, and the man sentenced to be hanged. It was the first time that such a crime had ever taken place in Edge, and the assignment according to Maine law was to be the undertaking of the presiding sheriff himself. "Do your job, you silly stupid fool," brayed a furious Thain. "Don't be a friggin' pantywaist! Hang the bastard! That's your job! Backing out of it, your cowardice reflects on me, and I will—I swear I will—*blackmail* you as weakling! You've always been a cheap funk of a poltroon, a yellow-belly! A dingo! A sook!"

He could not take his eyes from her hate-white face.

Then he blundered out of the room to try to save his soul. But she jumped up and went frenziedly barging after him spouting recriminations. "You're short and runty. That gun of yours is bigger than you! It gives you the feeling of power you lack!" He ran outside—and she followed, scoffing at him with a last disparaging shot, "You should die!"

"Stop it!" he cried. "Please stop it!" he pleaded, covering his head with his small hands as if from incessant gusts of a sudden frightful storm. "A milksop!" she screeched. "A mouse! A namby-pamby of a weakling. You know what you are?" It was like a merciless gust of black rain, a raging spate of hail. He could not bear it and quickly ran outside and slammed the door. But Thain again followed him, waving a sharp fork, her red seabird eyes glinting with hatred, "I said do you know what you are? They call people like you—a caitiff! She jumped into his space as he tried to turn from her. "*A caitiff! A caitiff!*"

In the far extreme, this lent itself to a foray or two, call them onsets, into the near occult—private incursions he faced. On at least two occasions, Mordaunt, always credulous, had the sudden, unsettling experience of having received urgent messages from the ramparts of a distant world beyond. In the first instance while alone in a cabin in a forest outside of Norridgewock, he underwent a near-death experience, the highlight of which was a brief interlude in the afterlife—a sort of cerebral vertigo in which a creature bathed in a douche of pure white light appeared waving a sword to whisper untidy and rather alarming revelations of wrath. He felt not only that he knew of the reality of that entity but that it provided answers to the mystery of life. It bore a shaft straight into his skull as if he were a human radio receiver or a seer taking dictation from a learned soul of the Fourth Dimension.

At another, alone as usual in a hunter's blind, or machan, designed to reduce the chance of detection by animals, where he sat thinking unnerving, peculiar thoughts, surrounded there by a thick coniferous forest, his spine was suddenly straightened by the sudden appearance hovering in a silver moonlit haze of the Seven Angels of Revelation 16:1 – 16, each bearing seven bowls of God's wrath consisting of judgements full of celestial wrath. These seven bowls of God's holy wrath, which were poured out on the wicked and the followers of Antichrist in an inundation or torrent spitting black fire, spoke to him!

Mustn't one *live* one's visions, as well as hear or merely ponder them, he gathered, dare bravely to "misread" weak pleas for passivity and apathy and take up arms to correct all injuries and infractions and infringements?

He listened, he heard, he hearkened, he would obey.

It was a predicament shared in common, determined by fate that way, but with this exception—one of them had to go.

After endless years of abuse and obloquy, for weeks now Mordaunt Hill plotted and intricately projected how to do away with his wife—it was an opportunity virtually handed to him—and he came up with an elaborately conceived plan, in its intricacy worthy of the knotted, twisted, and entangled life he led at home. He found support of his dark intention late one night poring over the Bible in an upstairs room in the library. He had to look closely to re-read the passage to be certain of the seemingly negative words. It was in Psalm 109, where the psalmist in desperation begs God for justice against his enemy:

"Appoint someone evil to oppose my enemy;
let an accuser stand at his right hand."

It was all of a sudden an astonishing message, a cogent Scriptural *sanctioning answer* to all his needs. In these few words, Mordaunt had been openly handed the validating privilege of retaliation and revenge. The entire psalm was a polemic against Thain, such people who do evil things and should be punished. It was just the kind if sanction that he had been waiting years to find, to justify, to defend, to validate, to sanction his long-held need for action—and if harsh, valid! Psalm 109 was unique, he read, because of its dark imprecatory nature. Imprecatory psalms are prayers that call for God's judgment or punishment on the psalmist's enemies! Was the psalm challenging for modern readers? Did it **contradict teachings** about love and forgiveness in the New Testament? Not for this man from Maine!

It was nothing less than an authorization -- a ratifying warrant from the inspired pages of Holy Writ itself, word for word -- finally to take a step into freedom!

"No fine things in my life have ever happened. I have always been late, forever passed by. I always get to the fire after it has gone out." Mordaunt was leaning against an oak, both of his palms for some reason shielding his ears as he whispered these words into a tree hole. "I have been deserted, defeated, and dumped."

A dark resolve began growing his head like a black cactus. Had it not been suggested in his proof-texting runs through Scripture, even from dark anti-visions he'd had in the woods, that Thain might have been born of those evil Nephilim mentioned in Scripture, twice, both in Genesis 6:1–4 and then in Numbers 13:33?

This gave him an idea, which suggested a scheme, that finally became a plan.

The plan. It had to be unique, something like a curve. He conceived it as a trick, an unexpected maneuver—odd—like a dogleg to the left. No one could suspect it. It seemed so strange, he found himself laughing and crying at the same time. He had *actually decided* something. Whatever he thought was the way he valued.

Merely having decided something alone proved its worth, He was going to make unleavened bread.

He sat up very late that last night in the jail, watching the prisoner. The echo of years of Thain's belittling remarks played in his head. He thought of yeast. When St. Paul wrote to the Corinthians, did he not admonish them, saying, "Don't you know that a little yeast permeates the whole batch of dough" (1 Corinthians 5:6)? Paul used fermenting yeast to illustrate how one sin leads to another in a snowballing effect. The waking world, unfortunately, was unaware of the compounding effects of the yeast of sin. Yeast equaled sin. In trying to scotch her merciless arguments that he was a lump, had he not told his cruel and intemperate wife—*adjured* her, for that was a Scriptural word he loved—that what leavened bread symbolized? Called to mind the notion of leaving old sin behind? That bread without leaven is a fresh start, a clean slate? Thain threw food at him in contempt, sourly spat. It was typical of the derision she heaped upon his every remark. She called him a drone. She sneered and scoffed, and over years her mockery of him, her spite, not only effected his habits—townspeople always smirked when he walked by—but also after time badly affected his mind.

Love seeks no record of wrong nor rejoicing in iniquity, he had read. A long, lost belief, thought Mordaunt. No longer a conviction. Love bears, hopes, endures, believes, and endures all things. Dead conceptions.

It was then that he offered a bargain to his prisoner, the Bangor thug, by which he could earn his freedom. Mordaunt went into the cell, and they sat there face to face, talking for an hour. He told the jailed criminal that he would release him if he would kill his wife. It all fit. He would let him free to go and do the job and then hide him in his own house, with no one the wiser. "I will let you stay hidden there as long as you want," said the sheriff, handing the man a house key. That was the boon for the condemned prisoner, he quickly realized, a safe house, with the protection, all along, of the very officer who was in charge of him.

He divined that under any circumstance, he held in his hand the assurance if complicity with law itself! It was airtight. Criss for cross! Tit for tat. A trade-off. Perfect!

"While you're sequestered there, free from the hands of the law," he was told, "you have to hold up your end of the bargain, remember, and will be held responsible for fulfilling your job. I want you to *take her life*. Fear not. The woman also has degenerative osteoarthritis of the hip and emphysema, even crabs. It will help her out!"

Right knows no boundaries, he believed, and justice no frontiers.

But of an equal spite, malice, and rancor had this dark, devious plan nothing to do?

True, a questioning Mordaunt fitfully reflected, but then came the answer in reply: was not Divine Scripture *itself* replete with scandalous examples of spite. Transports of a working passion control such perpetrators throughout its pages! Didn't the Hebrew prophet and wonder-worker Elisha, out of sheer spite give the servant Gehazi leprosy, cursing him out of hand in 2 Kings 27, crying our maliciously, "Naaman's leprosy will cling to you and to your descendants forever." Then Gehazi went from Elisha's presence and his skin was leprous—it had become as hideously white as snow." Didn't reckless David murder Uriah the Hittite by proxy, which is also to say by cowardice, by ordering all of his own soldierly comrades to abandon him in the midst of battle, whereby he was slain by an opposing army—and following Uriah's death, did David not take Bathsheba as his eighth wife?

Was not the entire Hebrew Bible an open proceeding of unadorned, shameless, and ongoing calumny against the people called the Philistines? Did not the Jews calumniate them at every turn as being bestial brutes?

And was that termed unjust?

When huddled into the crouch of his warped and ratiocinative theology to elicit some sort of salvation for his excesses, gave a perspiring Mordaunt the look of an odd ferrety but slightly demented medieval scholar, and yet while much seemed muddled and unsound—he was up at all hours of the nights by a pin-light in an attic room snapping the pages of his Bible back and forth—looking for justification.

But it worked for him

Spite defined all of those heedless bold, and extravagant sinners who paraded through the history of mankind, heretics, idolaters, fornicators, blasphemers, sodomites, whoremongers, revilers, all those corrupted in mind and conscience. The great variety of sin made it possible for all human beings to be atrocious sinners! It was a blatant sham, he felt, to believe respectability constituted goodness. Neither upright behavior nor exaggerated self-esteem can remove us from the sad, human weakness of sinning or can exempt any of us from devils.

The sheriff's prisoner, nodding, did not flinch. It would save his life. The two men closely colluded over the course of several nights at the jail, working out the details of the plan and determining exactly how it should go. "The house is the last yellow abode on Bone Lane," said Mordaunt. "Here, look, I have drawn an exact map for you." The sheriff pointed out to him just where to go, how to get there, where to find a rope, or the best way—noiseless—to dispatch her. His pupil, who was dead keen, was happy to oblige. He knew full well that was the one place that no one would ever look for him.

Did not the gulled prisoner realize that the sheriff knew the same, as well?

On the night of the murder, Thain had been sitting alone in the bleak kitchen before an enormous cup of watery coffee and an execrable-looking apple pastry. It was well past midnight, with a fierce wind howling wild outside. Quietly, the released thug who had found his way to the Hill house on Bone Lane let himself in the back door, as had been planned, and hid, waiting for the perfect opportunity to leap on the sheriff's cranky wife—he had seen the woman once at the jail when, wearing but a housecoat, she had barged in one night in a tirade to throw a cup at her husband—and to tie her up. She infuriatedly spat white wet, cursing him and wriggling ineffectively about in her stained housecoat. He worked swiftly, strapping her fat body with rope to a deal chair. It was impossible to gag her swiveling head.

There was only so much he could take before he had to shut her up. He raced up hard behind the perched, howling figure, raising both arms as high as he could with old coal-black cast-iron skillet, and brought down as hard as he could to duck-pop her with a flat clang on the head—*thuunngonggg!*—bashing her brains out.

It was a single stunning blow, immediately killing the woman outright.

The parrot in the cage, squinting, never squawked, as if implacably it was satisfied to see due process duly accomplished.

It was less than an hour when the sheriff, following fast the trail of the prisoner he let escape, arrived at the house where he found the prisoner sitting back in a chair in a dark room, his hands hung low, monkey-like, until without a word said he pointed to the corpse slumped rag-like in a chair, bleeding profusely from her battered crown. He hearkened to the words: *Appoint someone evil to oppose my enemy; let an accuser stand at his right hand.*

The criminal, impassive, was sitting on a stool, indifferent, munching on a wedge of apple pastry.

Attempting to collect his thoughts, the sheriff sputtered isolated words that said little. To describe the inexpressible joy of seeing the definition of spite a corpse flopped there, being free of the virago forever, charged him with a strange, soaring elevation. Without emotion, he looked to see a drooped body, her face like cold marble in yellow candlelight, one eye black, shiny, like an old, polished stone stared unseeing, her lips pursed in a harrowing way. Another ghastly eye had sprung out, and her tongue, purple, half lolling out, had been bitten in two. She looked as if she had swallowed a beet. She had shat. He almost laughed at her mustache that had taken on the effect of a smile.

While her weird fingers had curled at the moment of impact, the skin was now pale as campfire ash, sagging as if deflated rubber by some invisible valve that had been tapped and left open by mistake. It was as if he had entered an abattoir. A blood stench reeked, a putrid smell that hovered between that of a wet goat and algae decaying in a toxic pond.

Sweating, impatient, the sheriff wanted nothing more than to see her shoveled under dirt. But Mordaunt well knew, as he took a quick sip from the cup of watery coffee, that it was just a displacement activity.

For something else had to be done.

He stood there in place, looking at the murderer and the murdered and recited out loud, almost as if it were a required coda for yet another strange task about to be done that night, to fulfill as if by Scriptural fiat the concluding verse of Psalm 109,that had been speaking to his heart in the form of and by way of exequy, words of a penetrating fire simultaneously condemning the gullible prisoner while also redeeming himself:

> "Appoint someone evil to oppose my enemy;
>   let an accuser stand at his right hand.
> When he is tried, let him be found guilty,
>   and may his prayers condemn him."

It was an integral part of the solution that made freedom an obligation, for, inevitably, he saw, as the psalmist sang, it was required to kill this man who—as he would have to explain to the town—had killed his wife. Mordaunt quietly took out his revolver, and, aiming it, though he turned his head, not to look, shot the prisoner dead. Both deserved to die, for both were murderers. It was only fair. It was only justice.

It was by now late September. Rose mallow was in bloom in the marshes. Bayberries, gray-green, wax-covered, favorite food of warblers, ripening. Fog season over. Red Maples and Tupelo at their brilliant red peaks. Ospreys departing. Seawater warm enough to support hurricanes. Shorebirds—plovers, finches, dowitchers, and godwits—migrating south.

And Mordaunt Hill would follow.

On the last day, that final day, he could not bear to look to see what deep down in his heart he yearned to ignore and ached to avoid, yet already half in love with his own destruction if it meant having to plead remorse or seek contrition.

He abruptly left, fled, Maine that following month, court-directed funds having been granted to him for the tragic loss in the murder of his dead wife, allowing him at last finally to get away and to travel far. He never looked back. He wended his way south, to leave forever the world he knew, reaching by bum boat the sparsely populated remote island of Culebra in the Caribbean, a lifelong, a constant, dream of his.

But constant reminders, flashbacks, and dark recollections ruthlessly pursued him, as well, less by way of conscience than a single accusatory Biblical passage which, try as he might, he could not expunge from his mind; something was still badly going sideways. Restless in his travels, he heard again and again echoes from Luke 12, burning in his brain, the dire warning which Jesus in His parable gave, *"There is nothing covered, that shall not be revealed; neither hid, that shall not be known"* to a man who crowed, "And I will say to my soul, 'Soul, thou hast goods laid up for many years; take thine ease, eat, drink, and be merry.' *But God said unto him, 'Thou fool! This*

very night thy soul shall be required of thee. Then whose shall those things be,
which thou hast provided?'"

Over and over in nightmares, as well, he heard creatures—
possibly the two bodies come alive in the air like ghostly marauding
spirits to remind him of his misdeeds—chanting, canting, *"Freedom*
is an obligation, Freedom is an obligation," insisting that he was obliged
to meet the liberty he had momentarily found but couldn't face.

But that was not the killing detail.

What he had not foreseen, though he tried to forget, was
the memory, relentless in its insistence, almost like a vengeful voice
battening onto his conscience, month after month, the words all
along he omitted to heed, neither could forget nor ignore, nor soft-
pedal nor disregard, also taken from what he thought was his im-
mutable Psalm 109:

> "He found no pleasure in blessing—
>   may it be far from him.
> He wore cursing as his garment;
>   it entered into his body like water,
>   into his bones like oil.
> May it be like a cloak wrapped about him,
>   like a belt tied forever around him.
> May this be the Lord's payment to my accusers,
>   to those who speak evil of me."

The decree, alas, was not to be disregarded.

It was an unalterable decree.

At the beach, Mordaunt, a single distant and secluded figure
sitting on a dune, isolated, as usual, finally all alone, softly set his
Bible aside, having swotted over that passage, reading it over and
over, as his tears began to fall, for, at last, he understood that he
now reaped what he had sown and saw now what was required of
him.

Godly sorrow, he realized—for he knew 2 Corinthians 7:10 like the back of his hand—brought repentance that leads to salvation and brought no regret, whereas worldly sorrow, what he had felt, is solely the fear of being caught and brought death. The former was a sin, which could be absolved, the latter irresponsibly understood as a wrong to be escaped.

Therefore, culpable.

He had committed damningly felonious and dastardly murders. It was not merely inexplicable caprice.

Words of fire he recalled castigated him, words terrible, inevitable, and aimed at the heart of one who now felt a curse as his garment. He found no pleasure in any blessing, which was far from him. He began to question and doubt the visions of angels that he had witnessed when perched in his hunter's blind. Uncanny synchronicities no longer came to him.

As he waited, he wondered if he had been cursed, as he rued in a deafening stillness the pointless loss of his infinitely small, lost daughter. Why hadn't Jesus reached down to lift one of her tiny hands in his own, whispering "*Talitha cumi*," saving her from death, as he had mercifully done with Jairus's daughter? It was not merely that the wee child's life had been restored, but the lives of the mother and father who stood there with no words they knew how to say. The worst thing that had ever happened to them had suddenly become the best!

Mordaunt was now hearing certain formidable words with despondency and regret. Could these be the final, fatal words of the Olivet Discourse, the fierce apocalyptic language that included the compassionate Jesus's dire warning to his followers that they will undergo sorrow, tribulation, and persecution before the ultimate triumph of God's Kingdom when, in the predicted abomination of desolation, not one of those stones of Herod's Temple would remain intact in the building, and the whole and entire thing would be reduced to rubble?

For a grievous, endless hour, the beleaguered man walked up and down the strand, tears streaming down his face. He sat down on his haunches and looked up at the sky as if through a pressing ceiling to a roof that offered neither shelter not protection. Although he spoke, nobody answered, nobody replied, nothing happened to pierce the appalling silence.

The sun was sinking beyond the westward bay, flaming the raddled sky, darkening the ocean water, and he felt mercilessly abandoned to the darkness of the passing hour, with noisy jackdaws building high flapping and straddling their untidy nests in the dark ilex and portia trees behind him with a signature that spelled finality and impelled disaster.

A poignant visual memory, the moon face of his dead wife rose to view like a fat fish or flounder rising from the black liquor of the deep, as if mercilessly to call on him, yet again. The burning red seagull eyes, the upper lip hair of her mustache, the balloon of a belly, the slurry *S* of her carking assertions, which were nothing less than brutal accusations that always seemed to crown him with the dunce cap of a nonsense-monger condemned to a middle world. He grieved that he could not grieve for the now dead battle-axe who with her shrill pipes and incessant clamor had so long been the linchpin of his grief.

As the tide meanwhile ran shallow over the sands, turning backwards on itself and curling into waves of foam, the high swells in flood, the cruel white lips of the waves curling over the bowling rollers, where ominously behind them, long dark combers crashed in like snatching hands, thunderously spending themselves upon the sand and rocks, the roar of the breakers mingling with a biting wind that had blown up.

Mordaunt's head was wet with sweat. The yellow shine of sickness was upon him, almost as if a suet of tallow. Was it illness in him or traces of a ghastly odor from the rank vixen smell that he inhaled from unrelaxed hormones of his wife tainting the air, the flow and effluence of the bloody outflow of her horrible death? Now when out of desperation he again recalled St. Paul in 1 Timothy 1:13 "receiving mercy because he had acted ignorantly in unbelief," he felt in his extreme remorse—and with a cold shudder in his loins—it no longer applied anymore.

He concluded with a raw glare of grief, the essence of Jesus to comprehend, the truth beyond all truth, beyond the stars, past the firmament, that to live without Him is the real death, that to die with Him is the only life.

It was inevitable, he came to see. Divine will. A belt had been inextricably tied around him, the Lord's payment to accusers, just as curses had entered his body like water, turning his bones to oil. As he was forced to heed the corrective, he accepted the corrective he saw he had to heed.

Sitting there in sand, alone, he proceeded slowly to remove his watch as if by rote to set it aside, just as he set aside the holy book, to take off his shoes.

He paused a minute, skyward looking, then slowly stood up thinking *freedom is obligation.*

And he walked straight into the dark ocean, the sleeves of the dark beckoning ocean.

Over his head.

Forever.

Fr. Mario

"Essentially a man is what he hides."
André Malraux, *The Walnut Trees of Altenburg*

With the other washing piling up from her other children, Anne Racine was exhausted on most days, just trying to keep up with the masses of laundry she faced, the bulk of which were the stained sheets that Jean-Paul, her son, left for her to wash on just about every morning. He was a habitual bedwetter, an indisposition that seemed never to end, one lasting until he was twelve years old. Bedwetting, a problem also called nighttime incontinence or nocturnal enuresis, meant passing urine while asleep without intending to do so, an anomaly after the age at which staying dry at night should be reasonably expected.

The boy's parents had tried everything they could to stop it. Cajoling. Threats. Promises. Pleading. Persuasion of any sort, which seemed useless, gave way at times to anger. Nothing worked. No water after six p.m. Rubber sheets. A flat pad with a bell that rang when it got wet. He was sent to a therapist in Boston every Friday in the 5th grade. Every morning he woke up only to find the sheets in his bed wringing wet.

They had nowhere to turn, having neither the means of the access to professional help. Researchers, they'd heard, held that, although that most enuretic children with a genetic tendency to bedwetting were less able to wake up soon enough to go to the bathroom in time—and while deep sleep patterns in all likelihood were involved—most reports indicated that emotional and behavioral problems were often a cause of enuresis in normal child development. Enuresis that persists past the ages of eight to ten years are invariably associated with a lack of self-esteem or psychological problems in a child.

It is a taboo, bed wetting, with numerous effects on children, most of them adverse. Family relationships were often clouded by the increasing shame and guilt, while the victims who wet the bed, as genitals are involved, feel worthless, and a terrible anxiety is often the cause of bleak depression. Sufferers see themselves as different from others and avoid any possible embarrassment that might occur by never staying overnight at a friend's house. They may fear visits to relatives or staying in hotels where they may be found out. Overnight school field trips were out of the question. All these psychological harms are compounded if unsympathetic parents scold, punish, or embarrass the child.

Whatever the cause of bedwetting, while most parents and caregivers knew they had a special responsibility to avoid allowing the condition to scar a child's psyche, which could cause a lifetime deficit of self-confidence and self-esteem, it was much easier said than done. Anne Racine was never a strong mother, and the large size of the family only made her the more subject to stress, with few places to turn to alleviate or lighten it. Although difficult, patience and understanding are and were the desired response of parents to bed-wetting children.

Was it out of incompetence that they turned with an unlikely limit of choice to Fr. Mario, won over by his vociferous platitudes and that impulse in him of inexplicable but scoring vengeance? No, it was not; what gave them both over to what in the end was unreasoning discipleship was not trust but folly, not incapacity but need, not haplessness but despair.

As to the boy, he could not help but realize that, under the circumstances, it was an offense that he was committing on purpose, sinning even without intending to do so. Stress and trauma seemed to be a cause. A deep, profound sleep voyaging deep into the pillow—a face plunge—hoping to escape waking to the real world was a possibility. No matter what vows he swore or how insistently he prayed, it ended the same each morning. Swearing on his heart and soul that he would improve was a rocket that came whistling down a stick, always. Resolutions led nowhere. A firm purpose of amendment? Mere folly. The futility of it all had long replaced the resolve, made so often that it had become a mantra, that the existential burden of the disaster—a vulgar and personal crime, he felt—came down to the understanding that there were sins too subtle to be explained and others that were too terrible even to be publicly mentioned. He lived hourly in shame. It penetrated the very nature of passing time.

Jean-Paul had fought to be awake at such times, not to be lazy or give in to sloth, the strange word his parents always used. Not to be wet for him was to live in the enchanting sunlit uplands of his young, wayward dreams, free to feel the utter joy of knowing every day he was dry. The mere idea of stopping wetting the bed was so comforting to him and so constituted the very definition of freedom every waking day in the way of release that he truly knew, not merely felt, that he need not be given any other reward in life! That was enough of a world gift!

A visit from Fr. Mario, a priest in the family, became the occasion of Anne mentioning the strife she faced in the piles of dirty clothes daily mounting up that left her exhausted. She turned to her brother for helpful advice simply because she could find it nowhere else. The family always called him Uncle Louis—his pre-seminary name, the name his sister called him—and he said, "I have heard a number of serial killers were bedwetters. I could never figure out what correlation there could be in the parallel—what, pre-pubescent madness?—but frankly, delinquency comes down the pike in a number of ways nowadays. Is there any truth to it? I know a lady in Akron with five kids, four of whom still wet the bed, and she told me she wanted to run the hell away from it all and divorce." He puffed his cigarette.

Fr. Mario was a priest in the Carmelite order, a community located in Akron, Ohio. He was a stubby, roosterish figure, with a small inner grasp of who he was, which made his sallies into all relationships competitive and aggressive. Whenever he traveled home to spend time with his mother, as he did several times a year, he always took a short hop over to see the Racines, never without fanfare and a loud, sardonic presence, as if it were a Papal Visitation. Whenever he arrived, for the children dark clouds filled the sky. He was unpopular, because he could relate to children only by taunting and teasing, an acrimony that invariably took the form of comic badgering. A know-it-all, his need, indeed his capacity to commandeer a room, was always at its sharpest when his auditors were kids, children, as he explained life to them in the puffed-up way he had of telling them how the world worked.

Antagonism never drew its own portrait with a more all-inclusive stroke than with this basically insecure man. He was the incarnation of spite.

Sitting back in the best and biggest chair, he would remove his Roman collar and stretch out as if he owned the place. The black socks he wore, silk and long, the kids found particularly strange and eerie. He smoked cigarettes, heavily, one after another. He gave demanding orders, bossed the young boys to run across the street to the store to buy bottles of Moxie—and, with a scribbled note, to purchase packs of cigarettes.

Being with him, attendant in his lordly presence, was in a way somewhat like being a dog—he might take you out for a short drive, say for an ice-cream cone or to buy something, but you would find out where you were going only when you got there. You retrieved. Fetched. To say nothing, as he sat, of being muzzled, kept at foot level. *Sit!* Stay! *Heel!*

"You know what I would do. I'll tell you exactly what I would do," the priest told Jean-Paul's mother about the problem she was having with her son. He stabbed out a cigarette. "I would tell him right off, 'I'm going to hang your pissy sheets right out of the upstairs window!' Why, do you look so surprised? Don't you hear me, Anne?" His squinched face showed as hard and unfeeling as if carved out of a hard oak knot. "I *would* hang his sheets out the upstairs front window, draped down in public for all the neighborhood to see. That's correct, you heard me right! Think of the shame he'll feel—the shock of it," said with the priest, slapping hands with glee. "It will serve him right." Unmoved, his shelf chin shifted. "Do you understand what I'm telling you, the nature of his—*rebellion?* Don't you see the gain?"

Wasn't she listening? His nose swelled. "You tell me he's apologetic? You fall for all that crap. Bestir yourself! That monkey is streets ahead of you." He shoved forward. "Excuses are palaver! Sheer bunkum. Take no guff from the squirt. This is not my first rodeo. I've been around. Guess what happens when you don't stop something in the bud?"

He whooshed in exasperation.

"Like the slang word *pisher.* It's a Jew word, which means a bedwetter but also something like a useless good-for-nothing little idler giving you hard work! Do I sound I harsh? So be it! You need to learn exactly what disciplined care is. That's why custom fits out trousers with a belt! Don't you get it? The point I'm making? Cruel honesty is tough love."

Fr. Mario knew not a thing about children, for whom he had neither an interest nor an idea. To him, they were ciphers. Playthings. They were nothing but selfish, greedy, inattentive little robots to him who behind his back acted out and basically all deserved a good swift kick in the ass,

The priest crushed out a butt and lit another cigarette. "He is mulish and impertinent. You can see it. Don't give me any of that, that—that *children deep dreams and can't wake up* baloney. Pigheaded. He's making bad decisions."

Anne was confused by the remarks on her son. But as she pondered her dilemma of what to do, she thought: *he is still a mere boy. Changes can come. There is always tomorrow. And he is neither willful nor impertinent.*

Short, heavy, a creature full of himself, her brother had no neck and the kind of squat, nuggety body that in and of itself posed a kind of stubbornness. The thick eyeglasses magnified a look that gave his glare a crazy sheen. There were dots across his front teeth. He was impulsive and long-winded and given to maundering stories about himself. His every visit to the family was a blustering hurricane of a car racing up to the front curb, hastily followed hours later by car doors banging—and he was gone. It was drama he loved, less a visit than a visitation. He was a parataxis of boasts and rodomontades. He claimed that he knew, and was actual friends with, General Francisco Franco, and that he had once attended a banquet with comedian Bob Hope. He told everyone that every single year he finagled free tickets to the Barnum & Bailey Circus. "Last week, guess what? I met Jascha Heifetz. The violinist?" he waved a hand, disgusted. "You kids know nothin'." He had actually once written a cheap diocesan paperback book titled *I Thee Wed*, a farcical, out-of-date grumble of off-the-wall doctrines on the sacrament of marriage, one shot through with outworn paternalism and blatant misogyny, all of it of his own devising.

He derided Boston as a hick town. He was slippery, even shady, cadged tickets to shows, sought friendships with people who could help him, and almost anyone and everyone who was wealthy he befriended. He got "freebies." The children saw that he hoarded bags of sugar, rationed during World War II—and once three cases of rare port, what turned out to be old valuable vintages going back to 1919 (the deep ruby colors with garnet highlights attracting the kids) that he later falsely explained was Mass wine—in the backseat of his car, a sleek Packard that had been given to him gratis by a friendly dealer. He was given many complimentary things, not that he shared any of them with the Racines. The boys also saw a trove of expensive green glassware in the front seat and always remembered that, for, despite their expectations, the vain priest never gave anything like that to their mother.

Fr. Mario had a seducer's bent energy, a liar's gifts, and a magician's slight-of-hand. He loved to retail stories of his many worldly connections to well-known people, who were mainly third-rate celebrities and Broadway buffoons. He had once performed a wedding for someone famous in a singing group, the Four Coins or the Four Lads or the Something Quartet. His had read little and his education was meager, confined to closeted years in the seminary, which had only stunted him.

Among other of his claims was that that he could speak Homeric Greek. It turned out, however, he knew only a smattering of nouns—he could only decline the noun *skene,* for tent—and in the end, when he was tested on a later visit by Eugene, then in high school, he could conjugate only the verb *to be.* There were few subjects upon which he would not, could not, immediately pronounce, but virtually every subject raised proved him endowed less as an oracle than something of a blowhard.

The unavoidable fact was that the priest was hopelessly immature, even puerile, one of those who had gone off to the seminary at far too young an age, disallowing any chance to develop socially or emotionally or maturely.

By formal vows made celibate, Fr. Mario seemed in a guarded, mysteriously covert way a sexually incomplete and unfinished quiddity. He was crude, undeveloped, with an arrested juvenility, unsophisticated and awkward. He told crude jokes, felt free to pinch the bottoms of Franny and Daisy. Agatha, who never liked him, would not go near him. Nicknamed "Mule," she was leery of the priest, unlike Daisy who was so naïve it hurt. Agatha's slumbering dislike of him began when, once speaking to him, innocently, with a gracious little bow, had the effrontery to say, a brazenness at least in his view, *"Nous mangerons à onze heures et demie, s'il vous plaît,"* whereupon he heaped ridicule on her for being pretentious. And he pinched her bottom.

He had no sense of humor. His repartee was irony, his point of view an outflow of mockery satire and scorn that contained a grating undertone of contempt.

The kids in the family found him not only an off-putting curiosity, but a frightening and cruel bugbear, and no visit of his was not met with a good deal of dread. Remarkably, this was an ordained priest of the Catholic church.

He was manipulative. It was worse than a hidden agenda. He had a secret self, perhaps even an anti-self, a person within him that, for all anyone knew, he was unaware of himself, a perverted entity he avoided or could not face for the façade he was asked to present in the presumed piety of his vocation. It was like any other primary self but whether he was aware it was operating no one knew. That he was all along someone else, a dual self whose weird, complicated nature was obscured by the incongruous and competing ramifications of a priesthood overshadowed by the continuing bluster of an impious ego, obviously by his own choice, showed the lineaments of the bipolar to anyone bothering to look.

In a freakish way, the shameful secret that so beset Jean-Paul was matched all along by the closed past and clandestine backstairs led by Fr. Mario, a bizarre chiasmus of sorts. Everyone in the family suspected it, of course, detected it, as how could they not in the glaring, primary way it was always presented? But no one could comfortably acknowledge it, for doing so would have been unthinkable, a traitorous act. The façade in itself was bad enough, histrionics that virtually seemed to approach mental illness, for at the base of the priest's disorders in what seemed an ongoing enmity was a walking, waking grudge.

He *needled* children, exaggerated facts, spread gossip, belittled interrupted speakers, and despised Democrats, whom he dismissed as "brainless do-gooders." He cultivated various friends, always wealthy ones, whom, apparently, he kept handy in several parts of the country, people whom he would visit, not unlike visits made to the Racines. He was a scoundrel and a scapegrace.

Incorrigible. But worse, he was miscreant who in his capacity of behaving badly actually hurt those closest to him, a capacity born both of his energy and a warped sense of self, with a facile and frankly often underhanded way of looking at the world. It was far worse than his never hesitating to drive down the wrong way of a stated one-way street, which he always did. There was malice. His profession served him. He would boast how back in the city of Chicago, he would frequently put his stole over the steering wheel, so the police wouldn't give him a ticket. After his mother died, he returned to her house and stole back the Hummels he had so lavishly given her. He fought with several of his sisters-in-law. His dishonesty also consisted of his not paying taxes on several properties he had by way of third-party sources. Manipulation of this sort in conversation made him win every argument.

He loved to eat, craved salami and its broad categories, sausages of all sorts. of any sort in any variation. He scarfed whole bowls of chowder. Seafood was a specialty of his. He insisted specifically on haddock for his chowder, and he sucked winkles from a bag of them he brought along with bottles of Eau de Vie, only for himself, scooping out the flesh with a toothpick, while everyone watched with mild horror.

Jean-Paul's beleaguered mother always had to have a German chocolate cake waiting for him whenever he came to visit. Food played a part of his triumphalist narratives, for he often referred to expensive restaurants where he often dined, alluding to chefs who greeted and admired him. It was no exaggeration to say he owned the family with his visits, as being the only professional in the greater family—or what passed for one. He loved a Boston butt, bone-in for flavor, he explained. When he awoke, he asked for cheese-and-egg fritters and the hottest coffee with a special dish of black prunes in the morning, if ever he stayed overnight, which he did only once, unhappily waking up too early as it was too noisy, he said, and which he never repeated. Anne and her husband Al had given him their bedroom.

Al Racine, their father, always a quiet, reserved fellow, gave Fr. Mario a wide berth, and if and when the children in a willful, teasing, knowing way made inquiries about the priest, he merely shrugged, charitably responding, and said only that he "pursued activities not to be defined." Hesitant to be critical, to keep the peace, he chose to stand back out of decency in the way of accommodation regarding his wife's brother, making due concessions, but a propitiation in the way of appeasement that nevertheless burbled up like groundwater through a lawn.

Sometimes Fr. Mario offered a private Mass at the house, at a table in the dining-room. It was always done in a stagy way, one could say even operatic in the theatrical way he did most things. While the children were duly reverent, receiving communion, there was a sense of supercilious preening the performance gave him. In the light of his normal rough-hewn, indeed, often crude, boorish, and abusive behavior—constantly blowing his own trumpet—that holy mystery seemed incongruous. When the kids curiously ogled the chalice and vestments he had brought, he'd soberly chastise them for overreaching. Manipulation was his game. The priest's every act seemed to fit the nature of accumulation: wristwatches, wallets, even the weather. "This is the day the Lord has made," he would crow. "It is mine to love."

He collected Hummels, kitschy ceramic figurines with mold numbers and a Goebel trademark which he saw as "collectible" and which he gave to his mother, Jean-Paul Racine's grandmother. He was a worldly priest and conceived of everything as personal increase, food, travel, wristwatches, cigarette lighters, valises, even weather. "This is my day," he would say, stretching. "The day the Lord has made."

Fr. Mario was a man of neither mind nor matter. He had no little or knowledge of himself and so sought to cloth his soft brain solely with tired, shopworn thoughts borrowed from others, from adjacency, walking through life in the shadow of his neighbors with limited horizons and no sky to love. His ordination meant nothing.

He never learned to mint his attention into sympathy or understanding for any suffering souls.

He was buoyant, ruthless, and cruel. Shrewd was another
word that applied. A canniness gave him the feeling of being astute.
He was a glamor-lover, a publicity expert, a fountain of spouting
pretensions. He bought pricey bottles of wines, acquired paintings.
The shiny new car that he drove somehow emphasized not so much
its worth as the acquisitiveness of its owner, the rapacity, his covet-
ousness. His demand for fine things, especially in the way of jewelry, wristwatches, and rings, was fed by what seemed a kind of in-
stitutional larceny, odd especially regarding the vow of poverty he
took at ordination, a subject upon which he loved to boast, *plume,*
almost in the way of a good actor.

He took everything. He grabbed all the perks; he commanded all the glory and appropriated all the attention—he inher-
ited all that for himself. He kept it, not to share, not to allot, not to
split, not to commit or divide.

Around Christmastime, he always visited the family and—
it was virtually a ritual—they would all gather in the living room in
separate chairs, when he would sit in the center divan, like a pasha
an ashtray on his knees, posing questions to each youngster, turning
from one to another to quiz all the siblings, questions about their
pets, of school and their report cards, what chores they did at home,
and so forth. He would hold forth, smoking cigarettes, his glance
like the searchlight of a lighthouse slowly revolving, rotating, set-
tling on each youngster, Eugene, Franny,

Agatha, then Daisy, until it came to Jean-Paul who, waiting
for it, spot-lit, *floodlit.* He would be sitting in a corner, frozen in fear,
terrified for his turn to come, as inevitably it did, for the terror of it
was he knew that the priest, a single-motive puppet, knew the terrible secret of his bedwetting and how disgusting a creature he was
for the grievous fault. The desperate finger-crossed hope he fought
to be ignored was always dashed.

Once everybody had gathered around, when a proper circle was formally maintained, with all the kids sitting on their hands, chastened, awkwardly staring down at their shoes, Agatha alone bristling, glumly beleaguered, he would sit there in pomp like an Easter Island statue or *moai*, yet one perturbable, his face tilted upward in slight disdain, lips pursed, long flat nose, wide truncated chin, rectangle-shaped ears, and deeply dark eye sockets. He folded his hands and looked from one to another with a contemptuous appraisal. It was here he fired his boilers.

"I heard you bit a boy last week in a fight and play the radio after your father tells you to turn it off," Fr. Mario said to Eugene. With a lowered head, he said nothing in reply. They were all wingless chickens, mere poults, in the presence of a male peacock unfurling its tail. He then confronted Franny, accusingly, saying "You think you're Rebecca of Sunnybrook Farm with that plaid shirt of yours, don't you? Showiness is not attractive, for one thing, and you should remember your mother and father worked hard to pay for it all." There came a long pause. "All right?" Someone went to interrupt but he shushed him, as if compelling the atmosphere to assume the form created by his own thoughts.

He was nearly impossible to interrupt. Never mind not paying attention, even a mild reverie or looking away annoyed him. He demanded not merely attentiveness, but recognition. He was not a listener. The floor was his. He rarely waited long enough for anyone else to give a full answer.

All individuals who are controlling tend to be insecure and quite predictably come to resent even so much as a change in the expressions of any of his listeners. "Your mother also tells me you keep a diary. Why? To hide your real thoughts? Don't! And don't go trying to fool me because you can't. Indiscretions begin to appear in the way of entries. I know." Secrets, again. "Risks are run by rashness. Do you know what an 'occasion of sin' is, Miss? And stop making those silly faces at me!"

It was almost satanic that he could single out the one flaw in a person he or she found most cringeworthy. He skipped Agatha, whom he knew despised him. He seemed to pick on Daisy the most, pointless aggression. Was it because she was the prettiest? Or the most vulnerable? Or the most quietly sensitive in the family, her hold on herself so frail?

Small to begin with, Daisy was once sitting near him when a chance remark cruelly made about her weight crushed her so badly, visibly reduced her, that she never quite recovered and soon turned anorexic. Eating disorders very often proceed from a casual one-off remark made by an indifferent someone, often in an un-thinking way, which was exactly what happened in this instance. The debilitating, exhausting, soul-warping effect of it never left her, who already had a tendency to anemia. She would later become ad-dicted to drink, then drugs, and by the end weighed little more than the thin bracelet she wore.

Any civil or common need for empathy made this visiting priest only apathetic. In his unfalteringly obstinate and overheated impatience, intolerance, and irritability, he considered every child a malingerer. Ignorant in the most basic things, he would say "should have went" instead of "should have gone," could not remember the word *height* ends with a "*t*," no a "*th*." He demanded attitude adjust-ments. Complaints were, alone, all of your own making. "It's your own *attitude* that makes you carsick!" "Wind blows where *you* direct it!" "Be an adult!" "Don't try to fob off failure on anything or any-one else!" "Whiners are losers."

Fr. Mario's amateur sessions always solemnly ended in a wistful and death-like silence, with everybody quietly slipping away alone, embarrassed, with a kind of closed-mouth speechlessness, as if each had the experience of some haunting reverie. Nobody looked at one another. "Don't slink away, you—yes, you, come here." He would point to anyone.

"Get me a ashtray," Fr. Mario would brusquely command, extending the two fat fingers of one hand to Franny, simultaneously also sending one of the boys to the store across the street to buy him bottles of Moxie, his go-to drink. These were orders but he was also clearing a path to be alone with the boy. At this juncture, he told Jean-Paul, "Go over there." What did he mean in saying, please go over there? Where? The way the man baited people, adding feistiness to every situation, seemed savage. Jean-Paul despaired that his mother did not intervene, but she was in a sense helpless before her steamrolling brother.

Meanwhile, the boy had stood up and walked over to a corner, standing by himself.

"Do you still wet the bed?" asked Fr. Mario, staring straight into the face of the young boy. His eyes behind his spectacles shone with be-goggling severity like hot shellac. Jean-Paul blushed, his head scalded with heat, and tears filled his eyes as he stood there. Overhearing that question from the pantry, young Agatha angrily stepped out to drop on him like jaguar out of a tree, barking, "You should leave Jean-Paul be—*don't you see, he never hurt you?*" Bursting into tears, she ran out of the room. In the meantime, the boy stood mute, tight-lipped in the grip of shock, with his silence interpreted as cold insolence, or even weakness, both of which the interlocutor despised. The tension was sharp enough to cut. Asked Fr. Mario of him, "Do you think it very fair to your mother?" He paused. "Shall I put it another way for you?"

He waited, challenging jaw muscles bolting in and out.

"Have you any idea how much extra work you are heaping on her? Daily? At your age? My question to you is, are you a sissy? A homo?" His baleful eyes reflected behind the flash of his glinting eyeglasses. "Your mother works her fingers to the bone night and day. Do you know that? Have you the slightest idea? So, tell me, is yours the behavior of someone who has any sense of obligation or concern?"

Came no reply.

Those few vicious questions asked of him entered the boy like a sword, opening a wound that throughout his life never healed.

"Are you deceitful?"

Silence.

"Brash? Crafty? A sneaking conniver?"

He held fire. "Why do you not look at me?"

Because you are cruel
Because you are mean
Because you are wicked
Because I want the roof to fall on your head.

"I—d-don't know—why."

After the lighthouse sessions, he would scoot all the young-sters out of the way. That was the end of it for the other children. But not so for Jean-Paul, for at one point in mid-afternoon, pre-dictable as clockwork, he would with a nod—it had become stand-ard procedure, as if a rehearsal, a drill—summon the boy to the front door, without consult, in a proprietary way taking his arm to bring him outside for a walk. A panicky, hostile, dependent child is always putty in the hands of a manic firmness whose orthodoxies could not be contested.

Jean-Paul contested nothing, could not, did not dare. But one time in church, sitting in a pew turning through the Bible, he happened to read in the Psalms, "Break their teeth, O God, in their mouth!" and thought of Fr. Mario.

He would take young, Jean-Paul—it was standard proce-dure—for a long walk down to a local ballfield, Webster Park. It was a death march, silent for minutes as they trudged, with not a word said, but rather a tense and suspended interval like overhead clouds of boding rain filled with unspoken thoughts, when the priest would suddenly stop, grunt, and accusingly turn to the boy to inquire, "Are you a sissy?" Although he knew the routine, Jean-Paul was never quite prepared until the moment for the sense of alarm he would feel, the deep, traumatic disturbance. Although he tried instinctively to crayon his face as if to seem to care, he hated the man more than the question. "No," whispered the boy, looking away. "Do you want to end up peeing on your wife when you get married?" The boy's throat stuck. "That is what would happen, you know. Imagine what she would say? Do you hear me? I know another lazy person who wets the bed, and he is breaking his mother's heart." He coldly bent down and his large, closed face, scowling, came closer, damp with the effort. "You're an infection, do you know that? The laundry piles higher and higher every day. You're killing your mother?"

Jean-Paul felt panic, ice filling his heart.

A long silence held. The boy was thinking *please God, let me be somewhere else.* "Inside, you feel smug, don't you?" Fr. Mario poked his finger into the boy's stomach. "Deep down inside, right? Creamy as a cat. But you fool no one."

Silence was understood insolence.

"I'll bet you a monkey to a mousetrap you will never stop," said Fr. Mario, gripping his arm. "Why? Because you're a weakling. A namby-pamby. A coward." They turned to walk back home, with not a word more said, except, "A crybaby."

The boy's very soul had squeezed shut.

The humiliation of it!

He was mute, couldn't speak.

An irate railroad baggage-master destroyed young Thomas Edison's hearing by boxing his ears when the boy was twelve. Was this abuse any worse?"

The boy's voice stuck in his throat.

Although he was a small lad, Jean-Paul, in an uncanny out-of-body experience could see himself, could actually mentally stand-off, as it were, and witness it all– *watching,* as if he were his own accompanying angel, looking down in an attempt to interpret the mad complexity of this priest's unholy interrogations and admonitions. It was a survival action, less a mode to ride out the savagery than a defense against terror. His insides were spider-taut all the time. He felt he could get away only if he left his arms and legs behind. Yet while he could bewilderingly sense the priest's cruelty, and how wrong, almost prurient, his intentions were, he still looked upon himself as a criminal. Not to look back meant cordoning off all sorts of things of the non-suppressible present and to have to face, with almost mortal grief and deepening shame, the disgusting creature he knew he was.

Jean-Paul played the trumpet. He took lessons every Saturday morning. The fact was he not only had small talent but was listless about practicing, and also felt a sense of defeat in whatever he did. He grew up so hopelessly, desperately steeped in the recurrent fright of the constant of his every morning discovery—coming down from the attic, where he and his brothers slept, for the girls slept downstairs he would stand, sometimes for half hour in his wet pajamas behind the close kitchen door, holding his school clothes, with closed eyes, biding time, to hope to get to the bathroom, while everyone else was at the kitchen table eating breakfast—that he actually had to perform a mental adjustment to comprehend, yet once again, the agonizing, almost unspeakable, excruciating circumstance he yet again faced.

Although he shared with his brothers the bedroom attic upstairs that was sturdily built with crossbeam construction and ship-lapped floors, his siblings were too kind and sympathetic to show any adversity about his bedwetting, never choosing to vie with him as being superior nor mocked him for the fault. They kept proper silence, no doubt feeling as bewildered about it as was its victim. Unspoken, however, were many different approaches to things as they grew up. A lack of confidence characterized Jean-Paul's later behavior. He never went to camp or joined the Boy Scouts. At school, he did not dare to look at girls or seek to insinuate himself into their company. Dating was out of the question or—he lacked the social confidence—going to parties. No delirious sallies to investigate young love took place. It was always in order never to trust himself.

Any self-reliance over time had ceded to uncertainty. Certitude of any kind had been diminished, and, as to confidence or surety? Long lost.

But that alone was enough to plague him. The concept of being irretrievable, or even wholly absent, unremembered, or forgotten was disturbing, for he often thought *how can you get lost, when you don't even care where you are?*

Jean-Paul used to help his mother make a chocolate cake, a fail-safe basic recipe mix, and, breezily assisting her, he had no idea it was meant to be difficult or anything like a nerve-racking ordeal, that is, until one day two things happened. His Aunt Marie, a censorious cross-stick, who was visiting the family, asked him how he managed to be so breezy about it all, and Fr. Mario, reinforcing her remark, with full-faced ferocity chimed in with, "What business has he, or any boy, busying himself in a damn kitchen in the first place? The next thing you know, he'll grow up turning into a homo—a fruit!" From then on, the boy could scarcely bring himself to whip the batter or even add chocolate chips. Was it surprising? When confidence or hope is undermined, it can be difficult to do the simplest things, or even take enjoyment in trying. The boy never again, not once, helped to make a cake.

One morning, his trumpet teacher told him, quoting Gustave Mahler, regarding a problem Jean-Paul was having with cadence, "Any rhythmic structure may be organically adapted to any tempo"—and the first thing that he thought of, applying it elsewhere, was the finagling indirections of Fr. Mario and the deceptive adaptations he used guilefully to control him. The tricks. The maneuvering. The plotting. For it was these plaguing calculations, indicting him, that had become the bane of his life. The boy who was an irrepressible teen at a time when he should have been casting about for pretensions to adopt as his own, a thrilling hunt for identity that was usually done with joy at his time of life, was instead a solipsist who kept to his room in the attic or could be found in a church pew, crying.

His youngest sister, Daisy, the sweetest, was consistently the one person who in some kind of providential way understood his on-going grief, divined intuitively what he was going through, and was always there wakefully to open the door for him the right time, often with a hug of his arm as he ran to the bathroom to change. She once out of simple appreciating love gave him a miraculous medal. "Silver is the medal of redemption," she told him, whispering, with a gentle smile, softly kissing the crown of his hair. He realized even then that a person who expects everything of herself blames herself for everything.

Jean-Paul would never, ever, as long as he lived, forget the night that they lost her. The night that she died, he sat up all night in the murk of the close darkness of his room, shades pulled, playing over and over again a 45 rpm of The Cascades singing their hit song "The Last Leaf," one of Daisy's favorites, weeping bitter tears at her loss, holding one of her childhood dresses to his face, a blue striped jumper with buttons, rocking, choking throughout the night until the final break of dawn, as if in a desperate attempt to not let her go, with a sorrow filled with memories of her laughter, his eyes closed, his head in his hands, hearing

The last leaf clings to the bough
Just one leaf, that's all there is now
And my last hope lives with that lonely leaf, lonely leaf
With the last leaf that clings to the bough

Last summer beneath this tree
My love said she'd come back to me
Before the leaves of autumn touched the ground, touched the ground
My love promised she'd be homeward bound

Then one by one, the leaves began to fall
And now that winter's come to call

The last leaf clings to the bough
Just one leaf, that's all there is now
Will my last hope fall with that lonely leaf, lonely leaf
With the last leaf, the last leaf
With the last leaf that clings to the bough
Bough, bough, bough

Later in life, with a need to turn a penny, Fr. Mario, who aged poorly, growing into something of a white-haired dwarf, though never less feisty, made something of a living taking seniors and wealthy subscribers on private bus tours and upper-scale travel trips to "historic destinations," specifically to Rome and the Vatican, which he headlined—he was the expert guide—billing them as "engaging yet relaxed experiences, tailored to the specific needs of elderly folk." Yearly, the troupe of them went on pilgrimage to Lourdes, slower paced excursions arranged for a lower-pace, shorter duration, skip-the-line entry individuals, allowing even wheel-chair accessibility. The subscribers loved him. He could explain anything and everything.

After he reached his twenties, Jean-Paul never saw Fr. Mario again—that is, except for one last time. The particular event was a family wedding in the small town of Hamilton, Massachusetts, on the occasion of a cousin on the Italian side of the family getting married. That day, Jean-Paul had taken his little brother outside for some air after the service when suddenly in a walkway in late afternoon, Fr. Mario appeared in his Roman collar, wearing all black. The short, flabby, overweight Silenus quickly came up short, gasping from a sudden speed walk. A slight din of grief percolated through the pleasant atmosphere. "Ho," he barked, looking smudged and thumb-worn in his atrocious clericals. The veins in his neck popped up. Jean-Paul felt sorry for him, before anything else, despite the cruel history he had suffered at his hands. He looked shrunken and dry with a feverish, dislocated look in his eyes, orbs still hot with a manic shine. He was badly balding, sprits of gray hair springing up. A full decade or more had gone by. What had the years wrought?

Over time, Fr. Mario had inevitably come to see himself in the light of his own lack of importance, with the jaded perception from years of meting out the kind of counseling and advice that asked of him a morality he knew he never possessed in first place. It was a cognition in its failure, mocking the enterprise, of a hollowness he could not, could never escape, reducing him to the shape of irony his squatness almost visibly resembled. It was only a question of time before he caught sight of himself to detect the ignominious person he was. He knew this and recognized that the boy knew he knew it, as well.

The priest gestured to the little boy and asked, "Who's the shorty pants?" Jean-Paul stood tall but still, slowly guiding his brother behind him. He stared at the priest coldly, his eyes shining water clear and said, "Don't you dare come near him." The priest, blinking, had stopped, frozen in his tracks like some malignant elf or malicious little goblin and, with the eerie pallor of candle wax, said not another word but wandered aimlessly down the cloistered walk clubbed by the shadow of each pillar as he passed it.

That was the last he ever saw of the man who, seeking out the faults of others, blamed them for everything, very like an arsonist who, lingering there to do so, discovers a fire he himself had started. Late in life, Fr. Mario became a rabid Republican, sought to cadge favors from various of his relatives, and grew old poorly. He never came by for his visits anymore.

Jean-Paul became a writer—what else?—as do many wounded souls, turning to fiction and poetry to try to get the second chance in life that Art offers. The scars of his early experiences never went away, ever. A brutal scar never leaves without a pock of discoloration. His own would always linger in his consciousness as a sign of incapacity and impairment that fostered but somehow prevented yearnings in the same way that a coldly black and immoderate rain makes a plea for sun. Haunting echoes of that nightly default became the stage on which, never failingly, the grotesque play of it was ever in rehearsal, a run-though or going over in a drill so incessant that the iterations were actual reminders like a role of the one Original Sin assigned to him.

Memory, with its purple deeps, which he could never fully sound—or, on the other hand, escape—for him always had an obituary eloquence. Like Pericles, he needed a helmet to conceal the dreaded infirmity in his head. Jean-Paul as he grew up lived with the reminders of it in the way of spontaneous and unlooked-for reflections—it fairly beckoned with recollections—always with its reverberations within him stating that, no matter how tall he may grow, how much of an effort made that way, it was in its short-lived way an impermanence to hide a dwarf.

None ever forget what is absorbed in those early years of existence. The powers of vivid and insistent remembrance, slow-moving, makes time, indeed, very long for children. What can one say of thoughts, unstable in their course, weighty in their bearing—impressions made conceptions, notions metamorphosing to beliefs, fleeting perceptions transmogrified into studied and unalterable convictions—that fill the bewildered, agitated soul of the ponderer when he or she is but nine or ten or eleven?

Jean-Paul had stopped bedwetting at one point, of course, but the echoes of that indisposition never ebbed. He remembered when he stopped, not by the date or the time, but by the mere fact of it. It happened with no more explanation than when it started. Simply, the fact stood. He had no need for cheering dreams. Facts were better than dreams.

Over the years, he grew to read about many famous bed-wetters, Fyodor Dostoevsky, Franklin Delano Roosevelt, Jonathan Swift, George Orwell, the author Stephen King, among others. It was an ancient curse, going as far back as the ancient Egyptians who employed a potion made from sugar canes, known for the capacity of their tenacious fibers for liquid-absorption, to concoct an effective material to cope with bedwetting. The shameful secret of his past never left him.

Novelist George Orwell, who wrote about it, early in his life realized, as did most sufferers with the problem, that one can do wrong with no intent to sin without ever discovering what one has done or even being responsible for it. The existential, burden came down to the understanding that there were sins that were too subtle to be explained, perhaps including others of a related kind that were too terrible clearly to be mentioned. The effects of his indisposition Jean-Paul traced to problems he faced much later in life. He was shy in high school. He never married.

Whenever it occurred to him, it was swept out of mind. He sought jobs that kept him away from people. Security guard. Night manager. A multiple-choice test that he took in high school, one arranged to gauge what best profession he should choose, assigned him: *forest ranger.*

After one hurries down the ribbon of road that leads out of the heart of life, you would not see the figure of Jean-Paul—he was missing. He who was more aware than most people of the intricacies of appearance had given it a pass, thank you. At any public gatherings, he could not be found. At dinner, the chair was empty. At a school dance? It didn't happen. On a Pullman, a curtained berth? Not. Grand family reunions? Never showed up. Socializing? Nope. As an emissary? To nowhere, maybe. With a group, at an assembly, in the company of others? No way, no how. He was absent to the party. It was in its guardedness, stealth, reticence, and secrecy a legacy he paradoxically shared with the main tormentor of his life. Donation: Fr. Mario.

The family stayed in touch, by mail and occasional visits, small unions. They never mentioned Fr. Mario—or maybe once or twice in an offhand and dismissive manner, always in a sarcastic manner and always with the same charity he always showed them. Eugene laughed. "You called him 'a dirty old piece of chewing gum on the leg of a chair.'" Most all were anti-clerical, rarely going to church anymore. Agatha declared that if priests turned their pants around instead of their collars there would be less illegitimate children in the world. Snorting, Franny laughed and told Jean-Paul that she was compelled to believe in the Devil if only to account for the existence of Fr. Mario, O. Carm.

One day Jean-Paul, years later, living alone in Vermont, received a note forwarded from his sister Franny, who had married a wealthy hotelier, that included the copy of a begging letter that she had recently received—strangely from Fr. Mario, who was then living in a nursing home and who said he needed money. Over the course of all the intervening years, no one in the family—not a single person—had been in touch with him. Decades had come and gone without any inquiries made in that direction, even at Christmas. By his late eighties, he had become indigent, neglected, living at a retirement home for old priests in Cleveland. One of the sentences his nephew remembered reading as he brought the letter as close to his face as he could bear, went, "I will be broke soon. Real poverty is at my door."

Did his nephew send him a check? Airmail a box of fresh winkles? Send off a bottle of Moxie or a carton of Old Gold cigarettes?

No, none of those things.

Nothing, in fact.

But he did fashion a reply. For his one response, Jean-Paul that very week sat down and wrote a poem, and, having the return address of the priest, mailed it the same day that it was finished. The poem went as follows:

"Fr. Mario"

"The infant will play over the hole of the cobra, and the young child will put its hand into the adder's den."

Isaiah 11:8

Fr. Mario used to visit our house.
His eyes were crossed like a shit-house mouse.
He put me down for his own scenario.
A wicked priest was Fr. Mario.

He was our uncle and jimmy-jawed,
Pugnacious, tiny, and deeply flawed.
He drank bottles of Moxie, case upon case,
And spoke to people an inch from their face.

His collar was white, his mind was dark.
He once on a stroll to Webster Park
Stopped in the street, pinching my arm,
And hissed, "You're doing your mother harm!"

I wet the bed which he wouldn't forgive.
He sucked cigarettes like a Broadway spiv.
He sent us on errands across the street
And gave lordly advice with a nasal bleat.

He pinched girls' bottoms, squeezed our hands,
Took thirds at dinner, gave brisk commands,
"Study Italian!" "Don't fork the bread!"
"Get an afternoon job!" "Try using your head!"

He knew all the perks of being a priest,
Took subscribers on tour to the Middle East,
Collected Hummels, finagled free roasts.
Meeting Franco was one of his boasts.

He bum-sucked the rich, cadged tickets for shows,
Kept shelves of good whiskey, row upon row,
Got turkeys at Christmas, sometimes the trees,
And, of course, for Mass cards took standard fees.

From all that he told us he ran the Church.
People in Rome if you wanted to search

Knew him at once, he said, merely by name.
Was it for me to question that fame?

My weaknesses, anyway, got him quite vexed.
He constantly shamed me on the subject of sex.
"Sissy," cried Mario, wagging his knife,
"Get married, you? You'd pee on your wife!"

"You think a woman will turn a blind eye
While you hang a wet mattress out a window to dry?"
My heart almost stopped, missing a beat.
"Sleep on a bed with a cold rubber sheet?"

His mockery more by far than his screams
Polluted my nights with nightmarish dreams.
The church I soon saw, when I came awake,
Was as tricky and cruel as a ten-foot snake.

At family gatherings for the longest time
(I never go but know chapter and rhyme)
Thanks are made to the good God above
And someone is chosen to discourse on love.

The homily's Mario's, now pathetic and old,
And he offers up prayers like a hypocrite bold.
He'll die in a bed surrounded by candles.
His coffin will shine and have real brass handles.

But in hell when he's screaming, almost insane,
And he calls upon someone to lessen the pain,
Howling for help from the hole in his face,
My dream's to appear and administer grace.

It's a symmetry due him without any reserve,
A fate one can't say he doesn't deserve.
Let eternity balance time and degree.
Dante himself would be quick to agree.

I'll locate the priest in the midst of the fire,
Roasting like Dives in a scorching hot pyre.
Seeing me suddenly, what will he think?
There'll be no Moxie to give him to drink.

Why not then do what I'm good at, OK,
That which he knew me for day after day?
I'll prove myself useful, if somewhat uncouth,
Stand on his head, and say, "Open your mouth."

Raafat, the Hot Dog Vendor

"Punishment is justice for the unjust."
Saint Augustine

The hot dog water makes all the difference. It was a frequent thought of Raafat's as he stood by casually stirring the bobbing frankfurts in one of the buvette sinks of his mobile cart trailer and vending-stand kiosk with its tall scarlet umbrella on curb corners in and around busy 9th Avenue, his food concession. A poor immigrant from Gaza, the vendor had emigrated to New York City and was fortunate enough—favored, as he saw it—to have had a connected family friend to help get a vending unit license, hard to achieve, in order to run his food-cart, squeezing out a small living. Exterminating Gaza had always been Israel's plan, but when it was made official, Raafat and his family desperately sought to leave. The poor little slice of a country has been leveled flatly, with every last concrete building destroyed, and 75,000 or more people slaughtered. The safety he had found made all the difference. How was it that had he had the luck, unlike so many others, to find such security and protection? As his old professor once told him, "The only rule—is the exception."

New York City was a diverse, live-or-die city. Traffic was constant, honking horns and street-crossing mobs. There was constant noise and sirens, clamor and clash, a hubbub perennial, sidewalks teeming with roiling crowds moving like red-eyed cicadas. One is forced to *face* it there. Stick it out or leave. In your face!

There was much competition. Serving every corner of the big city, hot dog die-hards over time popped up on just about every street corner, guarding their aluminum carts like special workhorses. This was Manhattan, after all, where pace and tempo determined success. In a way Raafat had a leg up on the street rivalry, for he chose to serve not only classic all-beef but also pork hot dogs. It was true that beef offered a robust flavor profile with a hint of sweetness, but the pork franks offered a more subtle taste with a fattier, nutmeg flavor. The choice between beef and pork boiled down to individual preferences, of course, with most customers favoring the boldness of beef but yet others savoring the tenderness of pork.

He had done his homework, experimenting with popular brands. He tried Ball Park dogs and Nature's Promise, sampled Kirklands, and for a short while sold Sabretts. Boar's Head Uncured were tasty, yet expensive and wanting in snap. In the end, he settled on Teton Ranch Bun-Length Uncured Beef dogs and Wild Fork 100% all-pork bangers, slowly simmered in his "dirty" water. He sold them with black bean chili, purple onions, jerk sauce, squirt cheeses, fresh sauerkraut, and all kinds of exotic yellow and brown mustards. A truly great hot dog, to fit the perfect profile and appease the average customer without revealing any nasty or unlooked-for surprises, should be tender, juicy, and have a good aural snap to them. It also must be meaty, fatty, and savory but never too oily, salty, or greasy.

Most vendors, like Raafat, served a humble dog. He offered homemade chili, purple onions, and both yellow and brown mustards—seasonings were a closely guarded secret in the business—and had even tried blends of garlic powder, dried parsley, and oregano. A good hot dog, for a balanced spiced profile, should possess a subtle hint of liquid smokiness, one not too garlicky or oniony. It should not be hot pink nor sticky to the touch, but rather feature the natural brownish-red hue of good quality meat, having a skin with a nice bite to it, firm, yet juicy, never tough or chewy. On big holidays like July 4th or around Christmastime, he splurged and served "Danger Dogs," ordinary franks made alluringly delicious when wrapped in bacon and topped with jalapeños, bell peppers, and onions.

He learned to tailor for customers various kinds of MLB ballpark hot dogs—Arizona Diamondback hot dogs (four slices of bacon, tomato, and *salsa verde*); meat-sauce-topped Detroit Tiger Coneys (bell pepper, cumin, ground beef); LA Dodger-style Halo Dog (wrapped in bacon, topped with charro beans, *pico de gallo*, and shredded cheese); Chicago-style hot dogs (loaded with onions, relish, green peppers, and a pickle spears). He even perfected bratwurst sliders with a honey-mustard topping on pretzel slider buns!

Vendor's carts had to meet laws. There were rules and regulations. They all had to be kept 18 inches from a curb, with a 12'-wide clear path. A food-handler's permit was required, of course, and licenses displayed. Inspectors checked. A recent crackdown on unlicensed hawkers and bootleggers had raised the typical vendor permit fee for prime spots near Madison Square Garden or Central Park or the areas in and near Times Square to as much as six figures a year. An average price of a hot dog had jumped to $5 a pop. Every sold item meant a profit of $1 to $2. Sell 200 dogs a day at the average price, and you've earned upwards of $400. It was being on your feet all day. The work was hard

There were rules and regulations, indeed. A seller or street merchant in New York City could leave his cart unattended for 20 minutes only, a rule against tampering, but being gone longer than that would result in a vendor losing his permit. No carts could be left on a street overnight. A truly helpful benefit for Raafat was that over-night he could conveniently park his conveyances in his good friend, Midhat's adjoining alley

Raafat's fare was tasty, both pork and beef. He had sold 3,684 dogs in the first year. The water and steam pans in his portable cart were both heated by an efficient propane gas system, which allowed him the freedom to serve passersby anywhere, although his location was far from perfect on that score, not being near an MLB ballpark or wide city greens with tourists. He always rose early, before his girls headed off to school each day. It was his delight to capture the fleeting moment when the rising sun, like the splendid Palestinian copper coin he kept in his shoe, perfectly aligned with the city's s grid each morning. After two years, he had made many friends with the locals. His business was mainly street customers passing, including people from several synagogues near Alphabet City.

Hassidics were strange. They weren't permitted to drive or use any electric devices, or cook, shop, or even carry large amounts of money outside their houses. Men wore long knee-length black coats, wheels of fur on their heads, and long curls by their pointed ears. To ensure that they had access to kosher food at all times, they often carried plastic bags, which allowed them to lug their own utensils, containers, or packaged kosher food items, when not eating at home. Raafat rarely ever saw their women. Only the husband had the power to issue a Jewish divorce. The women could not even ride bicycles. As is the case with other Jewish Orthodox communities, married women had to cover their hair. Different Hasidic sects did so in a variety of bizarre styles. Some may wear hats (but never wigs), others may wear wigs (but never hats), and some may require the double covering of a hat on top of a wig. Then there were *tichels* (headscarves) and other forms of head covering.

He had heard that such couples always slept in separate beds, were not hygienic—they rarely bathed or showered—and he had been told that it is was virtually unanimous among halachic authorities that one could not even flush a toilet on Shabbat, because doing so would be a violation of a thing called *tzoveiah*, a Jewish prohibition whereby the water would be "colored" by the very act. Water, again! reflected Raafat, as he stood stirring the wieners pork and beef, in their adjacent buvettes. It somehow made all the difference, even with these very peculiar people who bought his franks, even if only beef ones.

Raafat understood and openly accepted the odd dress of the Hassids. It was part of their religion, and aspect of their faith, habiliments called upon by their God. And yet it was difficult indeed to believe any people could or actually would choose to dress like that in public, a "fashion," to use an extravagant word for it, so visually queer, so freakish, so intentionally deviant. It invited scorn as being a direct insult to any rational style of dress in history. A man wearing side curls, falling to his jaw below a ludicrous high round hat of fur, called a *shtreimel,* the black satin jackets and buttoned-up white shirts—no necktie—all hung over a fringed prayer shawl? Who could believe that any sane person would wear such an outfit? Pale bearded creatures, thin and childlike, with just a hint of facial hair? They were ghoulish.

Worse than capricious, it seemed grotesque. No wonder mirrors in their houses were covered to avoid distractions caused by their outward appearance! Taste, in an almost ringing, shape-changing hideousness, seemed to be banished in what seemed a mocking configuration of dress—it seemed less clothes than a visual punishment, so repellent in basic conception as to be almost a satanic fiction in the way of anti-style.

Lately, however, Raafat had had an unnerving experience. It was an inevitable contingency of trade, he thought. One man alone among his paying customers began giving him a hard time, a dissenter who began bothering him about his hot dogs, his country, his very existence. It was the same person who when no one was around actually bought pork hot dogs, although he was a Hasidic Jew. It was a marvel even one of them would do so, for as Raafat knew, it was an impiety, worse, a blasphemy—in this case it seemed to be a personal challenge for the stranger, to show that he was worldly.

Jews, he knew, ate no shellfish, pork products, or food that has not been slaughtered in the correct way, which was known as *shechitah,* or so he was told by his close Palestinian friend, Midhat, who had lived in Manhattan for years, ran the nearby newsstand, and whose brother had been the one instrumental in helping his get his "Hawker and Peddler" food-handler's license after he passed the food protection course for mobile vendors and for which he paid a fee of $200. A Hassidic who is faced with no choice but to use a toilet whose water will be colored by flushing, he heard, had very few options to choose from. There are grounds to be lenient with the disinfecting devices that are affixed to the top of the tank rather than the bowl of the toilet. This is because when the toilet is flushed, the water is not "colored" right away. The coloring only occurs after the water in the tank is refilled and reaches the top. The delay between the flushing of the toilet and the coloring of the water, a concept known as *gramma,* is what forms the basis for leniency in extenuating circumstances.

Raafat was bemused, smiling, as he stirred the aromatic hot dog water, redolent of meat and oil, and he savored its briny smell.

Water he knew about, he had crossed the ocean staring at the water. Thousands have lived without love, without shelter, but no one could live without water. Animals, too—except maybe the koala or the kangaroo rat, which never drinks water but gets moisture from the seeds it eats and also has highly efficient kidneys, at least so he had once read.

Nothing is softer or more flexible than precious water, the most valuable resource in the world, yet for all of its adaptability and pliancy nothing can resist it. It has a perfect memory, does water, and in its waking accommodation and give is always seeking to get back to where it was. We humans are made up of around 60% water. Our destiny is linked with water, for no water equals no life. Water is the driving force of nature in which we are all immersed, reborn in renewal, by baptism, with grace. Drizzle, mizzle. Sleet, stream. He had dealt with radioactive water for a thesis. The tree that grows beside the running water, always fresher, yields far more fruit. As a rainbow lifts over the ocean, it expresses thanks with its colors for the motion it has squeezed from the waters of its flight. Its blessedness is as eternal as its glory and is indestructible, Raafat knew, for the rising waters will one day come and eventually cover and remake the world!

Water holds memory, Raafat knew, just as acutely as he himself did. The phenomenon is maintained with the element possessing the ability to "remember" substances once dissolved in it—in the way, say, antennae can hold a frequency—even after those substances have been removed or diluted beyond the point of detection. Conscious, compassionate, essential to spiritual evolution. In Taoism, water is the Tao itself—soft yet powerful, always flowing, never resisting, as in Hinduism, where rivers like the Ganges are embodiments of the divine, washing away not just impurities but karmic burdens.

A Palestinian proverb goes, "Be shapeless, like water. If you put water into a cup, it becomes the cup. Put water into a bottle, and it becomes the bottle. Let water serve you the way you wish. Let the form be the figure." Be like water, thought Raafat, deliberating, counseling himself, making its way through cracks. Do not be assertive, simply adjust to the object, and you shall find a way around and through and between. If nothing within you stays rigid, outward things will disclose themselves.

Sturdy, Raafat was whip-thin. Rangy, muscular, and a bit short, with a fine forehead, eager questing eyes, and a face that registered every change of feeling. He was married, with two children, eleven-year-old girls. It happened that he had a crippled foot. He loved America and the opportunities it offered for enterprise. He was a sensitive man. He loved music, took his children to concerts. He was also deeply proud, even in exile, of his own country, Palestine, now so lost, which years ago had even allowed him to attend college for a year, where he had studied physics and quantum mechanics at Al-Aqsa University, before it had been bombed and leveled and utterly destroyed by the vengeful Israelis.

He demonstrated a strong aptitude, at least according to his teachers. His scientific field had been water, its variations, the nature of it, black water and artesian, hard, purified, distilled. He knew about osmosis, reverse osmosis, seawater, deionized, and grey water, and when the class began a study of atomic material, he accumulated a knowledge of "heavy water." He knew about aerial dispersal, chain reactions, fallout.

Although water shortage was a problem in Israel, that country managed to ensure the availability of clean drinking water for all its citizens, and also to hoard a surplus of water that it sold to nearby nations like Jordan. But with genocidal intentions, Israel, having bombed and bulldozed all of Gaza, had systematically weaponized water against Palestinians, including all electricity, food, and fuel sent there in the way of humanitarian aid. The entire infrastructure had been gutted.

At least 75,000 Palestinians have been killed in Gaza by Israeli tanks, bombings, and flamethrowers. More than fifty-four thousand children are presently malnourished in that small, beleaguered nation. The famine they are facing is entirely man-made, to which the USA is indifferent. Ten thousand Palestinians slaughtered by Israel were left buried in the mounds of cement rubble of their homes in the flattened strip of Gaza, probably the world's largest mass grave in history, all in the absence of an effective role by international organizations and humanitarian bodies, especially those concerned with the issue of missing persons, in light of the ongoing escalating humanitarian disaster.

The United Nations estimated that the average Gazan was living on only 3 liters of water per day for all needs—well below the United Nation's emergency standard of 15 liters. Palestinians were daily dying of thirst.

It was as bad, and growing worse, in the West Bank, Palestinian land but sections of which the "annexing" Israelis stole daily. Israelis, including those living in thieved settlements, use an average of 247 liters of water in a day of glut per person—three times that used by Palestinians there, which amounted to 82.4 liters a person. In Palestinian communities that are not hooked up to the water grid, average daily water consumption is a mere 26 liters per person, much like the average in world disaster zones. 92% of Palestinians in the West Bank store water in tanks on their rooftops to counter the chronic water shortage. In total, Israelis consumed 10 times the amount of water consumed by Palestinians in the West Bank in 2020—although the Israeli population is only three times larger.

Lamentation was fruitless.

There was no solution, and never would be, Raafat knew, because the problem went much deeper than politics. Here, two entities—two divergent worlds—collided. The Israelis, being Jews, can only comprehend—from the book of Leviticus—that a "neighbor" is defined specifically as "*a fellow countryman.*" Whereas the Christian concept of neighbor—a complete antithesis to that parochial and basically self-serving conviction, dogma to a Jew—is that of *a member of the human family*, which is made one in Christ, as believers understand from Jesus' specific teaching. To the Jew, this is an outlandish, indeed, subversive abstraction, absurdly foreign to him, impossible to grasp, and in many, if not most cases, actually resented as a false doctrine and, indeed, one born of a devious and corrupt theology. Christians, who have been asked to take off the "old" and to put on a "new self," are taught the opposite, to see the reflection of Christ in every human being, who implicitly demands our charity. To a compassionate Christian, there is no room for distinction between Korean and Frenchman, between Cuban and Greek, between Palestinian and Jew.

For his intelligence, Raafat's job as a street vender was beneath him. Findings over time repeatedly proved brave Palestinians to have a long-running reputation as the world's "best-educated refugees," a claim frequently made by international organizations. Particularly but not exclusively in the Middle East, the Palestinian people have long had a strong reputation as high-performing graduates, proficient most of them in at least two or more languages, with students frequently going on to pursue successful careers in science, medicine, business or engineering. At the same time, the Palestinians are the world's largest refugee population, with the longest-running case of protracted displacement.

The establishment of Israel in 1948 displaced and dispossessed more than 750,000 Palestinians, with large numbers left to survive in isolated, desolate camps across the region. As well as seeking immediate shelter and food, refugees quickly turned to the matter of education for their children in exile. Many camp refugees had been farmers in Palestine. Having lost the land capital that had once been their primary currency for generations, Palestinians now looked to education as an alternative form of social capital. They saw it as a necessary tool for reversing their displacement and dispossession. Refugees quickly coalesced on education as a possible route out of their crisis, both individually and collectively.

How did it happen, then, that a large-scale, desperate refugee population, many of whom survived for decades in detention camps, became so highly educated? The answer is simple. It was the direct result of Israeli cruelty.

But failure also clarifies what matters, teaches more than success ever could, instills resilience, builds courage. Failure ultimately means that you have tried. The umbrella set up over his cart meant Raafat would never surrender.

His red umbrella, some gaiety, had been a good idea, bringing attention to his hot dog deluxe mobile food cart, six feet high, with glass doors, including a special ice-bin with a drain for cool temperatures during the summer months, as well as room for bottom storage. It also had a catering trailer and a kiosk stand, for extra use. The hot dog pan was a sweet stew-water of salt and oil, with a scent of butter, redtop, and timothy. Herbs flavored it. He would sometimes drop in a bay leaf, occasionally a pickle spear for flavoring. It gave a heady, almost medicinal-type plant water, redolent of the best meat, with a beckoning warmth in which one could even steep tea or tisanes, a drinkable beverage in its own right. The fragrance! Rain-lily, a ferulic acid like mustard seed fungus with the fragrance of minerals! He has tested it all. Good hot dog water is slightly alkaline, because its pH is a bit higher than the neutral value of 6.14. At $100°$ C the pH of pure water is 6.14, which is "neutral."

One day, out of the blue, one of the Hassids in line—the same aggrieved man who, impatiently waiting, had often shouted out to demand of those ahead of him that the line keep moving—suddenly blurted out, "On November 9, 1938, in Nazi Germany 96 Jews were killed and a hundred more injured. My own uncle from Poland was one of them. A thousand synagogues were burned."

Everyone turned in alarm.

"What has this to do with me?" softly questioned Raafat, shocked, holding his frank tongs in mid-air. Onlookers stood with raised brows. A small group had taken notice. Many in line had seen this man before, howling at passersby about racism. He was a tall, bearded Hassidic fat man with thick eyeglasses, hair curls, fat liver lips wearing a long black coat over a tie-less white shirt and a peculiar cylindrical black hat.

"*Uncle*," whispered Raafat, hands high, in an attempt at humor, seeking to diffuse the scene and spreading out his hands in a sky appeal.

"Don't say stupid to me, stupid," snapped the grizzler and departed. A Mr. Gorson quietly put his hand on Raafat's arm in sympathy and said, "I have seen that same man do this many times with others—you must be careful, he is aggressive—and have devised a nickname for him: *Chevalier d'Epp*—Sir Stupid."

It turned out the objector was a man named Maggid. He was a well-known detractor among locals there and was the embodiment of spite. Queue-jumping and rudely butting in line in front of others he felt was his right. It was disturbing. More than a public scandal, it was cause for alarm. Customers had quickly begun to walk away. This kind of display had now become a daily occurrence, and the vendor's mind now, in an unsettling way, was plagued by disparaging, increasingly hostile treatment being often leveled at him by this one particular Hasidic Jew who had now started coming around almost every day, rarely stopping to purchase a hot dog without lingering there in order to make some kind of slandering and malign abuse. He was hugely fat and absurdly tall with an obnoxious, defiant, but alarmingly uncontrolled profile that had in it something of the cross, intrusive, menacing expression of a practiced stalker, which seemed to say he would brook no refusal of whatever it was that he demanded. A tortuous mind seemed to fit the mad Orthodox outfit, coat, and hat.

As many passersby came to wonder, tourists, as well, how did such a bizarre attire ever come to be, a garb of such freakish and uninviting regalia—a *fagotage* ludicrous in the extreme—that it actually seemed to *provoke* insult.

Always it seemed, by being the loudest, he seemed to be first in line. "You raccoon people, hawking is all and only what you do, *nu?!* *Links-shtivl!* Left-footed boots. A *luft gesheft* —a business founded on air." As time passed, the man's remarks became even crueler and more personal, for no reason whatsoever. *"Shvimers* and floaters!" he barked. "Who can say what you charge and don't? Look at this filth here. You, wrap my frank in a *brivke*, hokay? *Gornisht mit gornisht!* Nothink with nothink, is vhat!"

What did *hassid* mean in Arabic? It was strange. The word خَاسِد (ḥāsid) was equivalent to the active participle of حسد *ḥasad,* "to be envious."

Raafat tried his best to put it all in perspective. But he was soon nervous every morning setting up his cart. Was it not the fatal lot of refugees to suffer? Exile meant that. If expatriation did not mean that, what then did it mean? Did not Jesus himself go out of his way to leave the land of Israel for the only known time in his ministry when He walked to Tyre and Sidon, all that way to exert an act of charity? The only thing we know that Jesus ever did there was meet with a woman whose daughter was demon-possessed. And now in his own fugitive life, Raafat seemed to be facing a similar demon.

Raafat knew from his studies that the name *Israel* literally meant "He strives with God." *Competes with! Struggles against!* An unholy tribe, by definition, unlike his own people, he thought. That caviling and contentious people, he knew, even Our Lord denounced out of hand, saying, "O Jerusalem, Jerusalem, thou that killest the prophets, and stonest them which are sent unto thee, how often would I have gathered thy children together, even as a hen gathereth her chickens under her wings, and ye would not!"

He had never forgotten the facts of his own nation and its significance in the role it played in history. After St. Paul had undergone his dramatic "vision," and was knocked off his horse, as later he specifically wrote, where did he go? He rose and went to a self-imposed exile to *Arabia,* for three years—the kingdom of the non-Israelite Nabateans, just south of Gaza. St. Paul returned, it should be noted, not to Jerusalem, but to Damascus— and beginning his holy mission wrote predominantly to proselytize for Jesus Christ and His redemption to *non*-Jewish groups, Raafat's own people. These facts, almost never mentioned, are often ignored. He traveled in caravans of families and traders who came to be called "Arabs," steppe-dwellers, Semitic speakers—Ishmaelites, not Israelites—who spoke Aramaic in Syria and Nabatea, finding a provisional, constantly shifting domicile with, for, and among them, trying to square his new sacred, God-drenched calling with his murderous past, a revelation he'd undergone on a scale not unlike the announcement to Moses on Mt. Sinai.

Again, as his old professor had told once him, "Read the Epistle of Barnabas!" It was something that Raafat proceeded to do, who suddenly realized what the scholar knew. For him, the Old Testament was a Christian, not a Jewish book. The Jews misunderstood its teachings, and always had. A hardhearted, ignorant, willful, and disobedient people, they had been so since the days of Moses. When he smashed the first set of the Ten Commandments, that was the end of the Jews' covenant with God. It was never restored.

The central message of the Epistle is that the writings comprising the Hebrew bible were, from even back then, written for use by *Christians* rather than Israelites and, by extension, the Jews. Barnabas points out that Jews misinterpreted their own law—*halakha*—by applying it literally. Barnabas posits that the Jews broke their covenant from the very beginning and were misled by an evil angel. As Barnabas stated:

> "I ask you this one thing . . . to give heed to yourselves now, and not to liken yourselves to certain persons who pile up sin upon sin, saying that our covenant remains to them also. Ours it is; but they lost it in this way for ever, when Moses had just received it…But they lost it by turning unto idols. For thus saith the Lord: Moses, Moses, come down quickly; for thy people whom thou broughtest out of the land of Egypt hath done unlawfully. And Moses understood and threw the two tables from his hands; and their covenant was broken in pieces, that the covenant of the beloved Jesus might be sealed unto our hearts in the hope which springeth from faith in Him." (4:6–8)

But in his job Raafat had his own headaches, problems he had to deal with. Certain Jews, seeking discounts, questioned his cleanliness and complained that there were nitrates and sodium in the hot dog water. Others claimed the dogs were rubbery and flavorless meat sticks, usually the very same customers who were always demanding that he *never* give them pork. The only one who loudly demanded beef dogs, always calling for one as if by megaphone, was this same tall, glowering Hassid, sporting a bearded chin that would not take no for an answer, Mr. Maggid. The obscenity, however, was that in secret, with no one around—for he was a hypocrite of the first order—he would order *pork* hot dogs. Again, it so proved, the only rule—is the exception.

And once again he had cut in line.

"Can't you please wait, like everybody else?" asked a poor lady standing there.

Maggid sneered and grunted, "More everything forever."

The Orthodox Jew's insults were profane beyond the telling. The pinna of Raafat's ears reddened at insults, but he made no reply. "That frankfurter"—he pointed a nail—"should have a fucking inner temperature of 140 degrees Fahrenheit," said Maggid with a nasty bark. He was suddenly wagging an angry finger. "No, no!.

Look, dark! Give me *that one*, the rosy one, and use the tongs there, not your filthy fork."

Seeking to appease him Raafat, shrugged, saying, "Fully cooked hot dogs will have wrinkly skin, sir, and so *will* become darker in color."

Fat, untidy Maggid squinted at the sidewalk vendor. "You hawkers—"

"I am a vendor," replied Raafat, straightening his shoulders.

"—huckster, peddler, chapman, costermonger, same thing, wolf, cheat. *Shmegegge!* Fumble fingers A stupid business. *Luft gesheft!* A business founded in air! Water yellow. Shaved ice unclean!" He wailed, "I report you to Shop Safe Act the same as look at you." The Hassid conceived argument as monologue and found the process of learning only to be confirmation of what he already knew.

"Arab learn nothing!" sneered Maggid.

"Palestine having been the highway between Africa and Asia," softly replied Raafat who took exception to this, "allowed the Hebrews to absorb much of the custom, culture, and religious ideas of travelers from Egypt, by which Moses himself received much education. Read Acts 7:22. It was in this very same way that the prophet Muhammad in his early years gathered knowledge working as a humble attendant on his uncle's caravan journeys with merchandise to the market towns in the northwest of Arabia. For two thousand years, the Egyptians were looking forward to a new King, a great deliverer, the beginnings of a messianic vision—1500 years before it appeared in Israel! In your own Bible, Proverbs 23:1-3 is almost a literal quotation from ancient Egyptian inscriptions and proverbs. When Isaiah 10:15 asks, 'Shall the axe boast itself against him that heweth therein? Shall the saw magnify itself against him that wieldeth it?' it was borrowed from an early Egyptian tablet."

Raafat drew closer. "A papyrus in the British Museum, the 'Wisdom' of Amenemope, ancient Egyptian pharaoh of the 21st Dynasty who ruled from 1001 to 992 B.C., was translated into

Hebrew, and significant parts found their way into your Hebrew Bible. Jeremiah 17-5:8 was adapted from his writings, as was the first Psalm, as well. Egyptian wisdom literature served as an inspiration for several ancient Israelite books, including Deuteronomy, Psalms, and Proverbs. You see, ancient writings of priceless value were not limited to a 'chosen people' as the accepted sole revelation but handed down and channeled to the world by other proclaiming voices, like my people."

The New York City heat could be merciless, and the streets shimmering in haze rose like a thick invisible weed off the black tar. Then, later, it would be blue with rain. That was merely the weather, never not a factor of the job. Summer was passing. At noontime, Maggid appeared as usual, and, of course, always with a complaint, causing rupture in the waiting line. Now people hissed him. "I smell exhaust in the steam! Rotting bananas, burnt foil," angrily complained the tall, hovering customer, giving off an odor of what seemed like off-true cheese, but nothing at all like the white-brined *nabulsi* that Raafat, when a boy, had eaten fried in oil. This Maggid stood there, bulking in front of others, nagging.

The very own smell of the Hassid was acrid, with an ammonia cat-urine stink to it. "I want sweetness in nosh is what, you hear me," he grizzled, returning one hot dog for dressing, reaching out with an extended crab-like hand, its claws and long nippers bristling with hard, long, sharp, ramified, and menacing rugosities.

He demanded two more hot dogs, another bun.

"Thank you," said Raafat.

"More relish!"

Dubious, the Hassid held up what he was given, looked out of the pebble of a small eye, and commanded, "Give me a *brivke!* Putz." Angry customers walked away. Others behind him began to stare, openly shocked. "A parcel of *chazerai*. Junkfood, trash. Leftovers—*oysshis*," Maggid bellowed held out dollars. "*Nem di gelt!*" he cried, impatiently wagging the cash. "Take the money! *Nem di gelt!* Take it. Take!"

It was insufferable, the insults, Raafat reflected, as he stirred the fragrant hot water filled with juices. It was almost a basic *brodo*—or Arabic *maraq*—a gentle bouillon fragrant enough to cook, and flavor, gnocchi or semolina dumplings, an infusion, concentrated with some high-end spices and meat oil in the mix, a highly scented liquid, that was technically a stock one could actually drink. Raafat had done so very often.

At times, he added beef or vegetable cubes for flavor. A perfectionist, he also tried enhancing it with smidgens of avocado oil and even duck-fat. The longer the hot dogs simmered, he knew, the crispier they were. He quivered the water with his tongs. It unfurled and spread the sweet components in the water, a sweetening maneuver, and as he did so Raafat found it almost comic to reflect in sweet memory that when a mere infant he had even been bathed in hot dog water, and even growing up, when to save family money, there was no alternative!

Dark swirls of moving water, he contemplated, elemental runnels racing or bubbling in a swift darkness bearing a cockle boat, the immortal and infinite switchback thrust of water's elemental compound with its wild, wide-ranging, quickening capacities to buoy up, flood, or drown. Its *soif* for life was also part of water in the deep mystery of its blue-black needs! Raafat lived for memory—and to remember.

He knew well and remembered the old axiom: "*Corpora non agunt nisi soluta*"—bodies do not act, unless dissolved. Without fire, which liquefies and vaporizes them—without water, which dissolves them—there could be no action of bodies one upon another, no combinations or decompositions. Raafat leaned in to smell the fragrant warm water—*infusoriae!*—almost ocean-sweet with the heat increasing the phosphorescent faculty of these *noctiluques,* tangy, tasty, zesty, seasoned.

One sunny autumn morning, a stunningly lovely young woman appeared in line with a lilting laugh and a box of nougats for him. She was the pretty cousin of his best friend, Midhat

Kamal—her name, beautifully, was Fourth, a Palestinian Christian name. A yellow ray of sunshine filled Raafat's heart whenever she stopped by, as often she did when impulsively she skipped out of the building in which she worked. It left him with a guilty but concomitantly concerned feeling of joy and delight to see her beauty alone in such a big, noisy city.

"Buxom as fat badger," observed nosy Maggid, leering at her as she strode away.

"I don't like that."

"Oh, you don't, Mr. Hot Dog You? Your business *me*! Give me three wieners!" Maggid surreptitiously turned to make sure that no one was watching, or was at least close enough to hear him, before he ordered with a mutter below his breath, "Pork ones." Raafat knew that he had heard right. He held up a bun with a questioning pause. "This is what I say—you don't hear? *Trefah* food? I don't give this two shits, hokay?" snapped the angry Hassid, stepping back, pale, pimply face, his underlip extruded in a head butt gesture in reinforcing indignation, his enfilading eyes like bullets from a face of hairy ambush. He swallowed. "You judging me, *tchakh-chakh*? Maggid snarled, "I eat what I want, not like a dirty Arab who shun pork." He pointed, making slicing gestures. "Onions. Relish, lots." He tapped a hard shoe, waiting impatiently. "No, no, lots *more* relish, you! *Maroco sakin!*"

It was a mad corner, this area of the city, jumping with Hasidim. Many American Jews even feel a kind of uneasy cultural revulsion toward them, an unsettling faction who represented to them an atavistic narrow-mindedness. Broad hats. Long beards. Sidelocks. Dangling fringes. Raafat had begun to notice that many of them were characteristically impatient, arrogant, noxious, with an irksome sense of privilege, a long reach, and no end of inordinate demands to be served. They would be told nothing, paid no attention to other customers, jumping ahead in line, but this one was worse than others of his sect.

Maggid wolfed the first one, ate it, and farted. He placed his humid dollars on the console, took the two other hot dogs fatly encompassed in one fat hand, and headed across the street, only to look back to make a final salvo. "I know you park too far the curb," he snarled, his long ugly beard wagging with each pronounced word. It was essentially, existentially diabolical. He spread his hands. "Must eighteen inches from. You fool nobody!"

Spitting on the pavement, he proceeded to grind his big black shoe in the sputum and bawled, "*Rug merchant!! Palsbara! Arabush!—go back home!*"

That moment opened a deep wound in Raafat that was hard to heal, and it had now become a sore.

He expected politeness. Rudeness of this kind far exceeded anything that he had ever seen. It was way beyond the pale. Most often kindness was given, a phenomenon that over time exhibited periodicity, praiseworthy in passersby who in the busy city were usually rushed. Over the years, he had seen into people. He was quick to notice changes of mood or small betrayals of character. He could sense depression in his customers. Anxiety. Eventually, disturbed, Raafat Baroudi on a given evening in the community discussed rumors with Akmad, the flower seller, another close friend, that this same menacing Maggid in the long black coat had been bothering Midhat's pretty cousin. Akmad was dismissive of the fact. "Raafat," he said, negatively shaking his head, "I tell you the man is a neuter. A eunuch."

Maggid was a street monster. It seemed an almost uncanny fact that his one mission on this earth seemed to be notoriously singling out the poor street vendor for abuse, an ongoing and concerted racist attack against an Arab foe. He walked tilted forward as if he were walking uphill, with knees that never seemed to straighten all the way. His dark greasy hair fell against his face which he cast out of his eyes by jerking his head, as his unshaven beard bristled. Being near him was offensive, for he smelled of dirt, oil, and grease. Hanging by his ears were two curls. gray, hideous strands like snakes. Steam seemed to rise from his long black coat and tall queer black hat, called a *spodik*. He was an unremitting liar, a hovering boor, a bigoted falsifier. What evil magician, or devilish imp, had appeared in his life? There was something wrong, even histrionically, with a man wearing multiple hats.

Worse, even his fellow Hassids found him fearful, giving him wide berth. Many of Raafat's customers were kind and gentle Jews, and he scandalized them, as he did most of the other customers, for Maggid never hesitated to step rudely in front of them, shouldering them aside, to order with a loud voice and an extended arm at the end of which was a wagging finger—even, secretly, on the sly, a hot dog of pork, which was a taboo in his religion. Others always took Hebrew National beef.

Raafat had great affection for his customers and knew their tastes. Many of then ran out of buildings around noon, smiling, to make their purchases. Mr. Jesudowich, the hatter. The Collier twins. Ed Shields. Dorcas, from the apartment upstairs. Caro. Chet Klope. Youlgaroff, the butcher. Binx, his Yellow Cab friend. Donald "Duck" Duff. Cyril Estes. Alexandria Hong, a young model for whom he had great affection. They were, all of them, as loyal, steadfast, and tried-and-true as could be. Old Mr. Steenrod, kind Charlie Calhoun, Mr. Fanaritus, the Moon family. What signified, as well, there were also good-hearted Hassidic customers, who, gathering in the streets, offered him no trouble.

He had names for others who showed up daily for a hot dog and a drink. It gave a song to the day to name them. There was "Lionhead," Harry, Larry, and Barry, firemen from the engine house across the street, public sector people. "Moe Joe Rising," a black street sweeper who came by every day. One couple Raafat referred to as "10," husband and wife, because, when they came forward walking, the two of them resembled that number—he was tall and thin and she was short and fat. There was "Asterisk," a dwarf, "Flutie," a big blond, claiming that Nathan's Famous Skinless Beef Franks were too salty, enthusiastically maintained that the boiling weenie water that Raafat used was the best. He had long experience selling them and had long remained convinced that, while toppings are one of the great joys of a frankfurt, no truly great hot dog couldn't be eaten in a bun alone.

A grossly overweight twosome, ugly Kurt and Liz, tourists, from Philadelphia, vulgar rednecks, shovers to the front, would pound home three and four hot dogs at a time, stuffing their mouths, blocking other customers while loudly farting. There was angry Maureen, head-wrapped like Louise Nevelson, who bellowed for more onions. A grinning weirdo, Andrew Funn, was another muscling-in type, an elbower, impatient to eat. Mr. Schinz, whom people nicknamed "Left and Right," since he wobbled this way and that as he walked, insisted on pepper and onion relish, which Raafat had to buy to keep his business.

The worst of the lot by far, of course, was this obstreperous Maggid with his bobbing effrontery, always squeezing others out of the way. Mrs. Kern, a milliner, once hit him with her purse as he did so, and he slapped her, and she wept. A professor, an extremely loyal everyday patron, as well as a congenial one, who also had been often rudely pushed aside the very same way, remarking on the bully, waited until he left and, buttonholing Raafat, soberly quoted Shakespeare to him, saying "'Such whales have I heard on o' th' land, who never leave gaping till they've swallowed the whole parish, church, steeple bells and all.'"

There came another day that proved to be troublesome when Fourth popped up to buy a hot dog when suddenly, lamentably, in his pushy, presumptive way Maggid, leering, sidled up to her and began to talk. Pulling coins out of the pocket of his long enveloping black coat, he offered to buy her a hot dog. Raafat, who always pressed them free on her, with an interposing arm, objected, when Maggid, kicking the cart, sneered and pointed toward the vendor's cap and, taking in his club foot, also took the occasion to mock his faith. The Jew hated the hot-dog seller and said, "You an immigrating, jealous, vicious, satanically gifted dwarf, are a pilot fish of the Arab world, yes, you." He heaped ridicule on him as a towel-head. A profound hurt, mounting in Raafat, that day slowly increased from a sleeping distrust to a maximum need now growing in him to respond —somehow to right the wrong. For weeks it was but a minor insult. But to do what? How?

"You must respect and never hurt this woman," whispered a scarcely contained Raafat. Were not Hasidim supposed to be *religious*? Raafat said gently, "What you proclaim with your lips, practice with your life."

"Never say never," stated the Hassid, coldly.

Softly replied Raafat, "But haven't you just said it, twice?"

Customers soon took melancholy notice that, a once notably happy Raafat had soon stopped whistling or even humming the opera tunes he so loved.

Now, the unalterable fact was, whether Maggid was a "neuter" or not, he was a lecher with an anteater or pangolin's mammal need to abuse and belittle women—a long snout, a long tongue, a vile gaze. Pagan eyes. He soon had learned where Fourth worked and began waiting by the bottom of the outdoor stairs to see her, thinking, apparently, he could insinuate himself into her life. Soon, he was telephoning her. He began to maltreat her, and one day he climbed up to her flat and beat her almost to a pulp. She survived, having to stay in a hospital for months. No one pressed charges. Hassids didn't. They had their own courts. They were insular, suspicious, lived in cultish, tightly knotted communities known as "courts," in fact, meetings that centered around an appointed leader, always male, who was what they call a *rebbe*, an individual who combined both political and religious authority and who let few secrets out. They were all self-contained, clandestine, incommunicative.

What had happened in another set of tragic circumstances was that one day Midhat had purchased a silver wristwatch from wily Maggid in the hustle of a street deal but in doing so had inadvertently revealed the building and rooms he shared with Fourth.

Jewel pawning was a common street activity in Manhattan. It had been a great mistake of Midhat's.

But by now a line had been crossed. It was more than Raafat's close friend Midhat could take, who dearly loved his cousin with a bond that only those of strong family values can fully understand, he who had so often seen the Hassidic, locking arms, dance in the street, like sniffer ants, on certain high holy days. Midhat kept to one room for a week, behaving as if he were chloroformed. He took New York City to be a super Sodom and a grim Gomorrah. It had infected his reasoning, for he had come to blame himself as a repellent and worthless fellow. No one was in touch with him, and then one night in despair, so badly wounded by the girl's tragedy and deeply ashamed, he committed suicide.

News of the offense soon quickly spread by way of rumor. Maggid was widely held in contempt. His savageries made Raafat not only feel bad about his work, the way beer attracted slugs when placed in shallow bowls or dishes who crawled into them and drowned—often later killed with added salt or lime—but as if transmogrified by the enduring mistrust of this evil Jew who kept coming by his cart to order, and by each repeated appearance to show so boldly his abiding contempt and indifference. While he ate, hands always held high, like a praying mantis, long and thin and predatory, his surveying eyes, his eyes ever shifted, as he chewed his food with a tearing kind of greed. It suggested cannibalistic instincts. *God grant me justice against my adversary* had once been Rafaat's nightly prayer at the fall of dusk. Now, he found that he had been uttering the prayer over and over during day.

"Those wrinkled ones are bitter," said Maggid, pointing. He bought and wolfed three. "Give me free drink, you, just because," he demanded. "You hear? Gimme another. The pork ones!" He chewed loudly, mandibles working. "You Arabs can't eat pork, so I do, ho kay?" He added, "To spite you!" His laugh was like a horse's neigh. "*Chazir* is not as swine as you. I make the rules, which I obey. Let exemption apply to shlubs like you. What did you put in this?

Make it with? It's sweet." He grinned, his ugly teeth and open mouth filled with bread, munching and chawing as flecks of meat dripped onto his filthy beard. He slapped his hands free of crumbs, farted, and before walked away, he turned in a threatening way to say, "I heard you blame me for assaulting some girl attack, some *shiksa* no less. I could kill for that!"

And he dropped a dire word about the seller's children.

His blessed innocent children?

Could he have heard that right?

The words chilled Raafat's blood.

Later, Angelo, the fruit seller, another of Raafat's friends, called the man a "*scungilli,*" sordid, seedy, sleazy squalid, and said he knew of someone who could "take care of him." At first, Raafat had tried put up with his rudeness and hard shouting whenever that man ordered a frank. It seemed to him over his years of struggle to find his footing that humans are generally 50 percent sad and 50 percent happy all the time. *At the same time.* Insecure, sad, fearful. On the other side, they were fairly open, usually obliging. It was not complicated. Native New Yorkers all had a harsh growl, it seemed, and it was true. That was—is—the heft of the engine. But there were devils, he came to see who had to be stopped.

But this threat leveled at him was impossible to accept. It could not be overlooked nor disregarded.

It was now that Raafat was determined something had to be done. Things had some to a brutal, unacceptable pass that could be ignored no longer. Integrity was involved. The buvette on his cart was a portable four-compartment sink, adjacent to each other. Whatever gave him the idea to set one up as holding toxic water could only be speculation, but this was his bailiwick, and these were his tools. He had witnessed the exquisite pain in the dark liquid eyes of Midhat, his friend, after he had learned of the attack on his cousin and could stand by no longer. That was what set the dastardly but, he felt, necessary plan in motion.

Once sensed, the need to act broke within Raafat like a giant short circuit, arcing over the whole fraught issue of what correctionally had to be done for an unprecedented redemption, sacrificing himself though he might.

Simple was the plan, and the plan was plain justice, a word which Jesus almost never used, but when He did, it was to call upon his holy Heavenly Father as an interposing authoritative dynamo to right wrongs. *Dikaosuine*—"*adalah*" in Arabic—meant both justice and righteousness, a word almost exclusively connected to private morality. Raafat found the text in Luke 18:7–8 when Jesus declared outright, "And will not God bring about justice for his chosen ones who cry out to him day and night? Will He keep putting them off? I tell you, He will see that they get justice, and quickly."

Raafat's faith had displaced Raafat's fear.

Which word is repeated as many as 365 times in the Bible? The command "do not fear," he knew, is spoken in Scripture exactly 365 times, one mention for each day of the year. It is the most frequent command given by God, and it now gave Raafat the courage to prevent the wrongs and offenses he was facing, to help rid the world of evil.

It was brooding on Midhat's tragic suicide, while staring at the water he stirred, that had given him the idea of a plan that he had decided with a vow to follow. Given to neither violence nor treachery, Raafat had been slow in coming to terms with his objective. Trouble was not new to him, certainly. He had witnessed much of action in the street, confrontation of all sorts, violence occasionally, with the police often being called to make arrests. Security in the area was always tight. A constant presence by the New York police department was augmented by undercover guards and armed patrols that milled and wandered about. The area was also surveilled by a network of high cameras that, according to the 47th Street Business Improvement District, was funded by the Department of Homeland Security. He felt he had seen too much, often of the worst behavior in the world. It was what he called an unexpected element. That night he heard in concert Max Broch's profoundly moving, heart-stopping Violin Concerto #1 in G. It instilled in him, as he gripped the arm of his seat and swept his eyes high, across, and above the ceiling, a dangerous resolve. What it stole of affection in him was replaced with—what?

A truth, replenishing the rule that was—the exception.

Do not be assertive, simply adjust to the object, and you shall find a way around and through and between. If nothing within you stays rigid, outward things will disclose themselves. Solution available!

What Raafat knew about water, that elemental liquid so vital to and for all forms of life, the inorganic compound, its constituency, the chemical formula, its natural and supernatural substance, was bottomless, its fundamental glory. including the many facets of its face, not excluding of course the prayer that his mother, reminding him of the lance that pierced the Savior's side, had taught him to recite on *Eid il-Burbara*, Saint Barbara's Day, a Christian holy day Arabs celebrated, which went, "Body of Christ, save me. Blood of Christ, inebriate me. Water from the side of Christ, wash me. Passion of Christ, strengthen me." A practicing Christian—or Masīḥī (مَسِيحِيّ), as he preferred to be identified—Raafat, although in a foreign country, never forgot the tenets of his faith.

Water was the one thing in his life of which he had a working intelligence. Did he not cook his eggs exactly 4½ minutes long in a rolling boil, adding white vinegar, the precise length of time it took to hear the overture to the *Marriage of Figaro,* which is also exactly four minutes long, usually humming—the opera he dearly loved and kept a record in the kitchen expressly for that purpose— or reciting, slowly, although he was a practicing Christian, the short Muslim prayer, *"Rabbana 'atinaa fid dunyaa hasanat wafil aakhirati hasana taw wa qinaa azaaban naar"* (Oh Allah! Our Lord and Sustainer! Grant us good in this world and good in the Hereafter and save us from the Fire of Jahannam)?

It was his one passion, music. Raafat attended a concert once a month, to widen his horizons, to find some peace. Same-day rushed or early-bird tickets at Stern Auditorium, which he could buy as soon as they went on sale, were not expensive, and so, avoiding premium prices, he often took Sarah and his daughters with him, whereby looking about for mid-level seats and staying with them they saved money.

Autumn, its bright promise, always improved his business, and, as usual, coming by, Maggid checked to be sure that none of his co-religionist were near the vendor's cart to overhear his order. "I want the white," pointed Maggid, his euphemism for the pork hot dogs. Bright went his eyes upon a massive bite, his tongue slurping the gustation with a hideous chorus of loud wet noises. It was *muhrrham* in his own religion, among the vilest breach of faith. Now he had eaten pork—and so deserved it. "This is sweet," the Jew exclaimed, halving the dog in one bite, and then gulped the rest. "Make me another."

Raafat knew exactly why it tasted sweet. The dogs he served had come from buvette sink #4, in which—slowly, experimentally—he added a solution of deuterium oxide. It was the one sink of four in the cart so treated, he scrupulously saw to that. D20 is a natural element, the heavy form of hydrogen. (High deuterium levels in a human body can have a negative effect, causing chronic fatigue, metabolic problems, premature aging.) Maggid in a mouthful had tasted the molecules, ingested them. How was it heavy water tasted sweet? Simple. Water deuteration led to activation of a GPCR heterodimer to a level that is perceived by humans as, well, candied, almost cloying—a chemical treat sweet molecules. The vendor was disgusted at the profanation of Maggid's eating pork, but he was not surprised that his menace had found the hot dogs sweet, and so would use that against him

The only rule is—the *exception*.

It went back to basic physics. He knew all about "heavy water," had worked with it in the labs back in Gaza, well knew it contained a high concentration of deuterium, a heavy isotope of hydrogen, which is used as a moderator in nuclear reactors with natural uranium fuel. He had studied the very thing back in school. Of course, drinking it could be toxic for humans, but a large amount would be needed for poisoning to occur, flooding one's organs The effect is fairly strong and can last for hours. In his studies, Raafat with classmates had read up on it, and he was aware, by having paid close attention, that no effects with deuterium resulted until one reached something like 10–20% enrichment of all body water. At that level, general toxicity symptoms would start to appear, when it would become toxic at levels somewhat higher (30–40%). Natural chemical processes that occur often in the human body will be slowed by the heavier D2O molecules, badly effecting membrane function.

Where do you find it? Why bother to look? It could be *made!* One prepared it by using normal water in a prolonged process of electrolysis which separates deuterium from water and then treated with oxygen to form heavy water, heavier than normal water simply because the nucleus of each of its two hydrogen atoms contained not just a proton but a neutron, as well. Heavy water ice will sink in it. It tastes sweet, indeed, "sweet as a Sultana's kiss," a *jamila*, said his old physics professor with a wink.

Raafat tapped into his education here. He knew that there is a fairly well-known effect in physics/biology called the "kinetic isotope effect." Basically, he knew, proton exchange rates can slow substantially when substituting deuterium for hydrogen, which is clearly very bad for organisms that depend on those proteins/enzymes. It was a simple job to electrolyze water. Raafat had done it many times to purify the rusty water that ran through the pipes in his flat when he first moved to New York—to disinfect it by inactivating pathogenic bacteria.

Justice was called for, judgement demanded. Raafat, who dearly wished he knew how to bombard uranium with neutrons, now spent several days experimenting, spinning the fetid hot dogs

in the buvette sink like slugs in the frothy, gummy substance, looking long and eerie like the leg cases of insects. Should he add pyre-
thrum? Black Leaf 40, nicotine sulfate? Dowfume MC-2? Bromo
gas? Malathion? Cythion? He thumbed a few books. He set aside a
special box of pork frankfurters. Hot dogs are an emulsion sausage,
so the filling will always be finely ground and dense. System wieners,
made from pork and veal, are slightly smaller and thinner than a
typical hot dog. Raafat chose those.

Solution? Available! Lye, which is sodium hydroxide
(NaOH), is highly toxic if ingested, and, since it is a strong alkaline
substance, it can cause severe chemical burns to the mouth, the
throat, the esophagus, and stomach. Ingestion can lead to corrosive
burns and agony.

But it could be disguised not only by the sweetness of D20
but by relish and onions. A powerful 100% lye formula creates
enough heat to melt and dissolve grease, hair, soap, scum, and other
drain-clogging materials—scum particularly.

Scum most efficiently.

It was a late on a November afternoon, toward dusk, damp,
inclement, when tall Maggid appeared as usual as the same imposing
shadowy horror dressed all in black with his absurd black hat and
spit curls. He immediately barked to the vendor, "Make me three
glizzies"—he checked beside and behind him, to be sure he was
unobserved—"of pork." But Raafat was ready for him. In New
York City, glizzy gobblers, or glizzy gladiators, are people who wolf
hot dogs quickly, no hesitation, in a silly way, shoving the franks
way too far into their mouths. The vendor heaped on the relish, on
top of which he also piled onions.

It had all happened so quickly, as passersby moved along
the sidewalk, that in the moving crowds, nothing of consequence
was noted. A strangling sound came from around the corner, a hideous reverberating echo of choking and asphyxiation as if a resounding siren in the midst of mad traffic. Raafat never looked back
but kept his head down, although he distinctly heard a throng

gathering, circling a grotesque figure in black rolling in the gutter, his hugely fat arms biting into his belly as if madly to cramping his stomach, all the time his co-religionists recognizing him but, given who it was, closing ranks around the stricken body with their bobbing *streimels* and wagging *peyot* in the same suspicious way that they all tried to keep their strange, mysterious lives from public scrutiny—onlookers might have thought they were dancing again—but looking down upon him without pity. They saw a bully, revolving, humping the gutter, as he howled in execration. They felt he deserved his pain. But by then Raafat had poured all the hot dog water into a nearby street sewer, including the filthy, tainted money just tendered to him, quickly collapsed his small red umbrella, and locked his cart to secure it in Midhat's alley.

What dispatch happened may have been a deserved doom or a waiting death but, whatever the departure, it was delivery. Emancipation.

It was late Fall. That same night, a misty blustery one, after meeting his daughters, Raafat walked hastily through the crowded streets to attend a concert for which he had earlier bought tickets. A new but far less dramatic phase in his life was about to begin. All the while, he had with him in bracing and loving accompaniment his loving wife and his small children in hand, two small girls whose sweet natures, like the windy evenings of November, the fine drops of blown rain falling in the dark, the hectic tangle of bright leaves, and the uplifting perfume of the lovely Faqqua iris, the national flower of Palestine, which his wife, who'd known of his recent troubles, brought him that night, so calmly soothed him, in any crisis, as they crossed the swarming streets over to the Stern Auditorium, happily splashing through the puddles.

As they walked head, calling to the girls who plashed up the water with their boots, laughing, the hot-dog seller's mind was focused.

Water and blood, he reflected, had both poured from the pierced side of Jesus Christ, the blood of redemption, the water imparting salvation. Precisely which side of the Lord's had been lanced, the Gospels never state.

But as far as Raafat went, it did not signify.

He knew about both.

Dis-appointment at WNOT

"It is in the character of very few men to honor without envy a friend who has prospered."

Aeschylus

"Every man has his basic worth, from which must be subtracted his vanity."

Bismarck

Over the radio, "The Global Loop," a morning program dealing in the arts, ideas, and politics—called by sarcastic detractors "The Vocal Poop," "The Ignoble Goop," etc.—was a discussion show heard on the Public Radio International. It depended on listeners' donations and contributions but also received government grants. In fact, federal funding provided about 15 percent of the revenue for National Public Radio, which was a dubious investment of $1.40 per taxpayer per year. Theodore Creeple had been for years host of the talk show, which gave the daily news but basically featured flash to micro-light interviews. It welcomed all listeners' comments and call-ins, as well.

All topics fit his program's standard form of who, what, when, and why. Why do psychics have to ask your name? Why don't sheep shrink when it rains? Where is the audience sitting if all the world is a stage? What sits inside the Kaaba and why can't airplanes fly over it? Neither could unauthorized aircraft fly over the Pentagon nor over Taj Mahal. Why exactly is urine yellow? How could a Nash "Rambler" be a "hard top convertible" at the same time? When people hear the comedian Jimmy Durante sing the song "I'll Be Seeing You," why do they weep? Why are there cheerleaders in

Japanese baseball? How can women learn to counterpose instead of having to meet the demands of male ego? Where are the key Mesozoic fossil dig sites in Montana? And so forth. Mainly, "The Global Loop" was gauged to interview celebrities. Writers. Musicians. Politicians. People who moved affairs.

Ted Creeple, now in his eighties, was its broadcasting host. He was fairly well read and well educated (Brown University, '63). He was a good listener, quick to pick up the cast of an intense conversation and was an amiable interviewer—for such is what "The Global Loop" basically consisted of a two-hour morning show with a different chosen guest appearing each hour. Ted was quirkily alert, urging on his guests as they spoke to answer in depth by his encouraging semi-hum, "*Hmmm hmm.*"

The array of guests featured on WNOT's "Global Loop" varied widely, from local politicians to disgruntled feminists to celebrities. President Jimmy Carter once appeared on the show. Singer Nina Simone. The show was full of news, tittle-tattle, long stories—"chinwags"—scandalous tales, hearsay, gossip, and wonderful conversation. The New York chef Glib Stealth was a big hit in one hour, comically pointing out that the Countess of Beunchlingen squandered a fortune on her favorite delicacy, eelpout livers. "We're not talking about one of Marie-Antoine Carême's sublime babas or flans, mind you, right?" put in Ted Creeple, laughing and tugging on his bowtie, which he often wore. On one morning hour, the famous cellist Elissa Sue Shopmaker played Camille Saint-Saëns' Japanese Sonatas for Cello in studio, such sad music it was, and then talked emotionally about the "spoken unspokenness of music" and explained the nature of her instrument, mentioning that the oldest cello that exists to date is known as "The King," built between 1538 and 1560 by a certain Andrea Amati and which can be seen at the National Music Museum in South Dakota.

Seminar topics on the show included a multitude of subjects: "Dwarfism;" "The Awfulness of Sisters-in-Law;" St. Paul's dogma of sex and his preference for celibacy; the Popularity of

Coca-Cola as a world phenomenon"—a hugely-girthed company spokesman with a double chin, loudly gulping from a bottle on the air, wheezed with laughter, and boasted, "More than 10,000 Coca-Cola soft drinks are consumed globally per second"— and a seminar on the (winning!) characteristics of 1960s "Pop Art": banal (deliberately), garish, slapdash, funny (sometimes), satirical (occasionally) and vulgar (almost always), and its sources, namely, comic strips, circus posters, soup cans, beer cans, pinball machines, chocolate cream pies, animated cartoons, and girls, girls, girls.

A diabolist named Winter Sloath—he dubbed himself "The Anointed Cherub"—was featured on the show one hour, explaining that by the year 2040 all human beings through AI would be transformed into "next-level" technology, with computer cells in their blood streams, their brains working by nano-celluloids. He called Jesus a charlatan, saying, *"Lazarus was the first person to be raised from the dead!"*

More than one painfully boring show pivoted around UFOs, scientific approaches to near-death experiences, and paranormal matters touching on contactees and out-of-body experiences. A memorable hour one morning was the appearance of Archie Fellow-Bellows, the celebrated old English music hall performer who sang (and even danced) ditties like "The Miner's Dream of Home," "Down at the Old Bull and Bush," "The Lily of Laguna," and "Don't Dilly Dally on the Way."

Once asked about his religious faith by an inquiring Presbyterian minister, a guest on the show that day interested in his Christian outlook, an odd Creeple flabbergasted the man by citing as his mentor—of all people—*Ralph Waldo Emerson*! He whose heretical conclusion was that Christianity as practiced was dead! He who called it "a calcified institution with rigid rites that left an ossified legacy to the world." He who had not a working or single fideistic clue about Jesus Christ or harbored anything in his heart like a remote interest in the Savior! He who declared that "the prayer of the farmer kneeling in his field to weed it, the prayer of the rower

kneeling with the stroke of his oar, are true prayers heard throughout nature rather than the prayer of the penitent in his church pew."
"As to Jesus Christ?" said Emerson, "The dogma of the mystic of-
fices of Christ being dropped, and he, standing on his genius as a
moral teacher, 'tis impossible to maintain the old emphasis of his
personality; and it recedes, as all persons must, before the sublimity
of the moral laws."

To have to hear such a thing seemed ludicrous, and it
caused yet another breach with Aleister Porch, who was a practicing
Roman Catholic. Although he had studiously avoided interviewing
his friend on the show when his new book of essays had appeared—he had his reasons—Creeple never hesitated to invite on
his program many other authors, writers of debut fiction, African
American poets, politico-radical women novelists, and manufacturers of turgid semi-literate best-sellers and impossibly stupid "beach-
reads," all were openly welcome.

Was it not odd he neglected his own friend? But that was
the case. One invited writer was a fat fellow from Maine named
Edwin Sebba, author of the just published *Back from the Brink*, who
seriously swore on the air that he had literally passed away—
croaked!—and then had miraculously come back to life, with the
extra-extravagant claim that he'd swum in a pool of white milk in
heaven although being clinically dead! But was Aleister Porch now
invited to appear? No.

Never again.

An endless variety of celebrities appeared on radio WNOT,
and no end of topical subjects were featured on the show, controversial and not. One morning, a painter from Utah, B. S. Cowbyre,
brought along a canvas and his palette to the studio, choosing to do
a small living portrait right there of a delighted Ted Creeple and do
so while they talked of art. He muttered as he plied his brush, "The
great Michelangelo idealized himself in self-portrait as Nicodemus
in his Florentine Pietà in the Duomo in Florence." No reply. "In
Titian's painting *The Pietà* the St. Jerome who kneels before the

Virgin is a self-portrait," offered Cowbyre with a raised brush and a wink. "Think of yourself being memorialized in glory." Ted laughed heartily, although he had an ego and was embarrassed that he had a working knowledge of neither subject and urged the artist on, remarking, "Talk about it." Radical feminists were also popular guests on "The Global Loop." Ted thoroughly enjoyed their hard-core rants, gripes, political positions, and attacks on paternalism. Thelma Mothershed appeared, so did Anna Amelia Frame, so did muscular Doris Kommando, recently a month out of jail, who loudly proclaimed on air an angry half-hour lesbian manifesto. A mere hour was never enough for these firebrands. All the host had to say was "Talk about that," and they'd be off on a diatribe.

That odd phrase nettled one writer who was irascible and appeared only once on "The Global Loop," Canadian novelist Alfie Sheets, who brazenly demanded of Creeple, "What kind of expression is that?" asking his host to be more specific. "You're like Abdemon, the Tyrian," he muttered, "the one person who managed to puzzle Solomon with his subtle questions." It was a mortifying moment, having been said on air. "What is foxfire?" grumbled his unhappy guest upon leaving. "What is Prince Rupert's Drop? Who obtained divine rank by a leap into the sea? Who had their ears licked by serpents while asleep? What was the fate of Osceola? Who was the 'Old Man Eloquent'? When was Ichthyosaurus discovered? How do grasshoppers breathe? What general has two graves? How much did England pay per head for the Hessians? Who were the Budians? Where is Pompey's pillar?"

An amateur private publisher, a Mr. Weevil, a knob-headed anti-intellectual and pussy-footing "cancel culture" gepid, who issued particular books from his own house but who was a slave to his own specious and self-rightous whims, came on the show proudly to explain why he always flatly refused to publish—and would censor—any manuscript that he personally found socially or morally unacceptable.

"Including James Joyce's *Ulysses*?" asked an utterly bewildered Creeple. "William Burroughs' *Naked Lunch*? Anthony Burgess's *A Clockwork Orange*? Cormac McCarthy's *Blood Meridian*? Vladimir Nabokov's *Lolita*?" Edward Gorey's *The Beastly Baby*? Salinger's *The Catcher in the Rye*?"

"Right" said a smug Weevil, smiling.

"No?"

"Not a chance."

"Are you actually telling our audience that, as a publisher, you find truth indecent? That you honestly believe a writer in this country should not be allowed to say absolutely anything controversial without fear of punishment or censure or, worse, your own private and subjective disapproval?"

"Bingo."

"Not even classics like Willa Cather's *Sapphira and the Slave Girl?* Baron Corvo's *The Weird of the Wanderer?* Gustave Flaubert's *Madame Bovary*? You would personally reject those to publish? You cannot be serious."

The hack publisher preened and shook his head.

"Nope."

"What about a masterpiece like Dante's *Divine Comedy*? An allegory of darkness, terror, and chaos, of wild, raging, impenitent, sinful creatures, stripped of any hope, wailing in the dark, starless air, a kingdom of flesh and ugliness with battered souls punished on terraces of ice and fire for eternity in the midst of an unceasing pandemonium of freakish noise, strange tongues, horrible outcries, words of wrath, and shrieks of despair, exposing carnal sins, crimes, violence, and hellish dissension?"

Shocked, people in the studio all stopped to listen. Was this a man who ran a local publishing house or a plain, unmitigated dyed-in-the-wool ignoramus?

Astonished, Creeple asked, "Do you honestly and truly mean as a serious publisher, no matter how small, you wouldn't publish one of the western world's rare, proven, unparalleled treasures, a peerless and unsurpassed work of art?"

"Not a chance!"

"You don't mean it,

Weevil sat proud and grinning. His ludicrous baldness made him look even more stupid.

"Yup," he crowed.

 What about Mark Twain's legendary *The Adventures of Huckleberry Finn?*"

"That, too."

Ted Creeple's head jerked with a kind of chiropractic snap.

"I have six daughters," the hack publisher explained.

At that point, everybody in the studio, including the sound engineers and technicians, all burst into helpless laughter.

A New Hampshire poet, Paul Knific, whose series of modern sonnets, *Braiding Sweetgrass,* became a memorable show one day, poems which he unselfconsciously recited on air with a notable lisp, and which were a success despite the giggling and suppressed mirth off-mike of Ted Creeple's manager, Mary Mustardo Magoo, the chubby woman who did most of the behind-the-scenes work at the WNOT station, contacting guests, seeing to their schedules, and making sure they appeared on time. A gay man from England, Wallace Japazaws, author of *The Purple Tongue*, was a big hit for the fund of homosexual pick-up lines he happily retailed for the listening audience, old, out-of-date, but curious questions that in the gay underground were all actually true. "Oh yes, indeed, old gay openers in the UK were quite ingenious, even cryptic!" said Wallace, "'Do you know Naples?' was one phrase. Another was, 'How are the Horse Guards?' And yet another, 'Have you read *Winnie the Pooh?*'" Phyllis Grissim Panhead also appeared who had published an odd children's fable, "A Plot Against the King," in which an outraged harridan of a fishwife poisons her dog-loving husband, Justin, a circus dwarf, a crime mitigated when it is proven (by way of delayed revelation) that he had envenomed her first, all of it climaxing with a neo-Romeo & Juliet ending.

Alicia Mae Rumball, an expert on relaxation, was interviewed for her best-seller, *Do Less, It's Good for You,* explaining how bored, uneasy, or guilty people feel when they slow down and how we activity-oriented Americans lead frazzled lives and suffer from modern-day distractions but should learn to reframe what "counts" as rest. "The nation is far too cognitively intense," she said, advising, "Naps do wonders."

A certain Professor Osip Horrabin, a dedicated Zionist enthusiast from BU, on one political segment called for a scheme to marshal all of European Jews to colonize Gaza on the grounds of a committed and sincere national patriotism. Gloomy was a Mr. Elmo Lisinopril who disquisited on the bane of "swill milk" from cows in old stables fed on alcoholic distillery mash that killed children by the thousands in the 1850s.

Music took up many segments on WNOT. A Mozart expert, a fussifier by the name of Fridolin Pohl, his cheeks rouged red like faux-marbre—Porch happened to be visiting the studio that day—took up an hour lamenting the fact that the great composer died in poverty, plagued by creditors and with no end of accumulating debts, impoverished exactly as was his sister Maria Anna ("Nannerl"), age seventy-eight, her being almost blind. He said, "The small lodging where Wolfgang died at 1:05 a.m. on December 5, 1791, had been demolished, where in its stead today stands a department store, Warenhaus Steffl, with an ugly bust of Mozart crowded into a dirty, irrelevant, unworthy corner of the fifth-floor sports department."

Opera singer Katya Apostolova, a grand beauty, appeared on the show and said of *Aïda,* "The third act is very, very difficult for every soprano. It is not composed easily. That is Verdi for you! It is beautiful, but you must really watch out for the high C, for you need a lot of control there, because a high C in other places is easier, but, no, no, no, not there, not in that act. All sopranos—well, let me at least say many—are on guard for that moment and are afraid about it." Encouraged to hit that note, she laughed, obliged, and, placing a graceful hand flat on top of her head, sang it perfectly and almost blew out the mike!

Another day, a German opera singer Heinz Zuckerpuppe appeared on WNOT, not only to sing several Schubert lieder— "*Freude der Kinderjahre*" and the lovely cradle sing "*Wiegenlied*"—but took time to explain their subtle meanings. He said, "Note how the composer asks of the wind in his lovely lied '*Suleika,*' '*Was bedeutet die Bewegung*?'" In English, 'What means this movement?'" Many listeners telephoned in to request more. He lustily sang.

> "*Was bedeutet die Bewegung?*
> *Bringt der Ost mir frohe Kunde?*
> *Seiner Schwingen frische Regung*
> *Kühlt des Herzens tiefe Wunde.*"

One morning featured the music of jazz. A change from almost all jazz musicians of African American ethnicity was the fat expansive double bassist Norbert "Mugsy" Grimbolt, who, part Hungarian, Chinese, Native American, and African American, and who had grown up sucking-stone poor in Watts, L.A. resembled that ethnic mélange of his in his wild song, the groovy tone-poem "Groanin,'" an avant-garde pandemonium. Adoring Ted Creeple, who loved jazz, especially "Duke" Ellington, Lester Young, Ornette Coleman, and Illinois Jacquet, even Frank Sinatra, inquired about the origins of the song. Grimbolt looked at him, bewildered and plate-faced, only to say, "It is what it is, man."

"*Mmmm,*" hummed Ted Creeple, earnestly.

"Dig?" asked Grimbolt.

Creeple smiled and, prodding his guest, said, "Talk about that."

General interviews that he gave could endorse a cause, push an agenda, hawk a new movie, and of course sell a book—authors were to be found among the most popular guests—at least in the city of Providence, Rhode Island. Creeple was witty, at times insightful, completely with-it regarding politics, especially local, and loved anecdotes. But "talk about that"? No, there was something of a shortage there. Paucity, broadcast famine. He was a tall fellow, with a wide mouth, a short, forked white beard which he cultivated with the fond belief it gave him gravity, and shoulders that sloped. He dressed always in loose-fitting clothes, and more than one observer declared with a wink that he looked like a prosperous farmer. Hungry, aggressive, motivated, driving, determined and dynamic, he was energetically competitive, and a drawback related to that was that he could become combative.

And insistent. He was ambitious.

And jealous.

Spite was involved.

There is a need in an interviewing journalist to compete or—to put it bluntly—to win. It could become an obsession with him. Assessments can go either way regarding the takeaway, and while in an interview one can build or foster a relationship, there also remains in a way a confrontation that competes for a prize. Ted Creeple was always prepared and knew the ins-and- outs of the microphone and the mysteries of the radio studio. One person that he had determined would no longer be a guest on his show had been for years one of his closest friends, the poet, novelist, and essayist, Alistair Porch.

"'*Talk about that*?'" asked an astonished Aleister later, gently codding his friend for what he found an absurd remark. Always one who never hesitated to say what he thought, he had been visiting the WNOT station that morning, sitting by as he watched the interview through the glass and, simply by happenstance, decided to niggle Ted with a complaint that, irking him, he'd noticed Ted repeated in many interviews. "Isn't that what all lazy interviewers always say that to their sitting guests? 'Talk about that!' That is so weak! Let me tell you why, OK? It's because the interrogator cannot think of a good, solid *question* to ask! That phrase!—it is nothing less than confessing a foible! One only, *always,* hears it posed by hacks and fumbling amateur reporters with lapsed preparation. Face it, it's the mantra of the lame interviewer!"

He possessed an agile, self-deprecating wit, but his easy and high-pitched laugh hid a large and surprisingly fragile ego.

"Oh, come on, man."

"No, it's downright lethargy, Ted," Aleister contended. *"Talk about that'?* It's a sign of the times, my friend. Sloth! Worse than languorous—it's plain inert! The thing is, it not only allows for any open-ended response or off-true reply, but it *sanctions* in any interviewee the perfect right to blather on aimlessly, provided a wide-open field to pontificate, giving him or her carte blanche simply to take over and filibuster!"

Creeple, who didn't buy it, merely shrugged.

"You reject the concept. But an idea is not responsible for the people who don't believe in it."

Porch was exercised, "I call it pusillanimity, lame. As weak as that cottage publishing ignoramus, Mr. Weevil, whom you once interviewed on the air. Remember that knob-head? That self-important, mal-educated dwarf bowdlerizer who positively lived to edit out anything controversial in the work of the writers he published? Individuals with brains twice as large as his? I happen to have been in the studio that day. Call him a publisher? I'd have preferred as an editor *a blind white shrimp!*"

Porch twirled a finger round his temple.

"What is worse than a low-brow eunuch"—he shouted—*"who publishes books?"*

"That's not fair, not even close" squawked Ted, defensively, slapping shut his laptop. "Aleister, look, you know nothing about broadcasting!" The host looked preternaturally old. The haggard face, framed by a shock of unruly hair, seemed curiously appropriate to his broomstick of a body, and there was a peculiar flutter at the corner of his eyes, as if he were wincing. Creative people, he felt. put him in the shade. It had long been a sore point in his life that the books Porch published put him in the shade. Who was once a friend, became a rival. Once a Clark University scholar who was a guest on the show quoted the literary critic Van Wyck Brooks, saying, "The life that is not creative is spoiled and stunted and unworthy," which Ted, folding his arms in something of a harumph, sat back in his chair, and violently contested. It was an embarrassing sop to his own failure.

Did that note of criticism explain how their friendship ended and why Aleister Porch had been proscribed from ever again appearing on WNOT?

Partially, yes. Aleister and Ted Creeple went back twenty years and had long become friends in an uncomplicated way. Over time, mainly because Porch began writing and publishing books, while Ted did not, the relationship became frosty—not on Porch's part, not in the way of a major crisis or anything like a vulgar or dramatic showdown, but merely after he was never asked to appear on the show again—having been invited to do so would have been a boon in drawing attention to his books, a fact of which Creeple was well aware—and the subsequent years of truancy and disregard. The fact was that Ted was articulate, expressive, comfortable with language and could be eloquent and expressive as an effective communicator—he admired good writers and poets and collected books himself—and he very well might have become an excellent writer himself. Maybe.

The conspicuous—and in the end intimidating—fact, however, was that he never did, and never would. It would have been the last thing he would have ever admitted. It remained nevertheless something for which he could not quite forgive himself. In their early friendship, Creeple's assumption was that his newfound friend had a maverick, unserious, ultimately blasé and incautious harum-scarum temperament.

But that was a misguided notion of his, for in the end Porch proved to be stalwart, with a solid dedication to his craft, becoming productive and more than adequate as a successful novelist, and it did not go down well with Ted. He could be quirky and was a baffling combination of cool and high judgment, this coupled with a total submersion in blind emotional drives, and there always seemed to be an almost weird disconnection between his earnest judgments and his acts of will.

He had somewhat of an addiction to norms and standards, virtues in broadcasting and the way they should be levied—there was a canon to the observances of radio work—just as he had hoped deep down to be a literary writer, moving around on a varied festival circuit, enjoying a louche and notable lifestyle.

"Ted, the reason you know so much about standards," a critical acquaintance of his once observed, cheerily, "is that you have no character."

Porch had a writer's antic disposition, one open to deviltry, and always told Ted that the best parts of his interviews—his subjects' racy anecdotes—had been prohibited from being aired and never broadcast, like the time one biographer in a pre-show chat explained how a flying client of the early barnstorming Charles Lindbergh once hired the young pilot to fly over his hometown so that he could urinate on it, or on another occasion, when an author in a pre-interview detailed one of the many bizarre affectations of the silent film comedian Charlie Chaplin, a legendary womanizer—especially of young girls—who was not only a desperate hypochondriac, according to the silent film actress Louise Brooks, but out of sheer terror of contracting syphilis developed the habit of painting his genitals with iodine in the belief that it would prevent venereal disease!

In any case, Porch's criticism did not go over well. It was taken as carping and fault-finding—caviling, even. It amounted to censure, in any case. Sheer spite.

It also evoked an unwelcome image of Aleister Porch, who, on his side, was surprised to learn his friend could be so touchy. Disapproval simply for one crack? It was hardly outright denunciation. Didn't Robert Frost define *education* as the ability to listen to almost anything without losing one's temper?

Ted Creeple kept score—and he forgot nothing. He never forgot and never forgave Porch that one criticism, even though they had been friends for years. But it was not this simple remark that rankled him. What bothered him—what began to fester deep down in his heart like the gnawing of an inner wolf, what wounded him the most—was that Porch over the years had published so many books, topping him in prestige, and, in the comparison, he felt diminished in his own mind, felt small. It was even worse than that. The idea of having him as a guest on the show, simplicity itself had he wanted to do so, inevitably became a way of increasing the writer's reputation, which would only exacerbate the pain he had come to see as a rivalry. He had begun to look for an excuse in that negligence—and found one.

Broadcasters, talk show hosts, and radio journalists are commonly handed out free books, methodically distributed to them by publishers, over the transom, so to speak, in order to get some public play and any noteworthy attention, good or bad. Aleister Porch's small publisher had always compiled a prospective buyer's list which was sent out to readers by way of email for any who wished to buy copies in hardcover or paperback, highlighting a special 150 reserved in limited, signed editions. Over time, Aleister, who had published a sizable body of work so far, twenty-five books in all, eight titles with his new publisher, various books of short stories, early and new, a book of fables, and several books of poetry, by a simple glance at looking at the orders list was well aware of who did and who did not buy his books. It was among other things a barometer of who were his friends.

"I myself have only so many books to hand out," explained Aleister to Ted one afternoon as they were walking back from a book sale, where the former was encouraging his friend to invest in a set of the New York Edition of Henry James as being well worth it. Creeple assumed a bootleg smile. His eyes fluttered shut. His mouth snapped shut like something on hinges. *So that's how it is, huh?* He would remember that very day. It took place on an early Spring in the Wilcox Park in Westerly, Rhode Island.

It turned out that Creeple never ordered a *single* copy of any of Aleister's books. He typically published two books every year. But his friend bought none. Never ponied up. He could not find it in himself to do so. The fact was, as Aleister always had access to the publishers' list of prospective buyers, Ted stood out that way, even though the budget of the "The Global Loop" radio had allocations to pay for such things as part of programming. He never bought a book, not once—never thought of doing so. It was not merely that he was something of a tightwad, which he was; it was primarily that he felt getting freebies was his due, simply because, like journalists everywhere—they tend to see themselves as being in show business in a misguided way, even as celebrities—that was the order of the day. But even if he did now receive a free book, Creeple would not have invited him on the show.

Why, to give him free *publicity?* Wide-open promotion? Advertisements gratis? Not anymore. No how, no way, fat chance.

Was Creeple's unbudging personality a confession of personal failure or the result of, as well as an avoidance mechanism for, diverting attention from his inability to write books in a life he by that failure considered squandered? What did it matter? What difference did it make? All of it applied. Each of it signified. And the old truism held—*To have a truly good enemy, choose a friend; he knows exactly where to strike.*

Although he eventually came to recognize the affront, Porch harbored no resentment against his one-time buddy, nor even bothered to advertise the desertion. He merely attributed to a skill gap, much preferring that than to waste time slowly compiling a taxonomy of Creeple's ever-waking resentments. There is great strength in silence, he realized, and that strength is often proportionate to the difficulty of preserving silence.

A decade or so back in time, Aleister had in fact once appeared on "The Global Loop," had been interviewed, and had done well. This was in earlier, sunnier days when the two men were friends, but that was now long past, "history," as they say. Porch had appeared just that once, and it helped sell some books, but envious Creeple had by now determined no more, that was it. That affront opened a wound in Porch that never healed.

There is a well-known—and some go so far as to say identifying—trait among the American Irish that seeks to diminish someone else's accomplishments, an attitude that pours poison on the very nature of striving. It refuses to give praises to particular people who have achieved something while also seeking to belittle them. "It's about bringing them down," as critics describe carpers who are so ready with that bitter and unyielding remark, "I knew him when he was *nothin'*!" as they would say of someone now prominent who once was not.

Settle? Compromise? Make peace? Creeple was damned if he would bother. One policy held firm there at WNOT, and it became law: Aleister Porch was not to be appointed. It was not that he was terminated. For no terms had been set. Simply, he was proscribed. Excluded. Banished. Shunned. In short, he was disappointed. Better said, *dis*-appointed.

There is a sad and perfidious little game that we play when we reach a certain age. It is a form of solitaire. And, sadly, it is quite often timorous and pigeon-hearted. It consists of the kinds of evaluative dreams that we assume, looking back, the inevitable retrospective by which in an assaying way we gauge our value, when we—often in a melancholy way—start reviewing our lives, comparing ourselves with what we are and who we were in relation to our friends and what our classmates did with their lives. We begin to weigh, to evaluate, what we did. Looking back can be perilous. There is much to have to face in a self-assessment—an appraisal—when in and by comparisons we inevitably fall short.

We tend badly to want to become the audience we insist we hear in the process of assessing ourselves in hindsight, in the act of reminiscence possessed, or oppressed, by what Marcel Proust referred to as "a vast structure of recollection." When does the delicate act of self-appraisal, by which we classify ourselves—that delusional dance of reminiscence—not involve a subjective and selective approach, involving both how we come to choose that structure and how we come to tell our tale. It is often less a trial of honesty than theft. Deception is a trap ever tied to the process of seeking self-knowledge.

Self-defeated feelings of discontent, indeed, grief arise, a slow and resentful longing that is aroused by someone else's achievements, values, qualities, or luck. There is a specific word for that. It is not envy, in fact. Envy denotes a longing to possess something awarded to or achieved by another. Sitting in the midst of such a mood as that is a normal, if melancholy, aspiration. No, there is something more corrosive.

I am talking about jealousy, a vice in the extreme, which comprises an attitude of caustic resentment for another who has gained something that one more rightfully deserves. Jealousy is the unlived life in you crying out to be spent. It is the tribute that mediocrity pays to genius, as has been said. While troublesome to others, it is by far a much greater torment for its victim, for it is self-devouring. It is a basically fear of comparison, a mental cancer. As iron is eaten away by rust, so are the envious consumed by their own passion, although in a sense it less a passion than an obsession. Psychotic jealousy has in it a weird sense of clarity—for it actually *pinpoints* what it hates. There is nothing so self-destroying, and no emotion quite so despicable, as jealousy, the locus where vanity and pride mismarry and live in a subsequent hell.

It is worse than a mental cancer, becoming the tie that binds, and binds, tethering its owner as tight as a constrictor knot, the tightest of tight hitches.

Egotism, invariably a case of mistaken non-entity, invigorates the inner demon of jealousy, that dragon which slays love under the pretense of keeping it mercilessly alive and, in its metastasizing way, transmogrifies that devouring obsession into a strangling possessiveness—a mental cancer—which before anything else is self-tormenting. Jealous is the suspicion that eats itself out hollow in self-disgust. An African proverb captures it well: *"Jealousy was born in the same pot as a stone; the stone got soft but jealousy remained."*

Paradoxes prevail, for the vice of jealousy ironically looms large while it is singularly petty, and hideously small. It loathes what it feels—and this, all along, with an ongoing horror—*just as it loathes who feels it*, for it cannot free itself of the self-infected poison it yearns to spit. The irony within its depth is that it is driven to seek the very certainty it simultaneously hates to find! Weirdly, sardonically, its essential look is pathologically *inward*, not outward, its final revelation becoming the inevitable consequence that it is more than anything a self-estimate that contains more of self-love than love. What could be more damning?

It should be mentioned that Porch, in many a bewildered speculation of his own about Creeple's jealous motives of flatly refusing him any glory by scotching appearances on his show, often came to wonder if the crack-pated radio host, once his friend, did not by dint of desperate, ongoing defense mechanism, try to see their opposition differently and, marshalling his dream by way of projected wishes—seeing that *he* was the big success. But how could that be—since he had no brief against his friend. There was that, and then what would have been the basis of such a similar small-minded hostility.

Still, Porch was fully aware of the defiance, and it irked him because he saw that as his silence constituted a protest as much as a bellow it involved him as a participant in the antipathy, making the vileness mutual and so underlying the competition by simple—and ugly—contrast. The fact was that the two men by the queer arrangement of their personalities, at least in regard to any refusal to overcome them, by a complicated and pathetic ego arrangement so unnecessary created lives of mutual opposition, establishing the kind of contrivance in human affairs one never comes across in the natural world, and, in the process of pusillanimously attempting to X-out the reality of the other, trying to prove by sheer inflexibility Oscar Wilde's classic remark, "One's real life is so often the life that one does not lead."

"Ice splits star-wise," wrote Sir Thomas Browne. A single stab of the pick at the right point is made, a shuddering diamond glaze, when suddenly fissures begin crazily shooting out in every direction, as the solid crystal chunk falls in two at the star. Jealousy in its essential snarl radiates fissures almost exactly like that, spreading and tainting everything, affecting the living of life in the strangest, unpredictable ways.

The programming nature of "The Global Loop," with a different subject taking up each hour, was basically constructed on how to use a dibble: make a hole, drop a plug of grass, stomp the opening close, and move on. Guests chosen to appear were mainly writers, musicians, poets, people in the food-related world. Politics was an inevitable subject. Urban planning, mayoral candidates, radical feminists, and academics. News invariably ceded to entertainment, the latest celebrity news, headlines, and gossip.

We are now living in a modern world that is *augmented*. Nothing is joyful unless it is entertainment—iPads, iPhones that take photographs, video games. PlayStations, the Apple Vision Pro. TV screens the size of billboards. GPS Smart Watches. Pixel eyewear. Amusement, diversion, divertissement, recreation, and enjoyment are what matters. The gratifications of mirth. Much of the nature of entertainment is escapism and time-filling distraction. Extended reality. Virtual reality. Blockchain technology. Artificial intelligence, a wayward cutting-edge technology that has revolutionized industries by enabling machines to create content that resembles human-generated work. Technological immersion! Wasn't value now gauged solely by what has pel, sample bytes, pixels, bits, dos, and spot? Watching movies, playing video games—vivid video, digital, and computer games that transport the player into an alternative world where spiraling techniques are used to make them feel more like the character they're playing. and playing the immersive games on the AVP, watching television, going to the movies? Headsets are the new high!

Talk about that!

It was ironic, that phrase—one that had caused such contentiousness that, ironically enough, was *not* spoken. Never referred to, as the fifteen-year friendship between Ted Creeple and Aleister Porch foundered like a diminishing horizon at close of day, one that finally petered out in the grayness akin to the dark curtain of nightfall. Was it a case of classic binaries? White oak/yellow pine? Hamilton/Burr? Chaplin/Keaton? Who could say? As far as they went, Porch often reflected for comparison on the relationship between of the Army of the Potomac's Major General Winfield Scott Hancock and brave Brigadier General Lewis Armistead, the Confederate commander, both closer than brothers before the war—a rare and valued accord—that ended in a fatal fight at the top of Cemetery Hill at Gettysburg 1863.

The friendship with all the markings of a *ménage à trois* in a very real way had become a three-cornered one—Creeple, Porch, and the need for fame— precarious alliance in which a lot of curious, unusual emotions were given heed but allowed nothing like a place in the sun, with an immaturity factor having too high an influence. Porch's ultimate exclusion from appearing on the show to be interviewed led in its censure to the loss of friendship, a proscription in its pettiness that was less. He saw less as being expelled than relieved of pointless expectation. In the intervening years, Porch got married and had two children and continued writing. In the end, he could not find the space to need to care.

Soon it did not matter to either one.

Decades passed.

One day at the Stone Zoo, bewildered, one of his girls pointed to all the animals as they walked the perimeter to see monkeys, snakes, lions. "Look. They are all in cages. They are all separated from each other." Cages, walls of irreconcilable differences, Porch considered upon reflection, as he saw how bars which captured the animals also privileged them. We keep others out by the pusillanimity of an unbudging self.

"They are all detached," said his young daughter, concerned. "Divided."

To prevent Porch from any fame he could help boost—a project—eventually became an occupation for his radio host, indeed a burden. Would Creeple ever come to see that? Never. Nor would Porch ever come to see his friend again. No waking individual can comprehend an event in its extensiveness or fullness, he realized—neither the resonances of its depth nor the thinness of the tissues it rips apart—by seeing only one side of it. Anyone who observes the same event sees it from a different perspective. And so, it goes with witnesses. When taken all together, solid truth can emerge from a universal vision, yet no one here saw the truth intact. The truth, as close to it as mortals can ever get, is arrived at only when one went over all the different viewpoints and put them together in a synthesis.

Which never happens.

Jealousy consumes itself. It seemed that by such changes in their lives, fate reinforced what decisions had been made to alter it, for while Ted Creeple at WNOT obsessively kept up that wall, outside that very wall Aleister Porch in publishing more and more books, in the doing only kept himself more and more from any invitations to appear. Inconsistent behavior by a pal wounds, lack of a sympathy is bewildering, frequent criticism begins to pall, absence during challenging times untenable, often unacceptable, and in the extreme indefensible A person claiming to be a friend who does not read your books is not a friend.

Dissolution in almost every aspect is daunting regarding regrets, and it was a matter no different with Porch, for in fact he often thought about it. One of his reflections, probably the main one, was that only a fool should despise another man. No man can afford to despise another.

No one had the right to do so. Was not within each individual's life a history of hundreds and millions of years of descent, with a direct ancestral line to God himself. Was it is not written in the 17th chapter of St. Luke, verse 21, "the Kingdom of God is within man"?

Aleister tousled his little girl's pretty blonde hair.

Her bright insight made at the zoo was no small revelation.

"Good point," replied her father.

Reading Hartshorn

The one and only person in Scripture that Jesus
specifically called "friend" was, of all people,
the wayward apostle, Judas Iscariot, his betrayer.

See Matthew 26:50

I knew Reading Hartshorn very well. My favorite color is purple, and she once gave me a beautiful lilac bracelet that I still cherish. She was so pretty. Boys flirted with her all the time. It did them little good, as she was calm, dignified, and kept custody of the eyes. She was too gracious ever to complain about her ignoble and jealous sister, who in her treachery and unsubtle ways became the bane of her life. I can add that I myself witnessed much of it, later. I knew her from school. My being gay never came between Reading and me. It was not a factor, ever, as she never discriminated; as a matter of fact, her love soon brought us together in a strong bond. Her father was a physician, a handsome man, her mother a some-what ditzy, abstracted, not particularly alert, careworn woman with lots to have to contend with—and although in her stunning beauty she restated her father's good looks, Reading was not given to flaunt them. She always looked down on bigots.

She was the third oldest, with an older brother Donald, a much younger brother Alfred, and that cruel, overbearing older sis-ter, Maryk, a girl facially unfavored and consumed with resentment. The boys in the family were odd ducks, ineffectual and silent, and I called them "The Lost Boys," because they seemed to me whenever I met them, which was not very often, perpetually underwater. The two daughters never got along, ever, to say the least. Let me correct that, quickly. Reading tried, desperately tried to cope with her sister but with no success, for she was opposed, *repugned,* as my own mother would put it, repudiated. In a joshing way I was in the habit of referring to her as "Rapunzel," not only because she had beautiful glistening brown hair, but because she was—face it—repugned. I cannot emphasize that enough.

An egghead best describes Maryk. Her face was peculiar, for her nostrils, almost fully open nasal cavities, predominated over the flesh of the pokebone of nasal cartilage that seemed almost piggish in an unnaturally raised footplate. I honestly hate to have to say it, because I am exaggerating, but her anatomy, by way of that minor deformity, bore to a small degree a likeness to the hideous unmasked Phantom of the Opera, who with an elongated right nostril, missing right eyebrow, swollen lips, warped right cheek, different colored eyes, and partially balding head—one of which Maryk shared—was at least a creature who loved and one who tried to hide his awfulness with a white half-mask and wig.

Give the poor masked Phantom in his lair that much. Not so Maryk. Was it her sister's gentleness? Her quieter nature? The good looks? As I say, boys followed her like a beagle after bones—as if I myself wasn't a classic example!

In truth, Maryk was not at all unlike a monster. I cannot stress just how much she was in my case or to how a high degree from the first moment I met her she hated and detested me and everything I stood for, always flapping a mincing hand at me whenever I came in sight. Where to begin? She was impulsive, willful, and headstrong, and grew into her teens with, I want to say a hard edge, but it was worse and far more frightening, a browbeating right-in-your-face challenge, the kind of swaggering spite identified with angry punks. I myself live with such intimidating behavior. All gay men do. It is part of the penalty. I find a profile is in order here. Maryk was loud, attention-seeking, and smoked cigarettes. She was also a "clothes horse," which did her no good socially, at least in the way that style attracts comment. I used to see her on her way to play volleyball—all of us lived in New Haven, Connecticut, near

Yale—where in a short-sleeved jersey and wearing bulbous knee pads she walked like a duck.

I was seventeen, just a bit older than Reading. We had initially connected at a yard sale, standing beside each other, looking at a book on astronomy, wondering how much it cost. She spoke first, openly, innocently. That was me all over, ever the vain one. I need people to choose me, when I cannot even choose myself. We became close friends. I loved to make jars of passata for her and her family, a puree of tomatoes, not chunky, but fine as she liked it—three pounds of ripe plum tomatoes and salt, nothing more. She later gave me a copy of her own personal "Dream Manifesto," written out expressly for me:

> Respect all life
> Visit the ocean
> The more the body suffers, the more the spirit flowers
> Always be amazed by everything
> Gustave Holst's "The Planets"—*emollient!*
> Resist addictions
> Have few extravagances
> Persecution is a privilege in a believer
> I love all thatched dwellings
> Don't do anything that will master you
> Little details matter
> Paint with your heart, not fingers
> Belasco's brain: unique terroir
> Sing like a gust of wind
> Help homeless persons with donations

Reading had Dutch beauty, soft eyes, and at fifteen a fine figure. She had a voice so pure honest, and direct that you would always smile to hear it play back in your memory by way of echo. How many could say that of ourselves? She had a strong Christian faith. I often suspected that she harbored larger wants than others seemed to feel, but that taking things altogether was unable to single out or name, in spite of the glaring fact of her sister's blatant disregard of her, other larger, secret, solitary deficits that she sheltered or might have felt coming from deeper disappointments within. She constantly praised *my* intelligence, claimed that *I* was the brightest person she'd ever met. I was precocious, I've always known that, I was told so in school. But so was she, I mean, unexpectedly advanced! Clever herself. I am gifted, sensitive, *super*sensitive, disorganized, fearful, and, yes, a fanboy as queer as a fat lady's clutch purse or granny's handbag, or a bright fluttering maypole on the first day of Spring.

But we are what we are, do as we're driven, let who wants to deny it, so dare.

I am a paradox, I suppose, a walking contradiction that is the riddle of the griddle on which weirdly I sit. I am a left-wandering, non-traditional radical, a voyager on the liberal side. That's me all over, on the one hand involvement and engagement; detachment and reserve, on the other. No roof to the sky, no border to the land, as I believe westerners say about the Far Dakotas or Montana or Utah. Heart on fire, brain on ice.

I must say I suspect that Reading ascribed my "deviance," if you will, but without anything like repugnance—we never discussed it—to a misfortune or deformity created by the very kind of artificial or cruel conditions that she herself was encountering in her own life that had to be recognized, battled, overcome. Such things never mattered to us. We were too tight. A strange serendipity it is, whereby people, who should find each other, actually manage to do so, no? Is it Newton's Law of Gravitation? With the two of us, it was as case of an instant attraction—nickel, cobalt, and iron magnetically charged!

We are all of us afraid of love, face it, simply because we remain afraid of exposing our true selves. To handle such anxieties, we all if us fussily invent absurd categories—heterosexual, homosexual, Black, white—and categorize the groups that we don't belong to in order to avoid evaluating or, in the end, even recognizing ourselves. A breakout is too chancy for most individuals. My struggle, for what it's worth, has always been a struggle against pointlessness. I have always wanted to make myself matter, mold my mind to match. Our thoughts have bodies, do they not, the intimidating shapes of our fevers and focus and fitness, which are exacting and ever flourishing?

A quick twenty-minute drive from town, small Guilford is blessed with a delightful Long Island Sound coastline. We used to go down to Oak Street Beach, but sometimes dodged over to Hammonasset and Seabluff beaches, as well. I make mention of this only because it was my habit over summers to head out there with Reading, simply because her pain-in-the-ass of an older sister always flatly refused to let her accompany her whenever she herself headed out that way; it became an official sanction.

Maryk was so fastidious about her special beach towels that you would have thought that they were made of mink! She hadn't a clue about cosmetic sense, smearing and spreading her lipstick on like putty—I know a lot about foundation and mascara—but just as excess fat blurs the outline of a face, so can lipstick ruin the contours of a mouth. She also slathered herself with all kinds of suntan cream and beach oil and had a tan so dark, it was nearly audible. But it was no improvement.

I don't think I have ever seen a human face emitting—discharging—so much insolence, and at tomes even without recourse to speech, gesture, or contortion of features.

OK, I'm being catty, right? Well, in my opinion she deserves it. I remember how she would petulantly stamp her feet when eleven-year-old Reading followed in her shadow, tentatively, or even came close to her. It was at the beach where Maryk most liked to hang out. The small group of people of middle-school age that she ran with exuded massively dangerous male energy and exhibited, *radiated,* threats; they would get drunk and do things like punch-fists-through-glass-doors-kind-of-shit. It killed me that she was left out of the games and play of others, exiled, a state that I termed a "usurped damnation," denied even wearing her sister's clothing, which made her yearn to be elsewhere and otherwise.

Maryk's dumb party-girl friends, who would not only look at us, but actually *through* us, as if we were invisible—in a vacant, dumb-as-shit lip-glossed way while doing things like pretending to smoke by lighting up and inhaling rolled-up paper in the woods—had an effect on us as if we had vanished, when whole afternoons went by with us analyzing why she hated us so and would breeze by her and to spit on her shadow whenever she could. We would sit on a stoop, waiting, until they were all out of sight.

The premise Maryk used in judging her younger sister was conjecture, ill-bred speculation that because she disliked her, she could therefore conclude that she knew her—always the presumed postulations of the smug, the complacent, and self-approving arrogant people who feel superior. Assumption is actually presumption, the motives that one attaches to somebody's silence—the lowest form of communication.

It was a relief, not only a relief for us to be rid of Maryk and her gang, avoiding their open disapproval and tacky vulgarities, but a relief to be going to the beach, and always a relief to be with gentle Reading. I had no siblings of my own, nor was I ever personally popular, but, whenever I was sad or despondent, she never failed to cheer me up with a joke or an observation, sometimes even generously showing me a drawing or two of hers—she was a watercolorist—several of which she gave me. I tried to please her my way by taking her up the stairway, past my room, to the top of my roof where I kept my rare telescope, to show her the heavens magnified, for astronomy was my hobby.

I found a great nurturing comfort in showing Reading my lenses, my whole set-up, pointing out distant specks of light, faint stars—once or twice I had sneaked in to attend several college astronomy classes at Yale—and it was seventh heaven for me, and I believe also for her, to have spent so many evenings up there

together. Reading and I would pore over my volumes about con-
stellations and intriguing star clusters, which, because they thrilled
her so much, also elevated me to the very empyrean. She was fascinated with the firmament, the celestial sphere and all its vaults. I
explained to her that three stars made up Alpha Centauri, but that
only two, Alpha Centauri A and Alpha Centauri B, were like our
sun, locked in close orbit around each other. Circling this pair from
farther away is a faint red dwarf known as "Proxima Centauri." I
told her about some of the planets that astronomers had discovered
over time and that fully to claim a discovery, astronomers always
needed to find the planet again, either with the Webb telescope,
with another observatory on the ground, or in space. The Extremely Large Telescope, a European observatory under construction in Chile, could help. So could NASA's Roman Space Telescope, scheduled to launch by May 2027.

Reading was a great listener. I told her that Red China, now
leading in lunar exploration, surpassing the United States, would be
the first to populate the moon, but that America, with its concentration in the project, would probably do so on Mars, Ares, the Red
Planet, red for its coloring, which comes from the huge blustering
amount of iron oxide—known on Earth as rust—on the planet's
surface. She encouraged me to say more, adding, "Someday I would
love to live up there in the vast beyond!" I explained that the universe is a bizarre place, packed full of mysterious alien planets, stars
that dwarf the Sun, mysterious black holes of unfathomable power,
and many other cosmic curiosities that defied logic. I told her that
if you can spot the Andromeda Galaxy with your naked eyes, you
can see something 14.7 billion billion miles away! She was amazed
to hear that our Sun is 400 times larger than the Moon, but also 400
times as far away, making both objects appear to be the same size
in our sky, that stars don't twinkle until their light passes through
Earth's atmosphere, that driving a car to the nearest star at 70 mph
would take more than 356 billion years, and that if you drilled a
tunnel through Earth and jumped in, you would reach the other

side in 42 minutes and 12 seconds, and your top speed would be 17,670 mph. Reading would actually clap hearing each fact!

Reading was almost always happy, with herself, in herself, content within her world and satisfied in a godly way to be who she was. Almost always, I say. But one stone in her shoe was the source of her infinite sorrow and much pain.

Maryk.

Later, it rang in my ears by way of reflection, regarding my blustering pedantries and, you know, by going on to such lengths with so much chatty cheerfulness about myself and my enthusiasms, that I stupidly failed to recognize that the distress or suffering in other lives, as, say, in the case with Reading, might cause melancholy or depression by way of comparison, which would have been the last thing on my mind. She was so selfless, so considerate. A fondness for self-denial has always instantly won my heart—does this trait in me reveal some kind of female sensibility I should perhaps be ashamed of and so deny?—and will probably leave me a fated fool or simp for the rest of my life.

I'm afraid I am forced to have to number myself in this matter among those lacking the supreme quality without which a man can never be interesting to or accepted by other men—that is, the capacity to be overly sympathetic to or far too willing to think the best of people, a virtue disguised as a failing—or was it the reverse? How did I develop into gamer—a "Mary Ann," a "bog queen," a "shirt-lifter"—as Maryk always derisively called me—if not by a solicitude and a need—*especially*—to care?

I intuited her inward predicament as if it were my own and positively ached to ease her suffering and stanch the pain of her wounds, as I know she would have done for me.

I could always tell when Reading was blue, which often she was, invariably the result of her sister's repeated torments. She confided in me that her sister was a party animal. Maryk used all kinds of makeup and was relentless with her elaborate skin-cleansing routines, and always compulsively "did" her hair and nails. She would not share with her sister even so much as a bracelet or a bauble, a comb, a clip, or even a comment. When she reached her early teens, she shut her out of her room. Back then, her far, far prettier sister had only two school outfits. Being kept from joining her sister and her friends, she endured their bullying looks, with Maryk always playing the lead tease, their mean taunts and scoffing provocations causing her repeated emotional pain and distress.

A truly significant part of my friend's unhappiness and dejection was the complete bewilderment she had to confront that a sibling, a brother or sister, could act so cruelly to her, to anyone, to be so spiteful. Still, she was always hesitant to run her sister down, and, charity-prone, refused to diminish someone she called a friend.

"You can call her a *'friend,'* silly? My goodness!" I gasped, astonished, skeptical, utterly incredulous one night when we were together up on the roof. I took her arm and gently shook it. "No, you can't mean it. Look at me!"

"I do."

"I cannot believe my ears!"

"No, no, no, please, Belasco, it's true," she pleaded.

Reading wiped a tear from her eye, sadly searching up into the high celestial, heavenly empyrean, as if searching for an answer, dark as the mysteries confronting her in her own family. "I do, I *do* call her a friend," said Reading.

I look searchingly into her face.

"Isn't she my own sister?"

"Don't be a goose, Betelgeuse!" I said to the poor dear thing, hugging her as tightly as possible to commiserate. She removed her glasses and broke down, leaning into me, weeping on my shoulder. As I say, she wore rimless nose glasses, octagon lenses, so cute—but she also had a great round pair she liked, encircling orbs, which only added to the bewitching and ornamenting sparkle of her bright eyes gracefully to face-shape her astonishing beauty. I continued squeezing the dear girl's shoulders. I adored her. She gave off the paradisiacal scent of peonies, to me the most exquisite fragrance in all of nature.

Maryk loved jewelry. She was a "neat freak" and regularly, fastidiously dusted her room and all her little belongings. Even as a child, she was narcissistically proud of what she saw as her svelte legs and neat ankles, a delusion, but a dear one. She hated any kind of schoolwork, never tried hard academically, and was not much of an athlete, after a while out of lethargy and indifference giving up any interest in volleyball when the taller girls were obligated to make it clear her lax contributions added little to the team, which caused her to sulk. Nor did she have any personal creative interests. She was not a reader, not even of magazines or newspapers, and she had no hobbies, except smoking and drinking. Curiously, while I thought of Reading as *feminine,* I considered Maryk *female*, a subtle distinction, obviously, but one that nevertheless put me on my guard about her.

When Maryk got into her late teens, she began frequenting bars with her girlfriends, random alliances born of chance meetings that, for all her faults, gave her a notable confidence boost, and it was around this time, with her assuming a major big-time girl vibe, that she became a bit of a club kid, and in no time, upsetting her parents—a predominantly absent father, for his practice, and a mother, a woman basically oblivious and mainly inattentive. She was a woman with no education, weak, absentminded, and distracted. Maryk began staying out late, at all hours, and became brash and audacious. She cultivated bar slang she learned from hanging out in such places until late at night, often until closing time. She was a wicked flirt and would tease customers with snappy remarks of the quick-witted barroom sort, the kind of coarseness that made her feel right at home.

Reading owned a pet chaffinch, but Maryk had no interest in birds or animals as a child, although later, during one of her briefly hellacious marriages, she adopted a cat. I used to see her daily in high school. She liked standard music stuff, with average tastes. Whenever possible, Reading listened to those albums, but of course in doing so had to manage it stealthily and in secret—I was with her once or twice—for, as I say, she had been prohibited from entering Maryk's room on the penalty of probably getting punched out. One of Maryk's new friends—a Peruvian who had turned her on to Kate Bush—even fascinated young Reading as being somewhat cool, but whenever that girl even occasionally acknowledged her existence, Maryk intervened to fend her off.

Much later, after all the terrible troubles, which I must soon recount here, Maryk worked as a bartender for several years. I believe she also worked as a bouncer, no surprise to me, because she had always acted like one. She was not someone whom I would associate with anything domestic or culinary, but she could probably mix you any drink you wanted. At one point she was urged to buckle down and set out to get a degree, but she failed the coursework. It was during those bar-hopping days of hers that she began associating with a bunch of dumb, completely unreliable, loudmouthed boyfriends. Even her first husband was a gas-huffing, drug-sniffing alcoholic. Reading, who never understood what she saw in such company and never wanted to, avoided them as if they were Ebola victims!

Was Maryk a sex maniac—who could say? It's not that she was sexually depraved, it's just she was what she was. People came and touched her life, and she simply went with it. I don't see her as a victim. It's as if she became the predator after her beginnings, and she would set things up so that they'd fall into her lap. It didn't matter who she was dealing with, whether a woman or a man. It was a very subtle kind of aggressive behavior. Maryk a degenerate? Who knew? I have no idea. But from all the whispers and tidbits that I heard and came my way over the years, take a big guess? She was married two times, both of them total failures. An early marriage—an elopement with some indolent roofer—lasted a brief three-and-a-half weeks. The other one went a bit longer, but from what I've gathered many years later, it was a nightmare of bickering

and squabbles ending in divorce. She ended up living in concubi-
nage with a semi-moron named Gruntz.

I had the dubious occasion of seeing her both at the wake
and at the funeral after the tragedy I am about to tell you about,
when and where in her hypocrisy she was bent over like what we
call a craven, obedient futch, crying like a big, blubbering baby,
wearing slacks, mind you, a fact, I tell you, which would have been
positively comic in its shouting irony if it was not so nauseating, so
pathetically disgusting to the family, to me, to everybody. She was
always a "hard ass," from all reports, acid, tart and riddling, literally
perforating any attempt at warmth, except when it came to her father,
Dr. Hartshorn, whom she revered—Reading said she became a
boo-hooing, out-of-control nutcase whenever her father fell ill—
for I heard that she had all sorts of unresolved "daddy" issues, tons.

The tragedy to which I refer? I can scarcely gather the words
to say. What happened was this. One winter night, the word got out
that a cool party was to be held over in a low section of New Haven
called Newhallville, a gathering of hip people that stubborn, mulish
Maryk badly wanted to attend. At the time, Dr. Hartshorn was extremely busy and away on a trip to Canada for a medical conference,
a circumstance that allowed Maryk to badger her hesitant mother
for permission to attend. Reading was a fifteen-year-old at the time,
only a sophomore in high school. Her older sister was a senior, seventeen years old, and had promised to meet with her boyfriend, a
guy who was no longer in high school but who was living in a drab
old house in that area with two roommates who were local mutt
jacks, working stiffs down in the trainyards. That night Maryk lied
to her mother, who had initially refused her permission to go but,
characteristically wishy-washy, then weakly capitulated and allowed
her to go to the party on the strict condition that she take her sister
Reading along with her.

As I heard the full account from Reading's own lips, the
crimes committed against her that night will be imprinted on me
forever. She was originally planning to read and then go to bed. It

had already grown dark outside, and she was wearing a comfortable sweatshirt, flipping through a book in her living-room, sitting on the floor, leaning against a couch, and yawning. She told me she can still hear the muffled voices between Maryk and their mother: "Yes, her mother will be there It's just a harmless old party; all my friends are going." She was abruptly summoned by an impatient Maryk to quickly "get ready," for she was going to a party as her sister's so-called "chaperone," an event as something new, a "first" for Reading, and excited "beyond belief"—it was nothing less than Cinderella being invited to a ball. Reading raced to remove her glasses, hastily dressed up, excited to make herself as beautiful as possible, applying touches of makeup.

Not a word was said to her about the deception. Did their mother drop them off at the house, or had a dark car pulled up to take them? Reading couldn't remember. The fact was they arrived at a dark small low-slung house in a typical suburban neighborhood and walked into a dark narrow kitchen with a small corner nook at one side with built-in wooden seats where two young losers were seated drinking beer and yammering. Maryk immediately disappeared, quickly vanishing like a specter into a back room with a tall man whom Reading had never met and whom she barely got a look at in the hasty confusion on that party night. Reading was awkwardly left alone, somewhat stunned in trying to process what was happening. Where was the party, the food, the music, the dancing, the lights, the parents?

Reading was simply left to wait with two young guys, short, brown hair, non-descript baby faces with peach fuzz, one thin and one more husky. She remembered no names, just blurry images of shadows as vaguely just described. She was invited to sit down, when they taught her the game called "beer pong." She didn't like beer, had never played that game before, and felt uneasy as she sat there with strangers, killing time and waiting for her sister to finish whatever business had brought them there, ready to return home. She was offered no food. There may have been some dry kibble or peanuts on the table. The hours dragged on. Was it midnight? Where was her sister? Had she fallen asleep? When she enquired about her, she was put off. never checked on her. The guys were smoking pot and offered her some, which she took, being polite, accepting what was offered.

She recalled feeling sleepy, dizzy, and wanting simply to lie down to rest, while waiting for an eternity for her sister. Where was Maryk? Why had she deserted her?

I honestly cannot bring myself to spell out the details of what happened the rest of that night as Reading, crying, squeezing my hands, recounted it for me out of a desperate, galvanizing need to share it with someone, the better to have it said and quickly forgotten, for the men took advantage of her in the worst of all possible ways. She spoke, upon gentle prodding, as if trying better to process what had happened, having experienced what is called a "freeze response" or "tonic immobility." It was as if she thought what was happening was happening to someone else. She feigned to be asleep. She felt nothing, while the faceless, unnamed, anonymous, drunken rapists, high on drugs, typically behaved like the thieves they were, leaving as silently and covertly as they arrived. She was left alone there, clothed, as if nothing had happened until being abruptly wakened by her sister, barking, "The cops are coming. Come on! Get ready! We have to go!" It was by now three o'clock in the morning. Their mother had called the police.

Let me please briefly weigh in here, if you'll forgive me by way of point of view the chemical alchemy directing the range of my own sexual preferences—or deviance, if you must insist—on the much-vaunted, so-called rapture of coitus, an act paradoxical and ambivalent in nature, the "beast with two backs." Sex is biological, but gender is mental. As a subject, the topic is reductive—and boring. It occupies the thoughts of all, mankind has agreed to be silent about it. People become at their very worst when talking about it. I'm suspicious of individuals who discuss it in terms other than plain warmth or affection or fondness. Otherwise, it is to hold the knife on the sharp end. And, by the way, if sex is such a natural a normal and common phenomenon, how come so many books are written on how to do it?

I could feel Reading's pain but could barely bring myself to hear the details. I have never understood sexual intercourse as an inborn response to the erotic. The heat communicated by bodily excitement, its musky scents, its bright plumage, or skimpy clothing, seems all of it brainlessly triggered by the hormones of horn-mad grabbers and gropers who, while casting aside any personal or public decorum, go at it so instinctively half the time, they don't not even know the name of their partners. A pair is not necessarily a couple. The act has always remained for me a ludicrous cartoon of entangled legs and mooning buttocks, a non-mysterious conjunction between opposites.

There is supposedly a miracle bond of twoness in oneness, but to me the inherent oneness that is claimed in the achieved unity isa universal joke, when it is in fact it but a low deed of the grab and the snatch by an undifferentiated plenum, divided, not joined, rarely a loving but rather an ego experience and a metaphor of friction, tension, heating, plowing, planting, flying, riding, and swimming by shadowy pairs linked in an unconscious identification with a defiling psychological factor, as if with one's physical counterpart, with always the possibility of the two producing a "third." It is at its best a masquerade of aggression, appetite, predation, and rituals of dominance and submission.

I could overmatch that in spades in the way of passion simply by lying down on the grave of Nicolaus Copernicus, had I the power to do so, to leave after I departed a small prayer and bestow a laurel leaf and a white rose.

When has the flesh ever involved the soul? Appetite and hunger when employed regarding this subject are too nauseating to contemplate. One carries nothing going into sexual encounters but questions to be asked, answers never provided. Two-person push-ups. Heels to Jesus. Taking old one-eye to the optometrist. Parallel parking. Chesterfield rugby. Bedroom rodeo. Dancing the goat's jog. Yentzing. Bam-bam in the ham. It is nothing but double-dealing and exploitation. I could find more love and personal intimacy in satisfying my passion, physically, emotionally, spiritually, by planting a Ghost Orchid or Semper Augustus tulip in a silver vase or watching a Draconid meteor shower.

But in the case of the savage violation of Reading, it was an obliteration of innocence, worse than a sexual assault or thuggish ravishment, if one could bear to say so, but a kidnaping, an abduction, the hijacking of purity, goodness, and guilelessness, the obscene advantage-taking of ingenuous, trusting child, a virgin as pure as the snow on a Christmas roof! A songbird had been crushed by the squeeze of a moronic fist. She was terribly innocent of the world, I mean, of life itself. She was so pure. Her fragility was in her soul.

It was clear, a double crime, times two, had been committed in the silence and stealth of that ghastly night, for between the lusty whispering plans of the two co-conspirators, they picked her up and carried Reading from one room to another, and, as she told me, whether either reached climax in their wormy ways, there is no mistake it was nothing less than a brutal double-rape of a naïve and nonconsenting minor, twice done.

Reading had been rushed out of the house, and she and her sister proceeded in a furtive and clandestine way to make their way back home in the early morning hours without being sighted by the cruising headlights of police cars making slow rounds in the silent sleeping residential neighborhood. Headed back home on foot, they took a main road to get there. As soon as they started walking along that way, as fate would have it, a white police van pulled up beside them and ordered them to get in. The two girls were taken to the police station and fingerprinted—was that even legal?—with the cops snickering and making jokes at the girls' expense. Reading remembered saying nothing, but Maryk, glib and fast-talking, denied any shenanigans had taken place, claiming only they were lost and trying to find their way home.

She remembered pulling up in a police car where their mother was standing outside the doorway, on the top step, literally waving with a smile on her face to the police officer and thanking him with a laugh. The policeman joked, telling the parent as she stood there, that he had fingerprinted the girls only to scare them. As I heard the story—Reading and I were, as always, alone together and sitting out on a remote bench in East Rock Park—she was virtually lifeless at the time and mechanical of speech, almost robotic, traumatized, while I was left wondering, as I listened, exactly who were the criminals here, and, probably, more to the point, *who were not?* Her older, uncaring sister who, thinking only of herself, had abandoned a minor? The hapless mother for sending them off to some strange house? Or the police for fingerprinting them, while never bothering to investigate a thing, never mind the two vicious contemptible shit-sticks for not only illegally, criminally, plying a minor with alcohol and illegal substances, but entrapment, and the nefarious act of forced rape?

As we sat facing one another, what might have appeared there on the bench a gentle composition with a placid outward appearance would have revealed nothing of the strenuous exchanges being made there, as I tried to channel my friend's feelings, her sentience, neither be captured in excerpts nor indicate my attempts to contour time when everything that followed was an explosion of turbulence and pain.

Reading told me that her sister, who had more information about the people who did what they did, knew what happened but didn't care and preferred to ignore it, dismissing out of hand her sister's consuming guilt for the bad light shed onto her but not on the tramps, as if it were all her fault. Her sister Maryk's casual indifference and lame lack of response, constituting merely an impassive, workaday shrug—cold, unsympathetic, emotionless, and unfeeling, saying in so many words "get over it"—which only compound the unspeakable event with what has been referred to as traumatic invalidation, trapping Reading in a dizzy cycle of resentment and pain. It was and still remains "unspeakable."

Maryk's phony defense, airy as thistledown, she concocted on the spot and, hearing of the details that night, only rocked with laughter that she had been responsible. Reading had pressed her about the gravity of having left her all alone with the brutes she called friends. Maryk smiled, if the slight movement of her face could be so called.

Meanwhile, her sister Maryk had taken up with some obese beef-wit name Grontz, a thick-necked sociopath from somewhere like Oklahoma or Indiana or Iowa—I never bothered to learn his last name—whom she met in one of her nights of partying and with whom, last I heard, she now cohabits in a dilapidated old house over in Dixwell. Word is, at least what I've heard from people who know, they chipped in on the house to save money but never married. In the boozing world, I've heard, they call him the "pissing mannikin," for his habit at closing time to stagger drunkenly outside from one of the many bars in which he nightly gets fried to stop (often forgetting to unzipper) to urinate on the front steps, the way a rhesus monkey claims territory.

No one who knew her was surprised later that Maryk in a fit of petulance had badgered that ill-bred ignoramus to write a poisonous letter to Reading, in the very midst of her troubles, a bullying screed, which, despite its over-the-top pretensions, couldn't hide the donkey vulgarities of a born cipher, coming straight out of left field:

> I've heard from Maryk that you are now blaming her for your trouble at the party. Blameshifting is just what one would expect from you. Right? Admit it! We hear that you like a candy-ass and a coward are picking on her and blaming her for your own messes, when Marykhas spent so much time helping her parents while you just sit up there in your room with nasty thoughts that should be turned on yourself! You have done nothing but cause

trouble. Your baseless sniping and attacks in her just confirms that you don't own a mirror. You never look at yourself, do you? Once again during a very difficult time for the Hartshorn family, you have taken persistent steps to hurt rather than help. Perhaps your recent time criticizing and blaming others would have been better served answering your own questions about what kind of actual help you have for your own family. Wait, I can save you the time compiling the data, the answer is absolutely nothing. Unless, of course, you are counting your endless petty and misplaced criticism and whacky ideas in which you volunteer others to implement your idiotic plans. You are now notorious for pompously offering others to do your bidding while you do nothing, you and that dainty fag, Belasco.

In my life, I have never seen someone blather and pontificate so much while doing so little. You are a total fraud of the highest order and should be embarrassed. Big talk, no action. I think you have been locked in your bizarre world so long you simply do not realize how truly delusional you have become. In any case, your most recent nonsense is in keeping with your endless feuds with Maryk. No wonder they can't stand you. You are a carrier that make [sic] others around you sick while you keep on as if nothing has occurred. People urgently excise you from their lives, so they are not suffocated by your loathsome behavior or your blaming your sister for your own stopidity [sic].

Mercifully, please, keep your idiotic comments to yourself, OK? Clearly, you are delusional, intentionally or negligently disinterested [sic] and uninformed, uncaring for your mother as evidenced by deliberately not talking to her for months at a time and withholding communications. You haven't an ounce of common sense, probably the result of doing virtually nothing of consequence as you sit there, perpetually acting like a petulant know-it-all child who blames everyone else for her own mistakes and poor choices in life. Again, you need to shut up and keep your asinine comments to herself. If you have totally lost your common sense and moral compass, let me help by suggesting that you begin by simply shutting the fuck up. Stop being such an obvious jackass. If I was you, I would now quote some religious passage or platitude which I do not understand, believe or follow in a feigned attempt to paint myself as some kind of pious Christian. But I am a lot of things but not a hypocrite, so I will close by keeping it real, go fuck yourself.

Grontz

Reading showed me this letter that had come from a complete stranger, except though the wily knight-chess-move of Maryk. But by now Reading was facing many far, far deeper concerns. The rapists had broken at least two laws in Connecticut, she realized: (1) Statutory Sexual Assault of a Child Younger Than 16: A second-degree (defendant is 4–10 years older than victim) felony subjects a guilty defendant to up to 10 years in prison and a $25,000 fine. (2) Involuntary Deviate Sexual Intercourse with a Child Younger Than Sixteen. All cases under official law are considered first-degree felonies, and a conviction carries up to 40 years in prison and a $25,000 fine or more.

As to the "Mistake of Age" factor, unlike most states, Connecticut does not recognize a mistake-of-age defense for sex crimes involving underage victims in certain circumstances when the age of consent is 14 or older. It cannot serve as a defense where the victim is younger than 14.

I tried to tell Reading that together we could solve her problem, overcome and vanquish them. "We can dislodge an asteroid! Planetary defense!" I pleaded. "Cross orbits! Build infrastructures in outer space! Refuel way stations!" In my pleas to console her, I availed myself of cliches and resorted to platitudes and stupid maxims of the kind stitched on pillows. "Today is the tomorrow you worried about yesterday."

A concerned Elder from church whom Reading consulted earnestly advised her to press charges—she had become traumatized, spending long hours now and even days weeping alone in her room, having never told her mother—and, after due deliberation with him decided to take the rapists to court to pay for their crimes. Having learned of this, whether Maryk herself bruited it about to the culprits, for she knew both sods as bar friends—she was always loose-lipped and stupidly flannel-mouthed and perpetually indiscreet—or someone else's gossip had reached the ears of the two felons, the worst thing happened.

One of the two depraved rapists, a savage near-cretin by the name of Arm Henchy, upon hearing of a lawsuit being drawn up against him, in a mad fury stalked her and one night, hiding by her house, waiting for the right moment, stabbed and killed Reading on the spot, just as she stood. He was later found in a filthy back garage, having committed suicide by attaching a line to the running exhaust pipe of a dented old Chevrolet.

When the sudden news of this broke, such an utterly pointless, wanton elimination of one of life's purest, best, and innocent souls, it fell on me like cresting wave, risen to its own collapse, she who had all along deeply felt the burden of larger wants than others seemed to feel with such intense yearning but would never see

What had I not seen that in my small way I might have prevented? I had mistakenly seen in her naïveté a defense against trouble, not an inducement or incentive to it. I am ready to sit down and weep at my insufficiency of insight or understanding in the matter and of barely knowing even a fraction of her fears. As I pondered the advice I gave her, my words seemed so shallow, while the combination of egotism and presumption they conveyed embarrasses the part of me that still feels represented in them.

Reading's death was to me a crucifixion. It wasn't that I wept for weeks, I wept for long months, and I still weep in the darkness lying awake and being unable to sleep on many a pointless night. I spend much of my time alone, now, taking aimless walks out to East Rock where I end up sitting on our bench, alone. One gray afternoon, I left a flower on her grave, in her sacred memory, a Hacquetia, with shining green leaves, each cluster of whose tiny yellow florets, in spring, is surrounded by a ruff of green bracts. It is an endearing little oddity, unlike any umbellifer you have seen, but just like me.

I could not help but recall that same day, as I sat on the grass there, the old story of murderous Cain, who slew his brother, a violent conflict born of jealousy. Siblings, again. Cain, the firstborn, was a farmer, his brother Abel a shepherd. The brothers

made sacrifices to God, each from his own fields. God had regard
for Abel's offering but felt none for Cain's. Was it that arbitrary or
did God Himself condescend to discern the difference in virtue, as
He must have with Reading and Maryk? Cain's arbitrary killing of
Abel the God above considered an outright murder, cursing the vile
killer and sentencing him to a ratbag's life of isolation and transi-
ence. The guilty murderer, everywhere shunned and isolated, was
then driven to dwell in the land of Nod (נוֹד, 'wandering'), "outside
of the presence of the face of God"—this mysterious "land of
Nod," symbolizing the condition of all who forsake God, has no
other reference in Scripture and represents no known geographical
name or place—where he built a city and fathered the line of descendants beginning with Enoch.

   The irony remains for us in the unavoidable paradox we are
forced to face, doomed to reckon with, must recognize as our unalterable fate, that it is Cain, being the one who lived, the sole sur-
vivor of that pair, who has since become our own shadowy ances-
tor. Siblings, again, indeed! It is our legacy. Any naïve wish to deny
consanguinity with Cain only endangers the cohabitants not only
within our homes but within our psyche who perish as permanently
by our stabbing remarks and brutal repression and petty jealousies
as in a pool of blood.

   It is of small moment to others that part of my life disappeared with the loss of Reading. Life can go on in a foot-before-
foot way, but that is mere existence. Just this week I read in an
amazing newsflash that a Possible Planet had been Spotted Around
Neighboring Sunlike Star. Astronomers have found strong evidence that a gassy Jupiter-size world is orbiting Alpha Centauri A,
one of three stars in the solar system that is closest to our own. An
infrared image from NASA uses an amazing coronagraphic mask
to block the bright glare from Alpha Centauri A, revealing this potential planet orbiting the star.

   The planet, if it is one, has about the same mass of Saturn
and is, astonishingly—pause and take a deep breath—about the size

of Jupiter, and it orbits Alpha Centauri A every two Earth-years at roughly one to two times the distance between our sun and Earth, with a temperature of about minus 55 degrees Fahrenheit. Mild. Mild as the Seabluff ocean water my dear friend and I used to wade in.

But wait—*wait!*

Guess what? The color of this great discovery is deep purple—gay color, my color, hue of my heart and soul!—and is as round and as beautiful as the gorgeous bracelet that my Reading gave me as a gift! I could continue to weep, but I don't, because that lovely girl now is up there in a spiritual bliss much kinder than anything she found down below. The twinkle of a white star clear and cold smote my heart with its beauty, as I looked up out of the forsaken land for hope of any kind to return to me, beyond my reach.

It took time for that vision to settle. Lots of it.

Perspective has never been a gift of mine, as anyone will tell you. My judgments have always seemed like verdicts, my impressions skewed.

Yet I need only look at my gift.

And the glinting white star.

And I suddenly remember what it is like to be happy.

About The Author

Alexander Theroux has taught at Harvard, MIT, Yale, and the University of Virginia, where he took his doctorate in 1968. A Fulbright and Guggenheim grantee, as well as a National Endowment of the Arts and Woodrow Wilson Scholarship fellow, he is the author of four highly regarded novels—*Three Wogs* (1972), *Darconville's Cat* (1982), *An Adultery* (1987), and *Laura Warholic; or The Sexual Intellectual* (2007)—and of several books of essays, fables, poetry, and a travel book on Estonia. He lives in West Barnstable, Massachusetts with his wife, Sarah, and their two children, Shenandoah and Shiloh.

www.ingramcontent.com/pod-product-compliance
Lightning Source LLC
Chambersburg PA
CBHW052020020726
47501CB00004B/1151